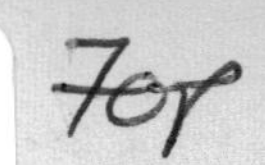

M.C. Scott was a veterinary surgeon and taught at the universities of Cambridge and Dublin before taking up writing as a full-time profession. Now founder and chair of the Historical Writers' Association, her novels have been shortlisted for the Orange Prize, nominated for an Edgar Award and translated into over twenty languages. Her most recent novel is *Rome: The Art of War.*

For more information on all aspects of the books, visit: www.mcscott.co.uk

For the Historical Writers' Association, see: www.theHWA.co.uk

www.transworldbooks.co.uk

By M. C. Scott

ROME: THE EMPEROR'S SPY
ROME: THE COMING OF THE KING
ROME: THE EAGLE OF THE TWELFTH
ROME: THE ART OF WAR

By Manda Scott

HEN'S TEETH
NIGHT MARES
STRONGER THAN DEATH
NO GOOD DEED

BOUDICA: DREAMING THE EAGLE
BOUDICA: DREAMING THE BULL
BOUDICA: DREAMING THE HOUND
BOUDICA: DREAMING THE SERPENT SPEAR

THE CRYSTAL SKULL

ROME

THE EAGLE OF THE TWELFTH

M. C. Scott

CORGI BOOKS

TRANSWORLD PUBLISHERS
61–63 Uxbridge Road, London W5 5SA
A Random House Company
www.transworldbooks.co.uk

ROME: THE EAGLE OF THE TWELFTH
A CORGI BOOK: 9780552161817
9780552161824

First published in Great Britain
in 2012 by Bantam Press
an imprint of Transworld Publishers
Corgi edition published 2013

A CIP catalogue record for this book is available from the British Library.

Addresses for Random House Group Ltd companies outside the UK can be found at: www.randomhouse.co.uk
The Random House Group Ltd Reg. No. 954009

The Random House Group Limited supports the Forest Stewardship Council (FSC®), the leading international forest-certification organization. Our books carrying the FSC label are printed on FSC®-certified paper. FSC is the only forest-certification scheme endorsed by the leading environmental organizations, including Greenpeace. Our paper-procurement policy can be found at www.randomhouse.co.uk/environment.

Typeset in 11/14pt Sabon by
Kestrel Data, Exeter, Devon.
Printed and bound by
CPI Group (UK) Ltd, Croydon, CR0 4YY.

2 4 6 8 10 9 7 5 3 1

To the memory of Rosemary Sutcliff,
Best and Greatest

Contents

8 Men equal a TENT-UNIT

10 Tent-Units equal 1 CENTURY commanded by a Centurion

6 Centuries equal a COHORT (480 men)

10 Cohorts equal a LEGION
(1 Legate, 1 Tribune, 1 Camp Prefect, 1 Primus Pilus, 5 Junior Tribunes)

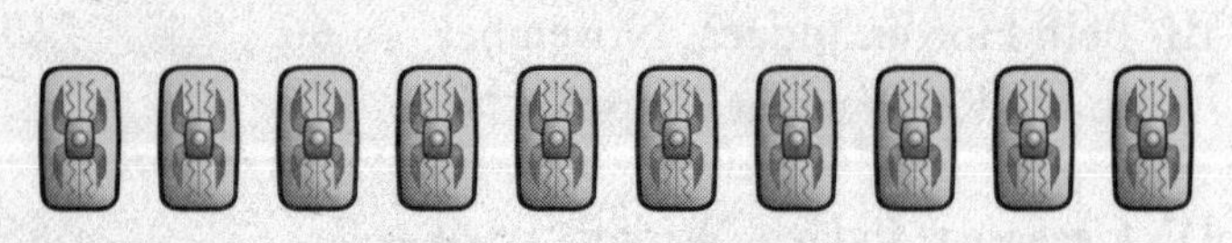

Total fighting strength equals approximately 5000 men

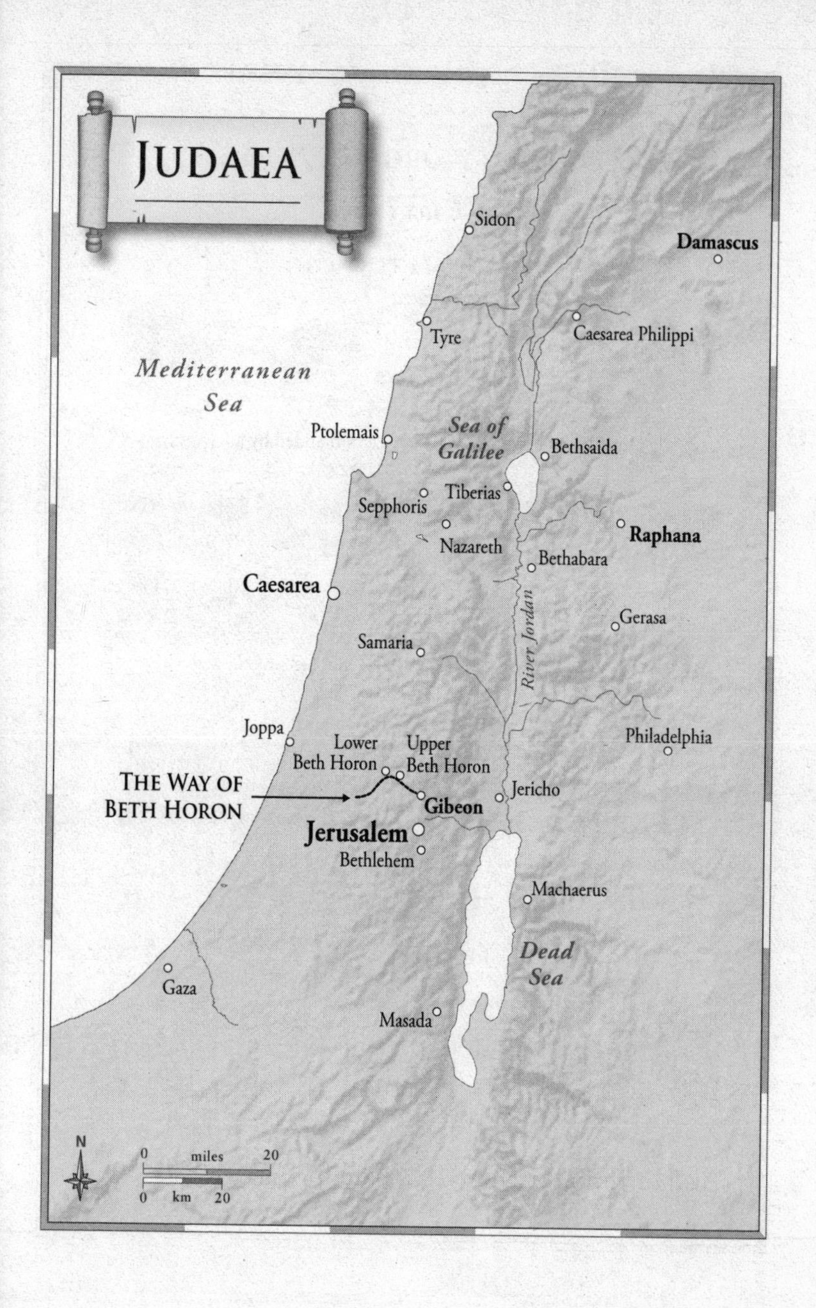
JUDAEA
Sidon
Damascus
Tyre
Caesarea Philippi
Mediterranean Sea
Ptolemais
Sea of Galilee
Bethsaida
Tiberias
Sepphoris
Nazareth
Raphana
Bethabara
Caesarea
Gerasa
River Jordan
Samaria
Joppa
Philadelphia
Lower Beth Horon
Upper Beth Horon
THE WAY OF BETH HORON
Jericho
Gibeon
Jerusalem
Bethlehem
Machaerus
Dead Sea
Gaza
Masada
N
0 miles 20
0 km 20

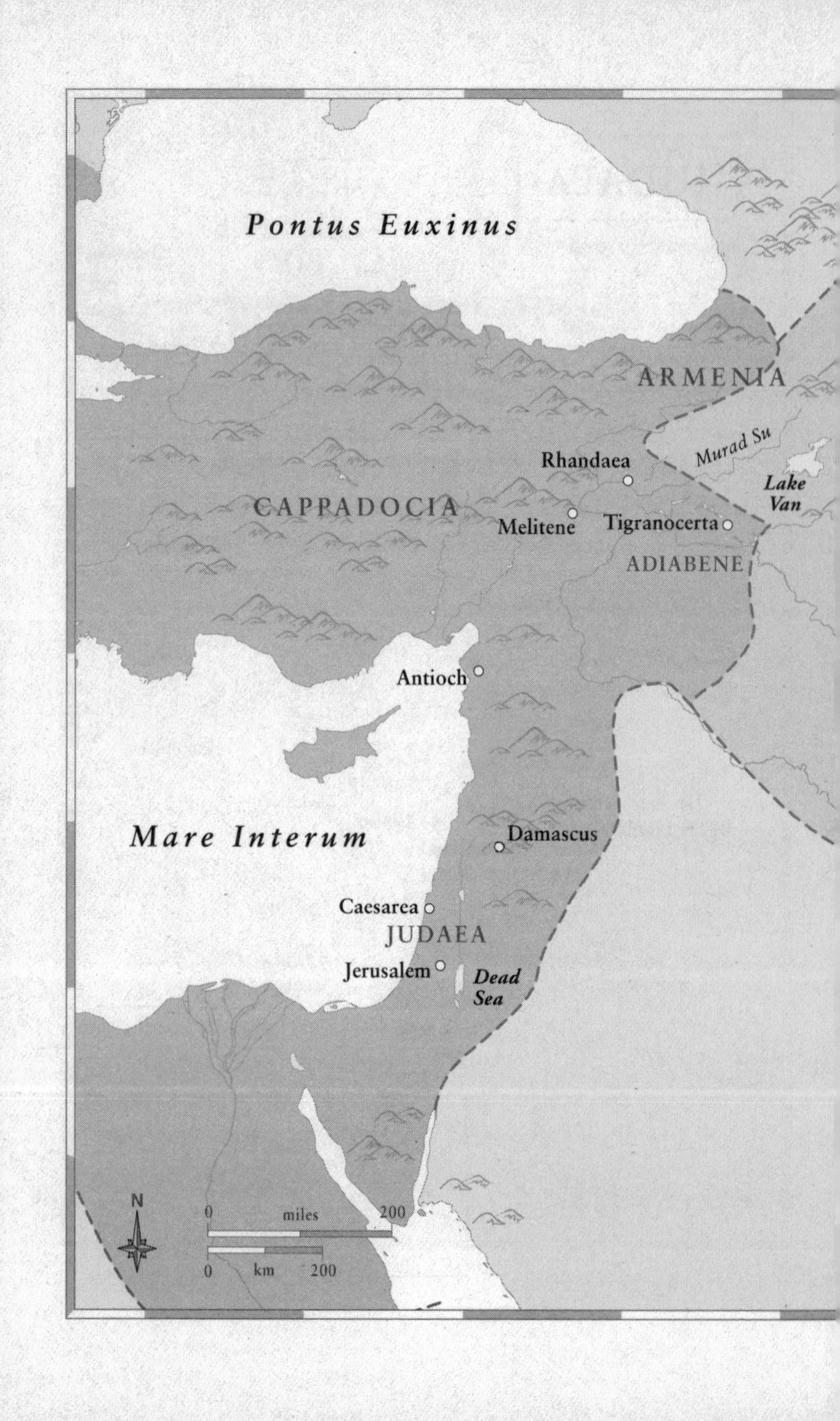

Pontus Euxinus
ARMENIA
Murad Su
Rhandaea
Lake Van
CAPPADOCIA
Melitene
Tigranocerta
ADIABENE
Antioch
Mare Interum
Damascus
Caesarea
JUDAEA
Jerusalem
Dead Sea
N
0
miles
200
0
km
200

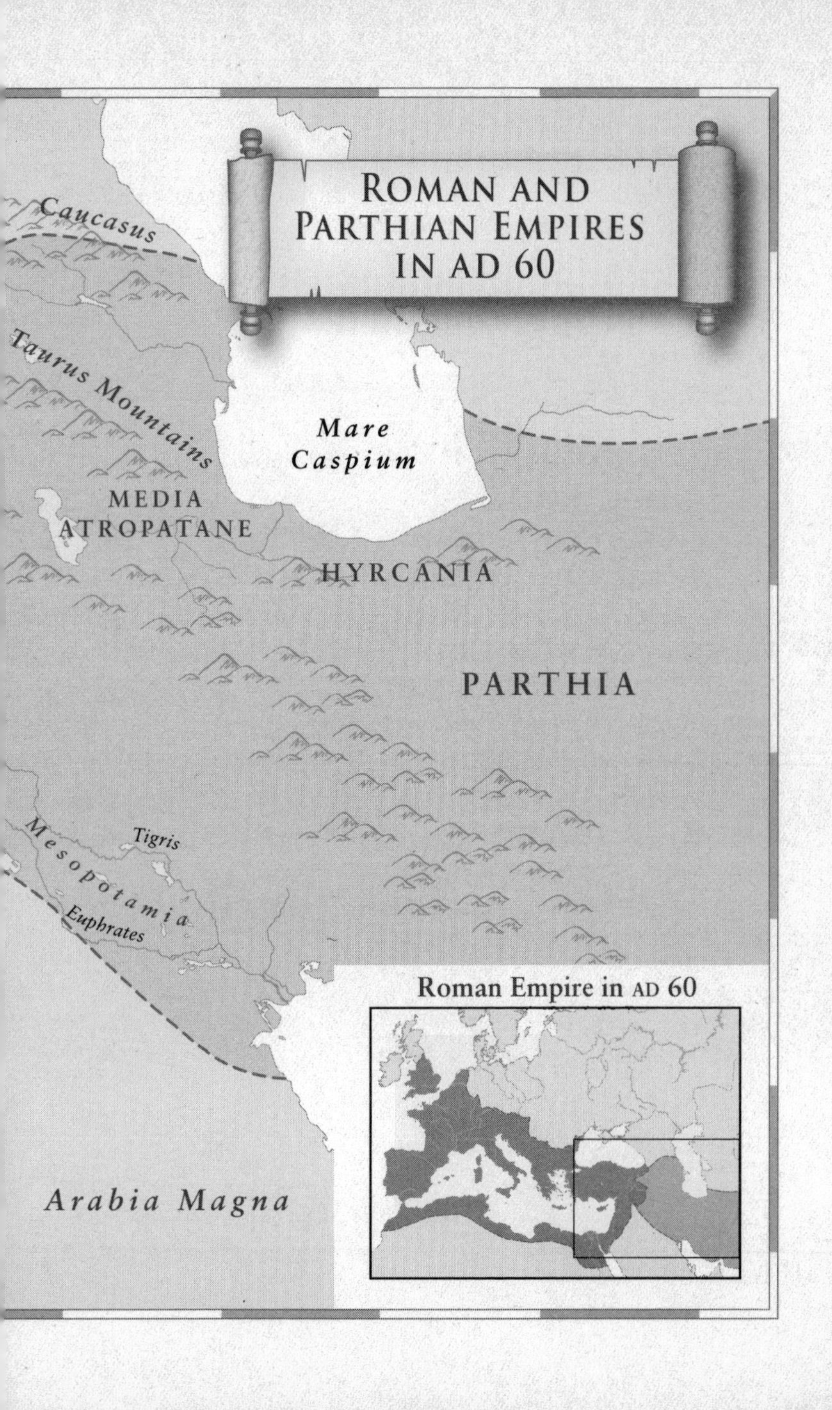
ROMAN AND PARTHIAN EMPIRES IN AD 60
Caucasus
Taurus Mountains
Mare Caspium
MEDIA ATROPATANE
HYRCANIA
PARTHIA
Tigris
Mesopotamia
Euphrates
Arabia Magna
Roman Empire in AD 60

Foreword

There is a generation for whom Rosemary Sutcliff's seminal novel *The Eagle of the Ninth* is the benchmark by which all other historical writing is judged.

It was our first taste of the ancient world, shaping images that have lasted a lifetime, and for many of us writing today it opened doors we had not known existed and asked questions for which we needed to find answers.

Certainly, I would not be writing the books I now write had I not been so enthralled by Esca and Cub, had I not so badly wanted to know what happened in the warrior tests and who exactly *were* the wild, dancing priests with the new-moon horns on their brows. The *Boudica: Dreaming* series was my answer to this last question and the *Rome* series has brought me to the brink of writing my own 'Eagle' narrative.

Sutcliff based her tale around the mythical disappearance of the IXth legion and the then recent find of a wingless legionary Eagle beneath an altar in southern Britain, but the point is that it was truly *mythical* – in reality, the IXth never lost their Eagle.

By contrast, both Josephus and Tacitus provide us with details of a legion that did lose its Eagle without any information on how it was recovered. (We can be fairly certain that it was, for the simple reason that the XIIth was not disbanded and went on to serve under Vespasian and later Titus in the siege of Jerusalem.)

If ever there was a fiction writer's dream, this is it. But where Sutcliff was able to concentrate solely on the Eagle's recovery, I wanted us – my readers and myself – to understand what it meant to the men of a legion for the Eagle to be lost. And so this novel, first and foremost, is Demalion's; his are the eyes, the heart, the mind that guide us through the troubles of the XIIth and we need to see and feel his triumphs before we can understand his loss.

For those of you who have come straight from *Rome: The Coming of the King*, please be patient – you will meet again in these pages the people you know, and find that story's progression. But in order fully to understand the enormity of what happened to the XIIth legion, we must journey back to a time before Pantera sailed to Britain. Fear not; all threads will weave together in due course.

I could not love thee, Dear, so much,
Lov'd I not honour more.

Richard Lovelace,
To Lucasta, Going to the Wars

Dulce et decorum est pro patria mori.

Horace, *Odes*

Prologue

Rhandaea, on the northern bank of the Murad Su, in the country of Armenia, October, AD 62

The last shreds of night held our backs. On either side, unscalable peaks held our flanks. Spread across the wide vale between, we, the XIIth legion, had the advantage of height against our enemy; not a great height, but enough that an olive placed on the stony ground would have rolled under its own weight down the four thousand cubits to the foot of the pass. Enough that when the sun's first edge cut the horizon and poured light across the tens of thousands of foot and horse who made up the King of Kings' Parthian army, we found ourselves looking down on to the tops of their helmets and they seemed to ooze towards us, thickly, like so much mercury poured into a dish; a river of shimmering metal, dancing under the sun.

Drums sounded their advance, and their thunder was

echoed by the roll of ten thousand hooves. They came faster than I had imagined. Too soon, the faces of our enemies became plain to see and the armoured heads of their horses turned the quicksilver to a darkling ocean with sheen-topped waves.

The gust of wind brought us their stench: a blanket of horse-sweat and man-sweat so thick that we could have cut it with our knives and eaten it to fill the hollowness inside. My own sweat flashed cold across my back, and I reached for comfort to the horn settled at my left shoulder, the brass nestled by my ear, the ready places for my fingers. A spray of notes crowded my mind, ready to loose into the wild air.

The sun edged up until it caught the first heights of our standards. I saw the raised fist of Jupiter reach for the first rays, folding the light into its majesty so that it blazed with a life all its own.

I raised my hand to join it and the cheer that broke along the line was deeper than the enemy drumbeats, lasted longer, grew louder, and harder. It reached the oncoming cavalry and I saw them check in their advance, saw the horses pitch and stumble as they took the first rise of the hill.

In that moment, I believed the gods were with us. From my right side, I heard Syrion suck in a breath and hold it, and let it out in a word: *Arianna*, the name of his woman – one of his several women – spoken as a benediction, in heartfelt gratitude, as by a man who is granted his greatest wish.

Syrion was the standard-bearer for our cohort, and no man deserved the honour more. He wore a muleskin, where others of his kind wore bear or wolf or leopard; for us, the mule spoke to our hearts of the time we had defeated a worthy opponent. He wore it for the first time now, and if it was the last, still, it gave us courage.

On my shield side, my heart side, stood Heraclides, known as Tears, who had been born into wealth on Crete, and had grown expecting to prosper as the owner of a dozen vineyards until both of his parents died, whereupon he had been sent to live with an aunt in Socnopaios, who had given him up as a conscript in payment of tax, in lieu of her eldest son.

Tears had wept for most of the first three months after he joined us, but he was too beautiful to be whipped for it and we had taken care of him and he had grown to be the best swordsman of our unit. He smiled at me now, and it was the smile of the young Apollo, or Zeus in his youth, readying himself for war.

Ranged alongside were the other men of our unit: Rufus, Horgias, Sarapammon and Polydeuces, known as the Rabbit, for the single act of hiding in a hole one winter's night, when we were camped in the Syrian mountains, with the IVth Scythians as our enemy.

None of us was hiding now. Ablaze at last, as the standard was ablaze, bright in our armour, with our scarlet tunics aglow in the sun, we held a firm line and the need to fight shone from us, I think; our need to prove what we could do.

I looked ahead again. The sun had flooded the pass now. Tribal banners in the coloured silks of the Parthian tribes wove across the oncoming tide in a clash of hues: jade and citrus, scarlet and emerald, cornflower, crimson, gold.

At the back on their far right was a silver elephant on a ground of midnight blue that was the King of Kings' own mark. Vologases rode a grey horse, not as fine as my bay mare – there was no better horse in his empire or ours – but he had thirty men around him on matched blacks that were good enough to keep him safe.

In the front, to their left, facing us, was the blue tern of Adiabene whose king was Monobasus, the fox-faced petty tyrant who had betrayed Parthia and Rome with equal abandon. I fancied he recognized me as I did him, for he spoke once to his men and they readied their spears, bringing them down in a flurry of silk and iron. Their tips hung level, aimed at our hearts.

A man's shout rose up from their rearmost ranks, and the enemy drumbeat changed. As one, in perfect harmony, the oncoming horses rose from a trot to a canter. I could see men's faces level with my chest, just beyond casting distance for our spears. In the centre of our line, eighty paces to my left, I felt Cadus raise his hand; I did not need to look.

'Sound,' he said. That was all.

As one born to this single act, I dipped my lips to meet the trumpet's mouth even as my hands raised it up to be taken. I breathed deep, set my lips tight, and blew the ripple of eight notes that Cadus and I had planned so many years before in a tavern in Cappadocia. All along the line, the trumpeters of each cohort did the same, and this morning, this glorious morning, we were note-perfect.

Ripe as riven gold, the sound poured out across the morning.

Four things happened.

On the first note, the front ranks cast their javelins and drew their swords and knelt.

On the second note, the second ranks cast their javelins and drew their swords and knelt.

On the third note, the third rank cast their javelins and drew their swords and did not kneel.

On the fourth note, every man in all eight ranks rose to his feet and took one pace to his right, then one pace back for each of the remaining notes, leaving behind hardened oak stakes that stuck out of the earth, angled upwards to meet the bellies and breasts of the oncoming horses.

It was faultless. It was beautiful. The gods themselves could not have done it more cleanly, more sharply, in better time or in more perfect unison.

A thousand drills, in daytime, in deepest night, in summer, in winter, on flat ground and bog, on hill and rock and snow, done over and over until each man could place his stake and step around it in his sleep; these drills proved their worth here and now and the men who had cursed Cadus and me for devising it, who had promised our deaths at their own hands on the first battlefield – now these men turned their heads to the front and raised their shields and set their short-swords through the gaps and I read on the face of each one the shine of such pride as made my heart burst.

Cadus brought his hand down, hard. We sounded

two more notes and each man pressed his shield edge firm against the one to his right and like that, as a solid wall, we stepped towards the stumbling, screaming, broken ranks of Vologases' cavalry.

I smelled sweat and spilled intestines; I tasted blood on the thick air; I felt my blood surf in my ears and my muscles bunch across my back and I was shouting, I who had not known I had opened my mouth, and it sounded to me as if my whole life had been building to that shout, that it might reach to the sky and rock the earth in its foundations – and that men might die on the end of it; other men than me.

I looked to my left and Tears grinned back at me and I saw on his face the mirror to my own exultation and knew that he was in love, as I was, with the promise of battle.

I screamed out his name as my battle cry, and then the name of the legion I adored. A spear came past my ear. I ducked under it, stabbed upwards and felt my blade bite through skin and flesh and liquid vitals. I howled as a wolf howls and did not pause. One man dead, and me still alive; that was enough to call myself a warrior. *This is life. This place, balanced on the edge of death – this is what I was made for.*

In five years, I had come to believe that we might win this battle. In doing so, unlikely as it seemed, I had fallen in love with war itself.

Let me take you back those five years, that I might tell you the whole from the beginning, for I did not, as some do, grow through my childhood wanting to be a legionary. The lust for war came slowly and if I was naïve in all that I did to begin with, if I see it now through battle-hardened eyes, I ask you to remember that one thing: I did not ask for this.

Hyrcania, on the Caspian Sea, February, AD 57

In the Reign of the Emperor Nero

Chapter One

February, AD 57

Blue-green, iridescent, gleaming in the hazy sun, the peacock feathers shone out at me from a stall in the heart of the market.

The feathers were glorious; bright motes of summer in this place of winter greys that spawned unexpected memories of bright Macedonian mornings, of flower meadows and foaling mares, so that I was left floundering like a landed fish, gagging on the stench of rancid seal fat and gathering stares from the almond-eyed, flat-faced men of the Hyrcanian market.

They despised me; I hated them: these things were taken for granted, but I had never previously made a fool of myself in their presence. That I had done so now gave me yet another grievance against Sebastos Abdes Pantera, the man who served as my superior officer while we remained in this foreign land, and who had sent me, Demalion of Macedon, born a better man than Pantera might ever be, on a slave's errand.

The familiar sting of ruined pride brought me to my senses. I blinked away the memories, snapped shut my mouth and, as I had been ordered, paid over a silver coin for twelve peacock pinions; six from the left wing, six from the right.

The trader tested the silver between his teeth before he parted with the feathers. His eyes were gimlets of suspicion, buried in the folds of flesh that made his face. His beard was brightly black, oiled with fish oil or seal fat or whatever repugnant mess it was that the men here used to keep the frozen sea-wind from splitting their faces.

I still shaved every day, and kept the cold from my skin with olive oil. The Hyrcanians deemed me no better than a woman for it and were only restrained from saying so because Pantera and Cadus did the same, and Vilius Cadus was a foot larger in each dimension than any of them, hewn from raw granite, with a pugilist's fists and a nose yet unbroken. None of them dared offend him.

Whether they would have been as impressed had they known Cadus was a Roman, indeed that he was centurion of the Vth Macedonica legion, favourite of the late Augustus, was an open question. Nobody knew Cadus was a centurion just as nobody knew I was his clerk. Here, we were Greek freemen, no more than bodyguard and scribe to Pantera the horse-trader; necessary parts of his subterfuge.

Pantera had a lot to answer for.

'Archer! Arrows?' The fat-faced trader was trying

to make conversation. His Greek was appalling; he chopped the words as if his teeth were hatchets, and murdered the vowels.

I forced a smile. 'Not me.' I made gestures to fit the words. 'These are for Pantera,' and, at the man's incomprehension, 'for the Leopard.'

'Ah!'

The Leopard was their friend, or so they thought. He brought them amber from the far frozen ocean to the west, balsam from the southern deserts, pearls from the Mediterranean that were larger, more lustrous than the ones from the Hyrcanian Ocean on whose shores they lived. Better than all these, he brought horses from all over the world; fast, good, tough horses that might survive a Hyrcanian winter, and carry their owners on many hunts through the balmy, rain-blessed summers.

'Give these!' The man thrust a fistful of whole raven feathers into my hand. 'Good arrows. Go fast. Kill many bear!'

'I'm sure.' I pressed my fist to my forehead, and remembered to bow as I backed away. Leaving, I wondered if the men here could read minds, or if it was always the case in Hyrcania that some shafts were fletched with peacock flights and others with raven, for I had been sent to buy both.

The peacock flights were required, so I had been told, for the lighter arrows that Pantera had fashioned through the morning, while the raven feathers were destined for the heavier shafts, with the barbed iron flanges at the tip, designed to stop a bear or a boar.

In Macedonia, where I had grown to adulthood, we

had used goose feathers for the lighter arrows and swan for the bear-hunters, but nobody had asked me what I thought and I had not volunteered the information. Rather, I had been stunned that Pantera had bothered to tell me anything useful at all; for the past six months he had told me precisely what I needed to know to get through each day and no more.

Cadus always seemed at least three steps ahead of me, but he was my centurion, and while he had never once used that to hold me to silence, I was too young to ask anything, too deeply imbued with a legionary discipline that did not allow a man to question his superiors, too in awe of his battle majesty: I was nineteen years old, a conscript with two years' training behind me, and I had not yet drawn blood.

My lack of a kill, more than anything, was what I read in the flat stares of the Hyrcanian men. In this land – in all of Parthia, as far as I could tell – the boys killed a man or a boar or they died trying. Those who lived became men in that single act and were given women and horses to prove it. If a man was mounted, it was because he had taken at least one life in battle or in the hunt; and everyone rode.

I despised myself for my weakness. I may have dreamed all my youth of life as a horse-trader like my father; I may have railed against my conscription and loathed the legions on principle, but even so, every morning in this place I cursed my lack of valour and every night, when I slept, my traitorous mind brought me dreams drenched in the blood of our enemies as my comrades in the Vth launched themselves into battle, taking risks, winning glory, rising in the ranks, killing the enemy and so becoming men . . . all without my being there.

The fact that it was winter, when the weather forced a kind of peace on both sides, and that my comrades were currently enduring endless forced marches over the mountains in western Armenia because their general had deemed them unfit for battle, did nothing to hamper my fantasies.

The Parthian merchants were staring at me still. I shook my head clear of imagined gore and continued on through the market, past the reeking stalls of dried and smoked fish, past bushels of shelled nuts that smelled of autumn and threatened more memories, past pickled eggs in stone jars and skinless seabirds packed in salt-barrels.

Near the shoreline, I found the stall marked with the red-stained ewe's hide where waited a bundle with my name on it that I had orders to open on the spot.

Inside, I found a tunic made of fine undyed lamb's wool, and trousers the same, and boots that might have been made of bearskin and a belt that certainly was, and a silver brooch the size of a duck's egg to pin the woollen cloak that was wrapped around the bundle.

All of this was my gift from the new, young, extravagant King of Kings, that a horse-trader's scribe might attend a day's hunting in the royal party without offending the royal proprieties. I should have been grateful, but I had had enough of Hyrcania and was churlish enough to disdain it as no more than my due.

When I returned to the tavern – in Macedonia it would have been counted less than a shack and free men would not have deigned to enter – neither Pantera nor Centurion Cadus was present.

They did not return that day, but both were there when I woke the next morning. Cadus lay on his back on the straw pallet, sleeping with the peace of a man who knows that the legionary watch-horns have no power to rouse him.

Pantera, as always, was awake. He sat near the window, fletching the last of his arrows by a thin, grey light that bled in past the shutters.

Pantera the Leopard, trader and friend of traders; Pantera the Roman spy who claimed to have come from the emperor himself, and had letters enough to persuade a legionary commander in Oescus to give him two men; Pantera, who had picked me from four thousand others because, alone of my century, possibly of my cohort, perhaps of my legion, I could read and write Latin as well as Greek.

Out of habit, I cursed my mother's father, who had paid for the tutor, believing that all his grandsons should be literate. For good measure, I cursed my father, and my father's father and all the way back up the line to the misbegotten son of a she-ass who had sold the great Bucephalos to Alexander and thus guaranteed that his descendants would be horse-traders for ever more.

Because that was the other thing that had sealed my fate: Pantera might conceivably have been able to find another scribe in one of the legions who could write Greek and Latin with equal ease, but there was none who also had a lifelong eye for a horse, and could ride as well as he could march; better, in my case.

I chose not to think about that; like Macedonian mornings, some things were best remembered through a haze. I drew in a breath and tasted ice on the air and threw back the bed-hides, so that I might not be tempted to stay long in the warm.

'You can open the window,' I said. 'It can't get any colder in here than it already is.'

'It may even be warmer outside,' said Pantera. 'They say spring throws itself on a man fast here, like a woman in drink, and you can never tell when the sun will outweigh the chill.' He threw open the shutters and leaned on the sill to finish his work. His tone was mildly pensive. 'Have you found the women forward here?'

Surprised, I laughed aloud. 'They wouldn't dare. Fathers give their girl children in marriage to their friends the day after their first bleeding, and if a woman looks askance at another man she'll find herself spreadeagled on a cartwheel and that cart pushed into the sea.'

'That's what I thought. It must be the women of other nations who are forward.'

The new light showed Pantera dressed in a tunic of the same fine-woven lamb's wool as the one I had collected from the market, except that it was black, so that the silver brooch – his was the size of a child's fist and bore amber at its centre – was shown off more brightly.

I watched him tie off the last of the arrows; a raven's wing flight on one of the heavy bear-killing shafts. He lifted it and it vanished and I, still sleepy, was transported temporarily to childhood, mouth agape, a little worried, a little charmed by his sleight of hand, until he stood and his good black cloak flew a little with the movement and I saw that the entire quiver hung from his hip and he had not performed magic at all. The peacock flights outnumbered the raven by two to one. In my disappointment, I counted them, and tried to think what the quarry might be.

Pantera had no thought for me. He had turned to look east, towards the place where the lowering sky pressed down on the leaden sea. The flat, crushed sun cast him in sulphur and citron, gilding his hair to the rich red-gold of the Gauls, and the peacock flights at his hip became as living jewels, ablaze with ice and fire in their hearts. By a trick of the light, his hands were a god's hands, and his face, caught on the three-quarter turn, held a like divinity.

It was more than a morning in Macedonia, that look; it caught me deeper, and twisted harder, so that I caught my breath.

Hearing it, Pantera turned fully round, one brow raised. This once, his features were clear, his gaze steady over a mouth that could hold a thousand expressions and currently held none, and in that moment it seemed to me that I saw the true man for the first time in half a year of looking; and that Pantera was taut as his own strung bow.

I looked away, down, at my hands, at my feet, at Cadus, rising muzzily to waking. When I looked back again, Pantera had stepped away from the light and was the Leopard again, lost in the lazy shadows that clung to the room's margins; a man neither big nor small, with hair the colour of the brown bears in the forest, and eyes the brown-green of a river I had swum in as a child.

Like that, he could have walked into a crowd and men would barely have noticed he was among them. I had seen him do exactly that.

'Are you ready?' he asked. His voice did not sound tight. I thought I had imagined the tension, perhaps had wanted it to be there.

'As much as I ever am.' I stood at the window and let the freezing air knife into my lungs, let it pare away whatever impossible longing might have taken root.

I made myself read the land, as I had been taught. To the north, layers of cloud lay draped across the horizon in a way I had come to know these past six months.

'Besides snow,' I asked, 'what should I be ready for?'

'For a hunt such as you have never known.' Pantera's smile was bright. 'Whatever happens, do exactly what Cadus tells you. His job is to keep you both alive.'

Chapter Two

The snow had not yet begun to fall when the boar charged from the forest.

A shout went up; the men who rode in the company of Vardanes II, King of Kings of Parthia, supreme ruler of all land from the Euphrates to the Indus, were nothing if not swift to recognize danger.

But the beast moved faster than any man could do and, from the beginning, it had only one target: it charged as if directed by the gods, straight for the new young King of Kings himself, mounted in his gold and glory on a swift bay mare.

In an empire where men lived, died, ate, drank, bargained, loved and killed on horseback, the horse that bore the King of Kings was the best to be found in all his eighteen client kingdoms; fleet of foot, sharp of eye, with the small ears, wide nostrils and compact jawbone that were said by Xenophon to denote the finest of horses, her hide was the rich, deep bay of a bronze dish, and her mane and tail were black as ebony. She was trained to war and the hunt; to stillness in the midst of battle, the speed of a wolf in the forest.

Nevertheless, she was not fast enough to outrun a boar, and even if she had been, there was no obvious route to safety, for the King of Kings, beloved of the gods, was hemmed in on one side by the bleak forest whence came the boar, and on the other three sides by such a collection of courtiers and guards and body slaves as to make three more walls.

West, which is to say behind him, forty matched Nubian slaves walked naked in the chill sea air, carrying whole on a trestle a pavilion of kingfisher-coloured silk, made large enough to enable the King of Kings to ride his horse in through the entrance and partake of his midday meal without the inconvenience of dismounting.

He had just done exactly that; the kingfisher pavilion was even now being readied to carry back to the palace.

North, to the king's left, between him and the just-thawed sea, thirty cooks and their under-cooks and pot-boys similarly tidied away the remains of the roast buck that had fallen to the King of Kings' own bow some days previously and had been the central part of the royal feast.

East, where the mountains curved down to kiss the sea, were grouped those merchants, councillors and vassal kings who had been granted rare permission to join Vardanes II in his winter residence, and further honoured by the invitation to join him in his hunt.

Only seventeen of Parthia's eighteen vassal kings were present; Tiridates of Armenia alone had not been invited. As uncle to the King of Kings, brother to the late king, Vologases of blessed memory, he was not perhaps yet sufficiently recovered from his mourning to enjoy the company of his nephew.

And besides, the Roman general Corbulo was camped with six legions on Armenia's western borders. He might have been fully occupied in putting all thirty thousand men through winter fatigues that made war look like a day of rest, but a king could be excused for choosing to stay and defend himself and his integrity, at least until the new King of Kings had concluded this war council and launched his own attack on the mewling, pale-skinned braggarts who so offended the integrity of his empire.

The war council had been conducted over the roast buck. A horde of mounted men to whom fighting was as necessary and integral as breathing did not take long to decide on a new war. When the King of Kings had suggested they make a late autumn attack on the Roman camps, long after the end of the fighting season had notionally ended, he had been roundly cheered by his vassals.

The seventeen client kings had fallen over themselves in the following discourse to promise horse-archers, heavy cavalry, light cavalry, infantry and, from the one who ruled the far eastern border with Mathura, elephants with which to grind Rome into the ground.

Weaving through their midst at his most effacing, and most efficient, Pantera had taken a dozen different commissions to source fresh mounts of sound stock at a good price for the coming battles. I, as his clerk, had written each one down. Against my better judgement, I found myself listening hard, making other, inner, notes of the tactics they proposed, and how much they knew of the strength of each legion.

They knew of the Vth, my legion, of their skill in battle, of how they had won Antium for Octavian, and then fought against Parthia for Tiberius; they were glad the Vth was not yet on their borders, although concerned that it was camped so close in Moesia. I may have loathed the Vth on principle when I was forced to march in its company, but here it was *my* legion; the men were my brothers. I caught myself smiling broadly once, or rather, Pantera caught me, and threw me a look that ensured I didn't smile again for the rest of the meal.

It was a rowdy, enthusiastic council; each man was testing his standing with the new King of Kings, and none had yet gained ascendancy. With all to play for, and the king known to favour courage in the hunt above all else, the lesser kings had moved their mounts swiftly away from the pavilion and towards the forest when the horns summoned them to the hunt, the mind of each bent on the ways he might outshine his brothers.

Still, when the boar charged from the forest, none of them moved fast enough to stand in its way.

I was one of the many who had shouted a warning as the beast hurtled from the thick, scrubby forest. I jerked my horse round, thinking to throw it forward and take the body of men with me, and at least look as if I was doing something useful.

A calloused hand fell on my wrist, skin on skin, holding me still. Vilius Cadus shook his head, and jerked his chin sideways to where Pantera had lifted his bow from his saddle horn. The usual pall of envy and resentment began to poison my reason – yet again, Cadus had been privy to our business when I had not – but then I caught sight of Pantera's bow for the first time, and was lost.

My great-uncle Demetrios, the last conscript in our family, had such a bow, and had brought it back home when he had retired after the Thracian campaign.

I may not have wanted to be a legionary, but all my childhood I had yearned to hold and to shoot such a weapon. It was of Scythian type, a war bow as much as a hunting bow, small, deeply curved, with a full belly, richly decorated, and polished horn at the tips.

With unhurried speed, Pantera leaned back and reached for the quiver that hung from his hip.

Three arrows sang in the clean, cold air.

Soaring high across the iron sky, they held their own fine tune; a chord played so close together as to make almost a single note. There are men who will tell you they could not have come from the same bow, but they had; with my own eyes I saw Pantera shoot them.

I did not shout now; nobody did. Even the King of Kings sat in measured silence, watching their flight. Afterwards, that was what the gathered kings remembered most clearly: that alone among the party, their king had not cried out.

The first arrow struck the boar behind its shoulder and sank deep, so that only the peacock flights stood blue-green against its steaming hide.

The beast barely slowed its charge, but then I had been taught that nobody had ever stopped a boar but with a ten-foot spear with a good broad blade and a crosspiece one third of the way down the haft – and a lot of luck.

The second arrow struck the beast in the eye and sank as deep as the first; the raven flights were lost against the black bristle, which meant that the heavy iron barbs had penetrated the bone of the beast's skull, exactly as they were supposed to.

The boar grunted once, a sound so like a man disturbed in slumber that I nearly looked away to see who else had made the sound. But I did not, for Cadus' hand tightened on my wrist, holding me steady.

Thus it was that he and I witnessed together the moment when its haunches ceased to power the boar towards the King of Kings and it toppled sideways to the turf.

'Good shot! What a shot! Did you see that? Did you—'

All around, seventeen minor kings gave enthusiastic vent to their relief, none more so than Ranades IX, the bluff, broad-shouldered king of Hyrcania, in whose country they hunted, and under whose hospitality the King of Kings had so nearly met his end.

If Vardanes had died, Ranades would have been required at the very least to take his own life. He might also have had to hand over his kingdom first, thus ensuring the deaths of all six of his sons. Such were the rules of sovereignty in the empire of Parthia.

The royal shouts ricocheted off the forest wall and rolled out across the sea. Shore birds fled, and a single raven rose from far back in the forest. As if at its command, the shouts of the kings halted, severed so suddenly, so completely, that the silence fell like a hammer.

I did not see the third arrow strike, but, forewarned, I turned to my right in time to see Vardanes II, King of Kings, by right of birth, war and parricide supreme ruler of Parthia and all her kingdoms, slide sideways on his magnificent bay mare.

There he hung, half dismounted, held by the trappings of gold about his thighs, with the third of Pantera's arrows protruding from the mail shirt above his heart, its raven flights black against the bright silver of his chest, its barbed point bloody at his back, where it came out a hand's breadth to one side of his spine.

'*Run!*' This time I did slew my horse sideways. 'That mad fool has ruined us! Run for your— *Oof!*'

That mad fool – Pantera – had slammed his elbow into my solar plexus, robbing me of breath, words and movement. From my other side, Vilius Cadus grabbed my mount's reins, so that even when I could breathe again, I could not escape.

Cadus' voice wove over my head, fine as a breath. 'Demalion, be still. Smile. Particularly smile at the king of Hyrcania. Do this, and we will live. Fail and we will die in exactly the manner you fear most.'

'And watch the kings,' Pantera said, from my other side. 'See who takes command. It may change what happens next.'

I knew what was going to happen next; it involved razor-knives and hot irons and hammers and pain made to last for days on end. I eased my free hand back, towards the dagger at my waist, trying to work out whether I had time to draw it and plunge it into my own neck before the men on either side could stop me.

Even as I did so, I found myself absorbed in the developing tableau ahead, where the seventeen client kings gathered about the bay mare, none knowing which amongst them had the authority to touch the sacred body of their supreme ruler.

Ranades IX, king of Hyrcania, settled the matter. Breaking free of the others, he pushed his own mount close to the king's magnificent bay and, leaning in from his own saddle, took the King of Kings in his arms with the care of a man for his most beloved brother.

They were not brothers, in fact, not even distant cousins. Ranades of Hyrcania was a man in his full middle age with six importunate sons who might yet try to depose him, while the King of Kings was one such son among nine, who had succeeded in deposing his father, killed three of his brothers and set himself on the throne.

Nevertheless, the king of Hyrcania's wide face was composed in lines of evident regret as he eased his supreme ruler free of the gold trappings that held him fast.

Holding the body across his arms as he might carry a child, or a woman, he stepped his horse neatly backwards; a man born to horsemanship. The other kings stepped with him in a ring of royal mourning, each man gluing his shoulder tight to the next, for now was not a time to stand out from the crowd.

Ranades IX, of course, already stood out; the murder

had taken place on his land, in his kingdom, by a man invited to his court: Pantera.

I felt the moment when seventeen kings turned their attention our way. I kept still only because Cadus held me, but Cadus himself was cursing under his breath, invoking gods and their progeny with a vicious invective that two years in his legion had yet to teach me.

Pantera was not cursing. Pantera, in fact, was leaning forward on his saddle, watching the kings with a kind of weary patience, as if he had better things to do, more interesting places to be. Two or three of the men opposite recognized the look and began to shout suggestions about how his death might be made as deeply interesting – and lengthy – as possible. Under Ranades' stare, they fell silent.

'Let the Nubians come forward.' Gilded by a new authority, Ranades' voice lifted over the shouts of his peers.

The forty Nubians hurried to his bidding, although for the first few yards they carried with them the kingfisher pavilion. Enough of them had died for letting it dip below waist level for the rest to have carried it into living fire and died holding it, had they been so ordered.

Ranades took a patient breath. He had grey eyes, the colour of iron, restless as the ocean, with not a shade of doubt in them that I could see.

'Set down the pavilion. Bring only the trestle. Our lord must be carried to the palace. You may not touch him. There must be furs, somewhere, on which he can lie?'

He looked around, his gaze already glancing over the

other kings as over lesser men, and it became apparent that they had missed their first opportunity, and that, did they not act swiftly, all authority would leak from the dead man to this one, living, who was giving all the orders when the others gave none.

Three of the younger men, contemporaries of the dead king, caught each other's eyes and, as one, stepped their horses smoothly back out of the royal group.

They had features sharp as foxes beneath their beards, and were clearly related. Their eyes had the same vulpine slant, but their cheekbones were neither as high nor as distinct as those in Hyrcania, where men from the king downwards had cheekbones jutting sharp as bridges beneath their eyes from which the rest of their face hung as an afterthought.

They wheeled their mounts, these fox-faced men with their black beards and hate-filled eyes, and pushed them at me, at Cadus, and at Pantera, the trader-archer who had slaughtered the King of Kings, and so signed his own death warrant.

Yet who still carried his bow, and had at his hip a quiver full of arrows, several of them fletched in black.

As one who lives a whole life between heartbeats, I saw him nock one, and draw his bow to its fullest.

'Which of you first?' Pantera asked, and smiled.

The three bearded men hauled their horses to a mouth-destroying halt.

'Do you *dare—*' asked the first. The blue tern on his horse's brow-harness marked him as Monobasus, king of Adiabene, a province to the south and west of Hyrcania.

Pantera arched one brow. 'I have killed a usurper, a traitor to the King of Kings, a pretender to the throne that was not rightfully his. Do you wish that I had not? Be careful what you say. There are many others present and they are all listening with interest.'

It was his calm that held them in the first moments. I had heard that voice before, and it set the small hairs upright down the length of my spine. I was relieved that Pantera was not speaking to me.

Covertly, I looked at him. In the spirit of wild detachment that had taken hold of me, I wanted more than anything else to know if Pantera's heart was beating as hard as my own.

It could not be, I concluded, because Pantera was holding a Scythian war bow at full draw with the arrow perfectly steady. But the knuckles of both his hands were green-white in the cold light and I saw a ribbon of sweat slide down the line of his jugular vein, to vanish beneath the folds of the lamb's wool cloak. He may not have been strung tight as I had imagined in the morning, but he was nowhere near as calm as he made himself seem.

'The King of Kings is dead,' said the king of Adiabene hoarsely.

'The King of Kings can never die,' Pantera said with careful patience. 'And in this case, he certainly has not done so. My lord? It may be timely now for you to reclaim your throne.'

He cast his voice over his shoulder, north, to the ever-moving sea, and there, from amongst the huddle of cooks and pot-boys and serving-men, a figure stepped forward.

He was taller than any of the servants, and, now that

he removed the cap that had hidden it, his stone-grey hair was full and flourished to his shoulders; the hair of a man who has fed well through his life, who has never had his head shaved to show his servitude. His bearing was tall and vigorous and as he walked through them the slaves and servants fell to their knees and pressed their brows to the turf.

Very shortly afterwards, the seventeen client kings slid down from their horses and did likewise. King Ranades IX of Hyrcania was not first, but he was most assuredly not last. He dropped the body he had been holding as a man might drop a dead snake, and his brow touched the turf and stayed there while the man they had believed to be dead these past eight months walked past to mount the bay mare.

Thus it was that Vologases, King of Kings, lord of all life, supreme ruler of the Parthian empire, may the gods for ever venerate his name, returned to reclaim the throne from the son who had done his best to usurp it.

Chapter Three

One month to the day later, I stood in the royal pavilion and watched a mass of armoured horsemen flow across a valley.

Bright as the polished moon, afire under the early sun, alive with rippling silk in every colour known to the Parthian empire, the heavy cavalry of Parthia, nearly five and a half thousand men, rode their horses at a hand canter from the mouth of a gorge to its blunt end amidst the mountains.

The earth rolled beneath them. Birds fled from the skies. It was said that the King of Kings could command the weather, that he ordered sun for himself, except when his subjects needed rain for their crops, and that he sent hail and snow, mud and thunder to plague his enemies. I stood less than a spear's throw away and watched him, as he watched the display of his army, and I believed every word of it.

Three hundred at a time, they rode by us, clad in

chain mail that chimed softly over the echoing beat of their mounts' feet. As they passed the pavilion, they turned to face us, and even the hardened warriors of the Hyrcanians gasped the first time, for every man *and every horse* was masked in polished iron, so that the men were silver-faced but for their eyes, which were black behind the gaps in the masks, and the horses were monsters, inanimate and terrifying, and I, who had never seen their like, felt my innards churn.

A thousand by a thousand by a thousand, they rode by, and now the last phalanx of three hundred horsemen came to take – perhaps to retake – their oath.

At their rear, a man shouted an order. Another blew a horn, not a curled one, such as we use to control our legions, but a long one that stretched to the high sky.

Three notes sounded, and the galloping men wheeled left in a single block, so that they were riding straight away from us. Another blast, and they turned left again, and another and they were riding straight for us, and this time I saw their twin-headed axes, which could kill a horse with a single blow – we had seen it done, earlier in the day – I saw their lances, the mythical *kontos*, ten-foot poles with long-swords affixed to the ends that might both slash and stab the enemy. Rumour said they had daggers on their butt ends, so that the riders might pierce a man beneath them should they have need. I could not see that they would have need.

They came at us, spear-swords levelled, and even though we had been subject to this seventeen times already I still flinched when I saw the eyes of the front rows flare white at the edges before the trumpet blasted one final time and, in the finest display of horsemanship I had ever seen, they brought their horses to a level halt.

Their leader stepped his horse forward. The silks at his waist and neck, I saw, were blue, and the sign on the funnelling banner behind him was a blue seabird; a tern.

Monobasus of Adiabene took off his helmet and the same fox-faced, death-eyed king who had wanted to kill us in the forest on the afternoon of what was now known as the Day of the Traitor's Death looked out at us.

Bowing to his King of Kings, he raised his right hand. 'We give our lives in the service of the King of Kings. Adiabene is ready for war, whenever it comes.'

He had a good, carrying voice, if somewhat nasal in its tones. Vologases inclined his head. He looked more massive now, as if kingship had given him layers of his own personal armour. 'Parthia is grateful to her sons for their sacrifice, and will honour their memory if death takes them on the field of battle.'

It was the same that had been said, by both sides, seventeen times before. All the eighteen client kings were here, for Tiridates had found that he could, after all, leave Armenia for the celebration of his brother's return to power. Each had brought three hundred cataphracts, the heavy cavalry of Parthia, so feared by her enemies.

Earlier, we had seen the lighter cavalry, and before them the horse-archers, who had shot their deep-bellied bows in the eight directions at targets in front, at angles on either side, behind. Having seen them with my own eyes, I can vouch that what men said was true: they could shoot a dozen arrows in the space of a long, slow breath, and do it as easily backwards as forwards.

Monobasus of Adiabene led his horsemen away in a jingle of mail and harness-mounts. A small brass gong sounded to end the display. The King of Kings rose. His courtiers rose with him, and then fell to their knees, brows pressed to the canvas beneath our feet. I was with them, Pantera on my left, Cadus on my right. I felt the swirl and play of silks as Vologases, King of Kings of all Parthia, walked down from his dais. His son, now dead, had used a litter to move amongst his subjects. Men respected his father more for rejecting it.

I felt him walk by, and then stop. An order was given in a language I did not know. The silks passed us, and the faint smell of frankincense, which was burned to keep the king free from ill intent.

A shadow remained over us. I looked to my right and saw a courtier bend and speak to Pantera. 'Be at the palace in the hour before dusk. The King of Kings will speak to you then.'

I bit my lip and offered a prayer to the local gods, begging that this might not be the final audience that saw us chained and impaled on spears in the market square for our actions on the Day of the Traitor's Death.

'I must leave this place and return to Parthia. Before I go, there is the matter of the bay mare on which the traitor was mounted. She has shown herself to be ill-favoured by the gods. She cannot remain here.'

Vologases let his words roll across the floor. His voice

carried an authority I had never yet heard from any man. Even Corbulo, Rome's greatest general, who many, even then, said should have been emperor, did not sound this comfortable with power.

Nobody answered; the King of Kings had not yet asked a question. I remained on my knees with my brow pressed to the oak boards. Cadus and Pantera held my either side. Neither of them moved. Together we three contemplated the fate that had befallen the traitor whom Pantera had killed.

There had been no pyre for the king's late son; his corpse had been left to lie in the forest as food for the wolves and carrion birds. It was the worst thing they could do to a man who had paid with his life for his treachery, for here even the stillborn children were given fire to carry them to the gods; even the women who died on the cartwheels pushed into the sea were drawn back out at low tide, and burned.

Nobody was left to the wolves, except this prince who had thought to usurp his father's throne and whose name was now unspeakable, whose own sons were . . . gone, and their mothers with them. No pyres had been lit for them, either.

The mare on which the traitor had been seated at the time of his death was, obviously, no longer considered the best horse in Parthia. It was amazing that she had not been served as stew at one of the banquets. There had been many banquets; an entire month of banquets without pause. I found it best not to think of those, nor the wine that had flowed as each minor king outdid his peers in celebrating his supreme ruler's return.

But the mare . . . she was young, and fit, and exceptionally fast. I knew her breeding and what would be lost to the world were she to die. I began to think how I might find a way to speak.

Pantera thought faster, and had more authority. Quietly, he said, 'If my lord might permit me to suggest an answer to the problem?'

I held my breath. The air did not fold about us. None of the nine men standing guard about Vologases skewered Pantera with a lance.

'You may speak,' said the King of Kings.

'It is necessary that I travel west again, soon; perhaps tomorrow. I could take the mare with me and sell her and return the gold – for she will fetch gold, I have no doubt of that – return that gold to your gracious majesty. In this way her worth will return to your majesty while she herself will not.'

'So you are leaving us.'

There was accusation in that flat, heavy statement, and a hint of a question. Or perhaps a request. Looking to my left, I found that Pantera had raised his head and was sitting back on his heels, still kneeling, but facing the king.

A quick glance rightward revealed that Cadus was in the process of doing the same. I joined him; it was easier to breathe if I did not have to appear to be kissing the floor, and there was some relief in being able to see the king, if not yet to look on his face.

Vologases was seated on a thick oak chair, padded with hides and velvet. He leaned both elbows on the arms, and the weight of his head on his steepled fingers, and he was staring at Pantera as if his eyes might bore holes in his skull, and thereby bring him to do his bidding.

Pantera had fixed his eyes on the king's feet. It seemed a prudent move. 'Majesty,' he said, after a pause. 'I am a trader. I have sold all I brought. With great regret, I must therefore leave your company to purchase more.'

'And you will return when? Ever?'

Another stretch of silence. Another moment to wonder that Pantera knelt before a man who was more powerful than Caesar, and appeared to be refusing him what he wanted.

'We would give you more than you can ever buy, did you choose to remain with us,' said Vologases, at length.

'Your majesty is gracious.'

'You accept?'

'You know I cannot.'

'*Why?*' Vologases' hand slammed on the arm of the chair. The entire room shook. Two guards stepped forward and then nervously back again. I dug my fingernails into my palms and kept my gaze hard on his magnificent seal-fur boots and let that vast voice boom over me. 'Because you work for Rome? Your heart is given to the thin-skinned, mewling children who rule there? Truly?'

'My heart is not given, lord, but I have given my oath and must keep it. What man would trust another who broke his oath to his liege-lord? My lord is too wise for that. I will take the bay mare and sell her and return to my lord his gold and it may be that in time I will be released from the burden of my oath and may return joyful to my lord's side. Nothing is impossible.'

Sweat soaked the armpits of my lamb's wool tunic as I watched Vologases compress his lips and close his eyes and saw him frame an order – and then reconsider it.

When he opened his eyes to look at us again, the yearning in them was less.

He said, 'She was your gift, was she not? You gave her to . . . him whose name is no longer spoken.'

'I did, lord. As I told you last autumn, it was necessary to come close to that one in order to stand any chance of success in our endeavour.'

Our endeavour? He had planned it for *six months*? I bit the inside of my cheek to keep my face still.

A tension changed in the air. I lifted my eyes and found that the King of Kings was staring at Pantera and Pantera was staring openly back. Which surely was not permitted.

'You asked of me a boon, when you brought your proposal,' Vologases said, and there was a new softness, almost an intimacy, to his voice. 'I agreed to it. Has anything changed?'

'Not that I am aware of, gracious lord. I asked that you not attack Rome unless she bring her legions east of the Euphrates. That remains my request.'

'Then I will keep to it. I, too, am a man who knows the value of his oath.'

Rising, Vologases grasped Pantera by the shoulders and raised him ungently to his feet. They were of a height, but where Pantera was slim as whipcord the king was a bear with bull's shoulders, a man born to wield an axe in war. His fists held Pantera upright. I could not tell if the Leopard's feet were touching the ground.

'Tell your Corbulo to keep his troops on his side of the river and I will keep Parthia's heavy cavalry and horse-archers on mine. In this way might our empires be neighbours in peace.'

The king's hands snapped open. Pantera rocked down on to his feet, and, with a tumbler's elasticity, converted what might have been a stumble into a bow. 'His majesty is wise as the eagle, fierce as the bear in protection of his people. I will convey to General Corbulo your message. If it is in my power, I will bind him to keep his side of the bargain.'

'It won't be in your power,' Vologases said sourly. 'Like all his kind, he is ruled by greed. And now he is ruled also by a mewling boy-child in Rome, who sings for the entertainment of others. There will be war. But not this year and perhaps not next. Leave now; we tire of your company. Take the bay mare and do with her what you will. We wish no recompense for such a gift.'

Chapter Four

'I don't understand,' I said. 'Vologases is as much an enemy to Rome as his son was. His brother is on the throne of Armenia and General Corbulo is about to start a war against him.'

We were no longer in the foul Hyrcanian inn; we were, in fact, no longer in Hyrcania, but in a tavern that spanned three storeys, a day's ride into Armenia, which nation, as I had had just pointed out, was currently ruled by Tiridates, brother to Vologases, whose men were assiduous in their care of us, as ordered by the letters of safe passage provided by the King of Kings.

These letters had provided not only our safety but also our luxury as we travelled; this inn was not the first to offer us its best rooms, but it was the first in which armed men had not shared those rooms with us, in order to 'ensure our safety at all times'. They had backed off now, just as had the snow that had harried us all the way to the border.

If the King of Kings could control the weather, he had done so well, for it had followed us faithfully until we had departed Hyrcania and begun to travel through Media Atropatene and Adiabene. Then the snow had dropped back and the sun had found its heart and spring had come, bringing snowmelt, and mud, so that there were times when we would have preferred the ice and snow. Armenia, such as we had seen of it so far, was little different.

I sat on the end of the bed tugging off my sodden riding boots and let fly the questions that had been held inside since we had taken our leave. 'What on earth were we doing back there besides trying to get ourselves killed?'

'Demalion, we're alive.' Pantera's voice was unusually clipped, as if his patience had finally run to an end. 'If we were trying to get ourselves killed, we three would have managed it, I think. Two officers of the Fifth and a spy trained by Seneca could manage that much at least.'

He was sitting by the open window of our room, facing west, to the old sun. As ever, he kept his back to a wall and his face to the door and the Scythian bow with the raven arrows at his side; he had never yet let it go, except when required to by the King of Kings.

He was resting now, turned away from us with his chin on his fist and his elbow on the edge of the window, and so did not see the mix of confusion and resentment on my face. Still, he must have sensed it. 'Cadus, tell him,' he said tersely.

Cadus was sitting on the bed nearest the door, teasing

a stone from the sole of his riding boot with his belt knife.

I turned on him. 'Well? Plainly you know everything I don't.'

Cadus tossed his knife loosely on to the pillow. Seeing him smile was like watching stone crack after frost; like having a friend return who had been lost. I don't think he'd smiled once all the time we were in Hyrcania. Smiling now, he said, 'Vologases is only an enemy of Rome if we make him into one.'

'But he put his brother on the throne of Armenia in direct defiance of Rome! What's that if not an act of war?'

'It's expediency. Armenia is a part of the Parthian empire and Vologases has the right to choose its king. If he fails, he will not be King of Kings for long – he has enemies inside his empire as much as he does without. General Corbulo thinks that Vologases can be persuaded to deal with Nero; he will be allowed to keep his brother on the throne, but only if Tiridates comes to Rome himself and asks for it nicely. That way, Nero can hold a Triumph, claim a great victory and not have to spend any more money in the east, at a time when the western borders are a sponge soaking up gold in the defence of Britain. Quite why anyone would wish to pour money into a swamp surrounded by sea, full of women who fight like harpies, is beyond me, but that's why we're here, you and me and Pantera: it's all about saving money.'

Cadus laid his boots to one side and began to remove his riding trousers, revealing thighs that would have made an ox blush, and very white skin. For his size, he was well made, and he had no difficulty balancing on one leg as he donned clean woollen trews. He glanced over his shoulder at Pantera. 'Am I right?'

'Close.' Pantera spoke without turning.

'But Vologases *will* attack the legions,' I said. 'He'll have to: the war council has met. If he goes back on that, they'll think him weak and he'll have another half-dozen traitors vying for his throne.'

I sighed and hunched my shoulders. I had thought we were in Hyrcania because Rome *wanted* a war. All the way across Armenia I had been preparing my report for the officers of my legion. I had new dreams in which I handed my notes to Corbulo himself, and was made flag-bearer of my century for my trouble. On the good nights, I became aquilifer, and carried the Eagle of the Vth Macedonica into battle. If I were going to be forced to march with the legions, at the very least I could march at the front, or so I had thought.

'Are you saying there will be no war?' I said, and heard in my voice a new hope; if peace broke out, who would have need of soldiers? Particularly those who would prefer to be herding horses. A cloud lifted that I had not known lay on me. I saw images of horse herds, and Macedonian mountains, and my mother welcoming home the unconquering hero.

Pantera threw me a bitter smile. 'Don't pack your bags yet. That's not what I was saying. If you want my honest opinion, I think war is a certainty; Nero doesn't have the self-control to keep his generals in check. But the fighting can perhaps be delayed if Vologases faces internal strife. To that end, I sincerely hope there is at least one king who'll be trying to take his place before spring. *That* is what we have been working towards—What?'

I was shaking my head; he must have seen it from the corner of his eye.

'Nobody's going to turn on Vologases this year.' I was scathing, which I had never dared before, but his tone had stung me. 'There are no sons left with any ambition and Ranades, who has the power, won't turn on him: the king of Hyrcania loves him like a brother and is loved in his turn. There's nobody left except—' I bit the edge of my thumb, thinking. 'The fox-faced king? Monobasus of Adiabene? You think he'll attack Vologases this winter?'

'Very good.' Pantera's voice was heavy with irony. 'The king of Adiabene is . . . intimate with Ranades' second son, who has just seen a way by which he might make himself at the very least king of Hyrcania, if not King of Kings. I wouldn't be surprised if Ranades found himself on the wrong end of an arrow in the hunt one day soon. And his replacement might find he had pressing business in Cstesiphon.'

'Where?'

'The Parthian capital. Where Vologases has his winter palace,' Cadus answered. He finished pulling on his trews and crossed the room to lay one ham-fisted hand on Pantera's shoulder. 'What's wrong with you?' he asked. 'You're moody and you're baiting the boy when he doesn't deserve it. That's not like you. Did the messenger say something you didn't like?'

The messenger . . . a short man with a hard-driven horse had met us on the track in a section of forest and spoken to Pantera as they squeezed their horses in opposite directions past the same fallen tree trunk. If they had shared four words they were short ones. If written messages had passed between them . . . that wasn't impossible, I thought; something small could have been transferred from palm to palm as they rode. I tried not to look shocked.

'What will you do if Vologases brings his heavy cavalry against your legion?' Pantera asked, rising. He sounded serious. He looked serious. 'If Demalion can stop planning his escape for a moment and accept that the Fifth *is* his legion, then the two of you might wish to consider this: Vologases has five and a half thousand cataphracts; you have seen them. He has as many light cavalry, who are still more heavily armed than anything of Rome, plus the horse-archers. The legions of the east have legionaries and minimal cavalry. What would you do if you were set against him?'

Run, I thought, but did not say it. To my left, Cadus poked his tongue into the gap between his front teeth, as if exploring it helped him to think. 'There are ways for men on foot to fight horses,' he said warily. 'Even the cataphracts.'

'Think on them,' Pantera said brusquely. 'I'm going out.' He pushed past us, out of the room and out of the inn.

We stood at the open window and watched him say something short to the guards and snatch the bay mare from the grooms. He mounted alone, neatly, hard, fast, with anger written on every line of his body. The mare tried to rear and he kicked her forward, cursing. He did not use her wrongly – I could not have forgiven him for that – but he let his rage be known and she left at a flat-eared gallop, heading out beyond the safe road to the unprotected forest.

It was the first and only time I saw Pantera lose his temper. I was only glad he had taken it away from us. I did not envy any bandits that thought him fair game, for he still had his bow, and I had no doubt that he would kill without thought any man who came against him.

Cadus and I stood together until the trees swallowed the sound of his passing, then Cadus turned away from the window, cracking his knuckles. His face was unreadable. In Pantera, that was usual; in Cadus it most assuredly was not. If I had not been certain that Cadus, at least, took only women to his bed, I would have thought myself caught in the heart of a lovers' quarrel.

'What do we do?' I said, lost.

'We sit here and work out the ways a legion of five thousand can stand against a mounted army of twice that number of cavalry and survive. When he's in that mood, we need to have some good answers before he comes back.'

'And then will he tell us what the messenger said?'

'He'll tell us when he's ready, but only if he thinks we need to know. Don't think about that. Just sit there' – Cadus nodded to the bed – 'and do what he said;

pretend you're in the front row when we're set against the Parthians and you want to stay alive. For a start, tell me anything you've been taught about the ways infantry might win against cavalry.'

Chapter Five

We had a plan ready by dusk, and laid it out for Pantera on his return, using our daggers and boots to show the cataphracts in their chain mail with their ten-foot spear-swords and our belts to show the layout of the legions.

Whatever his earlier temper, Pantera had recovered his good humour and approved our plan, suggesting minor alterations that we might consider. He joked with us, which was a novel experience, and we laughed, all three together; and in that spirit, with the excitement of battle almost upon us, we left the inn the following morning and travelled on.

The following days passed in a haze as we crossed Armenia from east to west, leaving the old volcano to our right and Lake Van to our left and then traversing the Taurus Mountains.

Each day, the spring grew stronger, the grasses greener, the flowers brighter. And each day, we studied the topography as if we were the forward scouts for the legions with Vologases' army a day behind, hunting us down. After a while, it began to feel true and Cadus and I searched out the places for lookouts, the open plains in these high, unfriendly mountains where a cohort, or three, or an entire legion, might hold a pass against an advance. We planned our anti-cavalry manoeuvres until we could recite them in our sleep. Only when we reached the western border where Armenia met Cappadocia – in effect, where Parthia met Rome – did we begin to relax.

That night, Pantera bought us wine, and we toasted our time together. I had lost my resentment, my envy, my bitterness. I was grateful to him for taking me out of a winter's quarters where I would have spent half of the six months marching over the mountains and the other half digging encampments in waist-deep snow. I told him so, and that I was taking back to the Vth Macedonica all I had learned.

And that was when he set his beaker down and looped his hands round his knees and I remembered the inn on the eastern border, and the messenger, and Pantera's temper.

'What?' I said.

Cadus answered for me, slowly, testing. 'We're not going back to the Fifth, are we? That was the message?'

'That was the message.' Pantera looked down at his thumbs. 'It was signed by the emperor; there is nothing I can do to countermand it. If it makes you feel any better, they're sending me to Britain, which, as you so rightly observed, is a swamp surrounded by sea and full of women who fight like harpies.'

'Perhaps the emperor thinks you can save him money there as you did here.' I looked down at the table as I spoke, and drew whorls with my fingertip in a puddle of spilled wine. I felt a kind of tugging grief in my chest and charged my voice to sound cheerful. 'If you can do what you did in Parthia, they'll make you a hero when you come back to Rome.'

'If I come back,' Pantera said. 'The chances are never high. But even if I do, spies are never heroes. We do our work unseen, behind men's backs.'

'What of us?' Cadus asked.

Pantera raised his head. He was too much a man of honour not to meet Cadus' eyes, and mine. He said, 'I am to leave you here and cross overland. You are to journey as swiftly as you may to Raphana where—'

'Not the Twelfth?' My hand splayed flat, loudly. The puddle of wine smeared across the table. I may have resented the Vth on principle, but I knew they were one of the most honoured legions in the empire and had some pride in that. The XIIth was quartered in Raphana with the IVth Scythians and both legions were universally despised.

I read the answer in Pantera's eyes, and his regret, which did nothing to make me feel better.

'I recommended you for promotion,' he said. 'It didn't occur to me they'd move you. They need good men in the Twelfth to strengthen its heart, and you are both that. At least you are accorded your worth. You' – he nodded to Cadus – 'will become first centurion of the sixth cohort, with pay to match.'

First centurion. It had a good ring to it. Of sixty

centurions in a legion, only ten were first of their cohorts, paid twice as much as the rest. And you might think that the sixth cohort was a long way down the line, with only four below it, but in reality, the layout of battle meant that the sixth was the veteran cohort, manned by the best of men, who held the rear line in battle and never retreated. If the legion had such men. From what we had heard of the XIIth, its men were worth less than sheep, but even then, you would have to suppose that some must be better than the others.

Pantera's gaze was turbulent, but Cadus met it squarely and I saw his chin go up. He was the fourth generation of his family to enter the legions: his great-grandfather had fought for Octavian when the Vth Macedonica had first been formed, and then for Antony. His grandfather had died in service as a centurion. His father had enlisted at eighteen and been raised to camp prefect before he retired. Cadus himself had joined a year younger, lying about his age, and been made centurion by the age of twenty-five. He was a man to polish mud and make it shine. I realized how much I would miss him. Both of them. In an act as unlikely as any that whole six months, I closed my eyes and prayed to join him at least in his cohort, if not his century.

I didn't see Pantera's face, but heard him speak from the darkness beyond my closed lids.

'Demalion,' he said, 'will be scribe and clerk to one Aulus Aurelius Lupus, centurion of the first century, second cohort. I suggested also that he be the cohort's courier, and that he be allowed to keep his horses.' There was a gap. I had my eyes shut still. He said, 'Demalion, I'm sorry.'

I was too numb to hear the care in his words, although I thought about it afterwards. At the time, all I could think was that the second cohort was a disaster; weakest of any legion. The new men were put there, the dispensable ones, left to die in the front line of battle, at no cost to anyone. If they survived, then they could move to a new cohort soon after. Small consolation, then, that I might be courier as well as scribe, allowed to keep my horse, to ride when others walked, a promotion that excused me from the outset from the duties every man hated: digging and filling the latrines, digging the ramparts at each new camp, setting and breaking the tents.

But still . . . the second cohort. The *second*. In the XIIth. I thought my heart would break.

I heard the slide of linen on skin and snapped open my eyes. Pantera had reached into his tunic. As he brought out his hand, he opened his palm to reveal a small scroll, like the manumission papers of a slave, only smaller. This he held out to me.

'I'm giving the bay mare to you,' he said. 'She will make you a good courier if you are offered the position. Think about that. Nothing is set in stone, and with the Twelfth in Syria, well behind the battle lines, you can carve your own niche to fit what you want of it.'

I took the scroll and Pantera stood, as an officer dismissing his men; he had been that to us. 'If you bear yourselves in service as well as you have with me, the Twelfth will lose its reputation for ill-luck long before

Vologases decides to wage his war. And if you can drill the manoeuvres we have planned into your men until they can do it without thinking, you'll come to love the feel of battle, and the men you fight with. Nothing is as bad as it seems.'

On his order, we retired to bed, and woke in the morning to find that he had gone without saying goodbye. I'm sure it was easier that way for all of us, but it didn't feel like it at the time.

Chapter Six

I named the bay mare Adiabena, after Monobasus, the fox-faced king whose mark was the blue tern.

In my bitterness at Pantera, I considered giving her to my elder brother, who had become the family's horse-trader since a colt had reared backwards on my father and killed him, but I grew to love her faster than I had any other horse; and while foot soldiers, on the whole, despise those who fight on horseback, and I knew already that I could not afford to set myself apart from the men at whose side I must one day stand, I did not want to part with her yet.

I might not go back to the horse fields of Macedonia, for they would surely hunt me down there, but as far as I could tell there was nothing to stop me mounting my new mare and riding back east, away from Rome and all things Roman. I was comely, I knew that, and I had seen enough of the fat-cheeked, almond-eyed men of Hyrcania casting their gaze at me sideways to know

I would have a welcome there, in the land between the leaden sea and the forest. And with my gold – the petty kings had been excessive in their generosity – I could easily have set myself up well as a horse-trader and continued the profession I loved.

I have no idea if Cadus considered the same, or if he simply read my mood, but from the moment Pantera left us he made sure I was so busy obeying orders that I had no time to plan my desertion.

He took us at a fast pace west to the breathtaking mountains of Melitene in Cappadocia. If ever a place was beautiful, it was there; a small town nested about by spring flowers that scattered the high mountains with hazy colour. Goats grazed there on impossible slopes, and the oxherds took their small, deer-like cattle high up to calve away from the hyenas on the plain, and to feed on the lichens and mosses and new sward that grew only in spring and gave the cheese a flavour of mint and citrus.

In this heaven lay the headquarters of the VIth legion, the Ferrata, named Iron-clad, for they were the first to use the scale armour down the arm that protects a man from the Parthian spear-sword.

The VIth was a hard legion of hard men: they had fought under Caesar, then Antony, and if they had been better used at Actium, then surely Octavian, who became Augustus, would not have won. Afterwards, the new emperor sent them east, because he was afraid of them, and they had faced the Parthians ever since. Tiberius used them when he was still a young man, and they won back two stolen Eagles from Vologases' predecessor by their displays of skill at arms.

In their camp, we met one known face: Gaius Tertius Aquila, third son of an equestrian family who had volunteered as a centurion and then chosen not to move beyond that rank. He had led the sixth cohort in the Vth when we had been part of it; now, it seemed, he held a like post in the VIth. He was tall, stately-looking, with a true Roman nose and pale grey eyes. His hair was nearly white, for he was long past the age when men retired from the legions.

We met him at the stables, where he was testing out a new horse, sent for his use, a blue roan gelding with a small white stripe on its nose.

'Demalion!' He clapped my shoulder. 'Sent by the gods. I think this beast is lame, but I'm just not certain. Tell me, am I right?' And to the groom, 'Trot him out again.'

We stood in a streak of warm sunlight, for the gods blessed Melitene with an earlier spring than the land around it. The blue roan trotted back and forth, back and forth, with an honesty that showed on its face. And it nodded on the right.

'Hold him,' I said to the groom, and felt the foot and the leg leading to it.

'He's got the foul matter in his foot,' I said. 'It makes it hot and causes the leg to swell and sets him lame, but if someone with a sharp knife can dig the point where it comes out—' Aquila's own knife was there, in front of me. I took it and dug the small pitted point on the horse's sole and, in due course, he jerked a little and the knife's tip broke through into the cavity where the foul-smelling black fluid dwelt. It oozed out, stinking, and I swept it away with a hank of straw that the groom had brought for the purpose.

'Keep him on clean straw and stand him in a clean-flowing river for an hour, three times a day, and he'll be fine in nine days,' I said. 'He's a good, honest horse apart from that. He'll see you well into your retirement.'

Aquila was not my officer now, so I could say these things with impunity, although in honesty he had never been a vicious kind of officer, and we had liked what little we saw of him.

He grinned now, and clapped me again on the back as if my father had known his in the baths of Rome, and then he took us on a tour of the camp nested beneath the snow-flanked hills and we saw for ourselves the changes General Corbulo had wrought.

Finding the men grown soft in their ease, he had sent one third of each century into retirement, drafted in new men from the surrounding provinces (Syrians in the VIth! The older legionaries hated that), and set them to work in a way men had not done since Marius' time.

Discipline was fierce: in the short while we were there, I saw men flogged at the post who would before have been made only to dig the latrines; and men who deserted and might once have got away with a flogging, at least the first time, were stoned to death by the remainder of their unit.

We left in two days, with gifts of food to see us on our way. Aquila came to stand at my bridle as I mounted.

'Are you going to Oescus?'

'To the Fifth?' I leaned forward and took the reins from his hand. 'There's no need.'

'What about your armour? Your sword? The quartermaster is holding them for you.'

'Let him give them to a new recruit. We have gold from our . . . recent trip.' Aquila had been party to our going, but I don't think he knew much about what we had done, and certainly he didn't know how much gold we had been given. 'Damascus is famed for its armouries,' I added. 'We'll buy something new there.'

'I see.' He held my eye a moment, almost sadly, and I jerked Adiabena's head away, thinking that he wanted me to go back and say goodbye to the men I had left, as if they meant anything at all to me.

I kicked the bay mare out of the gate and we left Melitene in a hurry, and did not slow until we were a day's ride away, after which we moved at a more comfortable pace, not exactly dawdling, but not hurrying either.

We reached Damascus just as the winter rains ceased and the streets were washed clean and the markets were alive in a chaos of colour and shouted Greek, and I felt at home for the first time in over half a year.

'Damascus supplies the legions and Parthia equally,' Cadus said. 'Their armourers are unequalled in either empire.' He knew his way about and led me on a fast route halfway across the city, past cross-legged men and high-browed women, past children who stared as us for our strangeness; we were not wearing armour, but we had bought some madder-dyed tunics in Melitene and so looked as if we had washed our clothes in blood before venturing on to the streets.

In an alley off an alley, a street so narrow it should not have been dignified by the name, Cadus pushed against a hanging piebald goatskin and we entered a dim space that smelled of honed weapons and oil and fire smoke, so that, momentarily, I was back in the legions, newly entered, buffing my helmet through the night for fear of a flogging after parade the next day.

My eyes sought light and, as we turned a corner, found it in three glowing braziers and a cascade of candles set in branched sticks around a room in which eight small boys sat cross-legged in a circle. The first two wound iron wire on to pegs, cut it, and swept the results on to a pile; the third made rings from the split loops; the last five looped those rings into others to make shining new mail such as I had seen on Vologases' cataphracts. In the legions, everyone wore old mail, mostly with the rings stitched to leather shirts which were hot in summer and held the damp in winter and stank of old shoes by the second day of wearing.

'If you're going to be a courier, you should have a good mail shirt,' Cadus said cheerfully.

I was sullen and moody, feeling like a conscript again, dreading the next day's journey to the camp. I turned away, unwilling to join in his cheer. 'I'm not going to be a courier. A clerk has to be with his centurion. I can't be riding post across the country if I'm also taking notes and securing the men's pay.'

'Even so: all you have to do is throw the spare in a barrel of sand and trip over it twice a day. At least look at what's on offer.'

Cadus spoke the local Greek better than I did; they

stretch the vowels here, and round them off, so that words that look the same on the written page sound as if they are spoken by a goat with catarrh.

He asked a question, wrapping it round with flattery; I could tell by the intonation. A nasal bleat came from the farthest, darkest corner of the room by way of reply, followed by the appearance of a man not much taller than the boys who worked so assiduously on the floor.

His back was bent. His face was long and yellowed with age. Beads of white matter gathered at the corners of his eyes, but he looked at me as if measuring my soul for the gods; I could feel the press of his stare down the flat of my ribs, my legs, my arms.

He nodded, gave another, more guttural bleat and turned back into the dimness of his demesne. I could see it more clearly now; shelves upon shelves of boxes, each marked with a carving on the fore, in the shape of a beast. His bleating dulled to a murmur, as of a man to his lover, or his horse, he reached into one marked with a stork.

'He says you are beautiful as a god, but taller than he is used to.' Cadus sounded amused. I was perhaps a hand's width taller than him and he, in turn, had been a hand's width taller than Pantera, although my memory by now had stretched the Leopard until he was the tallest of us all.

I think I blushed under the flattery. The armourer-boys watched open-mouthed as I stripped to my skin and then donned the layers the goat-man ordered, of linen, then padded wool, then a silk scarf to keep my neck from chafing.

And then he brought out not a mail shirt, such as I had imagined, but a leather shirt with strips of polished iron laid across and across, so that they overlapped like the ribs of a snake.

He held it out to me, grinning his gap-toothed grin, bleating encouragingly.

'He says this is a new thing. He has only sold one other, and he thinks it will be suitable for a young god to wear in battle.'

'Ask him who bought the other one.'

'He says a centurion in the Fourth Scythians.'

'Then you have this one,' I said. 'I can't go into the Twelfth and wear something that even their centurions don't have. It'll be hard enough as it is.'

Cadus didn't want it any more than I did, and for the same reasons. They argued back and forth, volubly. In the end, Cadus, grinning now, said, 'He wants you to keep it in your pack, for when you are a centurion.'

I laughed aloud, and meant it. 'Tell him I'll come back for it if I am ever made centurion,' I said. 'In the meantime, a mail shirt would be welcome.'

They wrangled some more, but in the end the little armourer brought out for me a shirt of rings so fine that it rippled like sharkskin in the candlelight. I stretched my arms high above my head, and let it slide down about my ribs and shoulders, link on kissing link.

The fit was perfect. The armourer lifted a shield of polished silver, and after a moment's embarrassment when I thought he was offering it to me to buy, and started to decline, I realized it was a reflector, like water in a bowl, and that I could see myself with the starpoints of the candles all about, and the red glow of the braziers behind.

I stood longer than perhaps was polite, for I had seen myself painted in water, or on the back of my knife, but never like this, whole, sharply, all in the right proportion. I am not, and never will be, as beautiful as Tears, but I could see now what the slant-eyed Hyrcanian men had seen, what women whispered at behind their hands, what my mother had wept to lose when I packed Great-uncle Demetrios' sword and took my father's second best gelding and joined the lines of conscripts heading east for war.

Time has worn me now, but then I had black hair, buffed to a high shine by the red glow of the brazier, and a lean nose, well balanced, that might have done good service on a statue in the Acropolis. I had fine, evenly matched brows and a clean jaw, half the width of Cadus', but not falling back to my throat as some men's are. The dark, smudged mark on my right cheek that my mother called the Kiss of Apollo was not so visible in the dim light, but still served to draw the eye, to break what would have been too great a symmetry.

And beneath all that, I shimmered silver, as Vologases' Parthians had done. In all, I was content, and more than content. I paid the gold that was asked for the shirt and did not think myself hard done by.

Nor did I later, when Cadus took me to other places, and we bought a helmet of the new design, raised about the ears and with iron there to stem a sword-blow, made in the factories of Gaul which are the best in the empire. We also bought two swords: a gladius and a longer cavalry blade, both well balanced for my reach; an oval cavalry shield, faced in bull's hide and red silk; and a square scutum faced in leather for infantry work, for even then I was determined to serve on foot, alongside my fellow legionaries.

Late in the evening, after dinner and wine, we bought ourselves tunics and ten pounds of madder, that we might dye to blood red the entire cohort, possibly the entire legion, for I had started to believe that this wasn't a disaster, that the XIIth was not so bad and that Cadus and I could singlehandedly turn it into something with a reputation as good as that of the Vth, which was now couched in memories of the same cherished flavour as the Macedonian horse meadows.

We were deluded, of course, and we knew it, but I think not even Cadus knew the depths of Hades we were about to plumb when we reached the camp at Raphana.

Chapter Seven

Raphana, in the plain of Abilene, south-east of Damascus

The permanent legionary camp at Raphana stands half a mile from the town, in the eastern crook of a mountainous ridge known as the Mountains of the Hawk that shelters it from the savage westerly winds, but does nothing to shade it from the sun until late afternoon.

Like all permanent encampments, it was built on a square, with roads that passed north to south and east to west and crossed at right angles in the centre. It had a hospital, an armoury, a quartermaster's stores, granaries, workshops for the engineers and stables for the horses. It had a parade ground within the walls and another around the outside. I knew the layout already, for each camp was the same wherever it was built, and a legionary comes to know every pace of interior and exterior as well as he knows his lovers' faces.

We presented there in the late afternoon on the last day of April. The watch guards at the gate gave us the names of the men we must find and waved us through, eyeing our pack mules, our horses – the bay mare had been pampered in Damascus and looked especially fine – our madder-red tunics and in particular my shining shirt of mail.

I loved the feel of it too much to pack it on the mules, and in any case we had decided to present ourselves as fighting men, not as weaponless recruits. I wore my armour, my cavalry sword and my rounded shield, and Cadus wore his helmet with full transverse plume, a thing he had not done since the last legate's demonstration over eighteen months before.

The camp offices stood in the centre, adjoining the shrine to Jupiter that held the legion's Eagle. In the camps of the Vth Macedonica and the VIth Ferrata, these buildings were of grey stone, dressed by Gaulish masons to such smoothness that a man could run his hand down them and not feel the joins. The legions' respective signs of the bull and the eagle had been carved thereon with such pride and perfection that men copied them on their shields and carved them on the bedheads in the barracks.

At Raphana, the camp office of the XIIth Fulminata and IVth Scythians before which we dismounted was built of the local baked mud, and some drunkard with a poor eye for detail had etched the Scythians' sign of the goat and the Fulminata's crossed thunderbolts together, so that it seemed as if the goat were thunderstruck, or else that lightning grew from its anus. Both applied equally; each was unthinkable in a legion which had any pride in itself.

The ache in my gut that had hit me when Pantera first named our destination returned and multiplied. The door ahead of us was closed only by a linen sheet with lead weights stitched haphazardly along the bottom; no bars, no guards, no sign that those inside took any particular care to protect the legions' wealth stored in the cellars below.

I glanced at Cadus. His face was set fast and hard. He shrugged, and jerked his chin at the doorway and I tugged aside the linen so that he could pass through ahead of me, wretchedly aware that this was the last time I might come under his order.

The clerk of clerks was a short, bulbous man named Munius Cattulinus, whose only narrow parts were his lips and his eyes. He sat behind a desk that was far more solidly built than the hut – I will not dignify it with the name of an office – that was his domain. He was writing when we approached, and, as is normal for small men promoted beyond their capacity, he made us wait before he looked up.

'You're late.' He spoke in Greek, with the caprine thickness of the locals. 'We expected you on the ides of March.'

I bit my lip and stared at my feet. In Cadus, I felt the kind of rising anger I had seen in Pantera. But this was a legion; we could not simply mount our horses and ride away.

'Then you underestimated by exactly one month and

a half the time it would take us to travel.' Cadus was Cattulinus' superior. In the crispness of the words, the perfect Latin used where the clerk had spoken Greek, he made that plain. 'We require lodgings. My clerk will need to be reassigned to his new commander.'

'He already has been.' A dry, acerbic voice came from our left, from the far corner, where the stairs descended to the cellar. A trapdoor stood open. I could not turn, for discipline said I must keep facing forward, but from the corner of my eye I saw the trapdoor lowered and heard a bolt slide and lock and knew that, if nothing else, our wealth would be locked safely away.

Steps echoed on the hollow floor. They walked around me, leading a lean shadow. I focused on the clerk's hands, on the flesh that bunched on either side of the silver ring with the garnet set into it that dug into his right thumb; on the ink stain on the pad of his fourth finger, on the quill that dripped ink on to the newly written document. If it were mine, I would have thrown it away and begun again. Already, I knew that Munius Cattulinus, scribe and clerk to my new legion, would send it as it was.

The lean shadow stopped on the far side of the desk. Its owner moved himself deliberately into my field of view. 'Aulus Aurelius Lupus, centurion of the first century, the second cohort.' He placed his palms on the table and used them as props, to bring himself closer to me. 'You, I understand, are my clerk, possibly my courier. Can you wield a sword on horseback?'

'I can.' My voice was as dry as his; drier. I looked up and, for a panicked moment, imagined myself desiccated to the point of the man opposite me; to see him was to think of summer dust, of plums gone to prunes too hard to eat, of toads caught out of water and drawn down to their hard, flat skins.

His face clung to his skull in a series of hollows, the opposite of the fleshy, almond-eyed Hyrcanian faces that I had grown used to. His hair was uniformly grey, not peppered like many men of his age, but as if he had once washed it in iron-water and the colour had set fast. His eyes were the same flat, iron hue and they searched me from my heels to my head.

'Your name?'

'Demalion.'

He ran his tongue round his teeth and I saw the purple tip of it slip between his lips, like a lizard's. 'Your tunic,' he said, at length, 'appears to be red. Why?'

Because we were going to set a fashion, and call ourselves the Bloody Legion. With more courage, that's what I would have said. But I read no humour in those grey eyes and my courage failed me.

'It's dyed with madder,' I said.

One wire-drawn eyebrow arced up. His flat eyes grew harder, and flatter. 'Then undye it. The men of my century wear wool in winter, linen in summer. Not dyed. Your armour also is not . . . standard.'

'It's all I have.' Truth lent desperation to my voice, so that he could hear it. Cadus and I were not completely stupid; we had bought other tunics, but already the shining mail shirt was my love and I had bought nothing to replace it. In the legions, men wear what they have, and are glad of it. I saw his eye go to the helmet I held under my arm, to the new design that men coveted, even in Rome. I said, 'I have a good horse and two mules and will care for them myself.'

Lupus gave no answer, but walked past me to the door. I did not turn. From the threshold, he said, 'You are billeted with the first unit, first century, second cohort, behind the workshop at the northern quarter. They, too, are late; they arrived three days ago. Ask for Syrion; he will assign your bunk and your stables. Your men' – his voice clipped Cadus – 'have quarters east of them. The Fourth Scythians have the southern side of the camp. Isodorus is your second in command unless or until you appoint another. He will, I am sure, find you a groom.'

So began our trip through Hades at the hands of the XIIth legion.

Chapter Eight

Raphana legionary camp, November, AD 57

'Wake up! Get up, you idiots! Get out of bed! We're under attack! Run! Run! *Run!*'

I erupted out of the bunk, reaching for my dagger, my sword, my sandals before I had even woken. In the dark about me, seven other men did the same, shuffling swiftly in small circles, taking care not to bump into one another, not out of courtesy or fear of another man's touch but because any untoward clumsiness made us slower and speed was everything.

In the past six months, I had learned to fasten sandals, belt and dagger faster than I would ever have believed possible. Whatever the heat, I slept in my tunic, after a time when I had been forced to fast-march naked into the mountains and back with my sword-belt chafing holes in my waist because I had dressed too slowly.

Now I was in full kit before the shouts that had

woken us had faded away: tunic, sandals, and my god-forsaken mail shirt, which might have taken one tenth of the time to clean compared to the ring-on-leather kind but took ten times as long to get into; a fact I had not considered in the calm of the armourer's shop in the spring.

My now battered gladius was strapped in place at my right side with a newly fashioned baldric across my shoulder attached to the tip of the sheath to hold it in place. I had found at the cost of a cracked rib what happened if it moved while I was negotiating a steep rock face. My dagger hung at my left side. At the door, I picked up my square-edged legionary shield, decorated now with the crossed thunderbolts of the XIIth legion, and a javelin.

This night, newly, I also picked up a stake of the same length as the javelin, with a fire-hardened tip and a flat iron plate nailed to the hub end, to keep the wood from splitting when it was hammered into the ground.

The stake was an integral part of the plan Cadus and I had developed back in Hyrcania at Pantera's behest when he had told us to design a defence against cavalry.

Cadus' men had demonstrated it before the camp prefect only four days before. His cohort was good and his century was easily the best in the legion. They would not have matched even the half-trained men of our old legion, the Vth Macedonica, but I was careful not to say that now: my new legion might have been universally despised, but the two people who could not criticize it on pain of 'accidents' that led to broken bones or worse were Cadus and me.

I wrenched open the door. Six men ran out. In the dark, I felt the seventh touch my arm.

'Demalion? I can't find my sword.' That was Tears, the Cretan youth who had come to us too young, and wept for three months. We hadn't called him Heraclides since the end of the first half-month. These days, he didn't weep any more than anyone else did, but his voice was lighter, as if he had not yet found the ground with his feet.

'Syrion will have it.' Syrion was our flag-bearer, and Lupus' second in command, a quiet man, a font of steady strength. The rest of us respected him for the fortitude with which he bore a role that nobody wanted. The flag-bearer was the first focus of any enemy attack; even in our play-practice with the IVth, we had learned that. Syrion earned twice the basic pay, and was welcome to every silver piece of it.

I found Tears' gladius in the safe place under Syrion's bunk. We were last in the room. I dragged Tears with me even as he struggled to finish tying his belt. 'Come on! Or we'll be last out.'

'But if we're under attack, that won't matter, will it? There won't be a parade line.'

'Idiot!' I cuffed him, and kept pulling. 'We're not under attack. Nobody's stupid enough to attack a legionary camp. Not even ours. This is a drill. I'll lay a denarius on it.'

'Done!'

Together, we ran into the parade ground. Exactly as I had feared, we were last out, but while I expected to stand in line under massed torches and have Lupus beat us in public for our tardiness, or the failure to polish our armour – he could find rust where no human eye could see it – or sandals tied awry, or any one of the thousand other things that a man might get wrong who had dressed in absolute dark . . . instead, we joined a heaving sea of running men, of the IVth as well as the XIIth, all streaming down the Via Praetoria and through the gate. Ahead, a horn blared five notes, sounding the call to defence of the camp.

'It *is* an attack,' Tears said, running. 'Who's insane enough to storm a legionary encampment?'

'Vologases? Maybe he's trying to take Syria for the Parthian empire while Corbulo is safe in Armenia.'

'But it's beyond the fighting season. Nobody fights after the rains start.'

'Vologases does,' I said grimly. I was still holding on to Tears' elbow, trying to see in the torch-studded dark so that I could find Syrion, or Horgias, Polydeuces – he was not the Rabbit then – Sarapammon, Rufus, Proclion, the remaining men in my unit. Attack or not, I knew the sting of Lupus' vine stick too well to risk their being in place before us.

'Northwest.' I hauled Tears with me. 'The second cohort is supposed to gather northwest of the gate. The others will be there.'

'But they're not.' He pulled me round, spinning on my heel. 'They're by the engineers' workshop. Look.'

Our unit carried a lit torch and ran on the edge of the others; six men I knew now as well as I had ever known my brothers. We sprinted to catch up. 'Syrion . . . I owe you.' I clapped his arm. 'Lupus would—'

'He might still. He's at the gate. Move!'

In the throng of an entire legion, amidst shouting, swearing, hammering men, we streamed out on to the hard-beaten earth beyond the gates. By instinct more than memory, we found the place where we had practised our defence against cavalry that one time with Cadus and set to hammering our sharpened stakes into the ground.

I was paired with Syrion: he held his stake, I pounded it with the butt end of my javelin, praying that I wouldn't miss and smash his fingers; we had already seen one man out of our century injured that way in daylight when last we did this.

As then, we were hammering into the parade ground which had been marched on by five thousand men daily for more years than I cared to count. It was set like concrete. I raised and smashed, raised and smashed. My fingers ached from the concussion. I felt the wood give a little, and again.

'Will it hold at that?' Syrion asked. 'If he kicks it?'

Lupus would kick it; even if we were attacked, he'd test it to see if he could find a reason to beat us. I felt the stake wobble.

'It might hold to a kick,' I said. 'But if the cataphracts come, they'll ride it down.'

I had seen Vologases' armoured cavalry. This fact alone had raised my standing in the unit; they trusted my judgement and I, in turn, found some respect for them if for nobody else. Syrion nodded. I pounded again. The javelin slipped in the sweat of my hands. I jerked it aside. Syrion swore, viciously.

'Your hand?' I asked.

'Missed.' Amidst the din I heard him swallow. 'Try again.'

I tried again. And again. And again until I felt it inch away from me, into the ground.

'Enough. It'll hold. Now yours.'

Another stake. Another frantic pounding, but this time I held it and Syrion battered it with his pilum. I braced my feet and held my arms rigid and prayed the same prayers for the safety of my fingers. Broken bones used to excuse a man from duties in this place; not now.

It had been different, we were told, before we came. Our arrival, with our wealth, or our obvious loathing of the legion, or the fact that Cadus had dropped from the heavens into such a senior position and might rob the other centurions of their easy promotions . . . whatever the reason, the XIIth had never worked so hard in living memory as they had these past six months. Only my unit did not hate me for it. Perhaps they could not afford to.

'Done.'

I stepped back. Syrion gave the stake one last, baleful smack. We stood in front of it, shoulder to shoulder, shield to shield. I felt Proclion press in on my left. He was largest of all of us, a bear of a man, from the south toe of Italy, where they have been Roman citizens for a dozen generations yet still speak Greek to spite their Latin masters.

Horgias fitted in to his left as his shield-man, then Rufus was left of him, and after him Polydeuces and then Sarapammon. Syrion held the century's standard, which had the open hand of a god (some said it was the emperor, but I chose to think of it as Helios) at the top, and the badges of valour underneath. We had few of those, and none won since Caesar's death.

Torches flared about us, bringing light to our hellish dark. Leontius, the aquilifer, who bore the legion's Eagle, brought it now to the fore and stood beneath it in such a way that the shadow of the bird fell on to the front ranks. He wore a wolfskin as his bearer's pride where others of his sort wore leopard or lion; that was done, we were all sure, to placate Lupus, for his name meant 'wolf' in Latin, although everyone on the camp spoke Greek unless forced to do otherwise by their officers, who themselves only did so to prove a point. A hundred paces to our left, the Eagle of the IVth Scythians caught the light of their many torches and spun it away to the dark.

By ragged starts, the sounds of hammering ceased. We stood in silence, bunched behind our shields, helmets aglow under the bouncing flames of the wool-and-pitch torches.

We were in the front and centre of the line; the place of dispensable men. I saw movement at my right and heard the trumpet's blast. To give him credit, Munius Cattulinus might have been a sloppy clerk of clerks – in my role as clerk to the century I had had occasion to read his writing and it was as bad as I had feared – but he was an excellent signaller.

The trumpet called clear and fine; eight strong notes.

On the first note, we cast our javelins into the dark at

an enemy we could not see and now knew did not exist, drew our swords and knelt.

On the second note, the rank behind us cast their javelins, drew their swords and knelt.

On the third note, the third rank cast their javelins, which was the point when we discovered that not all of the second rank had knelt yet; some were still struggling to draw their swords. Men shouted curses in the dark. Others cursed back, louder, so that, by the time the fourth note of the horn sounded, half the men were not sure if it was for them, and of those who did know not all were ready to rise and step to the right.

The remaining four notes, which should have timed our four paces backwards, descended into progressively greater chaos. An officer shouted for order; Lupus, I think, but there's a point when all angry men sound the same. As silence fell, we were a milling soup of disordered men, facing all directions but front.

Syrion held our eight-man unit together by force of will and a carrying voice. We had not stepped fully to our right, because there was no room to do so, and when we tried to pace back we were stopped after two paces by the men behind. So we stood where we were, shields locked in a wall, with two rows of stakes in front of us, half of which were not sound, knowing that if Vologases' cavalry rode out of the dark and charged at us now, we were dead men.

By then, though, even the dullest amongst us had realized that the Parthians were not coming. I wished that they were; standing there in the dark with the horn's blast dying in my ears, I thought it might be easier to face the fast-running anger of battle, the roar of death in my ears, the quick ending and release at last from this particular hell.

Instead Lupus came at us, but, this once, he was not first of the sixty centurions to rake along the lines; this time he walked two paces behind the two first centurions – and Flavius Silvanus, the camp prefect.

To us, it was as if the emperor himself walked out of the night. Nobody expected to see the tribunes or the governor, and even if they had turned out at the third watch of night they would not have been accorded any particular respect.

But the camp prefect was as close to a god as we had. Silvanus had been with the XIIth since his first commission and had risen through the centurion ranks, elbowing men out of his way, writing letters to Rome, doing favours for progressive Syrian governors until he reached the place where he led the legion in all but name. He had power of life and death over every one of us, and we knew it.

When he came to a halt and stood under the Eagle, we had to fight to keep our eyes forward, not to let them drift to him. When he raised his hand and the centurions began their walk down the line, we knew this was not the usual parade inspection, not even usual night manoeuvres; we just didn't know what it was.

Lupus stalked with his own particular gait. I remembered to breathe as he came close; I had been slammed in the solar plexus by his vine rod often enough by then for the crime of holding my breath.

When I was with the Vth, I had not thought Cadus a

particularly lenient centurion; there was not one man of the ten units under his command who had not felt the depth of his anger at one time or another, but he was always fair. He set standards and expected them to be kept and we knew it.

With Lupus, I found what it was to live under a man who changed his mind with the wind, so that it was possible I could be thrashed for not holding my breath the day after he had left me vomiting in the dirt for holding it.

I breathed in. The night was cold. I felt the air chill my forehead, felt my lungs bunch against it. I saw Lupus on the edge of my vision.

In six months, I had learned the skill of seeing sideways while looking forward. His orderly held his torch for him, a stooped man from Emona named Minicius. By its light I studied his dry-parchment face – and learned nothing. He could hold an expression of weary distaste through his own crucifixion, I thought, it was so moulded to his form.

He was nearly past when his eyes caught mine. Only for a fraction of a heartbeat, and I am sure without his intending it, but it was there, that human touch that lets soul meet soul, from which no man can hide.

And what I saw was more terrifying than anything I had yet seen: worse by far than his particular loathing of me, or his counterfeit rage; worse even than the moment of cold calculation before he changed his mind again so that what was right yesterday was wrong today. I knew all of those, and how he showed them, and none was present now: what I read in his eyes was terror.

Lupus was deeply afraid.

Knowing that, my own fear threatened to suck me away. I felt Syrion's shoulder forced against mine, as if by power of will and the friction of his tunic he could keep me standing. 'Careful . . .' He eased the word out under his breath, taking a risk even with that.

I leaned my own weight back against him by way of thanks, and the moment passed, but not my fright. I breathed in the cold night and in the time it took I saw us decimated, even Lupus drawing lots from the bag, fearing to pick the one black stone in every ten and the death by attrition that must follow. Or being marched to the sea and made to swim until we drowned; I had a particular fear of deep water that my journeys had never undone. Or . . .

The horn sounded a single note, high and long, the song of the moon. It caught my thoughts and carried them out into the black sky. Careful not to make a sound, I let out the breath I had not known I was holding. Beside me, I felt Syrion do the same.

Silvanus, the camp prefect, took a step forward. I heard his voice every morning after parade, but had never listened to the tones of it as I did now. He was not afraid, that much was clear; he was angry.

'Pathetic. I should cashier you all now and destroy your Eagles.' Silvanus spoke quietly; we had to strain to hear his voice. You could have heard the stars slide across the sky, we were so still and so silent.

'If General Corbulo were here, he would destroy you. He dismissed half of the Fifth and the Tenth and sent them home. The rest are billeted in tents in the

Armenian highlands with barley meal for fodder. He intends to make an army of them, to meet Vologases when he comes. I intend the same and therefore you will be treated the same as your betters in better legions. You will be proficient by the spring, or you will be dead.'

His gaze raked us, and we wondered which of us might die that night for the crime of being ineffectual.

His voice rocked us. 'To that end, you will spend the next three months in tents in the Mountains of the Hawk that lie between us and the sea. One hundred paces above the snow line, each century will determine an area suitable for three months' stay and build its own base camp. You will alternate along the mountains' length so that each century of the Fourth has a century of the Twelfth to either side, and vice versa.

'Each century will defend and maintain its own stocks against the men of the opposing legion; you are encouraged to avail yourselves of what you can. You may not remove stocks from camps belonging to other centuries of your own legion, and equally you may not aid in defending them against raiding parties from the opposing men. So that you may tell each other apart, the Twelfth legion will wear' – did I hear a note of distaste there? – 'red cloth tied about their left arms at all times. The Fourth will wear blue.

'You will be provided with raw fleece with which to wrap your weapons that they might strike but not bite. A man who is careless enough to be captured by the other side will be flogged and returned to his unit. Any man who kills another will be flogged until dead and any man who wounds another will be staked out beyond the boundary of his camp for two days and nights; if he lives, he will be returned to his unit. Any man who dies of hunger, cold or fright, or who falls off the mountain, will be deemed to have died by his own hand.

'You have until the next watch to make ready. You are dismissed.'

Chapter Nine

At the mouth of the stockade, crushed tracks sworled amid the night's fall of virgin snow; a stamp of sandal-prints and hoof-prints and the thick-edged blur of a heavy object, dragged without care.

Behind me, the tents of our century sagged under the new snow, and snow covered the earth rampart we had thrown up around them. Ahead, the stockade we had built to hold the mules had been dismantled piece by careful, silent piece, the stones piled neatly, as if by men at drill practice. And the mules were gone, all twelve of them: one for each of the ten tent-units, plus two for Lupus. Gone, too, was the firewood we had stacked to one side under the frozen oxhide.

I stood still for a moment, stealing the last vestiges of fire-warmth from the depths of my cloak, taking in the magnitude of the disaster.

Somewhere, a songbird hurled notes into the clear and empty sky. For nine days the clouds had hung over us, pressing down on our heads and our moods, but they had emptied all their snow during the night, leaving the sky such a startling blue as to make my eyes ache even when I looked down to the churned mess at my feet in an effort to discover who it was we must attack to regain what was lost.

'First century, first cohort of the Fourth. They left their mark on the gatepost. Unless that's a ruse to make us go the wrong way when we go to get our mules back.'

I wrenched round. Lupus stood behind me, wrapped in a black goat-hair cloak. He wore no helmet, only a heavy felt cap that covered his lead-iron hair and extended down beyond his ears so that he looked even more as if someone had lifted off his head and replaced it with a skull for a joke.

Nobody thought Lupus was a joke, but we were less afraid of him than we had been. He didn't push us any less hard, nor was he less particular on parade; we still had to present arms in the morning, and march for the duration of the first watch, but the perverse fury that had made breathing a sin one day and forgetting to breathe punishable the next had frozen away in the savage cold.

We were the sharper for it, and had a kind of fragile pride in our new capacity; at the very least, Rufus didn't play the fool on morning parade, risking a flogging to pull faces at the back of Lupus' head as he passed, or cocking his leg like a dog marking territory where he had been.

The IVth legion was our enemy now, and Lupus was on our side. But they were stronger than us. The first century of any legion was first in the line of march and full of good men of long standing. Even the IVth had a few good men, and many of them were in its first century.

I saw no point in dwelling on that; in war, too, you cannot always choose your enemy.

'They've taken the firewood.' I said. 'If we don't get it back soon, they'll slaughter the mules and build fires to smoke the meat so they don't have to hunt for the rest of the month.'

Lupus stared north, to where they had gone. 'Who was on watch?'

Of course he would ask that.

I said, 'Polydeuces. He was on guard duty last night. He's gone, so they must have taken him too. If Prefect Silvanus finds out, he'll be flogged.'

And if he's flogged, he'll die. I did not say that; there was a limit to my courage, and in any case it was obvious. Out of the ten units in our century, the men in ours had weathered the cold best, except for Polydeuces, who had taken the chill to his lungs in the first night's watch and was soon coughing up lumps of matter thick enough to mould into bricks.

I thought I saw streaks of blood in it one night, as we crouched round our fire in a circle tight enough for each man to draw in the outbreath of the one opposite. He had tried to hide it with a hank of the straw that he kept up his sleeves to sweep it away, but I saw what he threw on the flames.

In the blistering snow light of morning, I watched Lupus purse his lips a moment, and braced myself to hear him say that it was Polydeuces' own fault that he'd been captured – which it probably was – and that he'd flog him himself when the order came.

I was dizzy with cold and the sharp, knifing air that stole men's sanity. I thought of all the small things Polydeuces had done for me: carrying wood when I had bruised my hand trying to take a stone from a mule's foot; grinding corn when it was my turn but I was out hunting; cooking that same day, because I had caught nothing; grinding a new edge on my dagger when I destroyed it hacking at the frozen rawhide that held a broken tent peg.

He was a friend now, as much as Cadus had been, or my brothers back in Macedonia, in a childhood that seemed ever more a dream of someone I once knew in passing. It came to me that when Lupus spoke I might hit him, and that if I did so I would almost certainly die before Polydeuces.

I was braced for violence when I caught Lupus' gaze. The flat, iron grey was not flat any more, but alive with what in any other man I might have named joy.

'Silvanus won't come up the mountain until the full moon,' he said crisply. 'That gives us two days to rectify our loss. Summon the others. We'll get Polydeuces back. Whether we choose to take the mules back is another question. The longer they eat the enemy's fodder, the less you have to collect and carry up the mountain.'

The prefect had arranged for fodder to be left for us just below the snow line. Gathering it had become one of the most hated chores of our winter in the snow. At that moment, though, feeding the mules was not top of my concerns.

'Are we all going?' I asked, incredulous. 'The entire century?' Horror must have been written on my face for Lupus looked at me a moment, and his wire-fine brow rose a little higher. I saw his lip curl.

'That depends on what we learn over the course of today,' he said. 'Four units may suffice. It would be unfortunate if this were merely a diversion to pull us out of camp and we were to return and find we had lost everything for the sake of a dozen mules and a sick legionary.'

Not madness, then, but boldness, and forethought. I breathed in the cold air and felt less dizzy. I relaxed my hands, which had been ready for murder, at my sides.

Lupus continued as if I had not moved. 'On the other hand, however much we despise the Fourth, they are not weak men. If we go undermanned, we'll set ourselves at a disadvantage from the start. Intelligence is everything. We'll go at dusk when we're not so visible, and in the meantime you, Syrion and Horgias will spy ahead, find out what's in our way and where the ambushes are.'

He tilted his head, looking at me. Fire still burned in the heart of his eyes, and the quirk of his lip was deeper now. 'There will be ambushes,' he said. 'They will be expecting you and they will endeavour to capture you. I think we can consider this a declaration of war. Tell the rest that the morning parade and inspection will go ahead as normal.'

I was walking back through the snow to the tents when I realized that the curl of his lip had been the beginning of a smile.

*

'He smiled? Are you sure? Was he foaming at the mouth? Were his eyes rolled back in his head and showing white all across?'

It was Rufus who asked, our wiry, red-haired locksmith who swore he had Gaulish parentage, and it wasn't his fault he was barely tall enough to top the probationer's measuring stick and was half Proclion's width when any self-respecting Gaul would have been twice that size.

He was guarding our tents, and using the time to clean his armour against Lupus' next inspection; up here, where we could tickle the soles of the gods' feet did we but stretch our arms above our heads, the water had all frozen out of the air and we saw little rust, but the other side of the coin was that leather cracked easily, with the result that we all reeked of the sheep oil we used to keep it supple, and polished iron was soon coated in a fine film of grease and dirt.

Clad in a spare cloak over his own, with a felt cap hugging his ears, Rufus was seated on a log, warming his lanolin in a bronze mess cup over a fire made entirely of twigs. I crouched at it a moment, and held my hands out to the tiny, stabbing flames. I couldn't feel the heat through my gloves, except as a lessening of cold.

'First four units at least to go with Lupus,' I said. 'But not until nightfall. There's parade inspection first for everyone except three of us who are to spy on the Fourth. Where are the others?'

'Digging.' He jerked his head over his shoulder towards the area we had set aside for the latrines. 'Blow the horn; they'll come fast enough.'

My lips were too cold for that. I cupped my hands to my mouth and gave vent to the long, yelping sound, not unlike a wolf, with which we called each other. The men I shared a tent with ran to me like hounds to the huntsman.

Syrion led; in older times, he would have been an Olympian, running, wrestling, throwing at the games, and feted afterwards for the sculpted muscles of his frame. He had pale hair, the colour of cut wood, with flecks of bronze through it that spoke of more authentic Gaulish blood somewhere in his lineage than did Rufus' flaring red. Most of all, he was manifestly honest: he had a kind, open face that knew nothing of guile; what he said, he meant, and if you did not like it, still you could trust it.

Next to him was Tears, a hand smaller, a hand slighter, his hair dark, and moulded to his head as if he, too, were a sculpture, but one made for his looks, not the brilliance of his athletic feats. For where Syrion was an Olympian, Tears was his Youth; the perfect beauty, of impeccable Cretan breeding, temperament and looks. He was Syrion's for the taking, but Syrion didn't want him. Syrion had women – an uncounted number of women – in the town beyond the camp and Tears was left bereft.

I thought that Proclion might have liked him, but he was too vast for Tears and in any case Proclion had settled on his shield-man, Horgias the Silent, tall and lean and balding early on top, who had caught frostbite in an unfortunate place and let Proclion warm it for him one night and they had slept one atop the other ever since. We were envious, those of us who merely huddled side by side; they were warmer.

And so now these two were here, and last moon-faced Sarapammon, panting, grey-green about the eyes, who should have been sent to serve on boats, for he had been born on an island with sea all about and water was his love, the deeper the better; here in the high mountains he was as sick as I was on ship in the ocean. He leaned forward with his hands on his knees, fighting to breathe, as I told them that we were to consider ourselves at war with the first century of the first cohort of the IVth legion.

Syrion had already guessed the worst of it; why else was I standing there alone, calling men in? He listened while I sketched the bare bones of our disaster and then said, 'Four units isn't enough to take on the first of the Fourth.' He spun on his heel, looking out across the ruined snow. 'They were good men before we hit the mountains; they'll be better now. And they'll be expecting us.'

'Lupus knows that. In this, I think we can trust him. He knows we need to get Polydeuces back, but we need to teach them a lesson, too. They've been harrying us since we got here. We've only a month left. If we don't do something serious in retaliation, they'll be back.'

An idea was flowering in my mind as I looked at Syrion and he at me; our thoughts flowed along the same pathways, and we had come to recognize it in each other. He was watching me now, laughing. 'Demalion the Fox has an idea?' he asked.

Nobody had called me Fox before; I felt my cheeks burn

and dipped my head, to look at the marks my sandals made in the snow. 'Something I saw in Hyrcania,' I said. 'After Vologases returned to the throne, they had games and set us challenges. We were put in small groups and set to raid each other's wagons; it's a thing they do to sharpen the men.'

'Like putting us on the mountain,' Tears said wryly.

'Exactly like,' I said. 'There's a thing our leader Pantera did, with a few men against many. If Lupus will allow us, we can try it again.'

'That's the catch though, isn't it?' Sarapammon said. He was more flesh-hued now, less like a fish long dead from the sea. 'Will he allow any idea that isn't his?'

'At this moment,' I said, 'I think you will be surprised at what he will allow. Our centurion has just discovered what he lives for, and it is this.'

Chapter Ten

The camp of the first century, first cohort of the IVth legion was last of the line, a good eight miles to our north along the mountain ridge. Between us and them were five of their camps and five of ours, the last of these inhabited by Cadus and his men, first century of the sixth cohort of the XIIth. Our advantage was that there was a lot of cover between us and them. Our disadvantages were that they knew we were coming.

When we had been sent up the mountains that first morning, tasked with finding spaces that were large enough to sustain an entire eighty men for three months, we had been lucky – Lupus would call it his skill – to find a source of water near our camp, and a stand of cedars not too far below it that gave us firewood.

We had set our tents in the niche between two north–south ridges, with a narrow pass to our east that led down to the plain. On a good day, a lookout could see the officers leaving to visit Raphana, or the couriers bringing news from General Corbulo's campaign against the Parthians in the north.

We had news twice a month, at new and full moon, when Silvanus, the camp prefect, came up to check who had been captured, who had been injured, who had died.

He said that Corbulo went amongst his men bare-headed and clad only in linen to keep their courage high as they wintered in snow far deeper, far colder than ours; that the men were forced to eat only the flesh of cattle to sustain themselves, which every man knows is not enough. He said a man had lost his nose to frostbite, and that another, throwing down his pile of firewood, found that his frozen hand had come off with it.

We chose not to believe these tales, although when Horgias got frostbite in his member when he fell asleep while pissing against the wall we were quick enough to bring him in and send Rufus out to take his place; nobody wanted to see what happened if parts of us started to fall off into the snow.

On the day we lost Polydeuces, therefore, the three of us who had been sent out to spy wrapped ourselves in doubled cloaks with the outer one of pale, undyed wool. We wrapped wool about our legs from the knee down, and wove horse hair around our sandals, to lessen the sound of the nails without compromising their grip. We carried pads of bake-hardened barley meal in our belt pouches, and dressed in minimal armour. We took our swords and daggers and I tell you now that we did cover them in the raw fleece, and bind it tight with leather thongs. Whatever happened later, it was not because we failed to prepare properly.

The three of us left as the others were marshalling for parade. I led; I had spent six months in the company of a spy and my unit thought me trained in all the ways of subterfuge. I did nothing to disabuse them of their idea, for I enjoyed the little I had learned, and thought myself somewhat skilled – but there was nothing I could teach Horgias.

We called him 'the silent' because he could walk across a bathhouse floor in sandals and make no echo, which was the hardest test we knew. On the mountain-side, he was fast, quiet and easily our best tracker.

Syrion was not as naturally silent, but his gymnast's body made him supple and I would say that three quarters of subterfuge is in physical flexibility; the ability to mould oneself to the situation.

I was neither silent nor particularly athletic. I had my cunning from my father, the horse-trader, and on to that I had grafted everything gleaned from six months with Pantera, which was enough. If I say it myself, we made a good team.

The only mule path on the mountain spine ran high above the camps, almost at the roof-ridge of the range. We tracked the swath of ruined snow up beyond our camp until it turned hard right along the path.

There, I gave a low, looping whistle that called Horgias and Syrion up to me.

'It's too easy,' I said. 'Lupus was right: if there's going to be an ambush, they'll be waiting for us along the mule path; there are plenty of places to hide. But there's a goat path we could take that runs along the back edge of the peak; I found it while I was hunting earlier in the month. It's narrower, and more dangerous, but there's less chance of our being jumped and we can look over the top once every five hundred paces to be sure we're still following the mules. Unless either of you has a better idea?'

Neither had. In the thin, cold air, thinking was harder than it had been. The tents seemed like a hospitable refuge in comparison, the base camp an impossible luxury, beyond even dreams.

I pushed on up towards the mountain head, ploughing through the fresh snow, seeking out stone or ice to step on where I could, that we might not leave our own trail. At the peak, we passed through a narrow crack in the rock that ran perpendicular to the line of the range. At its widest, it was the width of a man's chest, so that we had to turn sideways, and edge our way along, and down, through the dim, frozen channel that the sun never reached, and then out again, into the same blinding snow light.

From here, we had a view down on to the clouds and through their gaps to the dozens of small farmsteads dotted about the plain below. The edge here was closer to our path; less than the height of a man from where we shuffled along the goat track.

I leaned in to the rock and began to pick my way along, and presently heard the quiet curses of the men behind as they saw the risk.

Without turning my head, I said, 'If you stay close to the rock, you're less likely to fall.'

Strained grunts were my reply. We each tilted in to the

mountain and, like that, pressed north, holding every piece of rock that came to hand, heads down, tasting ice on the wind.

Pantera had taught me to count as I walked, the better to estimate distance. Four hundred and ninety-eight treacherous, ice-laden steps later, I heard a man's murmured voice, and a moment later saw a cloud of breath in the air.

With my hand up, I halted, pointing. Horgias, who was closest, drew his knife, caught my eye, made a brief, simple mime, and passed me by, pressing close to keep himself clear of the edge.

It was rumoured that Horgias had barbarian blood in him; how much and of what tribe none of us knew, but when he slid up that sheer mountain trail with his knife between his teeth he looked like nothing and no one I had ever seen. I was grateful that he was on our side.

'He'll kill them,' Syrion said, from close in to my left.

I said, 'Not unless he wants to be flogged to death, he won't,' but even so, when Horgias came back, I looked first at his knife, for blood, and only when I found none did I back away into the shelter of a rocky outcrop and wait to hear his report.

At the camp, Lupus had said this was a declaration of war and I had thought him snow-dazed, but up here it felt as if a boundary had been crossed, and civilization was on the farther side of it.

Horgias crouched, to shelter better against the wind, and said, 'There's a full tent-unit of eight men watching the mule route, and an enemy encampment nested in the trees below. The mule tracks go on past.'

'The prefect said we couldn't combine our centuries to attack men of the other legion,' Syrion said.

'But I bet the men in the enemy camp know about the ambush,' I said sourly. 'If we were driven into it by men from up here, they might find it in themselves to take us prisoner. That wouldn't be against the rules.'

Horgias nodded, his lips drawn back in a smile that was a wolf's snarl. 'They want us all flogged. Why us?'

'Lupus,' Syrion said. 'The other centurions hate him, even among the Fourth. He's too distant. He doesn't drink with them or whore with them. They don't know who he is, and so they hate him.'

'He loves war,' I said, who had seen the ice melt from his eyes, and the fire behind it, and these two made sense to me now. I felt the truth in my marrow, and it warmed me. 'He's bored with camp life. The Fourth are making a huge mistake giving him a reason to fight them.'

Syrion thought that through, in the serious way he did, and nodded. 'Let's go on a little way along the ridge,' he said. 'They know Lupus well enough to know he's ruthless first and cautious second. They'll want to keep enough men in their camp at the mountain's end to hold us all off. A month's pay says they won't have left more than two other units in an ambush like this one.'

'Done,' Horgias said. 'If the next two enemy camps have a unit in ambush above them, and the one after doesn't, we'll know you were right.'

Syrion was right: there were only two more units waiting in ambush on the ridge, one above each of the next two blue camps.

Sometime shortly after noon, therefore, we three

turned round and made our way back along the goat path. The wind turned with us, and came from the west, pushing us to the mountain, gluing us to safe rock, away from the precipitous fall.

It felt like a good omen, and I told Lupus of it when I returned. I had never spoken to him of omens before. In a day of strangeness, that was just another new thing. He liked it and told the men, so that by the time the light was failing they all knew that the gods were with us in our battle against the IVth.

With our intelligence to guide him, Lupus had wrought a plan that was breathtaking in its beauty; elegant enough to be daring, but simple enough to work. We had used the remaining three hours until we were due to leave teasing it over, looking for gaps, and finding ways to plug them.

It was the first time we had truly worked together as a century. By the time we left, we were all that much closer to each other, all learning to trust each other's judgement, and all stirring to the first thrills of war. I, who had never killed before, nor even borne my sword in true action, found myself traipsing to the latrines eight, nine, ten times before we left, and still sick at the end of it.

CHAPTER ELEVEN

To take three men along the narrow goat path at the back of the mountain had been difficult, but not impossible. To take an entire century along there would have been impossible and we didn't try.

Lupus led the main party along the broad trail that linked all the century camps. The crushed snow was blue now in the late afternoon shadows, and freezing to ruts that made walking hard. He had us group into our tent-units and run at a jog-trot, with a distance of no more than twenty paces between each group.

In full armour, carrying our supplies of food and water, our mattocks, our mess kit – everything – we could walk twenty miles a day, forty if we were forced to double time. That evening, we wore our armour, but no helmets; carried no shields, but only our swords and daggers, wound around with fleece. We wound more wool on our forearms to act as shields, and kept our heads warm with the felt caps we had made in the harshest of the weather. Travelling light like this, even in the dark, I had no doubt that we could march the eight miles to the enemy camp before midnight; certainly that was our goal.

Syrion and I ran with Lupus at the head of the main group because we knew where the enemy units were waiting in ambush. Horgias, setting off earlier, had taken the other four men of our unit along the goat track, promising to reach the ambush places ahead of us.

We reached the first of their camps around time for the evening meal. It was nestled in trees, lower down towards the snow line than I think was legal, but they'd been there for over two months and Silvanus had not made them move it.

Their tents were set tight together in a square with branches across them to keep the snow off. A large fire was kept lit in the centre, and the men bunched around it, lightly armoured as we were, but with helmets on. They were still, silent, waiting. The fire's light blinded them to movement in the shadows as we backed away thirty feet.

There, I knelt in the snow beneath the first rank of trees and gave the call of the owl which was our signal for every man to halt where he stood. We waited a moment and heard Horgias call back, except that his call was not so much an owl as a man trying to sound like a wolf, and failing.

The men around the fire were expecting some such. Hearing it, they jeered amongst themselves and, gathering their weapons, rushed up towards the place where Horgias had seen eight men lying in ambush.

What they would have found there, if all had gone according to plan, was eight men bound and gagged, each one with the sign of the wolf carved on to the leather of his armour straps as a reminder of who had taken them.

We didn't stay to find out, but passed their camp at a dead run, and all were safely beyond it long before the main mass of the enemy returned carrying their newly freed comrades to the fire to warm away their frostbite.

They didn't send anybody after us. I don't know what Horgias whispered in the ears of the fallen IVth as he tied the rawhide knots, but it was enough to frighten them into stillness, at least for the first part of the night.

We continued on, running into the changing light. To our left, the sun slid down until it pierced itself on the mountain's highest spikes, spilling bloody light down the snow and leaving a long purple bruise along the ridge.

At the same time, the moon rose on our right, one day off full. It cast silver across the snow and ice, almost as bright as day, so that we could see our way as well as before.

The first century of the IVth had come this same route on a night of no moon, when the clouds sat on the ground and spilled snow waist deep in places. My respect for them grew greater, not less, as we travelled along the same path, even when Horgias and Tears and the other men tied the third enemy unit and whooped their wolf call high above the mountain as they carried on ahead of us.

Cadus was waiting for us on the path as we approached the last camp before our target, dressed in mountain clothes with none of the regalia of the parade ground, except that he carried his helmet under his arm, the plume crisping in the night air.

Under the moon's light, his hair seemed paler than I remembered it, strung through with silver, and his skin had the tight translucence we had shared in Hyrcania, when the cold pulled our flesh hard about our bones.

Lupus ordered a halt in good order ten paces away and went forward to greet him. After three paces, he said, 'Demalion. Follow,' and walked on.

'You brought all your men,' Cadus said, as we approached. No greeting, no clashing salute, no officers' exchange of gossip. 'None left to guard your camp.'

Lupus lifted one shoulder in a shrug. 'We disabled three units on the way. Our entire century therefore faces seven units of the best men in the Fourth legion. I decided it was worth the risk.'

'All or nothing.'

'I didn't come here to fail.'

'No.' Cadus ran his tongue round his teeth, thinking. They were of a height, he and Lupus, and both mountain-fit, but in all other respects they were as different as the moon from the sun. Cadus was a big, broad man, and given to laughter. He was not laughing now, while lean-faced Lupus, by his own standards, was vibrating with a kind of wild joy.

Cadus said, 'Do you need help?'

'Of course. And of course I cannot accept any. They will have us all flogged if we break the rules. Centurions will not be exempted.'

‘That may be their aim,’ Cadus said slowly. His gaze was fixed on Lupus’ face. They stood a moment, each lost in the other’s thought. It came to me then that the only centurion of the two legions who did not hate Lupus was Cadus, and that I should have noticed that before now.

At length, Lupus said, ‘They set ambushes above the first three enemy encampments, and I have no doubt that if we had not . . . disabled them they would have endeavoured to drive us down into the camps for the men there to take us prisoner. It could be, therefore, that we may drive some men of the Fourth in your direction. If they were to stumble into your camp, might you find it acceptable to take them prisoner?’

Lupus’ eyes were wide with pretended innocence. In response, Cadus grinned in a way I’d come to know in Hyrcania.

‘I’ll set men in a chain along the route. If they run past us, we’ll take them.’ He clapped Lupus’ arm. ‘Good luck. Your men are good. If you make it, you’ll have broken the Fourth; they won’t try anything else in the last half-month before we go back to camp. Not at this end of the mountain, anyway.’

Lupus half turned, and then wheeled back again. ‘It may be that I have read this wrongly, and that they do wish to destroy our camp. If your men would make themselves ready to block their passing, I would be grateful. I’ll send Demalion back to you if it seems such a thing is likely. That does not, I believe, contravene the rules as we were given them.’

‘It doesn’t,’ Cadus agreed, which might have been true

by the letter of our temporary law, but was decidedly not true to its spirit. 'But we shall keep this conversation between us three. And Demalion, if he comes, will be returning for treatment of a wound, not to bring news of an attack.'

'Agreed.' Lupus looked at me; they both did.

'Agreed,' I said, and followed Lupus back to our lines, grinning like a fool.

We smelled the mules before we saw them; a ripe, warm scent of old hay and urine and steaming dung that left me aching to go in amongst them and run my hands under their manes to heat my fingers, as I had done as a child on the coldest days of herd-watch. I thought I knew about cold, then.

With their smell like a wall before us, we inched round the last corner to the final enemy camp on our bellies, with our faces pressed to the ice.

It was as well we were already down, for the camp built by the first century of the first cohort of the IVth legion was not like all the others, a huddle of tents with an earth rampart about, set in a vestige of shelter.

Here, at the northernmost end of the Hawk range, the men had made the mountains their ally, setting their camp with its back in a natural corner, so that the northern and western flanks were solid rock with peaks that stretched up to scrape the stars.

On the southern and eastern sides, the Blues had not grubbed in the frozen ground to throw up an earth rampart as we had done, but had built walls of stone, setting each one against the others without mortar, but solidly, so that it would have taken far more than one night to pull them down.

The only gate faced southeast, on a scree slope so that any attackers must come uphill with uncertain footing and face an opening scarcely wide enough for two to go through; a nightmare to assault, and easily guarded from the inside.

The mule stockade was fenced with logs set lengthways and kept in place by posts hammered into the ground. It stood at the southwestern edge of the camp. If there were men inside, we could not see them. In fact, we could see no men at all; as far as we could tell, all the remaining seven units of their century remained in the main compound, hidden behind the wall's height, huddled in their tents – unless they had also spent the past two months building themselves proper barrack rooms; nothing seemed impossible.

Whatever it was, they had built themselves a camp to match the legionary fortress down below. And we had placed ourselves at war with them.

I lay face down in the snow and felt no cold. Blood hammered in my ears at the promise of action. I turned my cheek sideways and saw Lupus at my side.

'We could climb over the wall,' I said, 'if Horgias has remembered what you said and gives us the diversion we need.'

'He's remembered,' Lupus said. 'Look.'

I looked, and saw what Lupus had seen and bit my lip to keep silent, for Horgias had stripped to the waist and was wearing trews in the Parthian style that made him look even more the barbarian.

Blue-skinned with cold, he was sliding like a snake down the edge of the rock that was one wall of the stockade. I watched as he paused beneath the stacked lumber that kept the mules safe, saw him delay a moment, working in the shelter made by his naked form, then rise and throw what he had made.

He had made fire from the fire-pot at his belt and the wads of pitched straw we had woven in the afternoon, so that it might take the flame and hold it, and spread it in the mules' fodder.

In the stockade, a man shouted once: an order. I heard the sing of swords from their sheaths, many swords, and the dull ache in the air that comes from a mass of men moving to one purpose. Forgetting myself, I gripped Lupus' arm, and he did not prise my fingers free, but murmured, 'Steady, there . . . steady,' as if I were a startled horse. I had never heard his voice so mild. He said, 'If Tears and the others—'

'*There!*' I pointed to where Tears had appeared high on the stockade wall – a half-naked Tears, just like Horgias, except that he did not look like a barbarian; he was Apollo himself come amongst us. I had not seen how much he had grown in our time in the mountains, but saw it now, for he must have scaled the sheer rock that guarded the back of the camp and the mules' stockade, and jumped down from there to run along the wall of stacked logs, and hurl his own fire deep inside.

The fires caught and flared. What had been in shadow was cast in flaring flamelight and Tears was part of it. I saw his head go up as he went from secrecy to full display, saw him twist a moment, looking down to where Horgias must have been, then stand straight and take a breath and give voice to the long, looping wolf-call that was our sign.

Horgias had deliberately mutilated it. Tears called it now better than I have ever heard; truly, he was a wolf.

As they would at a wolf, the men of the IVth threw rocks at him, careless of the injunction not to injure another. I saw Tears laugh, once, head thrown back, and then he leapt down to join Horgias and the other three, for all of them were clustered at the stockade now, all with their blades out, crashing them against the wood, making enough noise to sound as if they were half a century.

Making noise enough for an entire cohort, the IVth sallied out against them. In their eight-man units, they charged from the stockade and the camp gate, their armour bright in the leering flames.

'Run! Run now! Horgias! Tears! In the name of all the gods, *run*!'

I spoke it into the snow, silently, but they did run. Laughing still, with Horgias at his one side and Proclion, the mountain ox, at the other, Tears took off like a hunted deer, sprinting back along a wide track that led away from the stockade, and then cut up towards the mountain peak. Hard on his heels, a horde of men coursed after him, dark and baying; the hounds of a hellish master sent to bring him down. Not one of them looked back at where we lay, nor stayed to protect their base camp.

'Go!' Lupus jabbed at my arm, but I was already moving, sprinting forward in a spray of ice and snow, hurling myself down across the scree slope and up to the open gate to the enemy compound.

I skidded the last paces and threw myself at the solid rock as much to keep from falling as to gain admittance. My shoulder crashed against the stone. I clung to it, pressing my face to the thin-grown moss, drawing in the iced air and with it the scent of recent cooking, of roasted meat, of barley, of warmth and camp and home. To the door's other side, Syrion mirrored me. He drew his gladius; mine was already drawn, although I didn't remember doing it. Their woollen covers made them fat in the moonlight.

I cast a glance back. Our fourth, fifth and sixth units were nearly on us. The second and third had gone with Lupus to the mule stockade, to take the mules and as much fodder as each man could carry. The seventh through to the tenth were holding off, ready to cover our escape. Syrion jerked his head at the opening.

'Ready?'

I nodded.

'Go!'

Shoulder to shoulder, we burst through the narrow gate, blades held forward like clubs. Four men waited for us, two on each side. I tripped the first, smashed the hilt of my gladius into the face of the second, bent and clubbed the fallen man on the side of his skull and stood, ready for the next.

There was no next: Lupus had trained us well and we had beaten our first true opponents in hand to hand combat. Not bad for a horse-trader's second son who had never wanted to fight. Exhilarated, I caught Syrion's fierce grin and returned it, then saw his eyes widen, and his lips form a silent whistle as he turned on his heel, and looked about.

What he saw was worth more than a whistle.

We had come into a small, warm compound, overshadowed by the mountain, so that it felt like a covered market, or a high cave: the IVth had, indeed, forsaken tents and built houses for each of the ten units, and one smaller, set back against the other wall, for the centurion.

I tried to remember him, this centurion; a thick-set man with a bull's neck, a sharp nose and a head of glossy curls much too like the images of the Emperor Nero for comfort. Gaius Hostilius Liccaius, I thought, but wasn't sure.

The houses seemed empty, which could not be: one of them had to hold Polydeuces and I did not believe they would have left him unguarded.

The plan was to find him before the IVth realized their mistake and came back from the wild hunt on which they had been lured. A dozen of our men joined us and more were pouring in through the gate, sent by Lupus who was holding guard outside against a renewed attack. I gestured two of the incomers to tie the men we had disabled and then waved the rest on; they fanned out and approached each hut in pairs.

Syrion and I took the first hut on the wall side of the compound. It was empty, although a brazier glowing in the centre showed two rows of four beds with hides and furs atop them, still crumpled as if newly vacated. The air smelled of harness oil and newly honed blades and the sweat of men waiting for war; I had come to know what that smelled like now, having been amongst it all day.

We left that hut and found the next as empty, and the next. Approaching the fourth, I heard the sound of a man's muffled grunt, through wool, or linen, or another man's clamped hand.

Syrion heard it too. He flung his hand up for caution, and we took more care to enter this hut together, hard, low, crouching down against the possibility of men with blades at the door.

They were not at the door. A half-unit of four stood in a line across the hut, with their beds pushed behind them, making a wall. And behind that, Polydeuces was stuck head first into a ruck of furs and hides, like a rabbit seeking its hole.

'Here! Fourth hut, wall line. Reds to me!' I called aloud over my shoulder; no point in secrecy now. The men of the IVth heard the same running feet as we did and knew what was coming.

Their leader was a small, wiry man with his lower face unshaved, which made him look like a haggard weasel. He spat an order in Latin and I, used to Greek, was slow to understand it, so that when they came at us, bunched in a boar's snout formation, two in front, two a little behind at the wings, I might have fallen to them but that my body acted faster than my mind, and I rolled sideways and down, below the level of their barely padded blades, and flung myself in a lengthways roll along the floor.

I had seen Pantera do something similar one night

when we . . . never mind, it was in Hyrcania and we were in no real danger. Not as now, when these men had murder in their eyes and were not remotely afraid of dying under their centurion's lash if they killed us.

Rolling, I toppled them. They fell in a clutter of stamping, cursing limbs. I bunched my legs under me and thrust upright, slamming my padded blade randomly at a calf, a heel, an elbow, as they came within reach. I felt a blow slice past my head and ducked under and slashed back, and struck out at the same time with my left hand at a shadow on that side and by the gods' luck it wasn't Syrion but one of the IVth who went down, choking, for I had caught his larynx and robbed him of breath. I saw another to my right and kicked at his groin, then brought my blade round in a full circular swing, straight for the great vessels of his neck.

'Stop!'

My gladius stopped, a hand's breadth from his throat. Even padded, it would have killed him. He stared up at me in mortal terror, and then looked past me with gratitude to Syrion, who had grabbed my arm, and was pulling me back.

'We're taking our man,' he said. 'If you let us go, we'll leave you here. Try to stop us, and we'll take you with us. You know what that means.'

They did, but still they did not stand and spread their arms and wave us past. 'Our centurion will flog us if we let you go and we are not injured,' said the leader, the unshaved weasel.

'Tie them,' I said. 'Cut the bed hides for ropes. They can't stop us if they're bound. We don't have to take them with us. Just do it now, while there's time. We have more to do here.'

'But . . .' Syrion caught my eye, puzzled, and then with slow comprehension. His smile grew like the rising sun, warm on his face. 'The Fox has nursed his plan to life?'

I grinned back. I was feeling more alive than I had for years, drunk on danger and the promise of success. 'Get the rabbit out of his hole and safely on his way and I'll tell you.'

The rabbit – Polydeuces – was warm and uninjured, if you forget the breaking of his pride. I sent him with the tenth unit who had waited outside to cover our retreat. They were men I knew by sight and hearing, but not by the colour of their souls; I had no idea if I could rely on them to guard my back in a tight corner. I told them to get him back to our camp if they could, or, if not, to stop with Cadus and ask for shelter there.

Outside, with Syrion at my side, I gathered the rest of our men.

'Our orders are to return now with the rabbit,' I said. 'But I have a different idea. Anyone who wishes not to be a party to it may leave now.'

'What idea?' someone asked from the back.

'One that might get us flogged, but will set the Fourth back for ever. Your choice. Go or stay. I won't say it until you've decided.'

Those that stayed did so, I think, for Syrion. We stood in darkness, with a nearby brazier glowing red. The tinted light caught him from behind, casting him in liquid bronze. He had thrown his cloak back and was standing square with his arms folded, so that he was the very image of a Gaulish chieftain, ready for the ultimate battle. It was a sight to strengthen the weakest heart, but even so, we lost two units. We watched them go, and did not mourn their loss.

I turned in a circle on one heel, thinking.

'Demalion?' Syrion was at my side. 'What are we doing?'

'The first century of the first cohort has charge of the legion's Eagle. We're going to find it and take it,' I said. 'It's the equivalent of taking a man, but nobody will be flogged for it.'

'They'll be flogged for losing it,' Syrion said cheerfully, 'all of them.'

And someone else, from the back, 'We can't steal their *Eagle*!'

'Can't we?' I felt their eyes on me, and saw their startled looks, and knew that, in that moment, I looked like Lupus. Just then, it was a compliment.

I walked past them all. 'We only need to hold it hostage, and see what they'll offer for its return. But we have to find it first. Shall we look and see?'

There was only one place a legion would keep its Eagle. We broke down the wooden door – they had built a wooden door, and barred it! – to the centurion's hut on the far side of the compound. Inside, a brazier was glowing orange, the colour a smith would use to harden a blade. It had not long been abandoned; its heat thickened our breath after the biting cold outside, and wrought the scent of cedar from the wooden walls.

A glance showed us the contents of the hut. The bed

was lifted off the floor, with the legs planted in bowls of water to keep vermin away, and set beside it on the wall was a shelf for the small things a man might take on campaign: a small hand knife with a bronze handle shaped in the likeness of a wren; a pouch of gemstones, still rough from the ground; a ring set with turquoise, and a dolphin etched on it; a scroll, half read: Xenophon, *On Hunting*.

In the corner was a cupboard, also bolted. I broke open the lock with the hilt of my gladius, and found inside a small shrine to Jupiter Best and Greatest, and another to the bull god, beloved of the Sassanids, and behind both, propped against the back wall, the flag-standard of the century with the open hand and medallions, and to the other side the Eagle of the IVth.

So much power in so small a thing. My heart tripped over. I had never seen a god, nor thought I might see one. I had never seen the emperor, to whom we renewed our oath each January. I had never even seen the governor of Syria, except at a distance from the parade ground. But daily I gave homage to our Eagle, watched its gilded wings glimmer in the rising sun as we said our prayers and renewed our oaths.

So, now, did this Eagle glimmer; its eyes gazed at us, and held us frozen. To see it was to feel the pride of our legion take hold of my heart and squeeze it tight, and I realized then how proud I was to be with the men around me, all of them, men with red armbands, men of the XIIth: my brothers.

I reached for the oakwood shaft, and stopped. Only the bravest of men carried the Eagle, for to them was drawn every enemy eye; every enemy archer and spearman tried to kill them. They were foremost in battle, and had to fight and yet keep the Eagle upright. To do such a thing was the epitome of honour. And to steal it was its opposite.

'They took Polydeuces,' Syrion said softly, from my side. 'There was no honour in that, either.'

I took a breath, tasted the cedarwood and incense of the shrines, felt the touch of the gods; both Jupiter and Mithras were martial, both valued valour above all else, neither was inclined to weakness.

'Take the furs from his bed,' I said tightly. 'Cover the Eagle. We'll take only that, and leave the standard. They'll know why.'

A bulge-eyed youth of the sixth unit looked at me and opened his mouth. 'Don't ask,' I said, but Syrion, who had more pity and patience than I had at that moment, said, 'It shows we didn't care enough about their century to take their standard; we only needed to dishonour their legion.'

It was done. I carried the Eagle; I could not ask it of another man, even Syrion, particularly Syrion, who carried the sixth century's standard with such honour. With a swathe of bear fur warming my chest, and the shaft pressed hard on my shoulder, we ran from the centurion's house.

Some of the other huts were burning; our men had tipped the braziers on to the beds as they left. Greasy flames peeped from doorways and smoke slewed after, rising sluggishly to hover in a thick wad less than an arm's breadth above the rooftops.

We cleared the gate in a dozen strides. The path lay ahead of us, and safety with Cadus, or the long march home. To our right, the mule stockade was empty, the wall of mule scent gone, and in its place the reek of smoke, and some blood. The entrance was churned snow, but inside men still fought. I heard a cry, just one, high and hoarse, like a gull on the sea shore, and knew the throat that made it.

'That's Lupus! The Fourth have come back and found him.' I had thought him gone ahead of us, and cursed myself for not knowing better.

I thrust the Eagle at the goggle-eyed youth. His name was Kalendinus, but I learned that only later. At the time, I simply took his arms and folded them around the Eagle, with the shaft angled back over his shoulder. 'Get this to the first of our camps along the path,' I said. 'Guard it with your life and tell Centurion Cadus that I said you were to do so.' I gave him more orders, secretly, that the others didn't hear, then said, aloud, 'The rest of you go with him, except Syrion, who comes with me.'

I was a clerk and a courier, not even the flag-bearer that Syrion was; I was the conscript who most hated being in the legion. But in spite of these things, or perhaps because of them, they listened as if I were the camp prefect, and left, running along the trail of our departing mules like a pack of schoolboys let loose from a lesson.

Chapter Twelve

Syrion and I ran back into the maelstrom of the stockade. The smoke was finer here, the fire nearly burned out. A clot of men battled in the left hand corner nearest the gate. Lupus was at their centre alone, set about by a full unit of the IVth. Their backs were to us; we had the advantage of surprise.

I flicked a glance at Syrion, saw him nod and raise his arm, and then, '*For the Twelfth!*'

We bellowed it with all the force of a full unit. I ran close by the wall and let my padded blade – the padding was less than it had been, I will own that, now – rattle along the wood so that we sounded like an incoming army.

Syrion simply bunched his Olympian shoulders and hurled himself bodily at the backs of the nearest men. Two went down with him, bowled flat and winded. I picked one and swung the flat of my blade at his back just below the shoulder blades, with a force that would have cut him in half had I used the naked edge.

He dropped as if dead. I did not stop to see if it were true. We were three and they were five and they knew now how few we were. They rallied and came at us shoulder to shoulder, big men with hate in their eyes, weaving their uncovered blades back and forth.

Their leader grinned, showing gaps in his teeth where earlier violence had taken them out. There was blood on his lips. In a moment's terror, I prayed it was his own, and that he did not feed on other men's death. He saw me and his grin widened. In northern Latin, with a Germanic taint, he said, 'Three prisoners for the loss of one. A good bargain.'

Lupus was on my left, Syrion beyond him. I felt him tense. In fast southern Greek, he said, 'Break to the left of Blood-mouth on my count. Three, two, one, *go*!'

As if our lives depended on it, we hurled ourselves at the hair's breadth space Lupus had divined between the blood-mouthed brute and the barely less terrifying man to his left.

I closed my eyes and made a missile of my body. I felt blows rain on my shoulders, my back, my hips as I rolled, but felt no pain. 'Don't fight – run!' How Lupus had breath to shout was beyond me, and in any case I needed no orders. I had seen the flame-lit gap where was the gate and nothing short of death would have stopped me going through it.

We broke out into cold, free air. Syrion was with me, Lupus a little behind, but catching up. I ran until my lungs burned, until I could taste blood in my spit, and still I kept running until the pounding of my blood in my ears began to echo and I listened through the spaces between the beats and heard footsteps, and a name; mine.

Blood-mouth did not know my name. I slowed and turned and felt myself sway with the sudden halt. I bent forward with my palms braced above my knees and dragged in air, hiccoughing and sobbing and swearing until all three came together and I was laughing, loosely, out of control.

Lupus was barely more sane. He crouched down and took a handful of snow and held it to a bruise on his cheek. Under the clean white moonlight, it was a black shape with no colour, but I could imagine it red-purple with greening edges when the sun fell on it in the morning.

I looked to my other side, where Syrion was standing with his head thrown back, dragging in air as if to suck in the sky. He grinned at me, and made the signal for success that we shared: a clenched fist.

I returned it, but when it was clear that neither of them had called me I walked back down the mule track away from them and the noise of their breathing until – *there!* – I heard my name called again, faintly, from far off.

I cupped my hands to my mouth and gave the wolf's call, not as well as Tears had done it on top of the stockade fence, but good enough. I heard a single yelp back, and walked on. The other two caught me up, silent now, and breathing with more care.

We met Horgias less than a spear's throw up the path that led back to the camp. He was holding his arm at an awkward angle and his face, even in moonlight, was more green than white.

'Who's been taken?' I could feel it, or I read it in his face. And I read the answer the same way, so that I was already reaching for snow to sweep across my face, to snap me to wakefulness.

Through the sudden cold, I heard him say, 'Tears. They have him in the centurion's hut. Proclion and Sarapammon have gone ahead for help. I thought you might be still at the compound.' He gave a kind of loose smile, that spoke as much of exhaustion and pain as of relief at having found us.

'It will need an exchange,' Lupus said. His left eye flashed from the centre of the black bruise on his face, wild and still at the same time. He took a long breath. 'Let's go back.'

'Why would they take one of us over him?' Syrion asked. 'They're as likely to take us all captive.'

'If we offer a centurion for a man, they'll accept,' Lupus said calmly. 'They've seen what we can do; they won't risk more getting hurt if they can gain me without battle.'

'But why would you . . .'

I laid a hand on Syrion's arm. 'He led us here,' I said. 'If that has caused a man to be captured, he has to do this, or he has to offer. For his honour.' I let go of Syrion and turned to Lupus. 'I think you're right, they would take you. But I think they will be happier if we offer them their Eagle back. And then no one is flogged.'

He looked at me a long time in silence. The white side and the black side of his face were perfectly still as his eyes raked me from crown to toe and back again. 'You took their *Eagle*?' he asked.

'We did.'

'Under whose orders?'

'Mine,' I said; and then, 'We're at war.' Syrion and I stood silent waiting for the tempest of his fury, and heard instead a strange, uncommon noise, and found it was laughter.

Lupus laughed until he choked, and we had to thump between his shoulders to help him breathe. Presently, when he could speak, 'Where is it?' he asked. 'The Eagle.'

'I gave it to a man of the sixth unit. He was to take it to Cadus and await us. If we haven't caught him up by dawn, he is to take it to our camp. If they're attacked, he's to throw it over the mountain, where it will not be found.'

His brows rose a fraction more at that, but he nodded. 'Horgias, go to Centurion Cadus, tell him what's happened and that he might need to surrender the Eagle to a delegation of the Fourth. Tell him that he is not to let it go unless they ask for it in the name of Jupiter Best and Greatest. If they ask in any other way, he may cast it down the mountain as Demalion suggested. And have his bone-setter take look at your arm. Syrion, Demalion, come.'

We three ran back to the enemy compound. That night, I believe we could have run the length of the empire and not felt it a hardship.

The smell that met us at the corner this time was not the lazy warmth of mules, but the ravages of fire. I ran through the smell of burning logs, of hides and furs, and, somewhere, of flesh.

At the bend in the path, Lupus dropped to a crouch with us at his either side. We were wild men now more than legionaries; any one of us could have been taken for a barbarian. Ahead, the men of the IVth were making a bucket chain, trying to put out the fire in their stockade. The compound that contained the huts was smoking threadily, but we had not fired it as badly as the stockade, and so fewer men were there.

Syrion said, 'If we walk to the gate, they'll take us and beat us. We might not have a chance to say why we've come.'

'Demalion?' Lupus was looking at me. I wondered if he saw the thoughts forming in my mind.

I said, 'We could try to climb over the wall at the back of the centurion's hut. We didn't fire that, so they won't be watching it.' I pulled a wry smile. 'If we don't have to give the Eagle away . . .'

'Lead us.' Lupus rose, wiping snow from his hand. 'On condition that if we meet them and there's any talking to be done, I speak and you remain silent.'

The route round the back took us over the treacherous scree slope, but I found the steps we had missed the first time, and I now knew must be there. I had seen their centurion's hut now, seen the lengths they went to for comfort and safety, and knew they would never leave their men to flounder on uncertain footing.

High clouds veiled the moon's face, making it harder to find handholds in the wall, but I had learned as a child that every dry-stone wall has places where a boy may climb, and where a boy can go a man may follow, has he but the nerve to go up, and not look down.

Syrion looked down. I was straddling the top when the clouds scurried away from the moon, and in the sudden wash of silvered light he made the mistake of checking that his foothold was secure.

I knew, because I could see by then, that what he saw below his foot was a great, yawning void; we had moved rightwards of the place where we started, and the fall was vertical and long. The ground was down there, somewhere, too far away to matter.

'Syrion!' I hissed urgently. 'Don't look down! Look up at me. Take my hand.'

There was a risk in that: our hands were not dry, but I could see a wave of weakness take him, and had seen men fall who would have been able to climb had not the height unmanned them.

I leaned over further. 'Come on, or I'll fall with you.' I felt his cold hand, and caught it at the wrist and locked my legs and held still while he used me as his climbing pole to make the top of the wall.

To his left, Lupus was already up, scrambling over the stone like a thief and then down in a long jump to the floor of the compound. I waited a moment, listening, but heard no shouts. I pushed Syrion and waited for his landing before I followed, and then led them out between the huts, through thin, acrid smoke and the reek of wet ash and wetter bedding. I imagined the IVth trying to find comfort in their stone-built luxury at this night's end, and felt an unkind satisfaction.

'Shh.' I put my fingers to my lips. The others stopped

where they were, mid-stride. 'Men ahead, three, perhaps mo—'

And then the night split apart, rent by a man's high, desperate cry, born of a pain so deep, so terrible, it could bear no real form.

'*Tears!*'

I ran as I had never yet run, without caution, without forethought, without an eye for the hidden traps, for the dangers, for the reasons why I was being summoned. For I was being summoned. In that cry I heard my name; however inchoate, however unintended, Tears called for me and, as Achilles to Patroclus, I ran.

He was in the centurion's hut, where the air was still warm, but not hot, and still smelled of cedarwood and incense and wealth, but now it smelled also of pain and blood and violence and Tears was flung on the bed, on fresh hides, naked, bruised, assaulted.

Two men stood over him, aroused and grinning as men stand over the women in a newly taken town. Another was climbing off – the centurion, by his badges – and one of the standing men was lifting the hem of his tunic, working himself to readiness. He was the same Blood-mouth we had faced in the mule stockade.

'*Tears!*' Screaming his name as my battle cry, I hurled myself at Blood-mouth with all the force and fury of a bull at a field cur, taking his chest squarely with my shoulder and ramming the hilt end of my gladius up into his solar plexus. As he went down, I jabbed my elbow in under his kidneys. He didn't even grunt, he had so little air to breathe.

Lupus and Syrion had taken the other standing

man, Lupus holding his shoulders, Syrion sweeping his feet out from under him. He fell lengthways, even as I swung myself past, using a set of shelves as a lever. I heard his head hit the stone floor.

The centurion was the last and slowest to respond. He was newly sated, dull-eyed, too fogged in his mind to think clearly. I kicked him in the gut with all the ache of Tears' cry behind it, and then reached for Tears who had risen and fallen again, or seemed so to have done.

But when I hauled him upright, there was blood on his hands, and a glimmer of iron, and the small, bronze-handled knife with the wren on the hilt was slick with crimson, and the centurion had a wound in his chest, over his heart, barely the width of my thumb. Blood oozed from his mouth. I saw death steal the light from his eyes.

'Give that to me!' I grabbed the knife from Tears, spun him away, saw in passing the marks of ropes on his wrists, the welts across his back where they had misused him before the centurion made him his own.

Ungainly, I shoved my friend back against the wall, and set my own naked blade against the centurion's chest, stripping away the last paltry strands of wool so that when I stood again, and Lupus was there to meet me, I could say, 'I killed him.'

Lupus said nothing, only pinched the bridge of his nose, and blew out a blood clot, and wiped the mess away with the back of his hand. Absently, he cleaned himself on the centurion's new bed hides.

Any man who kills another will be flogged until

dead. So had said the prefect, who was due to make his visit in a day's time.

Lupus' eyes fed on my face, then inched away. I heard Tears draw a breath.

'No,' I said. 'Be silent.'

'Yes,' Lupus said, 'be silent. Both of you.' He looked down. 'This man is a prisoner,' he said. 'We'll take him with us. You' – he pointed to Syrion and me – 'wrap him tightly and bind him so he can't escape. You' – this to Tears – 'dress fast. We must leave swiftly, before the others regain consciousness.'

We said nothing, any of us, only let our glances slide off each other, so that nothing was spoken between us, even silently. Tears was dressed by the time we had trussed the centurion as if he were, in fact, alive, and able to escape. We bound him in hides and Syrion and I raised him to our shoulders like a battering ram.

'Follow,' Lupus said, and led us out of the door.

We did not run from the enemy compound, but we marched faster than I had ever done before and came sooner than I might have wanted to Cadus' camp. There, we did not pause, but gathered Horgias and Sarapammon and the giant Proclion and poor Polydeuces, who had become 'the Rabbit' and already knew he would never lose the name.

'What will you do with the Eagle?' Cadus asked it of Lupus, but he was watching my face, trying to read me. I held myself unreadable.

Lupus said, 'If you could deliver it back to them tomorrow, I would be grateful; we have no need of it now. Tell them if they want their officer before the prefect's visit, they can bargain for him.'

We left swiftly, Syrion and I still carrying our bundle, which was clearly a man and perhaps not clearly dead.

I remember nothing of the march back. It must have happened, for we reached our own camp just as the first knife's edge of light cut the night from the eastern sky. I had cramp in my right arm, from holding tight to a dead weight, and I fancied I could feel warm blood on my skin, though it could as easily have been urine, or something more foul.

At the gates to our camp, we halted. Lupus had given no order, but we dared not go in, for fear of what looting might have occurred in our absence.

Nothing had happened – the earlier units had returned as they had been told and held our camp safe; we found that almost immediately. Lupus himself walked forward, and took the salute from the leading man and came out again. We could read him now, in ways we never had before. We saw his relief, his almost-joy, and we cheered him though the sound came ragged from our throats for it was over a day since we had rested, and we had fought hard in between.

He waited for us to be still. The sun was on him, lighting the bruise that marred half his face. He looked wild, and savage, and a far more genial man than he had been a day before.

He signalled Sarapammon and the Rabbit. 'Take the men inside. See to the wounded, build fires, cook whatever we have to eat. There is some ale in my tent. Share it out equally.'

'Where are you going?' It was a sign of how different we were that Sarapammon dared ask.

'We're taking our prisoner somewhere safer,' Lupus said. 'The Fourth may launch a counter-attack. I would not want him too easily retaken.'

Nobody argued. As they turned to go in, they, too, were avoiding each other's glances, preparing what they were going to say.

I still had no idea what I was going to say, except that I killed him, that Tears was not capable of it, that I would kill Tears myself with my bare hands if he tried to take the guilt to himself; better to die fast at the hands of a friend than under the prefect's bullhide whip.

Tears was not carrying anything, but Lupus made him come with us. We four left the camp and walked west, up into the high peak, towards the goat path that we had followed a day-become-eternity ago, to find where the IVth had set their ambush.

We squeezed through the narrow channel, barely wide enough to fit the centurion's body, and came out the other side, to the place where the mountain fell away and we could see down on to clouds still sunk in night; dawn had not reached them yet.

'Untie him.' Lupus moved away to sit on an outcrop of rock. He didn't look for it, but sat with familiarity, as if this was a place he came often to watch the sun go down, or to count the tiny insects that scratched and sprang along the valley floor, and were, in fact, goats, and antelopes, and the beasts that hunted them.

We untied the centurion and laid him out on the hides that had been his bed. He looked ridiculous in death, with his tunic still bunched above his waist and his member flaccid. His skin was perfectly white, blotched in places where he had lain against us. It was urine that had pooled on my neck. I swept it clear with snow.

Lupus stood and came across and with his own hands lifted the man by his heels and swung him round. It took him perilously close to the edge. Stepping back, he held on to the mountain behind with one hand and placed his sandalled foot against the dead man's head.

'*Given of the god,*
Given to the god,
Taken by the god in valour, honour and glory.
May you journey safely to your destination.'

It was the prayer spoken over the grave of a fallen soldier. Lupus spoke it like a benediction, as if the man had been his heart's friend. Then he shoved his foot out, sharply.

The centurion sailed over the edge. He was a log, turning end over end in a waterfall; a tree, falling from a precipice; he was a man, falling so far, bouncing, coming apart on the rocks, an arm ripped off here, a long peel of skin there; the snow was bloody to the snow line, and then the winter-dried earth was bloody beyond it. If he hit the bottom, we could not see it.

'He tried to retrieve his legion's Eagle and then escape,' Lupus said. 'It was an honourable act, worthy of the officer he was, but sadly he did not know the terrain and so fell. Such will be my report. A man who falls off the mountain is deemed to have killed himself, so nobody bears any guilt, but I will suggest that, because he was our prisoner, we will pay for a tablet to be erected in his name beyond the walls of the camp.'

We stood in a line; me, Tears, Syrion. We two held Tears between us, for I think he might have thrown himself over when the centurion went. Certainly, he was shuddering as a man with fever.

I swallowed. 'A good report,' I said. 'We shall, of course, be your witnesses.'

'Of course. Now get that man back to the tents and feed him. Parade will be one hour later than usual.'

We were marching away when he called me back.

'Do you have still the dye with which to turn your tunic red?'

'The madder? Yes, I do.'

'Enough of it for a century?'

'Enough for the entire cohort, if you want it.'

He twitched a smile then; I was coming to know it, and to revel in the sight of it. I was his then, part of the XIIth, and he knew it. 'Not the entire cohort yet, Demalion. The century will do. Henceforth we are the Bloody First. And I fancy we might have a mule's tail on our standard. See to it on our return.'

Raphana, Syria, Summer, AD 61

In the Reign of the Emperor Nero

Chapter Thirteen

We lost the first man of our unit during the siege at Tigranocerta, on the day I killed my first enemy and so became a man.

It happened in the summer after Corbulo became our commander, which was in turn three years after the first winter we spent in the Mountains of the Hawk, when I took the XIIth to heart, and ceased to dream of escape.

We were no longer the second cohort by then, we had become the sixth. Syrion was still our standard-bearer, with Proclion, that great bear of a man, as his signaller and me as watch officer, which gave me an increase in pay that I didn't need and a standing that I relished every time I took the password.

I kept my role as courier for the cohort and that, too, gave me a freedom the others lacked. I was lucky that they didn't resent me for it, but the events on the mountains had put us beyond petty squabbles and, in any case, I made sure to bring back gifts whenever I went away.

The ascending order of centurions meant that Lupus had nudged Cadus from his rank as centurion of the sixth and Cadus, in his turn, had leapfrogged three other officers to become primus pilus, first centurion of the first cohort, second only to the camp prefect among the ranks that counted.

In theory, the tribunes and legates stood higher than the prefect, but the fighting men knew that the officers came from Rome under sufferance and returned soon enough to their wives and comforts and politics while the prefect and the centurions stayed to fight with us and for us; they were the ones who risked their lives in the front lines in war and bartered with the local leaders in peacetime; they kept us as safe – and made us as rich – as they could, while not stinting on our share of the action.

It was a joy to see Cadus so elevated, but it was a sorrow also, for the pilus typically stayed in post only a year, from one battle season's start to the next, before he was promoted to camp prefect with another legion, or perhaps to lead an auxiliary unit, or to be personal bodyguard to some provincial governor.

His duties kept him more in the commander's office than on the field and we saw him rarely, so I took particular notice when he called me off the outer practice field one day after early weapons drill and asked me to deliver a sealed slate to Lupus.

It was a spring morning, I remember, not hot by the local Syrian standards, but warm enough for us to be out of wool and into linen. We were tired, but that was normal for the time of year; the lambing had started and, at the request of the local townsmen, our night watches were detailed explicitly to keep jackals at bay.

They gave us hides and mutton in return, and there were times when we could lie on the turf and get blood on our hands helping the ewes to give birth. I had experience with foaling mares and had found a new vocation so that I spent half my nights face down in the lambing fields and the other half marching their perimeters, listening for the sounds of hot breath amidst the night calls of the insects.

I should have been exhausted, but the feel of new life kicking under my hands in the night, the salt-sweet smell of the lambing fluids, the violent green of spring, all made the days seem more true, so that the sound of a single bird, singing, and the suppressed excitement in Cadus' eyes as he gave me the slate are etched with equal clarity on my memory.

I couldn't run – legionaries do not run within the barracks unless they particularly want to be flogged – but I marched at double time to the inner practice ground, the one that runs from the infirmary on one side to the far wall on the other, where Lupus was putting the latest recruits through the unnerving hell of pole practice.

It's hard to explain why slashing a weighted wooden sword at an oak post as thick as a man's waist should be a frightening thing, but when you aren't used to it the judder up your arm wrenches the muscles and sinews and there comes a time when you believe with absolute certainty that your shoulder is going to jump out of its socket at the next blow. Or the one after. Or the one after that.

And it is then, when you would give your left arm and your chances of life to be allowed to put down the sword and stagger to the water butts, that someone like Lupus will scream at you to hit harder, faster, because your life will depend on it one day.

Here, now, on this day, Lupus had them working in pairs, so that the entire century was spread out over the field. They were lined up, two men to each post, hitting alternately high and low, in opposing order; one man high and one low and heaven help you if you lose the rhythm and strike twice in the same place, because the tip is as likely then to catch your partner as the post and while it wouldn't take off a limb, a sword made of oak, with lead in the hilt to increase the weight, is a hard thing to control and might easily break his fingers. Or if not then his next strike, in retaliation, will break yours.

'Harder! Harder! *Strike* at it, for the gods' sake! It's a Parthian, not your grandmother! I swear if you don't put some effort into— *What?*'

He had always hated being interrupted. I gave him Cadus' slate without a word on the basis that he could read the crow's head seal on the front as easily as I could and even Lupus ceased his screaming for General Corbulo.

'Don't stop!'

It was a credit to their fear of him that the men continued hacking at the posts as if their lives depended on it while Lupus broke the seal and turned the slate over in its wooden bed. The words written on it were few, and, without craning to look, hard to see clearly. From the angle I had, I read . . . INSPECTION . . . LEGION . . . HONOUR . . .

Lupus grew very still. Presently, his gaze flicked sideways and settled on me blankly. I watched for the moment when he recognized me, and saw the ghost-edge of his smile. I think that, by then, he had begun to modify it, just for me, to see how finely he could pare it and I still recognize it.

The moment passed and he snapped his eyes wide, a sure sign of impending urgency. 'Your unit in parade dress within the watch. The entire cohort on the parade ground by the following watch, ready to practise the drill against cavalry. General Corbulo is coming to observe. He has been made governor of Syria. He is our new commander.'

Corbulo: a name to conjure with, a name to follow into battle, wherever he led; a name to have a man marching to the gates of Rome, crying *Imperator!* until the crowds and the idiot senate and the corrupt wax-brains of the Praetorian Guard and every other man with voting powers in the city came to understand what we already knew: that this man should be our emperor, that Rome would thrive under his rule, in place of the fool who presently held the throne.

Corbulo, who stood before us that bright, brisk spring afternoon and watched as our centurions bawled us through our paces, and then as Cadus took charge and marched us through the display that we had been practising, if we were honest, for the last four years, just for this moment.

Proclion and the other signallers blew for the thousandth time, and, for the thousandth time, all of us hurled our javelins, row by row, and placed our spikes and stepped back and did it as if we were one living breathing body, one mind, one heart, one soul, and that held in Cadus' cupped hands.

And then we stood waiting, panting, sweating, watching, and by his very presence our general held us in check, so that when he raised his arms we shouted his name until our throats hurt but we did not hail him as emperor, which would have started us along the inevitable road to civil war.

Had he unleashed us, so much would have been different afterwards, but at the time all we knew was that this man was Caesar come to life and walking among us; a man more at home in the legions, amongst the sweat and iron, the hard march and the killing at the end of it – and perhaps the dying – than he was in the senate amid the lethal politics of petty men who couldn't hold a line in battle if their lives depended on it.

He was not a large man, nowhere near as big as Proclion, or even Sarapammon. When he tucked his helmet under his arm, he showed how he was balding across his crown; he had skin that had chapped in winter and not healed, a largeish nose and pale blue eyes that looked as if someone had cut buttons from the sky and sewn them on to his soul.

He wore bare iron plate on his chest, none of the gilded nonsense that Octavian wore when he named himself Augustus and stole the name of Caesar. His sword was a legionary gladius, far from the usual dress sword of a governor or a legate, but we knew it had seen action, had killed, and saved men's lives; that it was a real sword, carried by a real soldier.

He did not draw it as he stood before us, mounted on an upturned flour crate, but as he lowered his arms his hand settled on its hilt as if it belonged there, and might at any moment spring to life.

That was when we came closest to hailing him *Imperator.* Even I could feel the word boiling in my throat, I felt it reverberate in the breaths of Tears to my left, Syrion to my right, I heard it rumble in the undertones of the rows fore and aft as we bellowed his name loud enough to wake the gods, to lift the skies, to call the heroes back to earth to see that one of them walked living amongst us.

'Corbulo! Corbulo! *Corbulo!*'

In time we grew tired, of course. At the cresting of the wave, our general raised his right hand with the palm out flat and the sound of his name died away, soft as the ocean's rage before Poseidon.

He spoke into the silence after, and I swear that every man of the XIIth heard him, though we were lined twenty deep in our centuries, sweating in our helmets, listening to the rush of our own blood pounding.

'Men of the Twelfth. When I first came here to lead the legions against the Parthian menace, I had heard the Twelfth was a poor legion, that it barely earned its name the Thunderbolt; that it was, rather, Thunderstruck.'

He paused. We did not laugh. We, too, had heard that. Some of us had believed it.

'And so I chose the legions I knew I could count on to face the King of Kings: the Third, the Sixth, the Tenth. I sent them to the Armenian mountains to harden them and fashion them into warriors again, after life in the east had turned them into goatherds and merchants, soft men with no heart for war.'

We shuffled in our places, we who had spent our nights up to our elbows inside lambing ewes, marching guard on the herds. But he was smiling, and his pale-sky eyes were friendly as he spoke.

'Even so, I sent some of the best men amongst you with orders to make you, too, into soldiers, and they have worked on you these four years, while the other legions have met the enemy and held him in check. And they have not worked in vain. I have witnessed today as smooth, as perfect a display as any general might hope for from his men. I have read the reports of how you conducted yourselves on the mountain each winter, how your skills improved, each legion against the other, how you have earned for yourselves the titles of the Bloody Legion, and the Ice-hard Men.'

We of the XIIth, dressed in our madder tunics, glowed, and then glowered. The IVth glowered and then glowed. I never cease to find it strange how readily a single word can call forth a dozen memories. In that moment of reminding, I heard Tears scream, saw him defiled beneath the centurion, saw the centurion falling down the mountainside, stood before his monument, which spoke of his bravery and not of his calumny, stood before the tribunal of inquiry later, and told my lies and was commended for them.

On top of these were layered three more years' worth of memories in the mountains, none of them as vivid, nor as enraging. Sometimes, we had lost to the IVth, other times we had won. But never again had a man of ours been taken prisoner, or a man of either legion died.

Corbulo waited for the almost-silence to become absolute, as he was used to. He was smiling still, knowing the depth of what he had done, and what it said of us.

'You are those men, blooded and ice-hard. It speaks well of you and those who have fashioned you, as iron on an anvil. And so now I have come to give you what you crave most: the chance to prove yourselves not against each other but against our enemy, against Vologases, King of Kings, against Parthia.'

His voice rose to the baritone shout he needed to soar over the roar of our approval. The lambing pens were forgotten, the petty feuds, the deaths, the injuries – almost the injuries: I did not forget, nor forgive, what had been done to Tears – but the rest was swept away in a joy I had never imagined would be mine and even now cannot begin to describe: we were good enough, strong enough, respected enough by a man we adored; *we were going to war!*

We were children whose every wish has just been granted; we were men who had not dared hope for this. If we had lovers who must be left behind, we did not care. If we had lovers who might be by our sides we hugged them in our euphoria, for this was better than love, this promise of action.

I kissed Tears and was met and held and kissed in return; not the first kiss by any means, but it was the first when I read only joy in his eyes. The shadow that had clung to him since the Mountains of the Hawk had cleared. I could have wept for happiness.

In time, we settled, hungry for details, and drank them in as they were given.

'As you know, our emperor in his wisdom has named Tigranes king of Armenia. As you know also, Tiridates, brother to Vologases, King of Kings, lays claim to that same throne. King Tigranes, in his wisdom,' that word had a sting in its tail; we laughed and he was pleased, 'has seen fit to invade certain cities of Adiabene that border Armenia, and has thus drawn on himself the ire of the Parthians.'

If I closed my eyes, I could see Monobasus, the fox-faced king of Adiabene, purple with rage at the invasion of his lands. I saw him kneeling before the King of Kings, begging his aid. I saw the shimmer-shine of the Parthian cataphracts as they massed and lowered their lances . . . I let my eyes spring open.

I was not in the front row, but I swear his eyes were on me as Corbulo said, 'Vologases, the King of Kings, is no fool. He has made peace with Hyrcania, and has sent his Parthians to attack Armenia. King Tigranes has withdrawn to Tigranocerta, his capital, which is a walled city, readily defensible. You will march now to his aid, and help him to hold it. A full wing of Pannonian archers shall accompany you, leaving your fellow legions, the Third, Sixth and Tenth, to cross the Euphrates and threaten Vologases from the south, thus splitting his forces. Vologases shall not take Tigranocerta. He shall not endanger Syria. Between us, we shall leash him and hold him back. You march in the morning.'

Chapter Fourteen

Tigranocerta, capital city of Armenia

By crisp starlight and a low moon, our unit passed in single file through the postern gate and out across the river. Our horses' bound feet scuffed on the wooden bridging boards, barely loud enough to cover the restless water sliding beneath.

The nights in Armenia were cool and dry and far more pleasant than the humid heat of day. Here, outside the city walls, the day's dampness had fallen from the air and gathered over the river in thick platters of mist that rose before us, like the shed skin of some great, forgotten serpent. Pushing forward, we let the mist swallow us, praying that it might keep us invisible to the watching Parthians.

Tears rode ahead of me, mounted on a liver chestnut gelding that was my bay mare's second foal. Its hide drew down the damp and grew so dark that it merged with the night and Tears became a half-man, birthed from the thick air. I set the mare to follow and felt the mist take me, and sent my thanks to the river gods for their gift of obscurity.

We left the bridge and crossed into open sward. Behind us, the rose-pale walls of Tigranocerta soared the height of five men and stretched, it seemed, from one side of the broad, fertile valley to the other.

This wasn't true, of course; the illusion fell apart when the city was viewed from a greater distance. If, for instance, you stood on one of the ranges of mountains that bordered us on north and south, you would see that the Armenian capital was not a vast city, not the size of Rome, say, or even Damascus, but it was bigger than Raphana, and the walls more strongly fortified, and both had been enough to awe us to silence when we first marched in.

Since then, we had come to know its weak points as well as its strengths. As a first task, Cadus had ordered us to destroy the bridge that crossed the river from the postern gate so that the only egress was over boards that were thrown across and drawn back with ropes.

When this was done, we had set bulwarks within the walls at the points where the gates opened out, then built up the stores of oil cauldrons, and firewood to heat them; we had seen to the weapons, the pike-poles that pushed ladders away, the city's swords, which had been left aside since the battle between Lucullus and Mithridates over a century before, the spears and axes and stocks of arrows for the archers.

Finally, over the course of a month, we had deepened

the ditch that completed the circle started by the river, and set rusted iron spikes in the base, and thrown down dead mules and rotting pigs from the battlements and left them to fester, so that any man foolish enough to attempt a crossing might die fast, impaled on hidden points, or slowly of the blood-fever afterwards.

We saw off three attacks; messy, discordant affairs with much noise of men and horses and the stench of burning oil and flesh and enough clash of arms for our unit to be awarded silver medallions to hang on neck chains for courage in holding the walls. But none of it was real fighting and if any of us killed the men who came at us, it was as much by accident as design.

They backed away after that, for it was clear that the only way to get in or out was when those inside threw down the boards across the river and we threw them down only when the units went out to forage, or to scout, or, as now, to escort in a mule-train sent by Corbulo with grain and fodder and bull's hide to patch our shields.

By now, we despised the men set against us for their pitiful prosecution of the siege. A Roman legion would have encircled the town and not one man, not one child, not a cur nor a rat would have left or entered it alive. The Parthians, by contrast, kept themselves well back, dug in at the heel of the northern range of mountains, where thick forest masked their presence, and they could watch us unhindered as we crossed the open, fertile plain, unless we travelled under cover of night.

It was a sad place to be at war; never in all my life have I seen corn grow so fast, nor grass fatten beasts to such weight. The herders of Raphana would have sold their grandmothers for such bounty, although they might have claimed them back again as recompense for the floods that were said to assail the land in winter.

We never witnessed any flooding; we were not there when the snows crashed down the mountains to bury the land, nor when the river turned to torrent, claiming land and lives and livelihoods at the gods' caprice. We met the river at its tamest, a fine silver thread spinning under the bridge and on down the valley. They tell me it joined the Tigris south of us, but I never saw that.

This night, what was left of it, we passed south and a little east, to where the mountains crowded dark against the sky. And what mountains! These were the southernmost Taurus ranges, that made our Hawks seem like wrinkles in the sand.

The passes through the peaks twisted like wool on a skein, but we knew the routes by then, and had no need of a local man as pathfinder. We felt safer without; one less chance of treachery, and one less man to guard if the Parthians came upon us, although we had only a passing fear of that; the scouts and spies said that Monobasus, who led the siege, was waiting for Vologases to come to his aid and there was no sign of that yet.

We reached the mountains just as Helios rode his blazing chariot to the horizon, and hurled his lance against the night. I cast a glance back over my shoulder, for the plain was at its most beautiful at sunrise, laid to emerald with beasts wrought as living jewels upon it.

Later, as we had found, the sun's heat drew a torrid dampness to the air that left us all short of breath. To escape, even for a day, was a blessing and we welcomed the shadows of the pass that wound through between the two tallest peaks, and the sharp, dry mountain air that settled there.

Trees grew thickly on either side for the first half of the rise and shadows wove in their depths, watching us; four-legged hunters, not men, but no less lethal for that. We had lost scouts to wolves or boar or both in our time in Armenia, and we rode through that forest with our blades unsheathed.

Still, we saw nothing, only breathed the blessed cool of the trees, the easy, moss-scented air, and were sorry to see it go as the path took us higher, beyond the tree line, to where lime-grey lichens and stunted grasses were the only sward and we had only to lean out over the edge of a path to see hawks sway and circle on the gods' breath below us.

Here, the air was thin and we breathed fast and did not push our mounts but let them pick their own route. They knew the way, the unexpected turns that seemed to lead over the edge of the mountain but in reality took us up and out on to another long, narrow path, with one side falling away to the plain and the other solid rock. In this much, it was like the Mountains of the Hawk back in Syria, except that the fall was far further.

It was two hours after noon when finally we crested the rise and stood at the place where we could look back to the distant city, sitting pale as a shell on the river's bank, or turn and look south down into the valley of the Khabur, which led to the Euphrates.

And there, moving towards us, was a string of flop-eared mules forging their way up to meet us, with a half-century of armoured men set about them as escort. They were led by a tall man on a blue roan gelding who wore a helmet in the old design, eschewing ear flaps.

I recognized the horse first, and then the man, for he was the last I expected to see here.

'Aquila!' Raising my hand, I pushed my bay mare forward, and he raised his hand in return, and sent his mount faster at the rise.

We met on a shelf of weathered rock. The lichens on this side of the hill were a pinkish grey that caught the morning light and softened it, gentling the stark blue sky.

'Aquila!' I was truly pleased to see him. 'I thought you'd have a farm in Iberia by now, with your life passing in a haze of fruitful olive trees and grazing goats.'

'And I thought you dead of a Parthian axe, or else driven to distraction in the bowels of the Twelfth. A year from now, you will be right. I trust that I will still be wrong.'

Grinning, I took the arm he gave and gripped it. His face was lined deep as oak bark by the Syrian winters, his hair the colour of the snowy rock about us, without any shade of grey. Even so, his eyes were still sharp enough to cut a man.

I said, 'The Parthian axemen all fell in the war against Hyrcania and the Twelfth is . . . a brave legion. Worth fighting for.'

He rolled his tongue around his teeth and had the grace not to raise his brows. Instead, his gaze slid past to the men behind me: Syrion, Tears, Proclion, Horgias,

Rufus, Sarapammon, the Rabbit. We were a unit in more than name, now, a union of hearts and minds and souls; where one went, we all went; what one felt, we all felt. A seasoned officer must have been able to read that. Aquila squinted at me, creasing his eyes against the sun. 'Have you killed yet?'

I must have glowered and he let it pass with a shrug, and another question. 'What's Monobasus done to assault Tigranocerta?'

'Nothing of note. He has archers and some cataphracts, but mostly light cavalry and a century or two of foot soldiers. None of them is suited for a siege. He's waiting for Vologases to come with the heavy cavalry and the engines.'

'Then he'll wait until the sky falls. We' – by that he meant the VIth – 'have the King of Kings fully occupied in the south. He risks losing all of Parthia if he moves. He won't do that for a walled city and a king he despises. The battle season will be over in another three months. You can go to your winter quarters then.'

A lift in his voice gave me a first clue as to why this man had come on escort duty, when he could have left it to someone half his age and a tenth of his rank. I felt my heart trip a beat, although whether it was for joy or grief I wasn't sure.

'We're not going back to Raphana?' I asked.

His smile was open, hiding nothing. 'Not Raphana. You are to winter in Melitene, in Cappadocia, where we last met.'

Melitene of the beautiful mountains, of the cold-clean air, and rivers like diamonds. I let myself linger a little in the memory, but not for long. On its own, this was news enough to bring Aquila here, a man with the authority to order Cadus to new winter quarters, and the heart to do it gently. But I knew him better than he thought, certainly well enough to see the shadow in his smile, and know there was more to come.

I peered at him, against the sun's high, knifing glare. 'What?' I asked.

This time, he did not smile. 'Corbulo has sent to Nero asking for a new commander for Armenia and Cappadocia.'

'Why? Corbulo is more than capable—'

'Stop.' Aquila's hand came up. 'Think.' His hand fell. 'And listen. Corbulo has requested aid in the protection of the east. He has kept the governorship of Syria. A new governor has been appointed for Cappadocia. He will be your general.' His face said *I'm sorry*, but his voice could not, even here on a mountain in the company of hawks and mules and seven men who would have given their lives rather than speak aloud any treason they heard. A company of the VIth was behind him and even here the emperor might have ears and the reports of those ears might lead a man to his death; it had happened before.

So I said only, 'Who is the new commander?' and gave no voice to the disappointment that curdled my guts.

To my shame, the name he gave was not one that conjured any feeling in me: not fear, nor revulsion, nor horror at a man who carried ill-luck with him wherever he went. On that bright summer day at the height of the world, I heard Aquila say 'Lucius Caesennius Paetus', and I shrugged and said, 'He who was consul in Rome last year?' and at Aquila's nod, 'So . . . Corbulo is making sure he doesn't hold too much power in the east. Is that it?'

'I have no idea.' Aquila's lined face was a mask of moderation. 'And if it were, I would not say. Paetus will join you before winter. So make the most of this siege and then meet him in Melitene, and spend your winter getting to know him. He will lead you in war next year. Now,' he clapped my arm, 'how long before we make the city?'

'Half a day. We aim to reach the plain as night falls, so that we may cross in darkness, unseen by the enemy. Once there, all that will hold us back is the speed of the mules. If you can push them, we'll see the city before midnight.'

'Oh, I can push the mules.' Aquila was himself again, bright as a polished blade. 'I've waited four years to see Cadus; this day cannot pass too soon. Let your unit lead us back over the path while we hold the rear guard; they say the route winds more than the bull-maze of Crete and this is not time to find ourselves lost.'

Chapter Fifteen

It was evening when we reached the forest on our return journey, and it was as unfriendly now as it had been in the morning; more so, as we soon discovered.

'*Hsst!*' Horgias reined his horse back and laid a hand on my bridle. 'To the left, past the bole of the fallen tree. Something's moving.'

'A boar?' I strained to look. Horgias is a wolf in the guise of a man; he can see in the dark better than any of us. With the moon barely risen, and starlight thin as slivers through the trees, I could perhaps have owned to seeing a shadow darker than the rest that moved faster than the wind-sway of the branches.

At my side, Tears murmured, 'Not a boar.' His sword scraped free of its sheath, scenting the air with lanolin and a faint tinge of iron. I would have said I was alert before, but I shifted into some new realm where my cheeks felt the lift of each leaf around me, my ears heard the shrews, the wood mice skittering beneath our horses' feet, and my eyes – now – saw what Tears and Horgias had seen: not a boar, but a man. Men, in fact; at least three that I could count.

Syrion was our leader; all three of us turned to him. Wordless, he raised his hand and made a gesture: three fingers, then three again, then two splayed out and down. At that sign, seven of us dismounted and slid into the forest, leaving Sarapammon behind to lead the horses on.

Old Aquila, who could have run through this kind of manoeuvre in his sleep, saw what was happening and rode up past the fifteen mules from the train's end to its head, bringing a dozen of his men with him.

His voice was loud enough to cross the Roman forum on a busy morning, never mind a forest at first fall of night, but its tone was conversational, as if we all still rode together and he had come up, with such noise, purely to pass the time.

'Demalion, how much further? My old bones ache at the end of the day and I would soak them before tomorrow's dawn.'

His patrician accent rang out like a piece of Rome transplanted, and Sarapammon, answering in my place and speaking Latin as Aquila had done, said, 'Not long now. See those trees ahead, where they part and let in the moonlight? That's the edge of the forest, where the mountain meets the fertile plain. We'll be there in a hundred paces and then we can get some speed on, and head for the city. It's dark enough now and the Parthians will never know we've—'

A spear passed within a hand's breadth of my head,

hurtling towards the voices. I felt the wind of its passing, and did not hear it strike flesh, but I didn't have time to look round, to see if Sarapammon or Aquila had been hit, for in that moment I was fighting for my life.

Three of them came at me, four at first, but Tears took the farthest; I saw the slip of his blade in the moonlight as he attacked.

As for me, I had my gladius in one hand and a long-knife in the other, entirely against our proper dress, but Horgias had been teaching us and we had drilled in these woods on each of our four previous forays and had learned the hard way that in the tight, dark crush between the trees a knife in the off hand was far safer than a shield.

I saw the pale flash of a man's face, mouth stretched wide in a battle yell that I could not hear. I stabbed at it with my left, my dagger hand, and even as the Parthian jerked back from the feint I drove my right hand hard at where his neck should be, the blank space between pale flesh and the odd greasy shimmer of mail.

I felt the blade bite, but not deeply enough to kill, and wrenched it away and barrelled forward, using my shoulders, my hips, and hit muscle and bone and heard a man grunt and felt him lose his footing and fall and had time to splice a swift backhanded cut across his throat to finish.

A kill . . . a *kill!* The boy in me exulted, roaring, at that final step into manhood. The man I had been for years had no time for childish fantasies. A gout of hot and savoury blood sluiced into my open mouth. I spat it away, and spun to where another shape leered from the dark and I was already moving, spitting, swearing, dodging a sword blow from my right, and then wrenching sideways, and up again, spinning round a tree.

'*Ha!*'

To this day I don't know if the Parthian cried out or I did or someone else, but the noise called my head round and I saw a blur of star-gloamed metal and some god's hand thrust me down so that I felt the kiss of its passing, but not the bite. It bit into the oak, a handspan deep, and pinned my hair with it. I wrenched free, ripping open my scalp, and tumbled away.

In Hyrcania, I had seen one of those axes kill a horse. It had been thrown as this one was, looping head over haft, and had ended neatly, in the solid bone of the colt's forehead. The beast had gone down without so much as a twitch, and the entire watching army had applauded the skill of the throw.

The King of Kings, I remember, had given the axeman a replica of his weapon in solid gold, but the man himself had been more proud of his elevation to the king's bodyguard, which had been, I understood, the point.

All that I remembered in a single moment, each image overlaid on the other, as I sought haven behind trees and struck out when I could and failed entirely to land a killing blow – any kind of blow – on the two Parthians in front of me, and felt my sword weigh heavy in my hand and knew that I was tiring, and that a tired man is dead.

I lost my knife soon after that. I was beyond thinking or planning by then; I saw a shape move, and I stabbed for it, and felt the jar of iron on bull's hide, and the tug as the blade bit, and there was a moment when I could have tried to hold on and been dragged with it, or let go.

I let go and rolled away from where it had been, round yet another dark, wide oak with scrub at its base, and rose with my gladius held point down, with two hands on the hilt, and stabbed down at the mass below me, where the Parthian had thrust against nothing and tripped.

My blade skidded on ring mail; I stumbled just as he had, and, falling, reached out with my left hand and found hair, a head, and grabbed it and wrenched back and by luck, not the least bit of judgement, my blade's slide kept on sheering sideways up his back until it struck the back of his helmetless head. I had to let go then, and roll away, and came up weaponless, spitting out the old blood that still layered my mouth from the first dead man, and the bile of terror that had flooded over it.

The miser moon rationed its light so that I had to feel for my sword's hilt in the near total dark. When I found it, I rammed the blade through the head of the man I had just hit. I have no idea if he was dead before that stroke, but he certainly was afterwards. So I was twice a man, and no more sure of living, for the forest was full of men and if only half of them were the enemy we were lucky: every man of our unit and of the VIth was fighting now, with a noise that rocked the trees.

I had to kneel to pull the blade out again, and stayed still afterwards. My heart was a bucking bull in my chest, my hands were slick with sweat, my face itched under drying blood. But for all that, I felt for the first time as I had the night we raided the camp of the IVth on the mountains; I felt *alive*, and glad to be so. If I had died in that moment, fairly, I truly think I would not have minded. And I would not have traded places with any man then, not for all the wealth of Parthia. I had heard of this, but had never felt it for myself; that this is what battle does for a man when he has trained for it.

Battle also brings him to kill his friends by accident, or almost.

I tugged my gladius free of the dead man's skull and replaced my lost knife with one he had sheathed at his waist and sought to find Tears and the others of my unit. All around me were the steps and grunts of men lost in fighting, the stifled screams of the wounded, the bubbling exhalations of the dying. Following the loudest of the sounds, I came upon one who bore Parthian mail and was still living, lying on his belly trying to push himself up to his hands and knees. I caught his head and stabbed my new knife into his throat and turned my face away from the gout of gore, not to swallow yet more of an enemy's life blood . . . and so saw a man's shadow sliding to my right, and the sliver of moonlight that fell on him, and the flash of blue that was exactly the colour of Monobasus' tern badge. Fast as a snake, I rose and took three silent steps across the clearing and slammed my dagger hand forward and—

'*Tears!*'

I couldn't stop the blow, but I could open my hand and let the blade drop, so that all he suffered was a strike to his back, and even that was less of a killing blow than it should have been, for he had turned towards me as I hissed his name.

'Demalion!'

He snatched my arm from the air, spinning me round. If I had been Parthian, the next move would have opened my throat as it lay exposed to his blade. He laid the edge of his hand across it to prove the point, but gently, with the humour that showed more often now, and always when we were fighting. After a moment, grinning, he let me rise, dusting me down. 'What are you doing? I thought I'd lost you.'

I was shaking all over, terrified, and he was just staring at me with that half-savage grin on his face, still with no idea how close death had brushed him. As far as I could tell, he hadn't even noticed that I'd hit him. 'Why in the gods' name are you wearing blue?' I asked.

'Is it blue?' He lifted a silk scarf from his belt and held it out between his hands. In the unlight that held us, it could as easily have been green, or red, or black. 'One of the Parthians was wearing it,' he said. 'I killed him with it when my blades were both gone. I thought better I should keep it than leave it behind.'

'Get rid of it before it gets you killed.' Even now, I was the more frightened of us, the more snappish, though it was he who had the bruise on his side that would take half a month to fade. 'We need to find the others.'

'There,' Tears said, and jerked his head back east to where the path ran through the trees. 'I was coming to find you before—'

A wolf's howl split the night, cut off at its peak.

Together, we ran towards it. In a small clearing, Horgias, the Rabbit and Rufus stood in a triangle surrounded by a knot of Parthians. Axes and swords flickered back and forth and it was clear that this would have been a good time to have a shield.

Tears and I hurled ourselves at the nearest enemy, stabbing at faces, knees, wrists, anything that was not armoured. I didn't keep count of the men I injured or killed, for we were still heavily outnumbered. I stabbed, I parried, I ducked. At some point, when I ducked, I found a dead Parthian's shield near my feet and picked it up. The grip was of a cavalry shield and the weight was not what I was used to, but it felt like a gift from the gods, and it saved my life as an axe bit deep into the hide by the boss. I shoved it forward and ran, to be Tears' shield-man, so that we might both be protected.

The Parthians were fewer now, but fighting like cornered rats. I stepped back out of the fray and raised my head and gave the call of the wolf twice, which is what Horgias had been trying to do, I think; it was the call to summon the XIIth and was particular to our cohort and our century. We needed them, and, more than that, we needed them to find Proclion, for our giant bear-man was not with Horgias and that spelled danger.

Sarapammon must have heard the urgency in the call; I heard his voice at the head of a troop, running, and Aquila's patrician voice urging them on.

Thinking we were saved, I let down my guard, and only Tears' speed saved me from the spear that came for my face. He slashed down on the haft with his gladius and the spear-head missed me and skidded instead past my shoulder.

Seeing a gap, I slid my blade up the spear haft to the man at the end of it. He backed away and I might have followed him and been caught behind enemy lines – a fatal mistake and one only made by the very green or the very wild – but that I heard Horgias cry out again behind me, a high, desperate keening that said he had found Proclion and the finding was not good.

I gave one last thrust with the shield and backed away, fast, then spun to my right where I found Horgias and Proclion fighting for their lives against six Parthian cavalrymen, each armed with two curved swords.

Something snapped in me then, some deep final cord that had kept me civilized. Bellowing like a madman, I ran at them, wielding my stolen shield as a club to break their noses, their faces, their heads. I reached Proclion and put my shoulder against his elbow, for he was that much taller than me, and became his shield-man and he, great bear of a man that he was, grinned down at me, as if we were on a routine training run.

'Never thought I'd hear that kind of noise from you, fox-cub. Shall we kill them, you and I?'

I was dazzled by his praise, for Proclion was a born fighter who had killed his man long before he entered the legions. Moonstruck and battle mad, I threw him a matching grin and took a breath and let out the animal scream building inside and we sprang forward to meet the Parthians.

We were a whirlwind, reaping death around us. We were gods, fighting mortals who stood no chance. We were welded together, two men with one mind, and that mind bent on murder. I remember one slice that cleaved the mail on my shoulder and would have killed me but for the skill of the Damascan armourer, and I remember the return back-handed strike of mine that cut the wrist of my assailant half off and left him bleeding to death – but the rest is a blur of hot blood and savagery that came to rest only when five of the six Parthians were dead; and Tears and Horgias were still alive and Sarapammon had come with thirty men who now surrounded us so that the last of our assailants had no choice but to surrender, or die on his own sword.

So we thought, all of us. We lowered our blades and drew breath and I felt Tears move up behind me and was about to turn to see if he was truly all right when the Parthian threw himself at us.

My shield floated up of its own accord and took his first blow but he was doubly armed and the second was hissing straight at my head. Tears blocked it, I think, but I never saw and never asked for the Parthian had rolled away from both blocks as if we had poured him full of power and in that roll he struck both blades, lightning-fast, at Proclion.

'No!' Horgias was on him even as the second blade struck, pounding his own blades into the Parthian's neck, his head, his throat, his groin. The enemy went down in a heap of macerated flesh, but too late to save our man.

'Proclion!' I fell to the turf at his side. He was our giant, our great bear of a brother, and he was not simply wounded: his life blood was spilling from a gaping flap in his belly and a second, sliced cut on his thigh, which might have unmanned him, but in fact had cut the vessel that pumped the blood to his leg, so that it pumped instead over me as I knelt at his side.

'Proclion?' I lifted his hand and felt the ridges where the sword had worn into them. His fingers dwarfed mine. He gave a squeeze and squinted to focus on my face.

'We'll get help,' I said. 'We'll bind your leg and—'

He gave the faintest shake of his head and forced a smile. 'You fought well, fox-cub. I'll wait for you where the warriors go. Don't grieve for me. You can have . . .' He coughed and stopped and his gaze lifted over my shoulder to where Syrion stood. 'Give the fox-cub the horn. Tell Lupus I said he was worth it.'

It cost him a breath to say that much, his gift to me – to us all – and then his eyes slid off me to Horgias who was kneeling at his other side, in the grip of such grief as I could only imagine, and did not wish to, for by then I knew that to see Tears dead would have destroyed me, and we were not yet as close as they two had been, nor might ever be after the damage done on Hawk mountain.

There were no words then, just the waiting and the numb beginnings of grief. The men of the VIth walked softly around us, stripping the dead Parthians, binding them up and setting boughs about them for a fire. It's not the Parthian way, but Aquila planned, he said, to signal to those left alive the magnitude of their defeat. They killed the prisoners.

As they worked, we who were Proclion's brothers stood vigil for the only man we had lost, at a cost of thirty of theirs, not knowing what to say, or what to do, except that we must not look away while he passed from us.

We watched his last struggle, saw his skin turn white and then grey and then a queer translucent blue, heard him speak Horgias' name, and the tenderness that was in it, and saw Horgias cease to weep at last, after the final shudder, and rise with Proclion's bloody blade in his hand.

He turned to look at all of us, and his eyes were not human, nor seeing us, I think. He said, 'Wherever they are, I will kill them. You will not stop me.'

I would have let him go, let him run into the night to hunt down every Parthian he could find, until he died himself, but Syrion had more experience of this and he had Aquila behind him, watching.

He stood in front of Horgias and gently pushed his blade down and said, 'Tomorrow. Tomorrow you can kill them all. Tonight, we are sworn to deliver the mule train to the city. It's what he died for. You can't dishonour him by failing in that. Besides, we must take his body back to the priests. We can't leave him out here for the wolves, nor throw him on the fire with the rest.'

That was what turned it – tending to Proclion's body. Horgias would not have stayed with us just to keep the mule train safe, but it mattered – just – to honour the mortal remains of the one he had loved.

I watched the inner battle and saw the one side win, and by how little, and said to him, 'We'll lift him on to his horse. You lead it, it'll follow you best,' and it was settled, as much as it could be.

*

We returned in sombre mood, and saw no more of Monobasus' men on the way back, so that we were all denied the vengeance we craved.

Once in the city, we left Aquila giving a full briefing to Cadus and Lupus while his men bedded down in a house that had once belonged to a merchant and had more rooms than our barracks back at Raphana. We gave our report as swiftly as we might and then excused ourselves and took Proclion to the temple of Jupiter where we gave him into the care of the priests.

Three old men with moon-silver hair and slow, ponderous movement took him in their arms and laid him on a marble slab and set silver coins on his eyes and swung incense over him, murmuring as priests do to fill what might otherwise be a god-sent silence.

We soon sickened of the noise and the smell, and took Proclion's horse, his helmet, his sword, almost all that could be carried, and retired with them to our own quarters, a barracks room that had once been a selling hall for corn. There, when we had lit the brazier and broached the ale, I saw a thing happen that I had heard about, but not witnessed, and certainly never been party to.

Syrion set Horgias on a bench with a jug of ale all his own, and bannocks saved from the morning's bake, then laid out Proclion's cloak on the ground nearby and set down all of those things that we had brought back from the temple.

Rufus went back to Proclion's bed and brought out those few possessions he had not taken with him: the battered copper mess tin that he carried on march, the one he used daily, not the polished one he kept for parade; the whetstone for his blades in a slick leather pouch; the pack of javelins and the pointed stake we all carried in our kit, to be ready at any moment for the cataphracts; his spare shield; spare thongs for his sandals . . . all were laid on the cloak for our inspection. All were things we, too, used daily, so that we had no real need for spares.

Even so, Syrion reached out first and took Proclion's shield, replacing it with his own, so that the same number of things lay on the cloak. 'It's better than mine,' he said. 'He had thicker bull's hide on his.'

I saw no difference, but did not say so, and Horgias, set apart from us all, gave a nod, as if his permission had been asked and granted.

Others chose in a kind of order: Rufus took the javelin and left his own on the cloak, saying that his was bent at the end and would not fly true; the Rabbit took Proclion's wooden stake, for the same reason; Sarapammon found that he needed to replace the thongs on his sandals, and did so, unlacing them with thick fingers, lacing them afresh with the new leather, tying the old neatly and setting it on the cloak.

I took his mess tin, and went to fetch mine from the store under my bed, saying it was wearing thin on the base, which was as true as Syrion's shield being thin, or Rufus' javelin bent, which is to say not true at all. In truth, we would all have been content with what we had, but this way each of us carried a piece of the man now gone, that we might remember him each time we ate, or walked, or marched into battle.

It was done without ceremony or displays of grief or any kind of comment to acknowledge that this man was gone, never to return, but it was our wake for him, and more fitting than any wailing of priests or mumbled prayers.

We slept poorly that night, listening to Horgias, who lay awake in the dark and would not weep, and in the morning, dull-eyed, we came before Cadus, who had us present arms and give a show for Aquila before he announced to the entire legion that we were leaving; that, faced by our intransigence, Vologases had agreed to lift the siege of Tigranocerta, in return for which Corbulo had agreed to grant kingship to Vologases' brother until such time as he could send an embassy to Nero and request that ownership be passed to Parthia.

There are those who said this was tantamount to surrender, but they had not been there and seen the pointlessness of the fight. Corbulo was a general who saw the greater scale of things and if he thought this was one battle not worth fighting we were happy to go along with him – all except Horgias, who nursed a terrifying hatred of the Parthians and would have happily attacked Vologases' entire army single-handedly.

He had no chance of that for our orders were to march west, to beautiful Melitene, which lay just over the border in Cappadocia, and there to settle into winter quarters and await the arrival in spring of our new commander, Lucius Caesennius Paetus.

Chapter Sixteen

Rhandaea, Armenia, on the northern bank of the Murad Su, AD 62

Imagine Melitene, land of plenty, under snow and ice and high blue skies; imagine it in spring, with the meltwater running off the mountains and the herds going up to the high pastures to graze and their milk scented with mint and citrus; imagine it in high summer, limpid in the day's heat, with the hawks circling high above and the mares full fat with foal, swatting flies with their tails.

Imagine that a man enters this idyll who does not know that he has come to paradise, who brings with him such ill luck as to make the statue of Fortune fall on her face at his passing and set the crows circling in murderous groups, eleven at a time, number of ill augur. Imagine such a man causing the minted milk to sour, and the men to sour with it, even before he gives the word to prosecute an unwinnable war, against the orders of his betters; or at least against Corbulo's explicit command.

Such a man was our new general and while you will have heard of the statue that fell on its face and the other ill omens – they became common enough currency in Rome soon after – you may not know that he disobeyed orders when he began his war.

I can tell you and I know it to be true because, although I had been promoted from watch officer to signaller, with Tears as my shield-man, I was still first courier for the XIIth. In that role, I had been present when General Corbulo had gathered his legates together and set the scene for the new autumn campaign.

Vologases, he said, had been rebuffed by Nero. We all knew that the emperor had made a grave mistake, but nobody said so. I will testify to that at my life's end, if need be: no man present said openly that Nero was wrong to thus provoke the King of Kings. No treason was spoken. The commanders merely accepted it as fact and went on to discuss how Vologases might be managed now that he was angry and had set his armies towards Syria.

I sat quietly and listened – a clerk is invisible at such times, and I was clerk and courier, and so doubly unseen – while they debated strategy and decided that we must hold our side of the Euphrates, and drive Vologases back; that Armenia must be kept neutral until all six legions could march on Tigranocerta and take it back, for we had been in there, and knew how readily it was defended by even a few hardy men, how large were its stocks of food, how infinite its water supply.

I heard the generals agree it, and plan for the ways to keep Vologases in check, if only the north might also be held steady. I heard it said of Paetus, our new governor of Cappadocia – he was not present, having claimed a head cold when invited – that he was inclined to prideful rashness, and might wish for more glory, faster; that, indeed, he had been heard to say that Armenia should suffer for its treachery, and be reduced from a client kingdom to a province, sooner rather than later.

I could have attested to the truth of this last if they had asked me, for Paetus had said exactly that in my presence, but I was not asked, and so held to my clerk's invisibility until I was needed, which came soon after.

I saw the scorn written on Corbulo's face, and saw him turn to me, and see me, and set me to take his dictation. In his words, I wrote to Paetus, my own commander, telling him not make enemies of Vologases or his subjects, and on no account to cross the Euphrates or its tributaries into any of the lands east of that river, but instead to hold fast and still and keep his men at peak fitness, as they had been when he had taken charge of them.

The black-dyed wax ran on to seal the scroll, letting loose a summer's breeze of bees and honey. Over it, Corbulo stamped his mark of the war raven with its sharp beak and bright eye and the ruffle of feathers at its shoulders. All this was given into my care and the following day I set out to deliver it to Melitene, to the land of high mountains and cleaner air than you can begin to imagine.

The journey back took me ten days, but the land

was still at peace when I placed the crow-sealed orders personally in the hand of our governor and general, Caesennius Paetus, although the statue had fallen long before then and the crows had circled and we had drunk sour milk and knew that he brought ill luck on all of us.

You can well imagine that only Horgias was happy when, in direct defiance of Corbulo's command, we were ordered to march out of our camp across the Taurus Mountains to assault eastern Armenia and its people for the 'crime' of failing to be Roman citizens.

We – the XIIth, the IVth and the two companies of Pannonian archers Paetus had brought with him – crushed undefended towns and villages who had dutifully paid their taxes to Rome in the past and might do so in the future. We slaughtered anyone who might conceivably have held any affection for Parthia, and so ensured that, whatever they had felt before, their families hated us, and loved our enemy.

We ruined their crops and spoiled their grain and were not even allowed to requisition carts and haul it back to camp for our own use, for, in Paetus' words, 'Why should Roman legions feast on the grain of defeated peasants?', as if this was not exactly what we had always done.

We did not take Tigranocerta, which was held now by Vologases' brother. We didn't try particularly hard, for we knew the inside of that city brick by brick and knew that such a thing was impossible with only two legions, and told Paetus so. It would still have been impossible even had he summoned the Vth to join us, but he didn't do that – he sent them instead to Pontus to 'recuperate' for the winter, which meant that he did not have to pay for their winter keep. That's the kind of man he was.

Left without a victory, we marched back over those high, deep-clefted mountains to Melitene at autumn's end leaving a hornet's nest behind us, and nothing good to show for it.

Paetus, of course, would not have it that we had failed. He sent a letter to Nero that . . . I can barely bring myself to tell of it, but I wrote it and so I have it verbatim in that part of my memory that cannot let go of the past. I repeat it here for you, with only the warning that not one word of it is true.

To the Emperor Nero Claudius Caesar Augustus Germanicus, from L. Caesennius Paetus, governor of Cappadocia, greetings.

To the greater glory of Rome, and in honour of your divine self, we have this late season assaulted all the key positions of the enemy as may have been reached in so short a time.

Next year, when the rains have passed and the season for battle commences again, we shall show our spirit and our power and take for you the foremost cities of Armenia. In the meantime, I send to you such spoils as we have gathered: they are a poor people, and have little of worth, but such as it is, I commend to your care.

The 'spoils' were a cartful of weapons, some mail, some poor gold plate that when scratched showed bare copper or even iron beneath, and a crown that had been made, I think, for some religious ceremony and had no official use whatsoever. All of these, Paetus sent to Rome in the care of the sixth cohort of the IVth legion, thereby sending away its best men.

The rest of us were summoned to the main square of our winter quarters. It was a mellow autumn day. Leaves made flags for us in a dozen shades of beaten copper, of bronze, of old rust and polished amber. The mountains stabbed the sky and it bled sunlight on to their ever snowy peaks, so that they shone too brightly to look at.

Our armour shone likewise, for we were the sixth cohort, vying with the first to be best in all we did. Cadus might not have liked Paetus any more than the rest of us, but he was not going to let one ill-starred commander ruin his legion.

He had us run through our display in front of him, and what amazed me then – and still now – is that we could do it each time with the freshness of a new task; we never tired of finding ways to be faster, sharper, more effective.

If Paetus was impressed, he did not show it. Rather, he affected boredom and paid more attention to a distant carter loading late hay on to his donkey cart. The hounds running at his heels caught a rat or some such in the ditch by the road, but even had they not they would have been more interesting to Paetus than us, his men, putting our all into our display.

We came to stillness, sweating in the cool morning air. Lupus was furious, I could tell by the tilt of his chin and the triple pulse at his throat that only came when he was grinding his teeth. Outwardly, he was as bland as a statue, and in any case, we were not centre front: that place was reserved for Cadus and his century.

Corbulo would have spoken to us of our display, would have noted the good points, the good centuries, the good men, the parts that needed more work, and we would have trusted that he was right. Paetus did not so much as acknowledge what we had done, but launched at once into his reason for calling us.

'Men! Winter is upon us and we have shown the enemy our mettle. Vologases, who is king of nothing' – how I ached to show him the glories of Hyrcania as he said that – 'has returned to his den to lick his wounds. We will see nothing of him until spring. I therefore offer to every man of you the opportunity to take three months' leave. The roads are yet fit for travel; those who remain will march with me to new quarters at Rhandaea on the banks of the Murad Su, but the rest, those who choose freedom, may return to your homes, to your families, or remain here and enjoy a winter in the town, unhampered by your duties. If the numbers wishing to avail themselves of this opportunity grow too large, we shall draw lots for it. But first ask your centurions and they shall say who must march with us, and who can stay.'

He had been a consul in Rome, the highest order a man may hold who is not emperor. He had spoken before crowds many times, and knew the jinks and tricks of rhetoric that pull men to cheer him as he delivers ordinary news. He tried them all now, and stood before us with his arms raised as the last words rang off the palisades behind us – and was met by a fog of silence so thick, it might have smothered him there and then.

The smile crawled from his face. His arms came slowly down. He frowned at us, as a man who has woken into the wrong life, and does not know how to get back to all he holds dear, and then he turned on his heel and left us in our ranks, without so much as a salute of dismissal.

We held our silence until he was safely out of earshot, then Cadus stepped to the fore and turned. 'Not a man of the first cohort shall leave this compound unless it is to war. The rest of you, decide for yourselves.'

Lupus did not have to say the same to us of the sixth cohort; he simply turned to face us and ran his eyes down our lines. 'The man who wishes to leave us, raise his hand.' It was thus understood that the leaving would be permanent, not three months' unpaid idleness in the town, gaining unfortunate rashes and making children and drinking ourselves to poverty while Paetus lined his own pockets with the money that would have paid for our keep. If we left, then when we came back we would find ourselves in a new cohort, probably the second.

No hand was raised. The eighth cohort was the same, and rightly so, as the next most competent in the legion, and, oddly, the second; but the third, fourth, fifth, seventh, ninth and tenth lost nearly half their men each.

The IVth legion went through the same process, to the same result, with the added insult that they had already lost their sixth cohort as bodyguard to some gilt shinings sent to Rome as victory spoils. The archers, I am told, lost not a man; they had their own code of honour, and it surpassed all but the best of ours.

Even so we were decimated by Paetus' hand, for, by the end of that day, we had two legions of just over half strength, where a month before we had been three, as fully manned as any in the empire.

Lupus marched us back to our quarters and set us to packing for the march east.

'Where's Rhandaea?' Rufus asked. 'And why are we going there? What's wrong with Melitene? We spent last winter here, and the town loves us.'

Rufus had a woman in town who was heavy with his first child and he had sworn to be with her when it came. Syrion, as ever, had a handful of different women all vying for the right to warm his bed. The rest of our unit, but for me, Tears and Horgias, all had whores or women they cared for in Melitene and were loath to leave.

Lupus swept his hand across his face. He was relaxed with us now, at least in private; we had fought for him and with him and behind him and alongside him so often that he was one of us. He had saved our lives and we had saved his, and we were owed his honesty.

'Rhandaea lies on the Murad Su,' Lupus said, and was answered by blank stares from us all. 'It's a river. It rises out of the Taurus Mountains and runs into the Euphrates. Paetus plans to set up camp on the north bank so that we are technically in Armenia.'

'We can't do that,' Syrion said. 'Corbulo promised Vologases that Rome wouldn't cross the Euphrates if Parthia would keep to her own side. If we do this, we will break his promise.'

'Which is exactly why Paetus wants us to do it.' Lupus

was taking apart his bedframe with a contained but brisk intensity. 'He thinks the battle season is over, and that we'll be safe in Armenian territory until spring, and that we'll have an advantage when the fighting starts again after the rains have stopped. He thinks he'll write clever letters to Nero, telling him how he faced down the enemy when Corbulo was hunkered safe in Syria. He thinks . . .' Lupus swept a hand through his iron hair. 'I don't know what he thinks, but I know that he's wrong.'

'Vologases will attack before spring,' I said, and I might have been looking at Lupus, at Syrion, at Horgias, but I was seeing a clearing in a forest in Hyrcania, with a group of vassal kings planning a winter campaign. 'The Parthians don't care if it's winter. If they know we're there, they'll come and fight.'

'Then we had better be ready for them,' Lupus said grimly. 'Be packed by dusk, and make sure your stakes are good and sharp and hardened in the fire. We might have need of them at long last.'

Chapter Seventeen

Mud.

What I remember of Rhandaea on the northern bank of the Murad Su, before the ill omens and the chaos, before the sea of cataphracts and the light cavalry and the archers and the slaughter . . . before any of that, abiding and overwhelming, what I remember is mud.

We marched there from Melitene in the first rains of autumn, across ground that was no worse than damp before the leading ranks met it but had been churned to slurry by the time the last man of the first cohort had passed.

Two legions and two companies of archers later, the last five hundred men were wading knee high through sucking, suppurating glue, and the bullock carts got jammed so hard and so often that it was easier to raise them up on rails and have teams of sixteen men carry them, four to each corner.

Our clothes were wet, our tents were wet, the firewood was saturated beyond any hope of a flame; we slept in wet bedding and ate cold, uncooked food and our mail rusted on our backs and when we finally reached the south bank of the Murad Su, we found it a swollen, churning cataract far wider than its tame little brother, which had so efficiently protected the city at Tigranocerta.

And so we spent our first half-day there hacking at wet trees with rusted axes to build the bridge that might give us access to the location that Paetus, in his insanity, had chosen for our winter quarters.

In summer, I'll grant you, it would have been acceptable; a wide, flat basin with a small town nearby for trade and girls, and, more important, with the river behind to hold us safe from the south and west and a good distance between us and the mountains to the north and the east so that even Vologases' fast light cavalry could not have come at us without half a day's warning.

Here, now, at the end of the battle season, we were faced by a flood plain laid slick with the first silverings of water. We gathered the bullock wagons on to the only high land and stood about them, trying to see places we could set our tents that might keep them dry for the six months Paetus intended us to stay here.

Our general, of course, did not sleep in a tent; our first duty, even before we dug ditches for the ramparts, pitched the tents or set the palisades, was to cut more timber for his living quarters, float it across the river and help the engineers to erect a house fit for a senator and his family.

Yes, his family. You will not believe me when I tell you

that his wife was there, but it is true. His wife, Antonia, who had spent her life learning how to manipulate the socialites of Rome, was there with his son, less than six months old. They sat together that first afternoon in nothing grander than a bullock wagon, stunned to insensibility by cold and mud and unimagined hardship.

We lost three days building quarters for them; three days in which our tents were pitched in a handspan of water, and we were not making dry our grain for the winter, or exploring the land, except for a few scouts – Horgias was one – who were sent out to check the most likely routes Vologases would take when he came.

When, not if – for we were certain that the King of Kings knew we were here; how could he not when we had marched two legions across the Euphrates? And we knew we were not yet ready to face him.

We finished the ramparts in the second half of the month. I remember stopping at the end of the last ditch some time in the late morning and glancing up at the wide winter moon that hung white as a slug in the sky.

I jammed my mattock into the mud at my feet, spat away a mouthful of dirt and took a long drink of gritty water from the skin at my belt.

Blood smeared where my hands had been and, looking down, I saw that the blisters on both palms had burst, and long, deep cracks ran from each.

The pain was old and hot, and I had not so much forgotten it as lost it in the greater discomfort of the day. I risked a glance down at my feet and was glad they were lost in the mud for they made my hands look pretty by comparison. I was walking on soles turned to waterlogged sponge and dreaded the morning when I woke to find the skin peeled completely away, leaving raw flesh and bone beneath.

The sounds of iron hacking at soil slowed around me, and stopped. At our feet, the raw earth was open deep enough to swallow a man, and wide enough for me to lie inside with head and feet tight to each wall. Above the ditches, on the inner side, earth ramparts rose eight feet above the ground.

Syrion gave a grunt of satisfaction. 'The river'll have to rise higher than a man to top that.'

'And even if it does,' said Rufus, 'the egress channels will carry everything away. It'll have to flood in here higher than our knees to reach the tents.'

'Higher than your knees, maybe,' Sarapammon said. 'That's barely past the ankles for the rest of us.'

That wasn't true, or not all of it, but it didn't matter; we were in jovial mood again, with the prospect of drier nights and a fire that might light and hold. I can't begin to tell you the relief of that; winters on the Hawk mountains might have hardened us to cold and endurance, but we had never before gone without fire and cooked food and the last half-month had worn us down.

Now, we had a watertight quarter-stores packed with enough food to last us the winter, and a sheltered paddock for the horses with stalls to one side and even they had begun to fill out on good fodder so that their ribs did not stare so through their coats and their eyes were bright once again.

A thread of smoke rose from just beyond the horse paddocks. I smelled the scent of applewood amidst the oak, and the first savoury rush of cooking, and my mouth flooded with spit just as my stomach griped, and I turned and—

'Vologases is coming! The King of Kings! Parthia's army!'

That was Horgias, riding my bay mare's youngest son, who had been born chestnut and was turning a fine rose grey as he aged. I gave him as a gift after Proclion's death, and wished I had given him sooner, only that he was not broken before that, and in truth I had considered giving him to Cadus.

Horgias had seemed grateful at the time, in so far as he ever seemed to enjoy anything these days. He had promised to take best care of him, and treat him as I might have done myself. Just now, he was riding him harder than I had ever seen a man drive a horse.

He hauled to a bloody halt by the standards and flung himself out of the saddle, calling the camp alarm.

We were already running; us and the rest of the legion. We got close enough to see the sweat running down man and horse, so that both were slick, and steaming, and near to broken in wind.

Horgias was wilder than he had ever been; unshaved and unwashed, his hair bound back by a leather thong, he could have been a barbarian come amongst us, except that he wore the red tunic of our cohort and the mule's tail was painted on the scabbard of his gladius, and in any case everybody in both legions knew Horgias by name and sight by now.

Everybody except Paetus, obviously. He emerged from his newly built house and stood on the top step, softly pink as from a hot bath, with his hair wet and his face half shaved, holding a towel in one hand and a pomegranate – *a pomegranate!* – in the other.

'Who is this man?'

Cadus was there, one step ahead of trouble. 'He's a scout, lord. He was sent to watch the Taurus Mountains, whence any attack is most likely to come. It would appear one is coming, and he has seen it?'

This last, he directed to Horgias. I was next to him by then, acting as his groom, giving water to man and beast.

Horgias saluted first to Cadus, and then to Paetus, as he must. And then he gave his report there, in the open, in a voice that bounced from one rampart to the next, and never mind that Paetus was trying to invite him inside to give it in private.

'Vologases, the King of Kings, rides at the head of his army. He has with him, I would estimate, ten thousand cataphracts, fifteen thousand light cavalry, five thousand infantry. They go slowly, held back by the pace of their marching men. In two days' time, they will traverse the Taurus Mountains south and east of here. There is a place we could stop them. At a fast march, we could be there in half a day. A legion, perhaps, could hold them, allowing the rest to finish the defences here.'

He spoke into a hollow silence. We sucked his words in and drained them dry of meaning and still we did not fully comprehend the size of the army that came at us. Paetus understood least of all. His gaze flickered from Cadus to Horgias and back as if he suspected both of some kind of conspiracy to unman him.

At length, Cadus said, 'Perhaps the senior centurions could meet with your excellency to discuss our strategy?' and Paetus was persuaded inside.

Horgias was dismissed without a second glance. We led him away to find food and water and wine, and Syrion and the Rabbit stayed back in case there was anything we needed to hear.

Horgias said, 'I'm sorry about your colt.'

Beneath the filth of four days living wild, his face was unreadable. He had never been an easy man to befriend, but since Proclion's death he had become a blank slate with nothing to see, nothing to know, except on those few occasions when we faced the enemy, when he became a lethal, screaming demon. The rest of the time he didn't talk much; the horse was his exception, he spoke about that.

I shrugged. 'He's fine. His tendons are whole; you didn't break him. In a while, when he's had fodder and water, I'll stand him in the river and let him cool off properly. For now, we'll light a fire and cook you something to eat.'

We reached our camp, the rows of tents with ours at the head of our cohort. We had firewood under a goatskin awning, and a fire pit that we had dug while he was away. I crouched and began to gather the tinder, and small twigs to start the fire. Horgias crouched with me, and caught my hand.

'Let me,' he said quietly. 'I haven't lit a fire in four days. I miss it.'

Even if it hadn't been Horgias, I wouldn't have argued with that; a man needs to light fires to keep his soul warm, or so my father taught me.

I let the twigs fall at the side of the pit, set down the bunch of fleece that I planned would hold the flame and set my fingers to my belt, where I kept the glow from the last fire in a pot.

'Have you fire to light it? If not, I can—'

A horn split the air from the far side of the camp. Three notes, rising, and two falling; it was the call to witness a sacrifice, which all men must attend who do not wish to call ill luck on themselves.

It came from the lines of the IVth legion. Horgias cursed softly, viciously, and tilted his head to look up at me. What could I say? 'We're going to war. Best not to offend the gods, even for the lousy Fourth.'

'Right.' He set his fire-making things down with careful precision and rose and together we ambled over at our leisure, drinking in the late sun, the scent of smoke, the sound of corn cakes frying.

In time, we came to a trench dug twenty paces in front of the tent lines of the IVth; the foundation for their quarter-stores. They had decided to build them in stone, an affectation they brought from the Hawk mountains. We didn't share it, but we failed entirely to talk them out of it, and it was, I think, a way for us each to show our differences, lest any man begin to think we were one unit.

Whatever the reason, they had dug foundations and someone had been into the town and bought a dark-fleeced shearling ram for the sacrifice. It was a fine, stout animal, with yellow eyes set with the vertical slit that makes them seem like demons, when in fact they are as terrified as any beast can be. Certainly this one was not being held with the calmness that is due an offering given to the gods. The young conscript who held it had evidently never done so before; in the time it took for us to fall into ordered lines he kept losing his grip and reclutching in a way designed to induce panic in any creature's breast.

The ram, for its part, had been dragged from the town to a place it did not know, amongst unfamiliar men who sharpened knives in its easy view; terrified, it fought its bonds fiercely. That could have been put to use if the priests and augurs had the sense to use its fighting spirit for our good, but these were small men with small minds and they were already drenched in fear at the size of Vologases' army.

So when they caught it up, and cut its bonds, there was a moment when neither the conscript nor the chief priest was fully holding it, and it lunged out with feet and horns, thrust the former to the ground and the latter into the priest's ribs and, with a kick and a butt, was free to leap out, over the foundations, past the tent lines, through eight ranks of men and away to freedom.

You could have heated the silence then, and beaten it flat to make a sword. Soon, though, the first mutterings rolled through, as men spelled out for each other the doom that was on us all. *A failed sacrifice. Failed! We're finished.*

The idiot priest made an effort to read something good in the beast's escape, but he was wasting his breath; every man in the empire knows that a failed sacrifice is the clearest statement the gods ever give that the endeavour – whatever it is that the sacrifice was for – is doomed.

So the IVth couldn't build their quarter-stores on those foundations. And we were dead men if we tried to face Vologases' army.

I turned, and found Horgias beside me. 'Let's go,' I said tightly. 'There's no good to be had in staying here.'

Back at our own tent lines, we set to making our evening meal. For a while, I watched Horgias as he devoted himself again to the fire, laid the tinder and the wool and shaved peelings from a dry block around them.

He borrowed my glow-coal and nursed the infant spark it gave him, feeding it small twigs that he had kept in the breast of his tunic and dried with his own body's heat. In time, he had a youthful, boisterous blaze that sent thin smoke spiralling to the sky.

He took wheat meal and water from his bag, spices, some dried rosemary, a little bead of lamb's fat, rolled and rolled until it was hard as beeswax. Mixed, they made a mash that he squeezed between his hands until it made small, flat cakes.

He oiled his mess tin and set the cakes to roast and it had the ritual feel of a last meal, shared amongst friends, amongst brothers, amongst men who knew their lives to be short, and yet still cherished each other's company. If anything, I thought Horgias looked at peace, and was glad for him.

I crouched beside him. 'Do you think he waits for you?' I meant Proclion, but did not have to say so.

'I am sure of it. I dream him often, standing at the river's edge, looking back at me as I live this half-life without him.' Horgias flicked a glance at me sideways. 'Don't think I'm in a hurry to die. He'll wait as long as it takes, and I will kill as many Parthians as I may before I join him.'

I shook my head. 'If you were going to die soon after him, you would have done so by now. There's been enough opportunity.' Not more than a skirmish or two as we left Tigranocerta, but sufficient for him to have thrown himself on an enemy spear if he had wanted to. 'I just wanted to know where he was.'

Other than my father, Proclion was the only man I knew well who had died, and I would have trusted him with my life in ways I would never have trusted my family. It was good to know he watched over Horgias.

I took out my own pack and set about mixing beans and corn and dried mushrooms and garlic, taking the same care as had Horgias. As they did in battle, my senses became sharper, so that I heard Lupus' footsteps long before I heard his voice and knew who came up behind me, and exactly when he drew breath to speak.

'Tell me we're not going to be stoking up the cook fires to build palisades through the night by their light.' I stood, turning as I spoke.

Gravely, he said, 'You're not going to be stoking the cook fires and building palisades through the night by their light.'

Something was wrong with Lupus. He had never in his life made a joke, and his eyes were not laughing; quite the reverse.

'What then?' Horgias was holding his dagger ready to

lift one of his meal cakes from the mess tin. He looked eager, ready to fight.

'We are to sally out tonight, before dusk. Paetus will lead us. All except the first cohort of the Fourth, which is travelling to Arsamosata, with the care of the general's wife and infant son as their only priority.'

'*What?*'

'He's sending the *first cohort* away?'

'But the palisades aren't finished. They aren't even begun. Is he *completely* mad?'

Syrion, Horgias and I spoke all together. Lupus affected a deafness which left him immune to the treachery spoken around him; then, in a voice so sharp, it would have cut through wood, he said, 'Our governor' – he spat the word – 'is of the belief that he was given command of men to fight for him, not wooden walls; that Vologases' army will be sleeping in their tents, so why should we not do the same? He would meet the Parthians at the Lizard Pass in the Taurus Mountains. He believes we can hold them there.'

'So we will hold the Parthians until Corbulo can get here?' I said. 'That, at least, makes sense.' After a fashion, it did; we had crossed the mountains through that pass twice in the summer, going out, and coming in. We knew it as well as we knew anywhere here.

Lupus shut his eyes. 'I have suggested,' he said faintly, 'that a message should be sent to General Corbulo requesting his aid. Cadus and the camp prefect added their voices. Paetus, however, is of the opinion that we will not need any man's help to defeat the King of Kings.'

Nobody spoke then; there were limits to what we could say and not be flogged for it, and in any case Lupus was distressed enough. The reason was obvious: Paetus was afraid of Corbulo's genius. To get himself into a crisis and then cry for help? It would ruin his political career.

To me, Lupus said, 'It might be that you could send a message to your old commander, wishing him well before you march out to die?'

'Aquila? But he'll send any message straight to Corbulo!'

'Who might choose to send us help. Or not. But at least he will know what has happened. I am sending a similar message to Hygienus, a centurion of the Tenth, and Cadus will write to a man he knows in the Third. We have need of a courier to deliver the messages. Would you—'

'No.' I faced him square on. 'I fight with my unit. Anyway, you can't send me away. I'm the signaller.' I fixed his gaze with mine. 'There are couriers enough in the other legion.'

He nodded, not surprised. 'Tears?' Tears had become our second courier, on the strength of my bay mare's second foal.

'The same,' Tears said. 'I'll stay. We fight together, all of us.' There were still only seven of us; they had not made up our unit after Proclion's death. It made us weaker in the battle lines, but at the same time it made us stronger of spirit.

'Right.' Lupus nodded, rising. 'You understand that I had to ask. We'll find another courier. He won't be as well mounted, but there are staging posts in Syria; he can find new horses on the way.'

He was turning away when Syrion said, 'When do we leave?'

'As soon as the tents are packed. Eat first. I said I would have none of my men march on an empty stomach. But be ready to move out by the next watch. He would have us march double time through the night if we have to.'

There are those in Rome who will tell you that the second of the day's ill omens occurred as we marched out of the camp; that our javelins caught the late afternoon light and shone, all in a streaming ribbon as we marched, so that we had silver in front and behind, and flashes of gold among us.

The naysayers will tell you that this reflected Parthian greatness, for it was known that the cataphracts loved their spears above all other weapons and the gods were saying that spears would be our death. But for us it felt like a benediction, a spark of light in the dark road ahead, a sign that the gods had not abandoned us so completely after all.

We marched faster for it, and long into the night, pitching our tents by the light of the falling moon, as it hung vast and gold on the westerly horizon, throwing shadows all about.

The light kept the watch sentries alert, while the rest of us slept with the stupor of men who will store sleep against famine later, and begrudge every moment of waking.

Chapter Eighteen

This close to death, time passed faster than it had ever done and it seemed I had barely risen before I was lying down again, this time face down beneath a stand of cedars high above a mountain pass a dozen miles from our camp.

Tears lay on my right and Horgias on my left and we watched in dreadful silence as four spears split the early light and four men of the IVth lost their lives in a trap as perfectly planned and executed as any I had seen.

The shouts that followed were Roman and Parthian mixed, but more Parthian, and louder, for while a half-century of the IVth had been sent out to scout the enemy's position they had been met by at least twice that many Parthians, and the speed and ferocity of the enemy attack had heightened their advantage so their numbers seemed greater.

The slaughter was fast and efficient and from our eyrie, a hundred feet up, it had the dance-like elegance of a mummery made for our entertainment, with pale faces raised and dark mouths opened in muted shouts and barely any blood spilled, except at the end, when the centurion of the IVth – first centurion of the eighth cohort, I think, but I hadn't looked closely at the men we were following – was decapitated by a Parthian warrior who rose high in his saddle and used his sword with both hands. That blood was a fountain; it soared and fell and stained the rock and the hard winter's earth beneath.

Horgias rose then, drawing both blades. Tears caught his arm, holding him back. 'Don't. We have to get back. Cadus needs to know what's happened.'

Our orders had been clear: our role was to observe and report, nothing more. On no account – none, on pain of execution – were we to participate in any action.

Cadus had been categorical when he had called us out of the parade lines. 'We need to know what's happening. It serves nothing if you give your lives and the rest of us are taken unawares. Ride a long way behind and don't let the men of the Fourth see you. If one of them is taken and questioned, they can't give away what they don't know.'

That had been in the morning's cold, with the unrisen sun spinning gold filigree along the horizon, layering it on the night's hoar frost. We had ridden out of the camp double-cloaked, with our horses' feet bound for silence, and our spears wrapped to keep them from shining as they had when we crossed the bridge; what had been an omen yesterday was treachery in the making today.

We carried no stakes, and knives instead of shields;

Horgias was slowly turning us all into barbarians. But good barbarians; we had tracked a half-century of the IVth and they never knew we were there. And now the Parthians did not know we had watched their slaughter.

'Let's go.' I touched Tears on the arm, and, with Horgias at my other side, we wormed backwards down a long, shallow incline, to the river at its foot where our horses were hobbled.

They knew better than to greet us with noise, but the bay mare blew a steaming breath into the nook of my neck. She liked it, I think, when we bound her feet. Whatever the hazards of walking – and they were manifold, and worse at the canter – she enjoyed the delicacy that was asked of her.

And so, quietly, led by Horgias, we stole out of the hollow. At a safe distance, we stopped to strip the horses' feet that we might gallop the twelve miles back across the plain to the camp where Cadus waited to greet us. He was not alone.

'All dead?' Paetus asked me; I had been the notional leader.

'All,' I said. 'And stripped of their armour. We would have gone to their aid but—'

'But I had ordered against it.' Cadus stepped up to my side. 'Without these three there to observe, the centurion and half his men would just have been lost and we would have known nothing of it.'

I said, 'The good news is that the Parthians were not yet near the Lizard Pass. They won't reach it until tomorrow, longer if they stay and celebrate their victory.'

'Vologases knows we're here,' Horgias said. 'He has no need to hurry.'

'How?' Paetus glared at us, as if all three of us had just confessed to treachery. 'How does he know we are here?'

'We killed one of his scouts on our way out,' I said. 'But where there is one, there will have been others. They couldn't miss two legions. And the smoke of your cooking fire would tell them soon enough.'

We of the XIIth had no fires: we ate cold food night and morning. But Paetus had refused to forgo his fire, even here, with the enemy a day's ride away; less.

The look he gave me was poisonous, but what could he do? I stared at the ground and said nothing, and in the end Paetus turned away. To Cadus, he said, 'Have my commanders meet in my tent immediately.' And he was gone.

We waited again, while our officers tried to talk sense into a senseless general. To pass the time I checked the bay mare's feet for stones, and groomed her and gave her some hard feed, for I had a feeling we might be moving fast, and while I marched she was made to run alongside the supply wagons like a cart hound.

'Demalion?' Lupus was grey-white, tinged red at the edges of his temples.

'What news?'

He shook his head and strode on past. 'Find Tears and Horgias. Bring them to the tent lines. You all need to hear it at once.'

Tears and Horgias weren't far; each was tending to

his horse. At the tents, we met the other four of our unit and the rest of our century and arranged ourselves as if on parade. Here, now, it mattered to us that we were sharp and well drilled; it gave us a sense of our own professionalism.

'Governor Paetus . . .' Lupus closed his eyes that we might not read the rage in them. 'Governor Paetus has informed us that he will return to our camp at Rhandaea with the Fourth legion, there to build the palisades and set up defences sufficient to deter the enemy. He will take with him the Eagles, and keep them safe, so that if a legion is lost it can be re-formed, and its honour may live on.'

There was a moment's silence as we all wrestled with the impossibility of what we had heard. The IVth leaving. And the Eagles going with them so that if *a legion* – our legion, there was no other one – was 'lost', which is to say annihilated, destroyed to the last man . . .

And that's when our discipline broke apart.

'*What?*'

'He can't—'

'How can we fight without the Eagle?'

And out of the clamour, my voice, rising, 'Lord, we *can't* fight without the Eagle. It's impossible.'

Lupus stared us down. 'You think yourselves so weak? So in need of aid that you cannot fight alone? I would say rather, how can we carry the Eagle to certain defeat? If it is taken to safety, then the legion still lives. Even if we all die, it will be re-formed. If, out of our own weakness, we keep it here, and it is taken by the Parthians, the Twelfth itself is lost. We will have the two companies of archers with us, which should help to hold the pass.'

'But why are we staying? I don't understand. What's the point?'

Lupus held up his hand before another storm of questions could arise.

'Paetus has had word from Corbulo that help is on its way. We have to delay the Parthians until that help can arrive. To that end, we, the Bloody Twelfth, with our cavalry and our Pannonian archers, will hold Lizard Pass for as long as we may, to buy that time. We know that the Parthians are not inclined to sit protracted sieges, that they will have poor supplies with them and no way of gaining any now that winter is at hand. We, on the other hand, have sufficient supplies at Rhandaea to feed two legions for six months.'

And only one legion left to eat its way through them, for we will be dead.

We each thought it, none of us said it; you could taste the words on the air. *We will be dead. And without our Eagle.*

'Quite so.' Lupus gave his half-smile, and today it was almost paternal. 'But we shall fight under the standards of our own cohorts. Those no man can take from us, save by our deaths, and I promise you we shall sell our lives dearly, and with honour. Cadus asked for this, and it was granted. The Twelfth shall be known as the legion that held back the Parthian cataphracts while others marched to safety.'

'Like Leonidas' Spartans at Thermopylae?' Syrion said drily. We were not Spartans, and Paetus was assuredly not a king. Laughter rose from the ranks, crisp as winter leaves, but real; after all the battles in which death was possible, but not certain, there was an odd freedom that came from the certainty of this one.

'Exactly like.' Lupus matched our tone. 'You have until the next watch to prepare. Whatever you do, in the gods' name, don't let the priests attempt another sacrifice.'

We broke camp together and set off in our opposite directions: we of the XIIth and our allies marched east, towards the rising sun, combat and honour; the IVth went west, to the setting sun, to ignominy and a wealth of digging. We sang as we marched. They did not.

Our horses were the happier too, and their number was increased by an old war-scarred gelding that carried Paetus' colours who broke ranks and cantered back to us, to join the fighting. We greeted him as a valued friend, and let him stay, and sent the colours back on a younger beast, though not one of my bay mare's colts; those all stayed with us.

The men of letters in Rome who have never ventured beyond the shores of Italy nor ever held a blade in anger will tell you that this was our third bad omen; that after the failed sacrifice and the way the sun caught our spears as we followed Paetus out of the winter camp, the retreat of the colours was the seal on our doom.

But we who marched east believed that the faulty sacrifice belonged to the IVth legion, that the flashing spears were for our victory and that an old war horse choosing to join us was the best omen we had seen all day, and that was with each of us scouring the skies for crows caught in groups of auspicious number, for circling hawks, or vultures. We saw none of those, but we set the aged war horse to our fore, ridden by one of the centurions, and chose to forget that our Eagle had left us.

We put up a brisk pace over clear, dry ground, hard with the first frosts of winter, and we were dug in and camped with our latrines dug and as much comfort as we allowed ourselves by the time the sun poured its last benediction across us.

A deep indigo blue spread across the evening sky, wisping to lavender and lilac at its edges with spear points of cinnamon, bronze and amber. I sat warming my hands at the embers of our cook-fire, watching the colours change.

'You're not sleeping?' Tears came to stand behind me; I felt the touch of his hand on my shoulder.

'Later.' I was going to sleep; I knew I would fight badly without, but it was hard to let go of the evening.

Tears came to sit on the log next to me, so that his warmth joined the warmth of the fire. His beauty made me ache sometimes, such perfection in a living man, and the thought that it must be marred, broken, deprived of life was too dreadful to contemplate.

He said, 'Are you afraid?'

'Not for myself.' I had been looking at him and so in that moment it was true; but then the moment was gone and I shook my head, and I said, 'Yes, of course I'm afraid. How could I not be? We're going to fight without our Eagle against Vologases' mounted cavalry. This is real fighting, not a skirmish in a forest.' The fire leapt a little, sending sparks into the velvet night. It gave me the courage to speak on. 'Even so, we do this for the best of reasons. If the gods honour courage, they will honour that. If they do not . . .'

'They would not be true gods.' He was mocking me, gently; Tears' gods were of river and vine and their gift was the spark that quickens a seed, not the moment of martial valour that lifts a man beyond himself. Mine had been the same, once, until a night on the Hawk mountains had changed me. I was not unhappy with who I had become.

I said, 'You could have taken the message to Corbulo. Nobody would have thought less of you for it.'

'I would. I couldn't live with myself if you died and I was not there to stop it, or had not already died trying to keep you alive.'

He said it so calmly, with such little fuss, that the words had sailed over me before their meaning struck my heart.

I shuddered then, I think; certainly my vision swam. In all the time we had lived together, eaten together, fought together, killed and been hurt, bound each other's wounds, slept within each other's reach . . . in all that time, Tears had never said aloud that he held me other than anyone else in our unit. I had not said it of him, either, but everyone knew.

I turned to him, away from the last light of the sun. I must have looked wretched, for he put out his arm and drew me in to lean against his shoulder.

Always, I had been the stronger, the one to look out

for him. To have it so very different left me worse than I had been.

I couldn't speak, and so he spoke for me, answering the question I could not ask. 'I'm your shield-man. Why else do I live?' His eyes sparked with a depth of humour I had rarely seen in him before, but I couldn't join him. I was too thrown.

I said, 'Only that keeps you here? Only duty?' It hadn't sounded like duty.

'No.' He was serious now. 'Not only that.'

'Why did I not know?'

'You didn't ask.' He kissed my head, dry-lipped, fast. 'And I didn't tell you. I was afraid, I think. And unsure.'

'Of me?'

'And of myself. Of how to be. Even without all that passed on the mountain, I am not Horgias or Proclion, to lie easily with the first man who asks.'

'I think you do them both an injustice.'

'True. Better to say I am not Syrion, to take a different girl to bed for each day of the month, and begin at the start again with the first at the next new moon and swear to her that the sun rises in her eyes alone.'

That was a gross calumny, but Tears was laughing as he said it, and so I eased free of his embrace and sat up, and saw him with fresh eyes. He was not a boy any more, broken on a mountain, but a man, with the heart of a warrior, and the quiet, easy laughter that had long ago replaced his fear.

'We have only one night,' I said, and my throat was so dry the words came out crushed to sand.

'I know. And if we don't sleep, we may not fight as well tomorrow.'

'I think . . . we'll fight well enough. We may fight better.'

I was lying, and he knew it. He raised one brow high, in perfect mockery of Lupus. 'Show me then,' he said, and, rising, took my hand and led me away from the tents to a place I had not seen before, that he must have found beforehand. It was quiet and dry and out of the wind, and we saw the last of the sun and its first faint rising and in between we let loose such passion as I had never dreamed of.

And I did face the morning more awake, more alive than I had ever been.

Chapter Nineteen

The last shreds of night held our backs. The Taurus Mountains held our two flanks. Spread out between them, we of the XIIth held a line as straight and true as any legion ever held.

Cadus held his first cohort in the centre. We, the sixth cohort, held the right flank. Syrion held the open palm of Jupiter to my right, and now, for the first time, he wore a muleskin draped about his shoulders, its head covering his helmet, its hooved feet crossed at his breast. He must have spent a hundred private hours curing it, softening it, polishing the hide until it gleamed a rich, deep oaken-brown. We adored him for that; the whole legion did. Our only regret was that the IVth had not seen it.

The enemy came towards us thick as mercury poured into a channel; a shimmering tide oozing from the furnace of the risen sun into the pass below us. I felt Syrion tighten his grip on the banner haft, we were that close, that closely knit. On my left, I felt Tears . . . I felt him breathe, I felt his heartbeat, I felt when he smiled, and when he did my soul sang in joy and glory and my only regret – I swear this to you now as the perfect truth – my sole regret was that the night could not have lasted longer.

I did not crave another night, only that the one we had might have been stretched a little, giving us time to learn more of each other, and perhaps with more privacy than a hollow in the woods where we could hear that other men were trying to sleep as easily as they could hear that we were not.

It was Horgias I felt for most. I had had trouble meeting his eye over the morning cook-fires, until he came up and hit me a glancing blow across the top of my head and said, 'That's for waiting so long, idiot!' which made the world right again. Which made it perfect, really.

And then Cadus had come to me as I was unpacking my horn, a sharp-edged Cadus, shining as if he, too, had spent the night bathing his soul.

He looked me up and down and it seemed he liked what he saw. 'You've come a long way since Hyrcania,' he said.

I nodded; what was there to say?

'Do you love battle yet?' he asked, and when I frowned at him, not understanding, he eyed me sideways and said, 'Pantera said you would grow to love warfare, given time.'

'He never said it to me.'

'What point, when you hated him?'

'I didn't hate him. I was awed by him. I wanted to do

what he could do, to be what he was.' I would have said that I loved him, but this morning my heart would not let that be true.

Cadus grinned. 'I know. And he knew. But you hated him too. If he'd said it, you'd have deserted there and then just to prove him wrong. Or got yourself killed for the same reason.'

'So you ask now, when death is certain.' I had rolled my shoulders and cracked my knuckles and looked about me at the camp; at our tents, left in rule-straight order as we left them every ordinary day, because today of all days we were not going to abandon discipline; at the horse lines, where the bay mare waited, the one that had been given me in Hyrcania, and would likely be back with a Parthian master by nightfall. I did not begrudge them that; the Parthians are good to their horses and she had served me well. A part of me hoped that Vologases, King of Kings, might know her, and recognize her sons by their brands, and take them all into his army.

Last, I had looked at Tears, who was waiting, ready to march. His armour had caught the smoky sunlight, so that he had been a mirage, only half there, a ghost-form already, waiting for me to join him. At any other time, that would have been omen enough to cripple my courage, but this morning it had left me heartened that he would wait for me in the lands of the dead as Proclion waited for Horgias. Not long, now, until we were all united again.

'Yes,' I had said, when I looked back at Cadus again, and lifted my horn to settle on my shoulder. 'I do love battle. I will love this one, until the moment it takes all love from me.'

'If we can manage the manoeuvre with the stakes properly, that may be a lot further away than the Parthians think. Keep your horn ready, and watch Lupus for the signals. He's a good centurion; he'll do his best to keep you all alive.'

'Sound.'

A single word. A single act. A single breath shuddered through my body into the horn, translated by the magic of brass into a peal of golden notes from the ten cohort horns that lanced through the morning and the thunder of the silver tide that was nearly on us.

On each note, three thousand men moved in flawless synchrony. The morning was shot with the spark of flying iron, with the reach and stamp as one legion and two companies of archers took one step to the side and four steps back and left their bedded stakes bare to the coming horses.

We felt the implosion of air as the shields came up and lay edge on edge together and we made our wall with our blades ready to force the gaps, and then they were on the stakes, the cataphracts, in their mirror-bright armour, and the men in their shimmering mail.

'Throw!'

On Cadus' command, we threw our spears in a withering rain of iron, that met the charge just as the charge met the stakes.

The carnage as iron and flesh met sharp and solid oak was horrible to watch, made worse by the storm of spears before, and the hail of arrows that followed as our Pannonian archers shot from the flanks into the centre. Horses fell, churning the earth with their dying feet; their riders died, crushed under so much armour.

The whole Parthian front rank fell, but they jammed the stakes and the next ones jumped them; they had no chance to slow, and so they met the second rank of stakes, and then the next wave met the third and suddenly we were held safe by a wall twenty paces deep of dead and dying beasts.

The force of the Parthian charge was broken, at least for now. On the far side of the stakes, they tried to form up, to remake their line.

'Archers, loose at will! Legion, step back!' I heard Cadus, saw his arm flung high, and sounded the high, keening notes he required. A storm of arrows fell and under their cover we all stepped back and back until we stood on the higher ground, with new javelins passed to us from the ranks at the sides, who held the stores. There, we stood firm and waited while the living Parthians picked their way through the dead, all the time dying themselves under the blanket of our arrows.

Even so, they outnumbered us by thousands and did not seem to fear death. With the sun at their backs, they came ever closer until we could see the eyes of the horses behind their face-helms, which meant, in turn, their riders could see ours.

An axe spun at me. I ducked even before I knew what it was, and heard it kill behind me, felt the gap at my back, and felt it closed, as men stepped together where their fallen comrade had been.

An armoured horse breasted the mass of men. I saw blue silk, and the mark of the tern, and screamed at it, but it was not Monobasus, only one of his men, and Horgias pulled at his spear as it stabbed through and Tears thrust his shield up, catching the horse on the face so that it half reared and I stabbed up under its flanks at the only place where there was no armour, and it fell, and Syrion stamped on the head of its rider, and broke it, and buckled his helmet.

He grinned at me, and we joined our shields, and the dying horse thrashed its way to the afterlife ahead of us, making a new part of our defences.

The day became a storm of killing of which I remember only brief flashes, where time slowed, and the air crystallized around a certain threat, a particular sword blade or spear point, or axe. I remember the moment around noon when our archers had spent all but a few of their shafts and Vologases sent forward his own archers to shower us with death.

If Lupus hadn't seen them, and hadn't roared the command at me so that I heard it over the tumult of battle; if I hadn't sounded the signal to raise shields, if we hadn't drilled it so often that men even in the act of killing or dying lifted their left arms without thinking . . . if not all of those, the battle would have ended there and then, with the Parthians only left to strip the dead and give final grace to the wounded.

But he did see and I did hear and the men did respond and, from fighting side by side, we were suddenly sheltering under a roof of shield-tiles with only those of us on the front rank holding our shields to the fore, and like that we weathered the storm until they ran out of arrows, or someone changed the command and the hail stopped, and we brought our shields back and the Parthians came forward again, who had drawn back for fear of dying under their own missiles.

The light cavalry came at us then, with horses unarmoured and men in short mail shirts who fought with axe and curved swords. They reaped us as if we were old standing corn, but slowly, and with losses of their own.

For each ten of our men killed we drew a pace back, and for each pace back, the pass narrowed and the incline steepened. The enemy cavalry had no room properly to move and so they sent the men in on foot with their spinning axes and their long-spears and we ordered our own archers to loose their last shafts on to them so that they, too, knew what it was to have to shelter from a killing rain; except that they had not drilled as we had, and more of them died.

As the day grew old, the fighting grew ever closer until we were battling hand to hand, face to face, knee to groin. The sun was behind us by then, shining in their faces. I remember seeing it glint on a Parthian shield boss and ducking, for fear of being blinded, and using that same shaft of light in my own right, raising my blade until the light bounced into the eyes of the screaming demon who came at me with his axe raised, but never saw the straight thrust into his mouth that killed him.

Dusk fell slowly, without our knowing, just that we had to strain harder to see the difference between mail and flesh, between skin and blood and bone. The sides of the pass became vast walls of unlight, and the blanket of night slowly drew across the Parthian forces, so that we no longer had any idea of how many were behind the battle line.

We had no one behind now to send for brands from the old camp fires; our line was one man deep, and not long.

A man fell in that line, away to my left. Lupus roared his command hoarsely now, and I sounded the horn and heard only one other match it, thinly, as we stepped back a pace, to keep our dwindling wall of shields intact.

But the other, thinner, horn kept sounding its long, rolling note, which was nothing at all like our three short, falling blasts that took us back.

'That's the retreat. The Parthian retreat. They're going back!' Someone shouted that from my left. I thought it was Sarapammon, but now I think it must have been Horgias. At the time, I barely dared lower my blade for fear of who would step in to take advantage of it, until I saw Syrion drop his head to rest his brow on his shield's edge and heard Lupus say, in a tone of weary, half-joyed disbelief, 'Demalion, sound the battle's end.'

We were three hundred, who had been three thousand. Our unit alone was reduced to five men: Sarapammon and the Rabbit were gone, lost somewhere down the pass. I had seen neither of them die, but Rufus had seen both, and convinced the rest of us that they were dead beyond all hope of rescue or recovery, and we must not venture out to find them.

Syrion, Rufus, Horgias, Tears and myself were left. In a tight knot, each cleaving to the other, we stepped back and back and back and at a certain point, when it was clear the Parthians really had departed, we turned and walked wearily together back to where we had left our camp in perfect order, never expecting to see it again.

It took longer than it might have done to kindle the fires, to gather water, to cook, to eat. When we were done, Cadus called us together in our centuries, to find who was left.

A good portion of the first century of the first cohort had held the centre; they really were a supremely effective fighting force. By contrast, only three men were left of the second cohort; they were the newest, the rawest, and while we had not left them in the front ranks – we valued our lives too much for that – they had borne the brunt of a light cavalry attack on our left flank, and then their centurions had failed to see the archers. Or had seen them and not been heard. Or their signallers had been too slow. Or they had not drilled often enough to raise their shields. All or any of these; what mattered was that the entire second cohort was gone, those who had not taken leave and stayed the winter out in the whore-baths of Melitene.

In between these two extremes, the rest of us were left speaking aloud the names of our dead, that they might know themselves gone, and so walk lightly away from this life. Nobody laid out the blankets and chose what to keep: there were too many dead, too many to remember and too few of us to take things from them. We chose instead to hold them all equally, and not single out one for more attention than the others.

We were tired as galley slaves, fit to drop, but Cadus did not yet let us go.

'We are three hundred,' he said, which we knew. 'We can hold this pass, perhaps for another day. We will sell our lives dearly, and they know already that they cannot send the cataphracts against us. But Paetus must know what has happened, and I will send a man also to Corbulo. This may be against our governor's wishes, but if I am dead there's nothing he can do.'

It was a joke, of a sort; nobody laughed. We watched him, fearful of what was coming next. He held out his helmet and shook it; we all heard the rattle of lot-stones. 'All those with mounts will come forward.'

I might have held back, but Syrion shoved me, and Horgias, and Lupus took Tears by his elbow and thrust him into the firelight. We and seven others stood there. Perhaps because of our history, certainly because of what Cadus had said about loving battle, I was the one who spoke up.

'I don't want—'

Cadus cut me off. 'Nobody wants to leave. You all want to die beside your fellows. But these messages must be sent. Ten stones are here. Seven are white; those men stay. Two are black. Those men go to Corbulo; two of you, because the road is arduous, even were we not at war with Vologases. The last is black with a white line down the centre; that man goes to Paetus with news that the Parthians are a day's march away, and we will be lucky to hold them beyond tomorrow's noon. That man must ride fastest.'

His eyes were on me as he spoke, but it was a lottery, a drawing of chance with only the gods able to influence the outcome. He could not have known it beforehand.

Even so, none of us was surprised that I drew the black stone with the white line down it. The surprise was that Tears and Horgias drew the black, which took them south to Syria.

'No!' I said. 'Three from the same unit? Only Syrion and Rufus are left.'

'There are units with fewer men left than that,' Lupus said, from behind us. 'Yours will join with others. Afterwards, you may be the seeds of a new legion, with a new sixth cohort and a new first unit of the first century. Thus will you remember us.'

I knew that voice, the solid implacability of it. Dismissed, I turned on my heel and made for the tent.

Tears and I passed that night in the warmth of each other's embrace, but we were too tired for more; we slept deep as the dead until dawn and left the camp with thick heads and tired hearts, and Syrion and Rufus stood at the tent lines to wave us on our separate ways.

For the rest of my life, I will remember them, and the peace that was in their eyes.

Chapter Twenty

I don't remember the details of the ride back. The bay mare knew her way without my pushing her and I didn't allow myself to believe that it was happening; it was only when I reached the camp, saw the state of the newly completed palisades, and spoke to the lead centurions of the IVth that it began to feel true.

Then they took me to Paetus and truth became a nightmare as he argued that defence was impossible and we were better to surrender to Vologases when he came, and depend on his better judgement, or his mercy, or his fear of Nero – all or any of these were suggested, and all were equally unlikely – to at least send the officers home alive.

I left him that first evening, heart-sick and desperate. I would have ridden back to the Lizard Pass had not night fallen and in any case what point when everyone left behind must be dead by now?

I was given a place to sleep in a tent with one of the

centurions of the IVth. Crescens was his name, third centurion in the fifth cohort, not one we had come across on the Hawk mountain, for which I think both of us were glad.

We of Lupus' century had a reputation amongst the IVth that made us out to be madmen and savages, or so I learned after the tense and fitful night which left both of us weary in the morning, and more inclined to speak.

'He needs a backbone, that one,' he said of his general, and nobody offered to flog him for it. 'If anyone can shame him into making a stand, it will be you.'

He was cooking me a meal; I was not going to turn him down. And when two other centurions of the IVth came to beg me to speak again to Paetus, I did as they asked thinking that if he had me flogged to death for the temerity, at least I would join the dead, amongst whom I now counted Rufus and Syrion.

Four of us went into the general's tent that day and the day after, and the day after that.

Slowly, we created for Paetus a plan, the first and most important part of which was the destruction of the bridge we had built across the foaming river, so that when Vologases marched here he might not have use of it to reach us.

Paetus agreed, as a weak man will do, not out of conviction or the need to see our plan through, but to keep us quiet. And he vacillated over every other thing that we suggested. I lost patience in the end, and told him that two men had already gone to Corbulo for help on Cadus' order, and that we only need hold out a few days; four at most, and we would be safe.

I thought he might order me killed then, he was so angry, and that was when we realized that, truly, Paetus would have preferred to lose us all to Vologases than to lose his pride to Corbulo.

Without being dismissed, I walked out. Crescens caught my shoulder as I stepped out of the governor's quarters.

'Don't do anything stupid. He can still have you flogged.'

'I'm going to destroy the bridge.'

'I know. He knows. He gave permission for it.'

'Then help me do it. We can't have long before they come.'

'I'll bring a unit. Any more and he'll stop us.'

He ran, I give him that much; he was a centurion and he ran across the hard-packed earth that had been our parade ground so few days before, past the unfilled foundations whence the sacrifice had fled, and into the tent lines.

Returning, he brought eight men equipped with crowbars, hammers, axes and ropes. I chose not to learn their names – what point to come to know men when we must all soon be dead? – but led them at a run to the bridge.

It was not built for easy demolition. Two of Crescens' men were engineers, part of the corps that had built it. They went across and back on their hands and knees, examining the intricate ties that held it. In other days I might have marvelled at their skill, to build a bridge fit to take two legions and all their carts, with no nails, but only wooden joints; now, I was impatient for it to be gone.

Coming back to us, they saluted me as if I were a centurion. They had heard, of course, of the carnage at Lizard Pass, and were ashamed to have been left out of it, even as they gave thanks, moment by moment, for the continuation of their lives.

The eldest, a man near to retirement, said, 'We'll need a man to go across to the other bank and hammer out the pegs or it won't fall.'

'I'll do it.'

Nobody argued with me.

I took a pole axe and crossed over the bridge, blindly. In my mind, I saw Lupus, speared through the chest; Syrion, dying with an axe in his head, Rufus cut in two by a sword . . . in the worst moments, I saw Tears and Horgias ambushed, taken, tortured; dead.

The ties that fixed the bridge were great wooden pegs as thick as a man's arm, hammered through the ends of the trunks and into the arch – three of them in all.

I swung the pole axe and felt it hit the first one with a noise like the crack of a tree in a storm. The peg moved barely at all. I swung again, and again, each time imagining a Parthian head beneath the axe, broken like a melon at each hammering impact. And again, and again; I slaughtered two units of them to get the first peg out. My arms were burning. My head was spinning. My ears rang from the sound. I began on the second peg.

Perhaps because I was thinking of the Parthians, I was slow to hear them coming. Or I wanted to die: in the time since, I have thought that might have been true. Whichever was the case, I didn't know to be alarmed until I heard Crescens calling me, shouting my name over and over.

'Demalion! Demalion of the Twelfth! Get back over here, they're coming!'

We had no archers for cover; they had all given their lives at the pass, on the first day, or the second. The Parthians, of course, had archers of their own.

As I hammered at the second peg, the men of the IVth threw their spears, their axes, their hammers, but the river was as wide as two trees laid end to end; few of the weapons reached the far side and even then they did no harm. I hit the third peg, and it was looser; it came free in three strokes. I shouted in triumph then, I think; certainly I felt the first of the logs begin to falter and to fall, and saw on the faces of Crescens and his men that I had succeeded in breaking the bridge. And that I was to die for it.

I spun, swinging the pole axe by the very end of its haft, and carried on spinning, so that I was turning like a child's toy, with a hammer's head of lethal iron describing a circle around me, eight feet out. In a battlefield, it might have worked for a moment or two, until a brave man blocked it with a shield and his fellows powered down its length to kill me. Here, a squadron of Parthian light cavalry made a circle around me, and simply leaned on their saddles, and waited until I grew tired.

Seeing them gave me strength for perhaps four revolutions more than I might otherwise have managed, and that, in turn, gave me time to find the gap through which I might escape.

An older man with greyed moustaches on a liver chestnut mare was flanked on both sides by his sons, men who were mirrors to the old man, but twenty years younger. Between him and each of them was a gap.

I picked the one to my right, where I might come at his sword hand, but his son's shield. Just before I had to give up my manic spinning, I lurched back, and then forward, and used the extra power to throw the hammer at the greybeard's head. I hurtled after, too fast to see if I had killed him or his son, concerned only with drawing my own blade in time.

'*Ha!*' I reached the horses, and stabbed up, towards the unprotected belly. The mare skittered sideways. I scented open air, and saw the remains of the bridge, and the men on the far side, waiting with their arms outstretched, as if to draw me over to them.

I heard the rush of the river, and a voice that hollered my name and—

Black. A torrent of blackness with pain at its heart. I remember falling. I do not remember hitting the earth.

'. . . doesn't matter. We have no restitution, nothing to do but act as we are told.'

'Or refuse.'

'And then die, yes. All of us. To no good effect.'

Two voices argued back and forth across my head. They were Lupus and Cadus, and I thought I heard Syrion more distantly, speaking of the battle, and so I knew that I had died, only I did not expect death to carry so many small discomforts, or so great a mass of pain.

A gritty, unkempt sheepskin lay beneath my unclothed skin. I knew by its smell that it was badly cured and did not know how the gods could possibly be so lax. I smelled vomit, too, which was as bad.

I felt stones dig into my ribs where the sheepskin ended and the hard, cold ground began. I felt the wind on my back, the sear and ache of four-day-old wounds from the battle we had fought that I had not noticed at the time, and the far greater ache, the thunderous, thundering pain of a wound at the back of my head. My hair felt tight, pulled by clotted blood. I thought of baths, and wondered that the gods did not have them.

I tried to roll over, to ask.

'Demalion! No!'

A dozen rough hands held me down. Cadus' face loomed close to my own. 'Don't try to get up yet. You're not fit.'

I struggled to make his face hold still. 'How not fit?' In my hampered state, I could not see how death was something for which a man had to prepare, other than stepping on to a battlefield. Or over a bridge. Memory came back to me in patches. I struggled to fit them to a whole.

Seeing it, Cadus said, 'You're in the Parthian lines. You are a prisoner, as we are.'

A long, sullen moment while I drank that in. Eventually, 'How?'

They told me, each hindered by his own shame, and I struggled to fit these patches, too, to a whole image.

When I had, it was not so very different from my own capture, only that it had taken longer, and the encirclement had been more savage, so that some men had died – one was Rufus, who had hurled himself at their spear-fence, trying to break it – and some men had been badly injured: Syrion's leg was broken and he was being carried on a litter provided by the Parthians. At least legionaries carried it.

But the rest were alive, who had expected to die, and nobody knew why unless we were to be crucified in a line facing the Roman camp across the river, which is exactly what we would have done to vanquished prisoners of an army that had dared to oppose us.

There seemed no point in mentioning that, when everybody knew. I sat with Cadus, who had a bruise the size of a goose egg on his temple and skin paled to a sweat-beaded green, but seemed otherwise unharmed.

'Does Vologases know . . .' I sought a way of saying what I needed, cautiously, in case we were overheard. 'Does he know of Horgias and Tears?'

Lupus said. 'None of us has told him.' He had broken his collarbone on the left. His face was a dirty grey-white that became simply white whenever he moved. He moved now, to fetch me water, when he could have called one of the others to do it, and when he handed me the jug with his one good hand he would not meet my eye, only said, 'You destroyed the bridge. That was well done.'

'Was it?' I drank, and felt cold trickle down to my stomach and was not sick. Lupus watched, still looking anywhere but at my face.

I set down the mug. 'Lupus, there is no shame in this. You offered your lives to the gods and to the enemy. It's not your fault that Vologases chose not to take them. Don't let him shame you by it.'

'Drink,' said Lupus tightly, 'and wait until your head is better. Then we can talk of who is shamed, and what might come of it.'

We languished half a day during which I drank a great deal of water, and ate sparingly, and began slowly to feel less ill.

Our guards did not address us, but they did not mistreat us either. We did not speak much amongst ourselves; men awaiting crucifixion find little to say.

Near dusk, a mounted officer approached. His face was compressed, top to bottom, his cheeks wide, his eyes small. He wore Vologases' sign of the silver elephant on a blue ground, but he also wore a badge of a bear's head in black and white that I had not seen before.

He dismounted and saluted Cadus, Lupus and myself. In sing-song Greek he said, 'Please to accompany me. The King of Kings will speak to you.'

Vologases' tent was larger than any I had ever seen, of silk so thick, so deeply hued, it was as if night itself lay on the tent poles. We were invited to enter the first of its many rooms, offered seating on benches padded with horse hide, and given peach wine to drink out of golden goblets. We ate dates and olives and small pieces of smoked ham that came apart in our mouths and spilled the taste of meat and spices freely.

'If they had given me this when first I woke,' I murmured to Lupus, 'I would have believed myself dead far longer.'

A horn answered for him, or perhaps a flute, for the notes were high and breathy, and rippled faster than I could have blown. At its summoning, we stood, turned, walked through a lifted tent flap.

Showered by sound, preceded by officers in silk and silver, with the sign of the elephant on its blue ground carried by each man, we came into the presence of Vologases, the King of Kings.

I knelt, because I had done so once before, because Pantera had done so, because it was natural to do so.

A half-breath behind, uncertainly, Lupus and Cadus knelt with me. We did not press our brows to the floor, but we did bow our heads to him, and then raise them again to look on his face, which was not, I am sure, how a prisoner was supposed to behave.

He sat on a seat of oak, marvellously worked, inlaid with gilt and silver, and lapis lazuli, and amber. He wore blue silk with silver and a filet of gold round the battle helm that held his head. His beard was longer than I remembered, and carried white through it, like frost on rock, but his eyes were the same: sharp, light and lively. They roamed over us now, back and forth.

'You, and you.' He pointed with a silvered blade. I saw something viscous run from it, and for a moment thought it blood, until I saw the fruit in his other hand, filling his palm, something green-skinned that I had never seen before. 'You have knelt to us before.' His eyes were on me, not Cadus.

'With Pantera, lord,' I said. 'The man known as the Leopard. In Hyrcania. After the death of . . . the traitor.'

His son, who had not been named then and was as

likely unnamed now. I watched a ghosted grief pass over Vologases' face.

'Indeed. We gave your companion a horse. A bay mare.'

There were men of my acquaintance who thought I had lied, that she had not been given as a gift by the King of Kings. I was glad, suddenly, that Lupus was behind me. 'Pantera gave her to me, lord, when he was summoned to Britain. I have her still. She is in the camp across the river.'

'Then you must return to her and keep her safe from harm. We are told there is a ford across the river.'

I could have denied it, but what point? 'Yes, lord. Although the river has swollen somewhat since we last crossed it. We had built a bridge.'

'Which you destroyed yesterday. We watched you. Our archers begged to be allowed to use you for their practice. They said a dozen men could have hit you three times each before you fell.'

'I'm sure they could have done, lord.'

'And you knew they were there?'

'My lord always has archers. In the past, he has always used them.'

This time he had not; and he had taken men prisoner, whom he could have slain. I could not ask why. He showed no inclination to explain, but only observed me, thoughtfully, tapping his knife on the gilded arm of his throne.

At length he said, 'You will ford the river tomorrow. Take from my army what men and horses you need to get you across safely. But they will return to our side of the river, and you alone will step on to the far bank. You will go to your commander, Paetus' – he weighed the name with the same kind of acerbic loathing as did Lupus – 'and you will tell him the terms of your surrender. When he has heard them, you will bring his acceptance back to us. Is that clear?'

'Most clear, lord.'

I didn't ask the terms of our surrender, and in truth I didn't want to know any sooner than I must, but Vologases said, in dismissal, 'Your General Corbulo gave me his solemn word that not a single Roman legionary would cross to the east of the Euphrates. In crossing the Murad Su, in camping on its northern bank, which faces eastward, your Paetus has broken the oath of a better man. He shall pay for it. His men, however, need not.'

Chapter Twenty-One

'Lord, they are taking everything, *everything*. We can't let them do it.'

So said Crescens of the IVth, first to speak after me in the commanders' meeting that Paetus had called on my return to hear the Parthians' demands.

Paetus stared him down. 'You misunderstand. They are not taking everything. We may keep the Eagles, and so retain the honour of the legions.'

'Honour?' Crescens' voice cracked. 'After a *surrender*! Lord, you cannot mean—'

'Centurion Crescens, you forget yourself!' Paetus seemed to have aged overnight. His shoulders fell round a concave chest; his hair, I swear, was whiter; his hands were skin and bone with no strength in the sinews. He held them together, blanching his knuckles, as if he they might betray him did he only let them go.

'I mean that I am not prepared to see the men of my command crucified before my eyes when by my actions

I can prevent it. Corbulo may arrive, but not in time to save the lives of First Centurion Cadus and his men. They are my priority.'

He turned to me and I found his gaze surprisingly sharp. This was a man who had survived two Caesars, who had kept in good odour with Nero when so many others had fallen from grace and paid for it with their lives. He was not a soldier, but he was a politician. 'As I understand it,' he said, 'we will be allowed to keep the standards. Is that true?'

'Yes, lord; all of them. We must march away leaving everything else behind, the food, the wine, the armour, the weapons, the horses . . . But first we must build them a bridge, to replace the one that was destroyed.'

'If we keep the standards, we have not fully surrendered.' Paetus' gaze had grown distant, seeing himself back in Rome, speaking to the emperor, setting the record straight, so that he, Paetus, came out of it shining.

He dragged his grey eyes back to mine. 'You destroyed the bridge?'

'I did, lord. At your order.'

'And with my help,' Crescens said. For a man of the IVth, he was remarkably decent.

Paetus' smile was thin as a lizard's. 'Then by my order and with your help, he shall replace it as the Parthians have requested.' He stepped in front of me. 'Clearly you will have to ford the river once more in order to give our agreement to the terms of surrender. But I wish you to return here afterwards, unless it is impossible to do so.'

Unless Vologases has had your head struck from your shoulders, is what he meant.

I swam back across the river, aided by a rope that the Parthians had already strung across. I delivered our acceptance. My head was not struck off.

As I was heading for the river again, the narrow-eyed general of the Parthians came up to me and caught my arm, turning me back to face him.

He had laid his hand on his heart and stared into my eyes. 'Amongst our people,' he said, 'that is, amongst the Parthian tribes from which comes the King of Kings, it is an unthinkable dishonour to take back a gift once it is given. His magnificence wishes you to remember that, in the time that is to come.'

'I see.' I thought of the bay mare and what she was worth and how far I was prepared to risk my life for her. Quite far, I thought, particularly if I had Vologases' backing. 'Thank you. I will not forget.'

I bowed from the waist with my hands on my breast as I had seen Pantera do with the kings in Hyrcania and the old man returned it as if we were not mortal enemies who had lately spent a great deal of effort and other men's blood trying to kill each other.

Soon after, I swam back across and helped the work parties to rebuild the bridge. It was lucky that we had wood enough in the camp without having to cross the river to cut more. Or perhaps it was ill luck. Cutting wood would have taken time, and in time, perhaps, Corbulo might have come and relieved us.

But under the Parthians' hard gaze we could not dally overmuch, nor could we pretend that we didn't have enough men, when the several centuries not working on the bridge were standing in clots around their tents, doing nothing.

The bridge was built in less than a day. That same evening, we stood in lines as Vologases had demanded, to receive him and his army.

He came in pomp, weighted in blue silk, carried on a litter at head height by men taller than any I had ever seen. His captains rode around him on black horses that sported silver and silk at their brows and tails.

After him, on horseback, not in a litter, came Monobasus of Adiabene, as smugly triumphant as any man I have ever seen. I could have killed him; I might have done so, whatever the consequences, had he not been leading Cadus and Lupus at either stirrup with leather leashes tied to their necks.

So, like the others, I swallowed my pride and my loathing and watched as Vologases and Paetus each approached the table that had been carried over and placed in the centre of the camp. There, the entirety of both armies heard read aloud by the Parthian herald the terms of our surrender. Vologases held out a quill pen and a block of ink and Paetus stepped up to put his name to the document.

We were finished then; even if Corbulo had come, we were bound by Paetus' word to leave without bloodshed, to abandon all of our goods, keeping only our Eagles.

Paetus stepped back and saluted – he *saluted* an enemy king! We gaped in disbelief.

There was a moment's hiatus before Vologases lifted his hand in a sign that was both acknowledgement and order. At that, Monobasus released the leashes holding Cadus and Lupus and they were pushed ungently forward past Paetus to join us.

I clasped Cadus by the arms, holding Lupus more gingerly, taking care for his fractures. A short while later, I saw Syrion lifted on a litter, and had the beginnings of hope that the day might not be as bad as I had thought, that Paetus had shown wisdom in not leaving these men to the worst of deaths, that we could walk out with our heads high and our Eagles to the fore and perhaps rescue something of our reputation.

Then I saw a movement from the corner of my eye; Vologases had dropped his hand – and that was when the Parthian army fell on us like a cloud of locusts, and set about pillaging our camp as if it were empty.

Cadus pushed me away. 'See to your horse.'

I ran fast, being light, with no armour. I saw my gladius taken, our tent ripped apart. My mail shirt was lifted, fingered, thrown from one laughing man to the next; the metal rings glimmered in the sick winter light.

But these were random acts by men who ransacked for the sake of it because that was what war expected and what Vologases demanded. A tighter, more disciplined group had moved almost before the order and made straight for the horse lines that were set beneath the palisade on the northern edge of the camp. Every one of the men was marked by the blue tern of Adiabene.

They went down the lines as my father used to, picking out the best mounts with a practised eye, tapping the tails as a signal that they were chosen, leaving their boys to squeeze in between the horses and free their halters from the tether bar.

My mare was last of the line. I reached her just ahead of the bearded maniac who threatened to take her.

'Stop! This mare was a gift from the King of Kings. If you take her, you dishonour him!'

If I screamed, it was a pouring out of the whole camp's anger, and my frustration that I had no blade and could not even strike him with my fist for fear of breaking the truce. I stood close, though, hoping to use my size and rage to overwhelm him.

I failed.

'Liar!' A gobbet of spittle struck my cheek. A leering face pressed close to mine. 'The King of Kings gifts no Romans. She is mine now. You can kiss her goodbye.'

Fury lifted me outside myself. I grasped the man by his clothing, pushing his shoulders back and back against the palisade behind. In a whisper, driving each word into his eyes, his nose, his ears, I said, 'Vologases gave her to Pantera in Hyrcania, after the Leopard shot the usurper. If you choose not to believe otherwise, don't blame me if the King of Kings has your skin stripped from your naked body this night, leaving you living to make your apologies in the morning.'

I had never seen that, only heard of it fifth hand, but it was enough to give the man pause, and me time to hear hoofbeats behind, and turn my head just enough to catch a glimpse of the man behind me; not enough to be sure who it was, but enough to take a gamble and pray that I was right. 'Or,' I said, loudly, and dropped him, 'you could ask your king, who stands behind me. He was present when the traitor died. He will confirm that Pantera made the fatal shot, and was richly rewarded for it.'

I turned as I spoke. Monobasus was still the fox-faced, narrow-eyed, duplicitous schemer I had first seen. And if rumour was correct, he had helped his third cousin on to the throne of Hyrcania the summer after we had been there, and might have helped him rebel against the King of Kings, although clearly Vologases did not believe that, or he would not have honoured him so greatly at our surrender.

He leaned on the pommel of his saddle. His beard reached halfway down his chest. His moustaches were half the length of his beard. Both were tending to greyness, salted through here and there with white. He smelled of garlic, and mustard, and wine.

Perhaps I should have fallen to my knees, as his men did beside me, but I had lost almost everything that day and was not inclined to throw away what dignity I had left.

I said, 'Shall I describe for you the moment my lord Pantera shot two arrows at the charging boar, and then at the one who pretended to be king? His name, as I remember, was—'

'It will not be necessary to name him.' Monobasus smoothed his hand down his chin. Hate lit his eyes. I was beyond caring.

I said, 'Then you will remember how the King of Kings gave to Pantera the bay mare that had been the traitor's mount. He gave her to me and she stands before you now. You may check her brands if you doubt me.'

'I don't doubt you. I placed those brands myself. I bred her.'

'Then—'

'She is yours.' He wrenched his own horse round with a savagery that would have earned him a beating from my father for ruining its mouth.

I called after him. 'She has given me three sons. Would you take those? Or are they not also gifts of the King of Kings.'

Monobasus did not pause. I looked at his man, who stood, uncertain. 'They have the brand of the leopard's paw,' I said loudly. 'If you take them, be prepared to answer for it to the King of Kings.'

It wasn't easy for a horse to move fast in the crowded wreckage of our camp; Monobasus was not so far away that he couldn't hear, or answer.

'Leave them,' he called back. 'Leave them all.'

All. Leave all the horses. The king had spoken and must be obeyed and so, slowly, as if working through mud, sullen men nodded at the sour-mouthed boys who in turn thrust their unwilling way back through the lines to retie the halters they had so lately untied.

I stood a long while after they had gone, talking to my mare, stroking her, checking her limbs, her mouth, pulling imaginary tangles from her mane, and then doing the same for each of her sons, who were jittery from having been so roughly handled.

Presently, I returned to Cadus and Lupus, who stood where I had left them, watching the chaos. A thin cloud had drawn across the sky, cloaking the sun that Helios might not be forced to view our indignity. It left the air thinner, paler, so that men seemed ill who had been only stoic before. Cadus and Lupus, particularly, looked as if the sky had fallen on their heads.

'What?' I asked as I reached them. 'I saved your horses for you. We march out now, and meet Corbulo, and go back to Syria and start again. It's bad, but we're alive. It could be a lot worse.'

'It is a lot worse,' Lupus said. 'We are to march out under the yoke. Us and the Eagles, both. You are to fetch your horn. It has been saved for you. The King of Kings requires that you sound the marching orders.'

I wet my lips. I blew. A faint, ugly whimper squeezed from my horn, barely enough to reach the first rank. Never in my entire life have I failed to sound the horn, but never in my life have I been so disgraced as to march beneath the raised spears of the enemy: the sign of ultimate defeat.

On the second effort, I managed a thin, stringy sound. It resembled the signal to march not at all, but the men behind, in their mercy, accepted it as such. I heard the centurions shout their orders, the clash of sandals that should have been matched by the clash of arms and armour, and was instead met by the odd, dull sound of three and a half thousand men coming to attention in only their linen tunics.

Ahead of us, two lines of Parthians used my horn as their own signal and raised their spears, holding them up and out, angled steeply so that they met in the middle of the line, forming a roofed channel under which we must pass.

The spears made long, knifing shadows that fell across us in spliced angles, like the bars of a gigantic cage. I stepped in, and in, and in, following Paetus, until I was completely within their shade, until I was surrounded by the laughter, by the jeers, by the spits and thrown stones.

I marched with Cadus on one side and Lupus on the other and I swear to you now that not one of us flinched, however we were struck. But in our souls, we knew we would have been better dead.

Two days later, we met Corbulo, who was of the same opinion. He sent us, the remnants of the IVth and the XIIth, to Syria with orders to rebuild our legions, while he took the 'fighting arm' of his army, the IIIrd, the VIth and the Xth, up to Cappadocia to overwinter in our beautiful camp at Melitene, there to meet Vologases in the spring, and bring him to heel. Tears and Horgias joined us again before the two forces split. It was the only bright light in our darkness.

Chapter Twenty-Two

The wounded died like flies on the march back south to Syria. To our continued shame, we left their bodies where they lay, for Paetus would not let us stop to build pyres for them. A centurion – often it seemed to be Lupus or Cadus – spoke the words of death that their spirits might go freely to the other life and we marched on by, hating ourselves more with each passing day.

Antioch, first city of Syria, loomed like a death sentence at the end of our march. The seat of Corbulo's power, it was acclaimed as the third great city of the empire, behind only Rome and Alexandria, and Corbulo had stamped his ordered, military mark on every part of it, from the pin-neat barracks to the governor's Spartan mansion to the markets, where neither thieves nor beggars plied their trade and every sale was decent, and the whorehouses, where the boys, girls and women were licensed by the governor's office.

We reached the city walls half a month after we had

left the camp at Rhandaea and it seemed our fame – our notoriety – had preceded us, for the people of the city shut their doors to us as we marched in and not a soul gave greeting until we halted outside the governor's mansion.

The steward could not pretend to be indisposed, but he took his time in opening the door and when he walked out on to the steps above us we saw that he had dressed himself in a torn tunic and thrown dust on both shoulders to show himself in mourning at our presence.

He was a tall, lean man with a bald pate and a patrician nose and he had the power to summon men from the locked and shuttered buildings of Antioch.

At his command, they gave us the barracks that had lately been occupied by the VIth; they gave us food and water for ourselves, our mules, and our mounts; they gave us weapons to replace the ones we had been forced to leave behind – second-rate weapons, that we would not have deigned to buy in the days when we had money – all of this they gave us at the governor's express order.

But Corbulo had not demanded that the people of Antioch make us welcome, and the lack of a single smiling face threw into painful relief all the other towns and cities we had camped in or near in the days of our ascendance, where we had been cheered, garlanded, wined and dined as men who came with silver to spare, anxious to find new ways to be parted from it.

Here, we of the IVth and XIIth found ourselves in echoing barracks, eight to a room and half of those rooms empty, so that the parade ground did not so much rock to our entrance as titter, and it was clear that at night we would be cold for lack of men around us.

Only the sick bay was full. As soon as I had seen to the horses, I went in to sit with Syrion; beautiful, elegant Syrion who was thinner than a starving street cur and lay for ever in a fever with skin blotched irregularly red and white and beads of sour sweat growing fat on his forehead. On the route down we had stopped for the night near a village and I had bought some rags of the kind they used for swaddling children and had boiled them in citrus juice to get rid of the smell of goat that had infested everything in that place. Whenever I could thereafter, I had used them to wipe Syrion dry.

I did it again now, leaning forward, stroking across his skin. Presently, he opened one yellowed eye in thanks and I lifted the beaker that stood in a dampened sand box at my side.

'Would you like some water? It's colder than snow. Well, almost.'

'As cold as our welcome?' His smile was a twitch at the corner of his mouth. 'I saw it from the litter. The whole city hates us.'

'The city doesn't know us. But once we have money, the people will—'

'Where are we going to get money from? We walked our Eagles under the enemy yoke. We're all down to single pay.' That was true; Corbulo himself had given the order: every man in the legion, whatever his rank, down to single pay. Paetus alone was exempt, but then Paetus was in Caesarea, desperately trying to find a boat that would take him back to Rome in winter seas so he could give his side of things to Nero before Corbulo's messengers ruined his life.

None of which was the point; the point was that, although we did have some money, nobody would take it from us. 'Cadus and I have gold from when we were in Hyrcania,' I said. 'It was left in the vault at Raphana, which is an easy enough ride from here. When we've settled in, one of us will go and get it.'

'Don't.' Syrion grabbed for my hand. The effort left him gasping, with his eyes flared wide. 'That's your retirement, Fox. Don't give it away to men who don't need it.'

I ignored him. 'We'll buy good weapons, at least. And armour for those who need it from the armourer in Damascus.' We had it planned; with Paetus gone, Cadus was the most senior officer. He couldn't leave the camp, but he had given Lupus and me permission to ride to Raphana as soon as the dust of our arriving had settled.

I said, 'We'll get you that new strip mail armour. You'll look like a god. The enemy will never dare assault you then, not even by the half-dozen.'

Eight of the Parthians had taken him down, so they said, and he had killed three of them. One of those who had survived had used an axe on his left leg and left it splintered so that he would have died had not Vologases ordered the battle's end just as the axemen were going to kill him.

Lupus and Cadus had carried Syrion from the field and he had not walked since. On the march back, the bone-setters said he might heal well enough to march again if the bone didn't go bad. They had pulled the leg straight at the cost of much blood and splinted it with rosemary on either side to keep it sweet. Even so, those of us who cared for him were ordered to lift the covers and sniff daily around the wound. They said the fruitiness and stench of old meat we had scented from the start were both signs of wellness, and that it was the smell of mouse droppings we should fear.

It had been hard to imagine the scent of mouse droppings when we were on the march, but mice and rats had clearly taken over the barracks as soon as the VIth had marched out. We had sent some of the younger men to buy as many cats as they could find. They had not yet returned.

I smelled something now, growing stronger as Syrion sat up to drink. I moved to lift the linen sheet that covered him.

'Don't.' He caught my hand.

'I need to smell . . .'

'You don't. Trust me; you don't.'

For the first time since we'd marched under the yoke, his eyes were the perfect blue-grey that I remembered from our first days in the Hawk mountains, when the sky had been the same colour and it had seemed as if we saw through him to the spirits of the place.

He said, 'Is there armour to be found anywhere in the camp?'

'There are six mail shirts in the quartermaster's stores. I found them when I did the inventory.'

'Would I be permitted to wear one, do you think? For only a short time. And a sword?'

'Syrion, why—'

'Because you're my friend and I can ask these things of you. Would you get them?'

I backed away from the certainty in his gaze, and all the things there that I didn't want to read. The stores were a dozen paces from the infirmary. I was there and back in a hundred heartbeats. I picked up a whetstone for the sword from the box by the door as I left; already a part of me knew what he planned.

There were tunics and sandals, and it took the time perhaps to turn a single marched circuit of the parade ground for me to dress him and sling the gladius at his hip. I settled the sandal on one foot but not the other; it was too swollen to take the thongs, and the flesh was green-tinged that had yesterday been reddish-purple. The smell of mice was no greater than the smell of sweat and leaked urine, but it was there.

He whetted the blade while I fixed the single sandal, and then he used my shoulder to stand.

'Where?' I asked, and did not dare say more. To be what he needed, I had to pretend not to know what he planned, even to myself.

'I haven't seen this place. Is there a high tower, from which I could view the sunset? Or a hill, perhaps?'

'The officers' quarters are in a tower. It's three storeys high. They're all in a meeting in the governor's residence half a mile away.'

'Perfect.' His lips were a reddish-blue; he pulled them into a kind of smile. 'Can you take me, do you think, without attracting undue attention?'

I doubted that, but wasn't going to say so. Instead, I offered a shoulder for him to lean on, and sent prayers to

Helios and the gods of death that we might pass across the camp unhindered by well-wishers or naysayers or anyone who might delay us.

The gods answered my plea; they always do, I have found, if the request is not impossible, and is asked with sufficient passion.

In a haze of thanks and grief, therefore, I brought Syrion unhampered to the three-storeyed tower that some former governor had built for his legions in Antioch. I opened the unlocked door, and half carried him up three flights of stone steps and then a half-flight that took us on to the roof with its low three-foot wall and the small sheltered standing box made of oak, in which the night watch might light a brazier and shelter from the elements and against which Syrion was able to lean, that he might stand facing west and see what was there.

It was worth having come for; all of it. Above the noise and murmur of the camp, we were held in our own silence. We were above, too, the many-layered stench of a city in the afternoon when the middens have ripened all day and leak their odour as an old carcass leaks blood. Here, we were bathed only in the scent of dusk that is the same everywhere: of dew falling, and the air growing cold.

And from the horizon, Helios' dying rays blessed us with a range and purity of colour the like of which I had never seen. Reds fired the core, scarlet, vermilion and deep, deep crimson, the colour of perfect blood, but it was the sky around that touched us; a haze of old blue and purple, of peach and apricot and amber so close and so vibrant that we could have reached out to grasp the threads and woven them into a cloak to keep a man safe for life. Or to see him into the afterlife.

I heard Syrion gasp a little, like a man who has found love late in life, and knows not how to ride it, and then he saw my face, and the pain that was on it, and smiled.

'I choose this. You know that.'

'I do.'

'And everyone else must know it too. Tell them I chose the swift death of a legionary, of a soldier, not the slow death of a sick man in a bed. And that I love the Twelfth and will not set my shade to harm it.'

I tried to speak, tried to say that none of us feared his shade, or thought he would trouble us, even if he had not died in battle. But my throat had closed and the words were a croak, and my vision blurred as Syrion lifted his new-whetted blade – so sharp that the sun itself split on the blade, and spun away in a thousand dancing motes of light – and raised the hem of the mail shirt so that he might angle the blade up beneath it, and rest the point just below his breastbone.

'Do you want me to . . .' Now, at the end, I had speech.

Syrion shook his head. His face was a mask of pain, but his smile was still true and certain. 'I've planned this for half a month. I can do it.'

And he did. He settled both hands on the hilt, took a breath and gave a small, sharp jerk in and up, hard, and pitched himself forward to fall on to his knees and then on to his face, so that the last fall pushed the blade on up through his heart and out of his back, to tent the chain mail away from his body.

It was good. It was fast, but not immediate. I knelt in the tide of blood that spilled from his mouth and nose, and gently took his shoulder and rolled him on to his side.

His eyes were open, and still aware as I spoke the invocation to the gods.

'Given of the god,
Given to the god,
Taken by the god in valour, honour and glory.
May you journey safely to your destination.'

We burned him on a pyre of Syrian wood; that much the local men gave us, ungrudging, when they knew what had happened.

Every whole and living man of the XIIth – all two hundred and eighteen of us – turned out to see him turn to smoke and rise to the night sky. The fire lasted a day and a night, so high did we pile it. When I go, I want it to be like that.

Lupus found me later that evening, sitting as near as I could to the blistering heat. He didn't lay a hand on my shoulder, or take my arm, or any of the things men did in sorrow, but there was a catch in his voice when he spoke. 'We'll miss him.'

'Yes.'

'He'll need to be replaced. Him and all the others. There are barely enough men left of the Twelfth to make three centuries. We discussed this in the commanders' meeting all day and we have a dilemma: we could put the bulk of your number into the first cohort, but then only two or three of you would be centurions when there are at least fifteen who are fit. Alternatively, we could spread you throughout the legion, with those fifteen each leading their own centuries. But that would mean that you would all be serving alongside new men.'

He was watching me, waiting for some reaction. I was watching the hot, red heart of Syrion's pyre, and not thinking at all of what might be ahead, only what was behind.

Dully, I said, 'Will we have new recruits? Or men seconded from other legions?'

'Some of each. Corbulo gave a number of relevant orders before we parted and this was among them: one third new conscripts; two thirds from other legions.'

'Two thirds?' That jerked me into the present. 'But they'll hate us,' I said. 'The men from the other legions. Nobody will volunteer to come to a legion that's just surrendered to Parthia and walked its Eagle under the yoke. They'll come to us as punishment from legions that want to be rid of them and they'll loathe the ground we walk on.'

Lupus stared into the fire. He ran his tongue over his teeth, found a gap, explored it. 'Syrion did well to leave when he did,' he said quietly. He turned back to me, 'Building the Twelfth again will be a nightmare that will make the past six months seem joyous in retrospect. But the only alternative is to let it die: to destroy the Eagle and join other legions where each of us will be one man amongst thousands and despised for ever. I will not let this happen. I will build this legion back up man by man with my own bare hands if I have to, but I would like to believe that I will have help.' He raised his brow in a way that was so familiar, so real, so raw, I could have wept. 'Knowing what we face, Demalion, will you help me? Will you be the core of the new sixth cohort? Or would you rather we took all the veterans into the first, and let the new men fill the rest?'

It was kind of him to ask, but I was bone weary in mind and soul as much as in body; too tired to think, too tired to make decisions that might mould my fate for the rest of my life. Other men made decisions and I acted on them; that was how my life ran. I had no wish to change it here and now.

Then, I said, 'The sixth is our home.' Which was true.

Lupus nodded. 'That's what I told Cadus and Crescens. The sixth is your home and you should remain there. I have proposed that Tears become the signaller; it's time he grew into himself. Horgias, of course, should bear the standard, although that will not stop him scouting when we have need of it. Each of them will need a new shield-man, but that can be arranged.'

He was watching me again, waiting for something, and I had nothing to give. For a fleeting moment, I had thought I was about to be given the standard of the sixth as mine to carry, and felt a stab of disappointment even as I rejoiced at Horgias' good fortune. But I felt nothing cleanly, or with any power: too many men had died, and too few were left to care who held the god's hand above their heads.

I felt Lupus' gaze resting on me, steadily. I saluted,

stone-faced. 'Tears shall have the horn tonight,' I said. 'Unless you would prefer it sooner?'

His mouth twitched towards a smile and I thought perhaps I had been overly wooden. And he could fuck himself, frankly, because I didn't care what he thought any more.

He was still smiling. I turned on my heel, ready to leave the fire and walk back to our cheerless, half-empty barracks.

Lupus stepped in front, blocking me. 'Tonight will be perfectly adequate,' he said. 'And if you present yourself to the quartermaster immediately thereafter, you can requisition a staff. Usually, we would have a new one made for you, but under the circumstances . . .' His voice drifted off.

I stared at him. 'What staff?'

'The vinewood staff of your new office. Did you think Tears and Horgias would vault over you so easily? You who broke the bridge across the river in the face of the Parthian archers?'

I hated that bridge. I dreamed of it nightly. 'I should have left it where it was,' I said stiffly. 'Then we wouldn't have had to lose a day rebuilding it.'

'Even so . . .' Lupus waited with the patience of a parent until I joined the facts to make a whole. Centurions held vine staffs. Only centurions. And they outranked both signallers and standard-bearers.

'I am to be centurion?' I asked, at last. 'Of what? Of whom?'

'The first century of the sixth cohort of the Twelfth legion. Of course, you should have held the standard for some time before it, to know what it is to have the entire cohort move to your signal, but that can't be helped. You'll have to work doubly hard to keep control of the men who join you, for all the reasons we have already discussed, but I'm sure that, given the right leadership, they can be knocked into shape. And when they have been, the Twelfth will be whole again. Not what it was, but whole.'

'What about you?' I was near to panic, who had not felt it at all in the face of the Parthians. 'Where will you be?'

'On Corbulo's orders, I will be camp prefect.'

Camp prefect. A station a man could hold until he was in his seventh decade, could he but hold his head high and his shield straight. Lupus had wanted that post all his legionary life and now, having got it, he spoke the words as if they were poison in his mouth.

Still, it was his, and if he was prefect, then someone else was not. 'What of Cadus?' I asked.

'After this year's campaigns against the Parthian light and heavy horse, General Corbulo reached the conclusion that each legion needs more cavalry of its own. Cadus is to be legate of a cavalry wing, in command of six hundred horse, plus whatever auxiliaries we can muster at any given time.'

I smiled at that, for the first time in months. 'He'll be good at that,' I said. 'In Hyrcania, he showed himself a natural horseman. And the Parthians taught us much of how they can be used in warfare.'

Lupus inclined his head. 'That had been noted. Although he would have been an excellent camp prefect.'

He laid a hand on my arm, which was as shocking as anything else. 'I know you'll miss him, but this is the best we could do under the circumstances. I hoped you'd understand.'

I did understand. I understood that good men were dead, and that I was not one of them. I understood that I had just gained a promotion I had once not wanted and later had not dared to hope for. I understood that the years ahead might well be a hell of our own making, and that I had just agreed to do everything I could to rebuild the XIIth.

When Lupus left me and Tears came to take his place, I understood, in a wave of feeling, that I had Tears, too, and he was to stay at my side.

But, new soldier that I was, I understood at last what Cadus had been trying to tell me all along: that life and love and rank were not enough. To be whole in myself, I needed honour, and I had lost it, and could see no way to get it back.

Beth Horon, Judaea, November, AD 66

In the Reign of the Emperor Nero

Chapter Twenty-Three

Four shameful years passed before the gods and a rabble of Hebrew revolutionaries granted us the chance to win our honour back.

In that time, exactly as Lupus had said, the XIIth was made up to strength by a mixture of conscripts and postings from other legions, with a small handful of young men who had actually volunteered. These last, oddly, were the hardest to handle, having dreamed of martial valour all their young lives and then found themselves in a legion that was universally despised.

That didn't make the rest easy. The bulk of our new intake were veterans of over ten years' standing culled from the VIth, VIIth and Xth legions. Greeks, Syrians and Germans for the most part, they were big men who bore big grudges and knew they had been sent to us only because their former legions wanted to be rid of them.

Every man of them had come to us loathing the XIIth

for its reputation and four years in camp being reminded daily of our shame had soured them to a gut-blackening hatred. I kept control because I used my vine rod hard and early on the most obvious troublemakers, because I flogged men for the least infringement of an order and twice had men tied to cartwheels and left outside the gates for two days and two nights.

I found in myself a level of brutality I had not dreamed of, and was not proud of, but even so, every marched step was taken grudgingly, every salute was wooden, with a perfect blankness in the eyes that hid the hate we all knew was there. I could drill them to a mechanical perfection, but it felt as if I pushed each man with my mind, and it was as exhausting as anything I had ever done.

They were united in their loathing of us, so that by the end of the first year we had two legions: the new men who made friendships amongst themselves, and we who were the veterans, to whom they never spoke a word unless they must.

Tears and Horgias had the worst time of it, for each of them had been allocated one of the new intake as his shield-man and didn't know from moment to moment if he was going to be shielded or stabbed in the gut.

Horgias was paired with a bull of a man, rightly named Taurus; a volunteer from Herculaneum with skills as an engineer who had been sent to us as his first posting and who, I thought, might one day become another Proclion if he could only get over his sullen ill temper. Tears was likewise protected, if that's the word for it, by Macer, a hard-bitten Athenian who had been sent to us from the

VIIth and resented every breath taken in the company of the XIIth.

For four years we drilled, and made mock battles against the IVth, and those of us who remembered the XIIth as it had been prayed nightly that we might see some real action, enough to weld us into a fighting unit, if not to forge the bonds of friendship that might make us something stronger.

Our chance came in the thirteenth year of the Emperor Nero's reign. By then, Corbulo had crossed the Euphrates and back, done battle with Vologases and forced the King of Kings to a truce that seemed likely to hold.

By now, the general's standing had risen so high in the east that if he had marched to Caesarea and declared himself emperor, every legion under his command would have followed him to the gates of Rome to unseat Nero and place their hero on the throne. Knowing this, Nero recalled Corbulo to Greece and sent Gaius Cestius Gallus to take his place as governor of Syria and general of the Syrian legions.

When I tell you that Gallus was a senate-climber cast from the same mould as Caesennius Paetus, you will know how hard it fell on the veterans of the XIIth who had fought at Rhandaea, but we suffered his generalship believing that it was transient and he could do us little harm.

And then a band of Hebrew rebels broke into an armoury in the desert south of Jerusalem, armed themselves and took the city, crushing the garrison that had kept order there for as long as anyone could remember. Overnight, our entire world was ablaze with insurrection.

By all accounts, the Hebrew king had abandoned his people at the first hint of violence. Certainly he arrived with us in Antioch barely behind the news, bringing with him a train of family and retainers all of them bearing tales of men armed with Roman weapons and fighting in Roman style; of a mint where men struck Hebrew coins swearing they would never be paid in taxes to Rome; of a god which threw off Roman gods, and would not acknowledge Caesar as its superior.

Cestius Gallus was no soldier, but faced with that kind of provocation he had no choice other than to hurl the legions at the Hebrews like a bolt, sending us in hard and fast before winter ended the fighting season and rendered a positive outcome impossible.

We saw our chance; how could we not? The governor had to choose between the IVth and the XIIth to spearhead his attack and even the most hardened naysayers amongst our men believed that we were the better legion. Overnight, men walked with more life in their step than I had seen in four fighting seasons. They began to mend things without being told. They lined up on parade with a crispness I had come to believe was impossible. They didn't smile, they didn't hate us any less, but by heaven they wanted to fight.

But then so did the men of the IVth, who had the same difficulties and as much to prove: they, after all, had not even attempted to hold Lizard Pass.

As camp prefect, Lupus held our future in his hands;

to him fell the job of persuading a weak man that we were his strength. There's a rumour that he knelt before Gallus, begging that we be allowed to march against the new enemy. Nobody believes that, but whatever he did, it worked: we were given our wish.

Three cohorts each from the IVth and the VIth accompanied us, with substantial numbers of allied foot and horse, so that forty thousand men marched out of Antioch in the end. But we of the XIIth, made up to full strength, trained to battle fitness and straining to be let off the leash – we were the only legion to march whole, entire, intact from Syria into Judaea to put down the Hebrew revolution.

In the beginning was no honour. From Zebulon in Galilee to Joppa in Judaea, we picked off the cities as we came to them, without ever having to resort to the siege towers and catapults, the sapper's kit and the ram that the mules pulled behind us every day.

We went in hoping for a battle and we came out disappointed. We lost two men of the second cohort to falling masonry in a city we demolished and one of the fourth to an unlucky slingshot when he removed his helmet in the heat of battle, but other than that we faced no more resistance than the pitiful defences of old men and women, for the young men had all run to the mountains, or so we were told by those few whose lives we spared.

They lied, although we only discovered that later: in truth, the young men had all gone to Jerusalem to swell the ranks of the Hebrew rebellion.

I don't think it would have made any difference had we known that. We marched twenty, thirty, forty miles a day, crushing the countryside and all who lived there in an orgy of devastation that left us sour-mouthed and irritable.

When, finally, there was nothing left to burn, we turned towards Jerusalem, taking the narrow, difficult pass they call Beth Horon that cuts from west to east through the mountain ranges north of the city and was said by our guides to be the most direct route. If we baulked at its difficulties, they assured us we could expect to spend ten days or more in detours to reach the same end, by which time, most assuredly, the winter rains would be upon us.

Like every other Hebrew who claimed to help us, they lied, but we didn't find that out until a long while later, either. At the time, our main concern was to find a means by which forty thousand men, their weapons, fodder, food, wagons and siege engines might pass through Beth Horon.

The local guides said that a lightly armoured man could run through from the western entrance to the eastern mouth of the godforsaken pass in a morning. Horgias and Tears came back after trying it and said that a fully armoured legionary could, indeed, do it at a fast march in half a day, but that there were places where the path wound along the lee of the mountain and was barely wide enough for an ox cart.

They said it would take us a full two days to cross; three or four if we took the ballistas, catapults and siege towers we had brought with us, for they must be dismantled and loaded on to carts. The ram, they thought, was impossible to take.

We didn't have three or four days to lose, not when Horgias had already killed two Hebrew scouts and they were only the ones he had seen; we all knew there were others and none of us wanted to come out of a nightmare of a pass to be met by a Hebrew rabble that had already annihilated the Jerusalem garrison.

After some discussion, we left the bulk of the siege engines at the wide westerly mouth of the pass, guarded by three cohorts of the IVth legion who had orders to wait three days and then begin to dismantle them, ready to move them across in stages if we needed them.

We took with us three light ballistas that fired stone shot the size of my head or smaller, half a dozen catapults with enough bolts for three days' shooting, and one siege tower that took us half a day to dismantle into numbered pieces and load on to the mule carts.

Two hateful days later, we emerged into the flat, open eastern end of the pass that the Hebrews called Gabao. It lies a bare eight miles north of Jerusalem in a natural bottleneck with forested mountains rearing up on either side, and the nightmare of a pass behind. Battles have been fought there for hundreds of generations and the men kept finding the debris of dead men's armour as they dug the latrines: a dented shield boss; a spear head; a clutter of arrowheads left where they fell and never shot, with the shadows of the shafts dark in the sand.

It was a perfect place to hold against a threatening army and we dug in there, building a full legionary marching camp with ditches and spiked redoubts and guarded gates at each quarter. With the mountain slopes rising high on either side and the sky unblemished blue above, it was almost as beautiful as Melitene, and ten times as deadly.

We doubled the watch and slept with our weapons naked by our beds and were glad not to have used them yet.

We woke to a fine, crisp autumn morning, not yet beset by winter rain, where the cook-fires sparked readily on dry tinder and the air rang to the bleat of goats herded in the near distance.

I was standing just outside my tent, fastening a new silvered buckle on my belt, when Horgias found me.

'Listen!' He jerked his chin to the south. 'What do you hear?'

I heard little that I hadn't heard all morning: the goats, of course, and beyond them the low grumble of armed men making ready for the battle we knew must soon be on us. Swooping birdsong wove through it all, fine as spun silver, snaring my attention.

But Horgias was never wrong, and if I let go of the light, high birds I thought I heard something else beneath and behind them, and then was sure of it: a deep wall of sound like the grinding of mountains across the earth. I wouldn't have heard it had he not spoken, but it was definitely there.

'Horses?' I asked, and when he nodded, 'How many?'

He looked round to see who was listening. Taurus was within earshot, and Macer, Tears' shield-man. Neither of them loved us, but both were ready for a fight.

Loudly enough for them to hear, Horgias said, 'Ten thousand? Maybe more. It takes a lot of cavalry to make that kind of noise.'

Tears sat on a log closer than either of the others, rubbing tallow into the straps of his shield. 'They can't be from Jerusalem,' he said. 'It's their Sabbath. They never fight on the Sabbath. Their god forbids it.'

We had men with us, first-born sons of the elders of Sepphoris in Galilee, who had come with us as hostages to their fathers' good behaviour. They counted the days in sevens and refused to do anything but eat and pray on one day in the cycle. They had told us all other Hebrews were the same and we had believed them.

'Maybe their god's given them special dispensation,' I said.

'Or maybe they've abandoned that god for one that allows battle any day they like.' Tears propped his shield near the fire where the tallow could warm its way into the leather and rose to grip my arm. 'Either way, I think we might have a battle on our hands.'

An actual battle. At last.

Around me, men were stirring with a new fire. I saw smiles, none of them directed at me. Then I looked at Tears and saw a look on his face of the kind I hadn't seen in four years.

'Someone had better tell Lupus,' I said, and Horgias bounded off, leaving the rest of us to prepare.

'It'll be a good fight.' Tears let go of my arm, but the prints of his fingers stayed, like living ghosts.

'It had better be.' I was grinning like a fool. I clasped

his shoulders in return. 'The men will mutiny soon if it isn't.'

Dipping into my tent, I caught up my shield, my helm with its red plume set crosswise, my neck chain with the rings I had won in the siege at Tigranocerta a lifetime ago, when I was a different man.

Normally, I had to shout simply to catch a man's attention. Here, now, the eyes of five hundred men followed every step I took and every man among them had surged to his feet before I turned back to shout the order.

'Get yourselves dressed! We have a battle to fight!'

They moved fast as mice in a corn spill, and not only my cohort. Around us, other centurions took up the cry and soon the whole camp was arming.

All around, I saw tight battle-grins on the faces of men who had spent four years barely managing not to spit when I passed. They were not my friends yet, but they were not the enemies they had been the day before.

Horgias returned, bearing the cohort standard of the open hand with the double thunderbolts beneath it, and the mule's tail hanging free. He wore a wolfskin, not the muleskin, for that had been Syrion's and had gone on to his pyre. The gape-mouthed wolf suited Horgias better: he had the same wildness in his eyes, the same white teeth to flash at the enemy.

Now, he held out his own hand, palm up. I laid mine on it, and Tears laid his atop both. 'Come out alive,' I said, and felt the pulse of each, above and below, and believed it a promise of the gods.

For the first time in four years, the cohort lined up

behind us without my asking. Not a man was out of place. Most of them didn't love their legion yet, but they were determined to march disciplined to war.

Like this, in tight order, we marched forward to take our place in the right hand side of the rearmost rank battle lines; the place of honour, where we would take most pressure, and must not yield.

We had a steep, treeless slope to our right, and two lines of men before. Behind was nothing but the ditches and spiked earthworks of our marching camp, and, a long, long way back, three cohorts of the IVth who held all our heavy artillery and had no idea what we were doing.

Chapter Twenty-Four

The sun was in our faces, not quite low enough to be difficult. In front, the Hebrew army was a ripe pestilence spread across the perfect land ahead of us; rank upon ragged rank of men marching in no particular order.

Some wore mail and helmets, some bore shields and swords and spears exactly as if they were just another legion, but the bulk of them were barely armoured, and bore the long-hafted spears of the sort whose heads littered the dry soil of Gabao, and short shields, and arrows with piebald fletchings. They looked like no army I had ever seen, and even at this distance, with more than an arrow's flight between us, they howled with a hatred we had not yet met in Judaea.

A proper fight. My hands were wet with sweat. I flexed my fingers on the grip of my shield and was glad of the soft leather there and the moss padded tight underneath it. My gladius was in my hand and I didn't know I'd drawn it.

To my left, I saw Tears wet his lips and raise the horn, ready to sound the advance. But not yet. We were the third rank and for now we had to stand firm, hold our place and watch the lines in front of us step forward into battle. Which they did, shouting.

The two sides met in a clamour of flesh and blood and armour. Men screamed in pain and fury. Horns brayed commands, sweeping great blocks of fighting men left or right or forward, to hold a line or pull it back.

Legion, cohort and century banners dipped and swayed, sending out orders that stitched together those parts of the lines where the din was too loud for the horns to be heard, and in the thick of it men died, and their killers were killed, and those killers died in their turn, some swiftly, spraying blood from wide wounds, some more slowly, of crueller strokes. Some lost their balance and died underfoot, which is the worst way to go in this kind of fight, lying in the dark, clawing for breath, seeing the nails come at your face.

Our men fought well. Even the second and fourth cohorts, which had been ranged in a thin line in front of the main battle ranks, had thrown themselves at the foe with a fervour I wouldn't have believed they owned, so that the first clash of men and iron had sent the carrion crows crying into the air, flapping raggedly off to less dangerous shelter in the trees that ranged the pass, there to await the evening's bounty of dead and dying men.

From the first clash of shields, the Hebrews came at

us with a screaming mania that was both more and less than battle-madness: more, because not one of them cared whether he lived or died; less, because not one of them truly knew how to link his shield with his neighbours' to make the sum of their line greater than its parts.

Even so, I watched them tear our front rank apart, shoving the valiant youths of the second and fourth back into the spaces made for them in the row behind. I saw the second rank, the first, third and fifth cohorts, take them in and step forward in a solid line, saw that line waver and hold and step forward again, but it was hard going, as if they pushed against the gods themselves.

I saw the signals sent and acted on, saw the enemy rally and reverse each gain we'd made, and through it all I knelt on one knee on the valley floor, gouging my shield into the dirt, biting my lip, reminding myself to breathe, to blink, to swill a mouthful of tepid water every thousand heartbeats, and above all to keep my gaze fixed on Lupus' standard so that I might see the moment when it sent us into action.

Now! And now! And now! But not now. A caught breath and a half-rise, and each time the crossed thunderbolts dipped left or right once or twice but never thrice and I must subside, dry of mouth and clenched of sphincter, to breathe again and drink again and wait.

The first two lines were spent. Even the good men of the first cohort who had stood directly in front of us at the start were tiring under the onslaught, but I could not move to help them for I had not Lupus' view of the action and could not see the whole field, only the small square in front of me, where the Hebrews had massed for a new attack, had formed themselves into a block, just as we would have done, and were charging now at the line of men who stood twenty paces in front of me, like bulls at a wall.

The line of shields wavered under the impact; men who had survived Raphana and the Parthian cataphracts fell now, screaming, and were lost.

'*Hold* that line!' Half rising, I shouted into a sound so thick that mere words bounced off it.

But the god heard me; from far to my left where Lupus held his stance, a flag dipped and rose three times. The high pipe of the cornet soared over it. Beside me, Tears reached for his own horn and bent his head to the mouthpiece. I let go the breath I had been holding, and sent out the words that had been crowding my teeth since the battle's start.

'*On your feet! Shields up! Third rank forward on my step!*'

The roar ripped my throat; I had no idea I could shout that loud. The wave of it tore across the body of the sixth cohort. My cohort. Mine to lead into true battle, to bring to victory, to wash clean of shame.

Horgias dipped and raised our standard. Tears took my words and wove them into brazen notes. A rising trip of three higher tones stripped away our fear and flung us into battle.

We surged forward, shields welded at the edges, swords spitting between; we were a storm wave sent at a shore. Four years of waiting went into those steps.

Nothing could have stood against us. In the first moments, nothing did.

As the bronze music shimmered overhead, I opened my mouth and found a new sound coming out, deeper than before, louder, and matched by Tears and Horgias. And like this, roaring the songs of our hearts, we crashed our shields into the enemy and our battle began.

But the Hebrews had brought new weapons against us. A lead slingshot skimmed past my cheek, drawing blood. Others slammed into my shield. I saw the first flash of spears and had time to shout 'Shields up!' and every second man stepped back from the line and swung his shield over his own head and that of his neighbour to the right.

They did it smoothly, free of the sullen rigidity of the past. To my left, Tears kept his horn ready and Macer the Mournful matched him step for step with his shield held high protecting them both, so that I knew that Tears was safe with him, at least for this fight.

To my right, Horgias looked past a screaming Taurus and caught my eye and grinned and lifted the standard higher just as the hard rain of spears pattered to silence. I had time to call 'Drop shields! Forward!' before the Hebrews were on us.

I took a running step to stab at a black-headed, rot-mouthed Hebrew who was striking at Taurus. Taurus, in turn, killed the man who was striking at Horgias. I struck down a prodding spear with my shield and sent my gladius spiking up at the eyes of the one who had sent it. He jerked back. I left him and let the strike skid sideways into another face, barely seen, just eyes that flared white and black — and then red, and closed and falling.

Another took his place, and then another and another and the part of me that was not simply fighting to stay alive was in awe of their ferocity, and not surprised any more that Lupus had held us back so long.

I batted down a spear with my gladius, stepped into the gap it left and, as no neighbouring shield came to block my way, stabbed in high, overhand, into the bared neck of the man in front of me. He fell, drowning in his own blood. I kicked him down, crushed his skull under my foot – no thought now for the horror of that death – sensed a space on either side of me, and stepped forward again, forcing the gap, and felt the wind of a slingshot where I had been, and then another so close that it grazed my cheekbone, and – I ducked – another.

Three, from the right, high. I looked up. 'They're flanking us. Slingers with lead shot high and right. Fourth, fifth, and sixth centuries wheel right! Form testudo! Forward!'

The three named centuries were moving almost before Tears got the signals out, making the square, with the outer men holding their shields around us and those on the inside raising theirs to make the shell of the tortoise, advancing up the rise at the slingers, who stopped using me for target practice and instead tried to kill the men behind the shields.

They failed.

We killed a dozen at the front, and saw the rest break and run back to form a ragged line a hundred long strung between one rocky bluff and another with bare mountain behind.

From somewhere in the block of men behind me, Taurus said, 'We can take them.'

'No.' I shook my head and my cross-wise plume multiplied the movement. 'It's a trap. See how they're looking behind them? Someone else is waiting behind those rocks.'

I watched a moment longer, studying the terrain and the scuffed earth beyond the bluffs, and then, more softly, said, 'Tears, signal to Lupus. Ask for cavalry.'

We had cavalry . . . by heaven, did we have cavalry.

When the Hebrews had fallen into revolt, petty kings all over Judaea suddenly found they had a need to show their loyalty to Rome. We had two thousand light horse from Antiochus Epiphanes alone, and a thousand more from Agrippa, the deposed king of Judaea, whose rank cowardice in abandoning his city had started the whole messy war. All of them were led by Cadus, who bore his command as if born to it.

Tears sounded a spray of notes that were not for our men. I couldn't see Lupus – the lines were too crushed and close for that now – but soon his signaller called out the fast, tripping beat that summoned our cavalry to action.

I heard the horses but did not see them, for just then the press of Hebrews in front was rallied by their commanders and for a few moments we were fighting for our lives, locked in the sweat-rimed embrace of battle, where each small fight mattered only to the men engaged in it, who had no sense of the greater whole.

I parried, I hacked, I grunted, I dodged, I thrust my shield forward and killed the man in front of me with a stab to the groin and a second to the neck and found a moment's respite when no one stepped in to take his place – and looked up to see if Cadus had cleared the open slopes above us.

To our right and coming closer, I saw his pennant cleave the harsh blue sky: a red pennant with the crossed thunderbolts of the XIIth in the centre and below them his personal mark of the white horse.

He had his men held in a solid line, sweeping across the fall of the slope. Spears flashed silver and red through the dust they made. Men fell before them and did not rise again after they had gone. The slope ran to mud-slurry with blood and urine and the soft parts of entrails that leaked out into the autumn dust. The churning wind brought us the iron-sweet scent of blood, and the sharper smells of death. That same wind carried a flicker of blue, a shade deeper than the sky, with—

'*Demalion!*'

Tears' voice. A blade coming at my face. I threw my shield up, put my shoulder behind it, heaved forward, and felt face bones crack on the boss. I thrust my blade in on instinct and felt it skitter off armour, and then bite in skin and flesh. A man screamed and the pressure on my shield grew less. I looked around it, saw a helmet, falling, and kicked the flat of my foot at where the face must be . . . and all the time my head kept trying to turn to the side, to look up the slope at the flicker of blue I had seen that was not the sky.

At the next chance, I looked back, and that was when I saw it – the blue tern against a white ground that had haunted my dreams since my days in Hyrcania.

Shock held me still and only Tears' fast action saved me. But then he saw what I had seen: that the peril was far greater than we had thought, for Cadus was fighting cataphracts. Here, eight miles north of Jerusalem. *Cataphracts!* Led by Monobasus of Adiabene. I threw back my head and yelled over the havoc.

'Horgias! Monobasus is here! Adiabene has sided with the Hebrews!'

The cry ran through the ranks like fire through straw. 'Monobasus! Adiabene! He's brought his heavy cavalry!'

The news spread like floodwater and reached Lupus faster than if we had signalled it. As my cry died away, we heard the blare of his horn and, acting on each signal as puppets to a master's pull, found ourselves faced about, with new centuries taking our place on the battle's front, so that we might lock shields and advance against the new-old enemy, filling the gap in Cadus' left flank, letting him move out and round, higher up the hill, to come down on them from above, which is what cavalry does best.

The horn guided us uphill and right to a place Lupus must have scouted out beforehand, where we found ourselves formed into a wedge.

Alexander used this formation in his battles, only his wedges were of cavalry. We were foot men, and I was at the apex, with five hundred men behind me, ready to widen any gap I could force with my shield and my body. This is one reason why centurions die more readily and in greater numbers than any other men on the battlefield: they lead the wedges.

I felt a flash of terror so fast, so fierce, so overwhelming that it was indistinguishable from joy. My body thrilled to it and drank it in, even as I knew that death waited for me in a dozen paces.

'*Charge!*'

The horn blared it, but I had shouted before the notes came, so clear was our moment of chance. Sunlight flashed on weapons and armour all around, blinding me to everything but the flash of a blue banner in the centre of the cavalry block, and the black horse that bore it and the fox-faced rider to its left, leaner than I remembered, but swinging his sword with the same savage carelessness, laughing as we came at him.

And then not laughing, as our javelins flew; we who had held them until the last, which was now. And not laughing as his horse stumbled, hit in the one place where it was vulnerable, on the loins, where no armour hung; we knew that, who had fought him before.

And not laughing at all, but shouting for order, trying to hold his men in line, as we ploughed on through their lines, and I did not die but let the force of the men behind me push me on, crushing on to horseflesh and manflesh alike, breaking bones and toppling riders by the sheer force of the wedge.

And then that force withered and we were left trying to re-form a battle line in the midst of an enemy whose own line was fractured beyond repair.

By the gods' will, I found myself still alive, and

fighting opposite the blue-bannered king who led his men in battle.

The air was drenched with horse-sweat, thick with blood and fear, and fury. I saw a black hide and stabbed at it, twisted and pulled free; I saw a flash of a pale unarmoured wrist, and stabbed for that, and felt the blade turned aside, and felt a hand grasp at my wrist, pulling me forward, and a gap where Tears was not with me. I saw a wall of horseflesh, rising, and iron within it, falling, and was spinning, trying to find my balance, when something more silver than iron was in the way, and I heard a horse's feet hit solid bull's hide and saw the blue tern banner of Adiabene fall at my feet, and the dead king beside it.

And then Tears was there, sliding in to my side, and I was safe in the shelter of his shield, with Macer to his left and Horgias and Taurus on my right with the silver of our standard between them, blistering in the sun.

Our shields made a new line and we took the long steps of a forward wall and heard-felt the smack of the bosses on armour.

I heard the enemy try to rally, but without their commander they failed, and within ten paces they were backing their horses away from us, step by bloody step, and I had time to pause and look to my left and found Macer grinning at me – grinning! – holding a stolen Parthian shield with silver worked thick on the boss and edges. So he was the one who had saved me, not Tears or Horgias.

'All right?' He hefted the shield, as if pleased with its weight.

I had flogged him five times with my own hand and tied him to the cartwheel for two nights as one of the worst thorns in my side. And he had saved my life in battle.

'All right,' I said, and smiled back.

We came to a halt at the edge of the bluff. With the retreat of Monobasus' cataphracts, the line of Hebrews facing us had fallen back and Lupus was not fool enough to send us after them. In the valley beyond us the Hebrews were retreating, as if their cavalry's defeat had knocked the fight out of them.

I signalled Tears to halt our men and we stopped where we stood while the slaves ran from the supply lines with water.

My arms were shaking. My whole body, in fact, was shuddering like a horse at the end of a race. My shoulders felt bruised; my knuckles bled where I had smashed my shield boss too often and too hard. My bladder was full and my bowels loose, and I wanted more than anything to find the blue banner that had fallen near the place where Macer had saved my life.

Horgias was there before me, standing over the still-warm body of the black horse. Its rider lay on his back, his eyes wide open. His armour was silvered, with gems on his gloves. His eyes were black. His face was fox-like, but a young fox. Horgias had kicked off his helmet. His hair shone sleek in the noonday sun – and it was red.

I said, 'Monobasus had black hair. Black going grey. It's not him.' I tilted the face back with my foot and we both looked down at a man younger than either of us.

Horgias said nothing. I didn't push him. Taurus stood nearby, watching with a new closeness.

Tears came to join us. He had a ragged cut on his cheek just below one eye. He saw me looking and shook his head. 'Later.' He nodded over to Horgias. 'He killed Monobasus. You took the horse, but Horgias took the rider.'

'It isn't Monobasus,' Horgias said woodenly.

'His son, then?' Tears said.

'Does he have sons?' Taurus asked.

'Bound to have,' I said. 'The way they are in Adiabene, he probably has half a village of sons sired on a dozen different women.'

A slave passed with a crate of water skins. Grabbing one, I tipped my head back and tipped half the contents down my throat and over my face.

'Well, anyway,' Taurus said, 'they're going. We beat them.'

I was halfway to agreeing with him when a scurry of wind caught my ear, and what I heard within it made me cough up the water. 'No . . . listen.' I held up my hand. 'Someone's still fighting.'

I turned, seeking the uncertain breeze, and heard again the sounds it carried so very faintly down the long pass from its western end half a day's march away, where three cohorts of the IVth held the rear guard.

Tears said, 'Is that smoke?'

It was: a sudden black belch billowing to the sky. I swung round. 'Tears, signal Lupus that the Fourth legion is under attack. Tell him we're going to their aid.'

Four notes, then three, then two, rising, and with

them our standard swung back and forth towards the valley's other end. And on that, we of the sixth cohort of the XIIth re-formed, grabbed what water we could and, taking a collective breath, threw ourselves into the open mouth of the Beth Horon pass, leaving our allies behind to keep the pass closed against rabid men who might regroup for a second attack.

Chapter Twenty-Five

The Hebrews didn't attack our front lines a second time, but many thousands of them had evidently used the original assault as a cover and, marching through supposedly impassable mountains to the far end of the pass, had laid waste to the three cohorts of the IVth who had not only been keeping our backs safe, but had been guarding the giant siege engines we had left behind.

The guides had been right when they told us that a lightly armoured man could run the length of the pass in a morning. Still fired by the fury of battle, we of the sixth cohort pushed ourselves to our limits and, having left before noon, arrived at the far end in time to see the winter sun layer itself along the western horizon.

We were too late, of course.

The battle, such as it had been, was over. The IVth was destroyed, not a man left standing. Worse, the siege engines and artillery had been either stolen or – those pieces that were too big to remove – broken up and piled together and set alight in a fire of such monstrous proportions that nobody could approach closer than thirty paces of it without blistering their skin. Dead men's armour melted on the bodies nearby, oozing like candle wax in the heat. Even as we watched, parts of our siege towers collapsed in on themselves with a crash and we had to spring back out of the way of the new, flatter flames.

The Hebrews were long gone. Setting light to the fire had been their parting shot, and even that had been done by men with fast horses. Horgias found their prints or we wouldn't have known of them at all, but there was no dust cloud to show where they had gone.

I sent men off to track the enemy, hoping to find some stragglers, while the bulk of us stayed where we were, to put out the fire and assess the damage.

In the first of these, we failed soundly. Hot as a furnace, it would have taken a lake full of water and ten units of Rome's fire brigade with piston-pumps even to stand a chance of quenching the blaze and we had no more water than the skins we carried with us. Not wishing to waste it on the fire, we found a store wagon that had not been destroyed and took thirty shovels and used them to throw earth on to the blaze, but we might as well have spat at the sun.

There was nothing to do but watch, and curse and count our losses.

On that account, I sent Tears to number the dead men of the IVth while Taurus and his engineers set to work calculating how many of the siege engines fed the flames, and therefore how many had been stolen to be used against us.

Taurus came back first. He was soot-stained, and there were blisters on the backs of his hands. His gaze was haggard, but not, now, with the shame of our legion but at the horror of what he was seeing: engineers can take the destruction of their equipment harder than they do the deaths around them.

He saluted, a thing I had never seen him do unprompted. 'Report, if you're willing to hear it?'

I found my face becoming smooth, as Lupus' did, not to smile at his new enthusiasm. 'I'm ready. Thank you.'

He ticked them off on his fingers, working from memory, and it was as if he detailed the deaths of his sons.

'Four out of five siege towers have been burned – the fifth, you'll remember, we took with us through the pass. So they have no siege towers, which is a blessing. Of the forty-four catapults we left, thirty have gone, plus all their bolts. The remaining fourteen are burning. Of the seven ballistas, the six smallest have been taken and the carts that carried their shot have gone with them.'

He paused to look at me, to see if I grieved as he did. I closed my eyes and tried to imagine the havoc that an army inside a city could wreak on its besiegers with that kind of equipment. The catapults shot spears the length of a man, and caused devastation when loosed into crowded cities. I could only imagine the horror they might wreak on a massed assaulting army.

The ballistas were no better. They shot graded stones from the size of a man's head up to the size of a balled tent bag; one volley could kill a dozen men if they were closely grouped, and injure as many more so that they soaked up the medical resources and reduced the morale of the troops. Nothing makes men nervous like the sight of their fellows with their limbs crushed to matchwood.

I opened my eyes. Taurus was watching me closely. 'What of the Son of Zeus?' I asked.

Son of Zeus was the largest of the ballistas, a wall-breaking monster that shot stones that had the height of a man as their diameter.

'They didn't move it,' Taurus said. 'It was too big.'

I smiled at that. 'Well, at least we still have that. If we can get it through the pass, then—' I caught sight of his face. 'What?'

'They broke the lever arm and cut the strings. It'll take days to make it fit for use.'

'We haven't got days. We've got about one night before they get home and work out how to use the things they've taken.' I bit my lip. 'What of the battering ram?'

'The ram is at the heart of the fire,' Taurus said miserably. 'The rack's more or less intact, but there are no trees near here anywhere close to the size of the one we've lost.'

The ram had been a thing of strange, unwieldy beauty. The oak tree that formed the ram itself was the length of three men, one atop the other, and as wide as all three tied together about the waist. The cradle built to carry it had consumed fourteen trees. The armoured rack from which it was suspended to give protection to the men as they approached a gate was drawn by a team of twenty oxen.

The oxen, I had already seen, had not been driven away. Some things simply move too slowly. By this stage, I was only grateful that they had not all been slaughtered, and wondered why.

I must have spoken aloud without meaning to, for Horgias, who had just come back from tracking up in the hills, answered me.

'If our oxen are still alive, we have to feed and water them and they slow us down. If they'd killed them, there'd be rotting meat here at the end of the pass through half the winter. The first Hebrews came down that way.' He pointed up to the steep, forested hillside at the south of the pass. 'But half of them cut across the pass at the place where it narrows halfway down so they could come in from both sides and behind. A third arm came at them from the west.'

'The Fourth was surrounded,' I said.

'Completely.'

Tears joined us then, with news that there were no wounded, ours or the enemy's. 'The Hebrews cut the throats of the fallen before they left,' he said. 'And there's a group of ten centurions at the far side who have been beheaded. Not very cleanly.'

'Gods.' I rubbed my hands into my face, kneading my cheeks. 'I suppose we should count ourselves lucky they weren't crucified. Everything else they've done is Roman.' I looked at Horgias. 'How many Hebrews did this?'

He took off his helmet and ran his hands through his sweat-sodden hair. 'Twenty thousand,' he said. 'At least. And if you allow that there were another ten, maybe fifteen keeping us busy at the other end, that's a lot of armed men.'

'Too many.' I kicked at a flaring lump of wood that had fallen from the fire. 'Hebrews and Parthians all working together. And disciplined, too. This took real tactical skill to conceive and to execute. The Hebrews aren't supposed to be like this. They're a rabble. They fight amongst themselves sooner than fight the enemy. Everybody knows that.'

'Not any more,' Horgias said.

'Exactly. That's my point.' Sparks hit my face; I turned away. 'Whoever's leading them thinks like a Roman. This is exactly what you or I or Lupus would have done.'

'If we had fifteen thousand men to spare for a diversion.'

'Which evidently they did. And now they have ballistas and catapults that they can fire at us from inside Jerusalem.' I raised my arm, and men began to withdraw from the stripping of the enemy. 'Tears, send runners to Lupus with the news. Let them go in pairs; they'll be running through the night. Horgias, we need to give the dead of the Fourth a proper funeral. Have the men gather the bodies while Taurus and I devise a way to get them on to that bloody fire without burning ourselves in the process.'

Chapter Twenty-Six

'Given of the god,
Given to the god,
Taken by the god in valour, honour and glory.
May you journey safely to your destination.'

I spoke from a platform built from the parts of six wrecked wagons. The XIIth legion stood in a semi-circle around, with the fire filling the gap.

The unarmoured body of a man I had never known lay in front of me on a bier made from two shields strapped together. At my word, Tears and Macer lifted him slowly, and slid him on to a chute greased with tallow; Taurus had found the quarter-stores of the IVth almost untouched and had bent his ingenuity to the problem of disposing of the dead. The result would have honoured an emperor.

Released, the body shot down into the blistering heart of the fire. There was a pause before the reek of burning hair and flesh hit us, and the oily black smoke that followed. We stood in silence until it had died away to the brilliant flame that had been before.

Two other chutes stood around the fire. I spoke the words of leaving twice more, over one man from each cohort to stand for them all, and then the men began the appalling work of feeding their comrades to the flames.

I stepped back after a while and let others take my place. I had never seen the men of the sixth push ahead of each other to volunteer for a task, nor bend themselves to it with such alacrity. They did not sing as they worked, nor even chant, but they were a team, a true welded unit; the thing I had prayed for these past four years.

I stepped back, and took my helmet off and ran my fingers through my hair, feeling the sweat cold on the crown of my head. Tears came to stand beside me.

'This could take all night,' he said.

'We'll be done by midnight,' I said, with a confidence that grew only from the men in front of me. 'We'll sleep and then go back.' I turned round on my heel. 'Where's Horgias?'

'He thought he saw something moving in the trees up there.' Tears jerked a thumb over his shoulder, south, to where the bleak, black wall of the pass rose up from the desert. Stark winter trees covered it completely. In the firelit evening light, they were a black fur that could have hidden half an army.

I felt a prickle of danger on the back of my neck and turned fully to look at them. And that was when

I saw what Horgias had seen: shadows of men shifting between the trees.

'Tears! Sound the alert. They're there. Call the first two centuries. Line on me.'

But even as I spoke, a clot of about fifty men were forming a line just below the last layer of trees – and to their left, a single pair stood on a small rocky outcrop, apart from the rest, directing, ordering: the officers.

Whoever's leading them thinks like a Roman. This is exactly what you or I or Lupus would have done.

But Horgias or Lupus or I would not have sent fifty men against five hundred, not after a day with such successes as this one, which meant there were more men hidden in the trees, waiting for orders from the two on their rock.

I tugged my helmet from under my arm and unscrewed the centurion's plumes. Three twists, maybe four, and they were out. I handed them to Tears. 'Form the men into a square, all of them. Lead them towards the rebels in the trees. Keep your shields up and hold the line. Get Taurus to hold the banners for you until Horgias comes back. If he does. Can you do that?'

'Of course.' He didn't ask where I was going; he had seen what I had seen. 'Stay safe.' He pushed me into the dark.

The night was not quite dark. I ran over rough ground, stumbling on stones and the debris of the day's battle. Near the trees, I came upon a small, round hand-shield about a foot across with an iron boss and a good leather front. Dropping my own, larger shield, I picked up the new one and slid it on to my left fist.

Ahead, trees held the western edge of the mountain and I reached them undetected, or so I hoped. The Hebrews were all watching Tears, who had donned my transverse crest and was putting on a display of formation skills that would have impressed even Corbulo. He had horns and banners showing clear in the light, and nearly five hundred men in a four-square block, advancing slowly, to the beat of hilts on shields, towards the rabble at the tree line.

Among the twisted shadows of the trees, I squirmed forward on my belly with my gladius in one hand and the small circular shield in the other.

The two lines clashed to my left, and below. The backs of the officers were in front of me, up a short, steep, bouldered rise. I was a dozen paces away, and all of them uphill. But I could run uphill. How often had I done so in the Hawk mountains? In the gullies of the Lizard Pass? In Antioch in all the years of shame?

'For the Twelfth!'

Running like a lunatic, I smashed the boss of my shield into the face of the officer on the left, and thrust my blade at the open neck of the second.

They stumbled, but neither fell, and came back fast as vipers, with blades hissing at my ears, at my calves, so that I must twist two ways at once to get my tiny shield against their weapons.

I heard the clash of iron on hide only once; the second sound was iron skidding on armour, and striking flesh. I felt the sting of a blade on my calf, but in my rage I did not care.

They were on either side of me, left and right. I

bellowed and thrust out my fist-shield and hit the one on my left hard enough to knock him over. But that exposed my back to the one on my right and I felt a blow to the back of my head as I spun round and wrenched sideways and caught his blade on my own and slid it on, down, iron on iron until the hilts caught and I could wrench it up and twist . . . and fall back.

A lesser man would have lost his blade then. This one twisted free and sprang away and looked round for a shield. But even then he was watching me, waiting, with his head cocked, as if I might at any moment fall over, and I did not know why except that my head was ringing and blood from the wound on my calf was running down my left leg, oozing between my toes. I dared not look down.

He smiled at me through the almost-dark, a wide, mocking smile that drove away the last vestiges of my sanity and tipped me into a true blood-red battle-rage for only the second time in my life.

I threw my little disc-shield edge first at the grinning face in front of me, and hurled myself after it, which at least wiped away his smile and gave me time to bend down by the fallen man and pick up the sword he had dropped and stamp on his head as he tried to raise it, and feel his nose break and his teeth after, and then I was facing the one still standing, two swords to his one, and breathing thanks to Horgias who had made me practise with my dagger hand until I could use it as well as the other.

The Hebrew was good; in fact, he was exceptionally good. If we had been evenly matched, I would have lost;

I will own that now to anyone. But we were not evenly matched, for I had the two swords to his one and it took less than four strokes, blade against blade, high to the head and then low to his legs, for me to find the weak line in his lead and cut his sword down with my right hand and slice in at the back of his right knee with my left.

He dropped like a sack to kneel on the rock, looking up at me in shocked surprise, as if his god had promised him a long life and only now did he see the lie.

I killed him as I had killed my first man so long ago in the forests of Tigranocerta: a single backhanded cut that opened the whole side of his neck and sprayed blood in a spectacular arc across the stone.

My rage died as he did, leaving me gasping. I caught my enemy as he fell and held him until the last life left his eyes and then laid his body on the rock with his blade flat on his chest as I would have left one of our own.

Only then did I discover that my head ached savagely, and that I could not stand as easily as I might, but must kneel there beside him a moment to catch my breath while the small battle, that had never properly started, wound to its close below.

Horgias found me.

'It's over. Demalion? Did you hear me? It's over. The rabble lost heart when you killed the first of their leaders and fell apart completely at the second. I asked a man their names before I killed him. The elder was Jacob, one of the sons of Giora. His cousin is Daniel, who led the assault on us this morning. They came to see what their brethren had done and saw us weeping over our dead and thought they'd take advantage, but—Demalion?' He shook my shoulder, I remember that. '*Demalion!* Tears! Over here! Help me carry him.'

Chapter Twenty-Seven

The roar of a thousand voices shouting shook my skull. Pain speared down from it into the depths where I hid, piercing me awake and dragging me, unwilling, to the surface.

I opened my eyes into darkness and heard swords beat on shields and the discordant stamp of a thousand men on the march.

War. I remembered it distantly, as if it were a tale I had heard of men I once knew. *War against Jerusalem.* I felt for something to hold that I might pull myself up, and wondered how I was going to lead a century into battle when I was blind, and the ache in my head made me want to be sick. In fact, the sickness wouldn't wait . . .

I found an edge, and leaned over it, and puked a thin, sour muck that felt as if it had come from somewhere down near my kidneys, and my stomach had turned itself inside out to be rid of it.

I spat, and wiped my mouth with the back of my

hand, and was trying to find a way to stand up without being sick again when a brilliant light lanced my face with a pain beyond imagining. I screamed, I think. Certainly I fell. Cautious hands caught me and drew me upright again.

'Tears?' I knew his smell, his feel. His arms curled round in the dark, crushing me against his chest. I struggled free.

'I can't see you.' I lifted my hands to my face and touched my fingertips to my eyes. I felt my own pulse there, raging through my head to my eyeballs, but saw nothing.

'Wait.' Tears pressed down on my shoulders, as if I might otherwise leap off the bed, and I felt the chill of his leaving and then again that lancing light, which hurt more than the noise.

'Sorry.' A goatskin flapped and the light became less. 'You're in a tent; we kept it dark because light seemed to pain you.'

'It does . . . What happened?'

'You got a sword cut on the back of your left calf but that's healing. More important, you were hit on the back of the head. The second man you killed – Jacob ben Giora – he had a sling. Your helmet saved you, but even so I don't know how you stayed standing long enough to kill him. The physicians say it only caught you a glancing blow, but truly, we thought you were . . . gone from us.'

His voice caught on that last, and he bit his lip, hard. I saw him do it, and so, slowly, saw the rest of him, blurred about the edges, older, harder than the guileless boy who had come against his will to join the XIIth, but still the beloved of the gods.

Memories flapped at me like fire-sick moths: of a day's fighting against cataphracts; of a run through the Beth Horon pass; of men burning, their armour melting like candle wax; of a strange small battle on a hillside and then, hazily, its reason. 'How long have I been like this?'

'Six days.'

Six? And I remembered none of them. 'Have we taken Jerusalem?'

'Not yet.' Tears smiled down at me, full of pity and concern. 'In his wisdom, General Gallus decided to wait for three days after we got back from the pass. Agrippa, king of the Hebrews, wanted to send a peace envoy into the city. He swore he could bring the rebels back to peace without further bloodshed.'

I snorted. It hurt my head. 'What happened?'

Tears smothered a grin. 'The first one was decapitated and his head was fired at us with one of our own catapults. His ears and his genitals had been cut off and stuffed in his mouth before he died.'

I stared at him. 'Tell me there wasn't a second.'

'There was. A man by the name of Borcaeus with great courage and little sense. He escaped with only a broken arm.' Tears ran his tongue round his teeth, assessing my mood. 'We waited another day after that and then Gallus allowed that we might attack Jerusalem. We took the outer walls two days ago, almost without a fight. We're camped inside now; if you look out of your tent, you'll see the ruins of the wooden markets. Gallus had us fire them, but the people had already pulled back to the old inner city, which has walls as thick as a house. We won't get to them easily. But there are still some good things here. When you're ready to look out, you'll see the temple and the tower of the Antonia and Herod's palace that Agrippa claims is his own.'

I wasn't interested in palaces, not then. My mind was full of jumbled imaginings of siege engines and artillery. 'The ballistas,' I said. 'The catapults. The ones they took . . .'

'They haven't used them against us yet. Lupus says they're waiting until they really need them, in case it's a long siege. Which it might well be. At the moment, we're making no headway at all.' He caught sight of my face. 'If they do, Taurus says you're out of range here, even if they draw them up to the walls.'

'They won't. Lupus is right. They'll hold them till they need them.' I pulled myself half upright. 'Let me look outside.'

I screwed my eyes shut as Tears brought me to the doorway and edged the goatskin aside. Sunlight bathed my face and my guts heaved so that I had to stop and clutch the side of the tent and swallow back a mouthful of vomit.

'Demalion, are you sure you want—'

'Absolutely.' I kept my eyes on the ground that I might see less of the sun, and so instead I saw more of the devastation: the blackened stumps of houses and market stalls, the charred remains of bodies piled into heaps and incompletely burned; the same carnage, in fact, that we had wrought on other cities across the land, only here it was held within an unbroken city wall that circled us on all sides, while ahead was the Hebrew temple that the prisoners and collaborators had spoken of with such awe.

From this side, we couldn't see the fabled jewelled doors that represented the worth of a kingdom, or the steps leading up to them that had caused so much comment with their height and width. All we could see, in fact, was a long, majestic wall the height of five men with a barred gate set into it near the northern end that looked solid enough to last a century of attacks and a tower at its southern end called the Antonia that was a further three storeys above the height of the wall and at this moment was housing a veritable horde of Hebrews, armed with slings and spears and arrows to be hurled down on the men below – men who were doing their best to push forward the single oak-boarded siege tower that we had brought across the pass in our first march to Gabao.

I saw the capricorn of the VIth legion and the vine leaves on yellow of King Agrippa's auxiliaries amongst the units gathered at its foot. The siege tower itself was bigger than any I had seen before, but the Antonia still dwarfed it, and even the walls of the temple were as high as its roof.

Beside me, Tears said, 'It took less than a day to subdue the outer city, but the hard nut is here. Our ballistas have loosed all their shot, our catapults are out of bolts and still we haven't touched them. Taurus and his men are breaking up bits of the houses so at least we'll have something to fire tomorrow. But you should take a look at this.' He turned me gently by the shoulders until I was facing the other way.

'What in the god's name is *that*?'

'That,' Tears said cheerfully, 'is the king of Judaea's palace. It was built by Herod the Great who wanted it to outmatch anything in Rome. It does. There are baths in there. We have use of them.'

I should think there *were* baths in a place like that; public baths and private baths and small individual baths for the king and his wives. Or wife. I was never very sure with the Hebrews how many wives they took. Whatever it was, the palace was quite easily the largest, most opulent building I had seen in my life.

Four storeys high, faced in unblemished white stone, it had guards set at the foot of its marble steps and an oak palisade stretching beyond one wall, from behind which came the sounds of—

'Is that a beast garden?'

'Well done.' Tears was grinning widely enough to split his face in half. 'They have Berber horses in there, and hounds from Egypt. Horgias says . . .'

Berber horses! I felt my jaw grow slack. My father would have given his right arm even to see one of those. And to have a foal sired by one . . . I tried to remember where the bay mare was; I had left her with the cavalry, so Cadus must have brought her—

'Demalion?'

'Sorry.' I was swaying like a tree in a storm. I caught Tears' arm and made myself stand upright. 'What was it that Horgias said?'

Tears was already moving me back towards the tent.

'He said that until very recently there was a cheetah in a cage in the beast garden, but it's gone now. He plans to find who's taken it. Look . . . you need to lie down.'

'No, I—'

'Yes.'

He took me back to the cot, laid me down and pulled the sheepskin over me for warmth.

'I'm glad you're alive. We'll get you well now you're awake. And when you can stand for the count of a thousand without falling over, Lupus has a gift for you that'll make it all worth while.'

'A spear?'

It lay across Lupus' hands, living silver in the sunlight, its shaft of dark walnut smooth as the skin of a newborn foal and pearled with grain marks. About the neck was tied a scarf of scarlet silk that rippled in the wind.

I tore my eyes from it to look at Lupus. 'I don't understand.'

He didn't sigh. He didn't smile, not even his ghost-smile with the half-raised eyebrow, but then there were twenty-three thousand men standing behind us, arrayed in front of the king's palace in Jerusalem, and we had little time before Gallus wanted all of us at the walls for a fifth day of assault.

'It's a spear.' Lupus drew out each word, slowly. 'Strictly speaking, the Ancient Unadorned Spear granted for extreme valour in the face of the enemy, that valour having been displayed in a battle or skirmish that the recipient was not ordered to undertake. I have adorned it a little.' He tilted it so the red scarf flickered. 'I believe the gods of maniple and century will not be overly offended.'

'Not ordered?' I wasn't thinking clearly; that was obvious to both of us.

'I didn't order you back through the Beth Horon pass. You went of your own volition and then, I am told, single-handedly attacked the ben Giora cousins. You have won honour for yourself, your century, your cohort and your legion.'

There was a gap, when I was supposed to speak, and could think of nothing to say. My gaze drifted to the Hebrew temple, which remained intact, unstormed, impervious to everything we had thrown at it.

For two days I had lain still, listening to Taurus and his engineers telling the centurions how to do their jobs, for the command post was less than ten paces away from my sick tent.

The conversations had become sharper, shorter and less amicable as the days went on, and still there were Hebrews on the temple's heights and nothing we could do to them. Our ballistas were hurling Taurus' reclaimed pieces of masonry, but the wall had not so much as shown a crack.

With the ram we had brought with us, the one that had burned at the end of the Beth Horon pass, we could have—

'Centurion?' Lupus sighed and scowled together, both of which were surprisingly unfrightening. 'Just take the spear. I will assume your extreme slowness is as a result of your injuries and excuse you from the assault on the walls today.'

That got my attention as nothing else had. My head still ached, I vomited at unpredictable intervals and the cut on my calf, which was an inch deep along its length, had opened at its lower end and was oozing a clear, straw-coloured fluid, but now that I could stand unaided I had no intention at all of leaving the sixth cohort to assault the wall alone.

I held out my hands to receive the spear.

The whole XIIth legion cheered, and all the auxiliaries. Three days before, when first I woke, the thunderous noise they made would have driven me to my knees, weeping. But time is a great healer and the sight of a spear such as this, the chance to hold it, were worth even more.

I ran my hand down the haft, feeling the beauty, and tilted the head to catch the shimmer sheen of true silver. By accident, I caught sight of my own reflection there, a wedge of dark-hollowed eye and nose and the corner of my mouth with lines of pain and tension all round it.

'Thank you.' I glanced sideways at Lupus.

He smiled a rare, real smile. 'You earned it. Now go back to your tent and drink some water, and if you can hold it down you can lead your cohort into the assault.'

I drank water. I kept it down for first time since waking. Horgias, who held the water jug before and after, said, 'Amazing what a bit of silver can do for a man's health.'

'A bit?' I hefted the spear. 'This is solid silver. Melted down, it's worth a small farm in . . .' I drifted to silence. 'Not anywhere you'd want to live.'

I had been going to say Hyrcania, but I was talking to Horgias, and anywhere in the Parthian empire was anathema to him.

So we left the spear in the wagon and I dressed and still was not sick and together we walked to the head of the century. Tears had been ready to lead them. Macer was there, holding his horn. I saw them both shrug and get ready to swap Tears' shield for the horn.

'No, stay as you are,' I said. 'It doesn't hurt to have someone else learning the signals. Tears can stay as Macer's shield-man. Taurus, stay with Horgias.'

'And you?' someone asked.

'Don't worry about me.' I grinned, careless of the listening gods. 'I'm indestructible. I'll outlive you all.'

I remember very little of the assault on the walls of Jerusalem that day. The men of the VIth who had been at the left flank in the battle at Gabao were still taking the brunt of it; they had a dozen centurions all wanting to earn a crown that would trump my silver spear.

The first attack was competent enough; we had Taurus' siege tower and any number of ladders, and engineers on hand to make sure the latter were the right height so that they were tall enough to reach the top of the walls, but not so high that they overlapped and so were easy to push down.

When the ladders made no impact and nobody had yet won anything but a blade or a slingstone shot at his face, then, exactly as I had heard done on the last two days, we rolled forward our three ballistas and hurled bits of masonry from the broken parts of the city at the walls, and when that made no discernible impact we hurled them over the walls at the defenders.

At last, when nothing else was working, we turned our attention on the gate to the northern end of the temple wall, which was at least made of wood, even if that wood was half an oak thick, studded with iron and solidly barred from the inside.

One look told us that it needed a proper ram to open it, which was one reason, I have no doubt, why the Hebrews had destroyed the one we'd brought with us.

In default of that, an enterprising centurion in the VIth had found some roof beams and lashed them together to make something almost as thick as a tree. Three times I saw him and his men try to get it near enough the door to ram it; three times they were forced back by the sheer number of stones, spears, arrows and – after we used the ballistas – great pieces of masonry that were rained on their heads.

We abandoned the assault at dusk and spent a frustrated night barely sleeping, with whole centuries of men set on watch in case the Hebrews tried to sally out of the gate and destroy our one remaining siege tower.

Lupus was outside my tent when I woke in the morning, before I had time even to walk to the latrines. He was carrying a length of dark brown, rough-woven wool, and what looked like a spear jutting beneath, and joined me as I threaded my way through the tents, talking as we went.

The morning was warm and cloyingly damp with a crimson tint to the clouds on the eastern horizon. I looked at them and made the sign against evil, for, more than anything, we wanted this to be over before the winter rains came.

Seeing me, Lupus nodded, tight-lipped. 'Taurus and his engineers have been building us a new ram, a proper one on slings with a good thick roof over it, not the twig the Sixth were prodding away with yesterday. Gallus has given permission for a full-out assault on the gate at the northern end of the wall. He'll deploy archers on either side to give us a chance at least to bring the ram within reach of it.'

It was what I would have done, only I would have done it five days previously. I pushed past a tent-load of auxiliaries to reach the latrine ditch and stood on its edge, pissing into the lime-dusted depths. Beside me, Lupus did the same.

'Who takes the ram?' I asked.

Lupus stretched a tight grin. 'The Twelfth. The Sixth had their chance the past four days and failed: it's our turn now. The first cohort will take the left side. Your men of the sixth will take the right, both sides in testudo. Horgias will lead them. Tears will take the standard and Macer the horn.'

I stared at him. My head ached as if someone had tied iron round it and was tightening the screw. 'I'm well enough, I swear to you. I can—'

'I'm sure you can. If you're finished, come with me.'

I wasn't, but I wasn't going to squat at the latrine's edge with Lupus standing over me frowning. I settled my tunic and followed him to the place behind the tents where the mules were tethered.

He turned abruptly to me. 'Cadus says you can shoot a bow.' And when I stared at him, 'Apparently a spy called Pantera told him so when you were in Hyrcania.'

I frowned. Pantera hadn't seen me shoot once. But Lupus wasn't interested in my past; he was too busy enjoying my reaction to his own sleight of hand as he dropped the scruffy cloth he had been holding and revealed that what he held under it was not a spear, but a Parthian cavalry bow.

It was made of honey-coloured ashwood, deeply curved and sprung back at the ends, with a full, rounded belly wrapped in ramskin for a hand-hold and luck-marks of gods and heroes poker-burned all along the inner length of the pale, perfect wood. The string was horse sinew, rubbed with beeswax that sweetened the air between us.

It was alive with power and the promise of death; a weapon to die for, or at least to kill for.

'Where did you get that?' I asked.

Lupus' grin had a satisfied air. 'I won it in a game of dice from a centurion of the first cohort. He found it on the battlefield after Cadus had decimated the cataphracts. You were occupied at the other end of the pass at the time or I'm sure you'd have had the chance to win it in fair play. Here.' He passed it to me. 'Try it.'

Nobody had asked if I was an archer when I first joined the XIIth and I had been too sullen to volunteer the information. Later, when I might have offered, we had our own companies of Pannonian archers who were jealous of their lines in battle. In any case, it had been over ten years since I last held any bow, still less one as good as this, and I had no idea if I could hit a horse at ten paces.

I was going to say so, but my body knew better than my mind. Just looking at it made my arms itch as if I had shot it yesterday and must do so again to stay sane. I braced my hand against the ramskin on the belly and felt the padding under it, which had moulded to a hand larger than mine, begin to ease to my shape. I flexed the string and let so much honey into the air that I heard bees dance in my head. I eased it back to stillness.

Perfect. As good as Uncle Dorios' bow had ever been.

'Cadus said you learned the skill in your youth?' Lupus ventured.

'Did he?' I was fumbling in my belt pouch for a spare thong to wrap round my wrist as a makeshift guard, not paying attention to Lupus, or what Cadus might have said, or to anything that wasn't the bow.

Wordless, Lupus handed me an arrow. It was goose-fletched with a small, unbarbed point, not enough to stop a boar or a bear – or a son who had usurped his father's throne – but enough to test out the bow's strength and my skill.

I licked my finger and held it up and found there was almost no wind, just a gentle, tugging breeze blowing east to west that could easily be managed. I looked about for a target.

'The goat hide, perhaps?' Lupus waved a vague hand at a skin draped over a sack of straw about thirty paces away; the kind of thing men set up to shoot at of an evening, when the dice games have grown cold. I didn't ask if he had put it there; his expression was so bland as to be an admission.

Hissing wearily through my teeth, I nocked the arrow, drew and loosed all in one movement and was barely aware of the sting on my arm as the string snapped back; I was too busy watching the arrow's flight, how it bucked a little because I had jerked the loose, and so flew wider than it should have done.

I hit the goatskin a hand's breadth high and a foot to the right of the centre. I lowered the bow, slowly. 'Not good enough to kill a man.'

'Good enough to keep him from killing us, though,' Lupus said. 'The bow's yours if you will use it. We have fifty arrows per man. Use them wisely, but don't be miserly. If we don't get through on this assault . . .' He looked at the horizon, at the gathering rain, and didn't have to finish that thought.

'Who will I lead?' I asked.

'Syrians. We have two complete companies of archers, more or less. They're mostly from King Antiochus' personal troop. They know nothing of how we make war, and even if they did, they lost their commander to a thrown spear at the mouth of the Beth Horon pass. That's why I want you to lead them today. Stay alive, and while you're at it, do what you can to make sure we can ram that gate. It matters.'

'Testudo . . . shields up! Raise the ram!'

Horgias' voice rebounded off the walls. Ahead, the temple wall reared high as a cliff above us, and on its height men stood with spears and bows, slingshots and piles of rubble, just as they had before.

Until now, they had not faced archers in a solid block, but men scattered through the legions, King Antiochus of Syria not having wished to put his archers in the line of fire until specifically requested. Now that he had been made to understand the urgency, I had one hundred bowmen with fifty arrows apiece placed under my orders. At my request, I had a part-century of the VIth in attendance as shield-men, chafing under a strange command, and sour because their assault had failed and ours might succeed.

I stood alone in the centre of the rank, holding the bow Lupus had given me. I had no shield, nor any intention of having one; we were out of range of all but the longest bowshot and I needed to show that the men of Rome were not afraid. That was a lie, of course; my mouth was too dry to swallow and my guts were clenching and unclenching with horrible regularity, but I was learning how not to show it.

The archers stood in two ranks, fifty to my right, fifty to my left. They were Greek-speaking Syrians, dark-haired, dark-bearded men who looked, dressed, ate and thought exactly like the Hebrews – and who would kill any man who said as much in their hearing, for they loathed their neighbours with a passion unmatched anywhere in the empire.

As bowmen, they were not the quality of Vologases' horse-archers, or even the Pannonians we had fought with at the Lizard Pass, though they were easily as fond of finery. They wore ivory guards on their left forearms to counter the slap of the string and tabs of leather on the fingers of their right hands to ensure a smooth loose. I had been loaned the same, and took it as an honour.

'Ram, ready!' Horgias' voice came back in time with his horn signals. Macer was almost as good as Tears at that.

I raised my bow. The men needed no command: they had orders to shoot as I did, unless told otherwise.

I drew. The air about me hissed to the sigh of one hundred bowstrings. I smelled honey again, and heard bees enough almost to drown out Horgias' cry.

But not quite.

'Forward!'

I loosed. My men did likewise. The air sang. One hundred and one arrows soared up to the top of the temple wall. I heard screams. Some of them were Roman. Most were not. I was already drawing on the next arrow, raising . . .

Boom!

Taurus' new ram hit the temple door. I loosed again and this time the song of the arrows was lost in the deep belling note of the ram on the door and the deeper shuddering hum of the sling-ropes after it. Caught in that tone, with my whole body reverberating to its song, I loosed again, and again and again until—

'Stop!'

I held up my hand. My men held their bows still. Ahead of us, not a face looked over the temple wall. No man stood on the heights of the Antonia. I had no idea how many we had hit, but nobody could have survived that barrage for long.

‘Is that it?’ asked a Syrian from my left. Artacles, his name was, I think.

‘I doubt it.’ I squinted up at the top of the wall, shielding my eyes from the sun. ‘Unless we’ve killed the man who sent the Hebrews to take our siege engines, then he’s still inside there, and he’s not stupid.’

‘What will he do?’

‘What would you do?’

There was a pause, and the ram struck again. As the thunderous noise died away, Artacles said, slowly, ‘I would find shields to keep my men safe.’

‘Exactly. Or broad oak boards, which are of greater length and take fewer men to hold. I think, if you look up at the southern corner, you’ll see they are bringing some up the steps there now. If we shoot at once, we can delay them a while longer . . .’

I nocked, raised, loosed and hit the lead man who was carrying one end of a wide, flat board across the top of the wall. He fell outwards down the wall to lie still at its foot, so that I could be sure of the kill. In the flurry of arrows that followed, three others, I thought, went the same way, but they fell inwards, and so were uncertain. And by the time we nocked again, the boards were in place, raising the height of the wall by four feet.

‘Hold.’ I raised my hand. ‘Let me test this.’

I took three paces forward and tried one shot at a far steeper angle than we had before. It soared over the barrier, but, for the first time, an answering arrow came back. It struck the ground near my feet and skittered back towards me so that I had to take a step sideways to let it past.

'They'll get our range soon,' Artacles said. 'Best get yourself a shield.'

'Later.' My head still ached dully, but I was feeling expansive and calm. The buzz of bees was constant in my ears now and a knot had taken hold of my stomach that was beyond the usual stir of battle. I had an idea and wished I had not.

A ray of weak sun lanced through the clouds and, as if invited, I stepped forward into it and turned round to face the bowmen behind me.

'The Hebrews will try to use the boards as cover to shoot back at us. If we step forward and aim high and long, we can keep them back from the wall.'

As if to test my theory, a man's face appeared at the barrier. A sling whirled in a blur by his head. I drew and loosed without thinking, as Uncle Dorios had taught me. I missed, but so did the enemy slingshot. A small lead pellet big enough to break open my skull cracked on to the ground between me and the wall, kicked up a small plume of dust. The next did much the same, and the next. With my fourth arrow, I struck the slinger in the throat and he toppled backwards, out of sight. If he screamed, I didn't hear it: we couldn't hear anything over the thunder of the ram on the door, but I was still expecting—

'Look out!'

It was Artacles who called, I think, but it was Tears' voice I heard, and in any case I had been waiting for this. I threw myself sideways, rolling on to my shoulder to keep my bow from harm. A ballista stone the size of my head hurtled past where I had been and gouged a hole in the solid earth big enough to hide a sheep in.

'Loose!' I screamed, over the noise of the archers' shock. 'Shoot as fast as you can along the line that stone came from before they—'

'*Look out!*'

Two pairs of hands wrenched me out of the path of the second stone. By the third, we were running backwards, by the fourth we were just running, all tactics gone, all ideas abandoned, all chance of success fading with each running step.

And then the Hebrews brought up the catapults. They had taken thirty, plus fifteen hundred bolts that were the length of a tall man's leg and nearly as thick, tipped with iron shaped to penetrate armour. Shot by a man who knew how to sight and loose, nothing could stand against them.

These, I thought, were aimed by an expert. The first volley were rangefinders and scattered on to empty ground. After that, every one was sent to kill.

I saw one pierce a bowman through his mailed chest, come out the other side and kill the man behind him, pinning his body to the hard earth. After that, they came in a volley so fast and so hard that all we could do was run as far as we could, and each of us try to find somewhere to hide. I ended up in the armoury tent, set far back against the beast garden, as far back, in fact, as one could go without leaving the city.

And among all the many deaths, there were perhaps only half a dozen of us who thought to look to the ram – and so discovered that the catapults had been a diversion, much as the attack on us at Gabao had been a diversion, and the real attack was on the ram as it tried to break through the gate.

The stones that had so nearly killed me had been the most distant from the wall. The rest had been sent at progressively steeper angles until they were dropping from the heights of the sky, just on our side of the wall.

They fell in volleys of three at a time and crashed on to the ram and the men about it, and these were not the small stones the size of a man's head but massive rocks big as bulls' heads and bigger; one in six was so wide a grown man could not wrap his arms round half the width.

The first volley crippled the ram. The rest – I counted thirty shots in all, but there must have been more – smashed into the men around it, crushing their shields to tinder and their bodies to bloody pulp.

'Sound the retreat!' It was Lupus who called it, although it should have been Gallus. 'Call them back! Retreat in good order! Now!'

Nobody was listening to him. A broken horn lay to my left, waiting for one of the smiths to have time to weld the handle back on. I hauled it out of the clutter of other broken kit, hitched it over my shoulder and blew the retreat as loudly as I knew how.

It wasn't pitch perfect by any means, but it was a rhythm every man knew second only to the order to advance. I wasn't sure anyone would hear me over the screams of dying men, and was thinking to run in and haul them out bodily when Horgias and Tears emerged – alive! Both alive! – bellowing orders at the survivors that sent them running like hares for the safety of the tent lines.

'That's it,' Lupus said, as the senior centurions gathered at the flags; only twelve of us were left. It felt like a repeat of Rhandaea, only that we had not yet surrendered.

Lupus, though, thought we were close to abandoning the fight, which was the next worst thing. 'We're finished,' he said. 'Gallus had little enough heart for this at the start, but he's lost it all now, and more. He'll have us marching out in the morning.'

Everyone but me seemed to have been expecting this; but then everyone else had seen Gallus dither over the assault in the first place. I stared at Lupus. 'I thought you were worried about the weather closing in.'

'That too.' He turned away. I turned him back.

'Then we have to break through the gate today,' I said.

Eleven of my fellow officers looked at me and laughed. All except Lupus, who was the only one who counted.

To him, I said, 'Fire. All we need is fire. They've just turned the ram to matchwood. If we can pile it against the gate and set fire to it, we can still weaken it enough to get through. We know how well a ram burns now; trust me, they make a good fire. Nothing will stand against it if we can make it hot enough.'

Lupus blinked once, slowly, then nodded. 'Do it.'

I asked for volunteers, and then had to turn half of them away. My century came, what was left of it; we had lost thirty-two men to the missiles at the gate, of whom at least half were dead. So that I might not seem to be favouring my own, I made up the numbers with men from the first cohort and brought along the first century of the VIth as well.

I set signallers on the rise by the palace with particular instructions to watch for missiles and let us know as soon as they saw them. We arranged different calls for stones and catapult bolts and a brief, easy system to let us know roughly where they were aimed. I set the archers to keep men from the temple heights while we worked, so that they might not attempt to put the blaze out too early, and while I did that Taurus led his engineers in gathering every bit of flammable material that could be found, plus the tallow, lamp oil and tinder to start a fire and keep it going.

The sun was a glowing orb behind Herod's palace by the time we were ready. Taurus brought me a small green-enamelled ember pot with ties to fix it to my belt.

'There are twenty of these,' he said. 'We found them in the king's palace. As long as even one of us lives, we'll get the fire going.'

I clapped Taurus on the shoulder. 'Stay safe,' I said simply. 'And keep Horgias safe for me.'

I'm not one for speeches, but something was needed for the men and I could not address them all singly. To that end, I climbed halfway up the steps to the palace and turned to look down on them. They gathered in good order, effortlessly, even now when they were burdened with bags of wool and straw and the cloaks of dead men.

I raised my hand to speak to them, as Corbulo had done once, and if that was hubris I apologize, but it did not feel like it then: I was shaking with the battle-fear that I always felt, but pride, too, that we had come this far, that we had grown to be a fighting unit against such bitter odds, that these men – each of them – believed in me enough to follow me back to the carnage at the gate.

'We have suffered enough at the hands of this rabble. Now is our chance to give them back the fire they gave us. And to rescue our wounded. Each man has his task. You know what to do. Do it well, and we will win this city before sundown.'

They cheered a little, but it was not a time for cheering. I jumped down from the steps, found the head of my small force, raised my right hand, and stabbed it forward.

'*Go!*'

I carried a proper shield this time. Running in its shade, I saw only the churned ground beneath my feet. I jumped ballista stones that lay like hail in the dirt, and soon after jumped dead and living men, and splintered lengths of wood.

The air around the ram stank of blood and entrails and fractured timber. I pushed through until I reached the iron-capped head, where the great tree that Taurus had found and felled lay cracked on the ground in a mess of broken beams. Four men sheltered me with their shields as I dragged and threw and kicked fragments of wood, some of them longer than a man's arm, into place around the ram.

'Fleece,' I called, and men passed me what they had carried bundled up under their shields, and soon, from the back, came jars of lamp oil taken from the palace, and then tallow, and behind me others and others were doing the same, so that soon enough we had the whole thing padded and wadded and ready to burn.

Horgias' face grinned up near my own. 'Have you the ember pot?' he asked.

He was one of the twenty flame-holders – I had seen Taurus give him a red-coloured pot – but he was giving me first fire and I was not about to turn him down.

I unhooked the pot from my belt, and blew on it, and saw the charcoal glow to cherry red and blew again and it was the colour of fired apricots, and again and it was the noonday sun. Surrounded by the smells of tallow and oil, I fisted a hole in the wadding and leaned in and tipped the brilliant fragments on the bed there, and blew as on the face of a sleeping lover and saw a flame rise and dance and leap and catch.

'Hold. Hold the cover. Don't let them put it out yet.'

I nursed that flame as if it were my only son, and all round the ram nineteen other men did likewise. My small group leaned in over it with their shields against a volley of missiles that blasted down on us, for our archers were running short of arrows and saving their last for the time when the flames needed the greatest help. Men fell at the edges, but for every one that fell, another stepped in to take his place until the fire was no longer dancing but roaring, sucking in air, giving out heat that made my sore heart heal again.

And then, cutting over the havoc, a long, high note from the signallers on the palace rise—

'*Run!*' I screamed it, or Horgias did, or someone

else back down the ranks who knew the calls we had arranged. 'Hot sand!'

Before the threat of sand heated almost to melting point, we scattered like sheep before a wolf, like hares before hounds, only faster, and came to a stop at the tent lines, where Lupus had the archers shooting long, endless volleys until their fingers bled and their arms were strained out of their sockets.

I snatched up the pale Parthian war bow and joined them and, together, we killed men by the dozen, by the hundred, but there were tens of thousands in the city of Jerusalem and we had only twenty arrows left apiece.

They came to an end, as they must, and after that we could only wait and watch as the flames of our creation, the beautiful, vast, roaring fire that we had built, was quenched first by sand and then, later, by water.

I watched the final embers blink to darkness. 'We've weakened it,' I said. 'It wouldn't take another day of the ram.' And then, remembering, 'Did Tears get all the wounded away?'

'Before you ever lit the fire,' Lupus said. 'That was well done.'

'But not the fire.'

'It was well done,' he said, woodenly, and then with more feeling. 'It *was* well done. We're fighting against men with talent in there, and we are led by one with none.'

Lupus stayed with us a long time, watching the smoke die to damp ashes before he bade us good night and took himself to Cestius Gallus' tent, where our commander waited with our new orders.

Chapter Twenty-Eight

We marched out of Jerusalem with the dawn on the seventh day after we had entered it.

The XIIth legion had lost over two thousand men out of a full complement of nearly five thousand, with another eight hundred wounded drawn in ox wagons behind; the VIth had lost half their number, though with fewer wounded. The three cohorts of the IVth, of course, had been wiped out to a man.

Cadus' legionary and allied horse were almost intact, barring the losses at the mouth of the Beth Horon pass, which had been few. The allied infantry likewise had lost only eight hundred men, most of them in the skirmishes and battles before we ever reached Jerusalem, but were otherwise largely untouched.

But the XIIth had sought the glory and the XIIth had borne the loss. In poor heart, knowing how failure further sullied our already desperate situation, we neither sang nor spoke to each other as we marched.

*

The rebels fell on us before noon, harrying the rear centuries who were guarding the wagons. Gallus gave us no order to break ranks and go to help them, but Priscus, a centurion of the third rank who had command of the VIth now, turned his men round anyway, to marshall a defence.

Thus it was that we lost half of the remaining men of the VIth, ten of the supply wagons and all of the wounded before nightfall.

We ran the last miles to the safety of a small legionary fortress at Scopus, halfway to the Beth Horon pass. I had lain unconscious through our first stay there, and would as readily have slept through this one; it was a dreary place with little to recommend it save that it put stone walls between us and the Hebrew spears, which meant at least we could light fires, cook food and sleep.

We slept badly and woke to a dull, damp dawn that threatened rain but did not deliver. We cursed the sky for that; it helped us to think that a good downpour would have hurt the Hebrews more than it hurt us.

We left Scopus, fervently hoping never to see it again, and began the rapid-march beloved of Caesar, who could get an entire legion with all the baggage across forty miles in a day. We made the four miles to Gabao, the battleground at the mouth of the Beth Horon pass, before Gallus called a halt.

Gabao is not a fortress, but we had built redoubts and staked them on the way down and those remained in place. I had rather more confidence in them than I had in the defences at Scopus, but that was little enough.

We centurions were so few now that we were all invited to meet Gallus in his tent. It was the first time I'd seen him close up and the first time I'd seen him at all since we set out for the Beth Horon pass.

My first thought was that he was sick with fright. My second was that he was simply sick: close to dying, in fact.

Always a tall, lean man, he was thin, now, to the point of emaciation, with the skin of his face stretched tight over his skull and his eyes sunk so deep in their sockets they seemed to glow from the back of his head. His hair was almost gone, but what was left, in plumes above his ears, was a rich, dark colour, as if it were twenty years younger than the man himself. His eyebrows, too, were thickly luxuriant.

I stared at him until Lupus, who was beside me, trod on my foot and brought me to silent attention.

Gallus began with no civilities. A brazier stood between him and us and he clasped his hands behind his back and paced back and forth on his side of it as he spoke, sending his shadows dancing against the far walls of the tent.

'As you know, the pass of Beth Horon is a death trap. The enemy have already shown that they have a different, faster, route through the mountains to its further end and the heights are a gift for any man trying to ambush those going through. Still, with them harrying us as they do, we cannot afford the time to march round, which means we must run for it, literally.'

He waited for someone to say something. When

nobody did, he paced the breadth of his tent and back once more and came to a halt behind the brazier. He swallowed, as if his throat were too tight. He looked the way I feel before battle, although I hope I hide it better. I watched his larynx bob up and down behind the drawn skin of his neck.

Drily, he said, 'This has the merit of being a defensible position and therefore we will stay here for the rest of today and tonight. We will march out at daybreak tomorrow, by which time I want the mules and oxen dead and their carts destroyed, particularly the siege engines. Destroy every one and if necessary burn it. We must leave nothing to the enemy that they have not already got.'

That was it. We were dismissed moments later, with no time for questions, or discussion, or any plans beyond that.

Killing mules is a foul task and one best left to the butchers. Every cohort has half a dozen men whose skill is in killing cleanly and fast but even they hate mule-killing.

It's not that they are harder to kill than horses, but they are so much more intelligent that after the first one, when they know what's coming, they become almost impossible to handle. The oxen, by contrast, stand eating corn from a bucket and each one killed seems as surprised when the pole axe hits it between the eyes as the one before and the one after.

I stood apart from the slaughter, listening to the sounds of men cursing in the dull day. Lupus came to stand beside me.

'Thank you for not speaking out,' he said. 'It would have gone badly had you said what was written on your face.'

'Did he see it?'

'Of course. But it's different if no one says anything. He can manage it better then.'

'What's wrong with him?'

'I don't know, but he passes blood when he passes anything at all and he barely eats now.'

'Bloody flux?' I gaped at him. 'Then we're all—'

'No. He's been like this since he joined us and none of us are the worse for it, nor any of his body attendants. At a guess, I'd say he has ill humours gnawing away at his bowels. If it were flux, we'd all have passed our innards into a bloody ditch by now, and no thanks to the Hebrews.'

'But he'll be dead by winter,' I said.

'I thought he'd be dead by now and I was wrong.' A mule broke free and ran at the ditch and staked itself. Over the ear-harrowing screams, Lupus said, 'He's doing his best to keep us alive. It's not good, but he is finally listening to us. If we can get through Beth Horon alive, we can run for Caesarea. He won't try to do anything else.'

'Was there anything else he could have done?'

'He wanted to take us back to Antioch. Be grateful that he knows he hasn't the strength.'

Without the wagons to slow us, we did actually run from Gabao into the Beth Horon pass, much as we of the sixth cohort had run down to the relief of the IVth, when we still thought there were men of that legion left to relieve.

There was an odd strength in the running, in the sweating, panting thrust and pump of it, so much like training that we could lose our minds in the count of stride and breath, staring at the man in front, listening to the men behind.

And we who had run it twice knew the places where we had to walk, where the path narrowed to a shelf along a precipice, fit for one man on a horse, or a narrow cart, but no more. Heading west now, as we were, the sheer rock wall reared up to our right and the cliff fell away to our left, while on the far side of the canyon the thick wooded slopes could have hidden half the Hebrew army.

We sent the cavalry along first, and then the men in single file. Lupus was way to the front. I found Horgias behind me, bearing the cohort standard. He came up until he was just behind my left shoulder. 'What would you have done last night if you were the Hebrews?' he asked.

'I'd have sent men on above the pass through the night while we lost time killing mules. I'd have them waiting with rocks and spears, ready to force as many men off this ledge as I could.' It wasn't a new thought: I'd been playing it over in my mind the way a dog plays over a bone since we'd left in the morning. 'There's no way out but forwards.' I slapped a hand on the rock wall to my right. 'Even you can't climb this.'

'So we have to be ready to run,' he said. 'Soon.'

'Can you see them?'

'I saw the spark of sunlight on armour when we—'

'*Down!*' I pushed him sideways, clinging on to him at the same time, to keep him from falling off the ledge. The rock that hurtled down from above missed him by a hand's breadth. Tears was wrestling with his horn a dozen paces behind. There was no time. I took a breath and screamed my lungs out.

'*Run!*'

Like hunted deer, we ran, and like hunted deer they picked us off, one by one, harrying us ever forward, so that even when we made it off that bloody ledge and on to something approaching flat ground again in the valley's depths, we were never able to come together in proper formation.

Their slingers and archers picked on the cavalry and then on the infantry, driving us from side to side across the pass and killing, killing, killing from mid-morning until the end of the afternoon and into the evening.

We should have been through and out the other side by then. We should have been halfway to Caesarea, but we had spent so much time scurrying for cover that we had made less than half of the progress we had done the last time we ran in this direction.

Only darkness saved us. When it was too dark to see, the Hebrews stopped wasting their spears, their arrows, their slingshot, their rocks, and we were left huddling in our units, waiting for instruction.

We lit no fires in the beginning, but sat where we had stopped, and Lupus had to walk amongst us, calling in the centurions.

We had no tents, and so met at a place only a little apart from the main body of our men.

Lupus gave the losses first. The allied infantry and cavalry had taken the greatest losses this time, for they were least armoured and least able to manage the constant unpredictable assaults. Most of them were dead. Out of a force of forty thousand that had left Antioch, and of twenty-two thousand that had left Jerusalem, we were reduced to ten thousand.

'And by tomorrow we will all be gone,' Lupus said. 'There is no way out of here alive.'

'Unless we go by night,' Gallus said. 'Now, in fact.'

'No.' Priscus was dead. The new leader of the VIth was named Festus and he spoke before Lupus as if rank had no meaning any more. 'They'll know. If we don't light fires, if we don't set guards that they can see, they'll know we've gone. And if we can go, they can surely follow.'

There was a moment's silence. I thought men were embarrassed at his intervention, but then I saw that Lupus was looking at Gallus and Gallus was looking back and there was an understanding between them.

'The XIIth will stay,' Lupus said. 'We are less than a thousand men now. We shall stay here and light a thousand fires, so that it looks as if ten thousand men have camped for the night. The Hebrews won't realize the deception until dawn. You should be clear of the pass by then.'

There was an uncomfortable moment in which nobody but me met Lupus' eye. Then Gallus, nodding, said, 'Name three centuries to escape with us. To carry the

Eagle and the cohort standards that the XIIth might live beyond this night, and be honoured for your courage.'

'*No!*' Lupus and I spoke together.

I said, 'We fought once before without our Eagle. We will never do so again.'

And Lupus, in much the same breath, said, 'The Twelfth will never survive the shame of a second defeat. Let us die here, and be honoured at least for this much courage, and let our legion die with us.'

A new silence held the other men, of a quite different quality. Men touched their brows, in a mark of silent respect.

'It will be as you wish,' Gallus said. 'We shall reach Caesarea and we shall return in spring with enough men to bring Jerusalem to its knees. Your sacrifice will not be in vain.'

Chapter Twenty-Nine

We were eight hundred; all that was left of the XIIth legion, not including the cavalry. Cadus had begged to be allowed to stay, but he was the only surviving officer of the cavalry and Gallus had ordered him to lead his men safely through the pass.

And so we were left, we veterans who had lived through the humiliation of Raphana, and those who had joined us since, and we were not divided now; only by thinking hard could we remember that we had not always been as brothers.

I don't think any man amongst us begrudged those who were leaving. In that, if nothing else, it was like the battle at Lizard Pass, when we counted ourselves lucky to be allowed to face Vologases' cataphracts while others fled. This time, though, we intended that those who left us must get clear away, and so we threw ourselves into the deception.

Taurus organized five hundred men in groups of four

to forage for firewood, noisily. The rest of us built fires, lit them, stood around them, spoke quietly, laughed, cooked and shared a meal, then passed on to the next one and did the same again, all with our standards in the centre; not so close to any fire that they might be counted, but close enough for the Eagle to catch the light of a dozen fires and be burnished by them, so that it hung over us, suspended in the black night, casting its own light back down on our helms and our armour as we moved and talked and moved again. None of us slept.

I found Tears just before daybreak; or rather, I allowed myself to go to him, when I had not through the night. He was sitting on an upturned shield with his knees hugged to his chin. He said nothing as I came near, only shifted a little by his fire as if to make space in a crowd and handed me a new-baked oatcake, hot and steaming, scorched a little at the edges, as I liked it, so that I could taste fire and corn and the melting sweetness at its heart, where the dough was still soft.

I had the Parthian war bow with me, slung over my shoulder. He had still not seen me shoot it, not properly; he had always been too busy.

'Have you any arrows for that?' he asked.

'None.' I unhooked it and held it balanced on my open palms. 'I could burn it. The wood's strong and true. It would hold a flame a long time.'

'No, you couldn't.' His smile flashed and was gone. 'If you were going to do that, you'd have done it half a night ago, when the cold began to bite. Let someone find it. A good bow deserves to be used.'

'Even against us?'

'It won't be against us. We'll be dead. We won't care, and I don't think the bow will care either. You've killed enough with it to balance your side of the scales. It can help another man to do the same.'

'Maybe.' Firelight rippled the white wood in colours of amber, copper and bronze. I watched it a while, seeing the glyphs on the inner face march up the length of the body to the curved horn tips and back again. I still had no idea what they said.

Presently, I put it away and we sat in silence, watching the flames and each other until Horgias and Taurus came to stir the embers of a fire nearby and we joined them, to lay on more wood. When, shortly after, Macer joined us, and then Lupus, we felt complete.

Taurus, too, had made oatcakes, which we shared, along with those from Tears' fire, as if it were a god's day, to celebrate.

I had two in my hands, and was steaming myself in their scent, when Macer lifted from his tunic a small fired pot the size of a hen's egg, with honey bees marked in scored lines round the sides.

'I have this,' he said, and we all looked at him, for the shyness with which he had said it; Macer had never been a shy man.

'Honey?' Tears laughed. 'Have you carried that all the way from Antioch, just for this?'

'Further than that.' Macer was grinning like a fool. 'I brought it from Moesia when I was ordered to leave the Seventh. I thought that if I ever had occasion to share it, I would know I was a man of the Twelfth at last.'

He stopped smiling. 'In Antioch, I thought I would die of old age and never have reason to open this. Many times these last days, I have feared I might die with it still in my tunic when we should have had it already.'

He held the jar on the flat of his palm, near the fire. It was sealed with dark red wax that stood in a blob over the top surface and ran down in uneven runnels about the bees. With all eyes on him, he drew his knife and cracked it open, and the smell of honey drenched us, like the smell of waxed bowstrings, multiplied a thousandfold.

As a priest at a sacrifice, Macer used his knife to lift a nugget of comb from the pot. He offered it to Lupus, then a second to me, then Horgias, Tears and Taurus. Last, he helped himself and spread it on his oatcake.

'There was just enough,' he said. 'Some god guided us to this; just us.' He raised his head. I had never seen his eyes so clear, so set in their purpose. Macer the Mournful had gone in the night and a new man inhabited his skin. 'I would help to hold the Eagle,' he said. 'If you will permit me?'

'Every man will hold the Eagle,' Lupus said, 'All eight hundred of us. It's the only order: that we die before it is taken. But if you wish to be shield-man to Horgias' shield-man, you are free to do so.' He stood, a little stiff from the cold. 'We'd best make ready. I can see you all by more than firelight. And if I can see you, the Hebrews will soon see how few of us there are here. It won't take long. By noon, it should all be over.'

*

I stood at the heart of the increasing crowd who gathered about the standards and there was a sense of quiet competence as we fastened buckles and checked the grips on our blades. There was none of the fire, the zeal, the heroism-in-waiting that had attended us at the Lizard Pass when we faced the King of Kings' army; just a job to be done and then peace at the end of it.

Day was coming on us more strongly with every heartbeat. The sky was heavy with the scent of rain, and a low, thick cloud held the valley walls, hovering just above our heads. We knew that it had been sent by the gods to aid our subterfuge; for a long time after true dawn we were still no more than helmets flashing in the mist, swords and shields scraping into position and units of men muttering amongst themselves, giving thanks to Jupiter, to Mithras, to Helios.

Lupus walked quietly among the men. 'Hold the Eagle as long as you can. There is no other order.' I heard his voice echoing back through the mist, over and over, impossible to tell its direction.

'What will you do?' He spoke in my ear. I jumped, and snatched away my sword, which had stabbed upward without my asking.

'Fight,' I said. 'What else?'

'Do you have your bow still?'

'Yes. But I have no arrows.' The bow lay near the fire where Tears had made his oatcakes. I reached down to pick it up and held it out to Lupus. 'Do you want it?'

'Regrettably, now is not the time for me to learn how to use a bow with true skill. But you have the skill. And I have a gift for you.' From behind his back,

Lupus brought a fistful of arrows. Even at a fast glance, I counted eight. In the grey light, their shafts were dark, almost black, and the feathers sullied, but still intact.

He read the question in my eyes and gave a brief, almost shy, shrug. 'They're from the bodies of the men you hit the other day. You and the others. I went back in the night and took them out. I thought you might have use for them.'

His brow rose as it always had, but there was an honesty in his eyes that stabbed me with sorrow for the first time since we had made our decision to stay.

'I won't waste them,' I said, and heard the thickness in my own voice.

'Good.' He looked about us, frowning. 'The mist is lifting.' He took a sharp breath. 'This is it.'

We were already in position; buckles fast, swords out, shields to hand. As one man, in stillness, we watched the mist thin and rise until, at last, we could see this place where we had chosen to die.

Wide and flat and shallow, we had come without knowing it to a bowl in the very foot of the pass. The path to freedom meandered up the mountainside before and rose steep and narrow behind, but here was the perfect battleground, a plate of turfed earth with little by way of boulders or rocky debris to hamper us.

The heights were hemmed about by winter trees, blowing ragged in the coming breeze, shading the grey hillside with copper. The scent was of dying fires, and oiled leather, and iron; the scent of any army in the morning; the scent of awaited death; a scent so peaceful, I could have lain down with that as my shroud, and slept.

And that was when the sun scraped through a finger's width of mist and Helios cast a single ray, spear-straight, at our Eagle, washing it with living light, the breath of the gods.

Horgias took hold of the haft and raised it up so that it flew above us, our guardian and our care, ours to protect until death.

We cheered, how could we not? And so revealed how very few we were.

There was a moment's raggedness, as the wind caught the last hurrahs and tore them to shreds. Then I caught a glint of sun on iron somewhere on the hill high to my left, and another along the valley, and another on the shoulder of the mountain to my right, and another, if I craned my head to look behind, along the pathway that led out of the valley, and another and another, as our enemies rose from the places in which they had been hidden, and so revealed how very many they were.

They began to group together, moving easily through the scrub and debris of the pass as if they knew each bush and rock. The first we saw were not the Roman-clad men we had faced before, but lean warriors in rough tunics belted in plain leather, bareheaded and barefoot, carrying long-spears, small shields and side swords. Each one carried a sling, and a pouch of lead shot over his shoulder.

They took stances above us on left and right, before and behind, and one among them put his fingers to his mouth and whistled, as a boy does to his goats.

What came then down the wide, meandering path that led from the east was not goats but men on horseback and on foot, men in mail and helmets, bearing shields and spears, men mounted on . . .

One man mounted on a Berber mare, milk white in her coat, with her mane down to her knees flowing black as a Parthian heart and she as beautiful as any living thing might be, with a long, loose-limbed walk that made my heart turn over and my eyes sting, so that I had to dash away tears with the back of my hand and even then I could not tear my eyes from her to see whom she bore.

'There's gold on his helmet,' someone said nearby; Horgias, I think. 'That's the king.'

'Demalion, is there any chance . . . ?' Lupus was still close by. His voice snapped me back into myself. The bow lay at my feet, but even as I eyed the distance, I knew there was no point in picking it up. 'Too far,' I said. 'I'd only waste an arrow. But if he comes closer, I'll take him.'

'Take the ones near him, too,' Tears said. 'The giant with the axes near to his right is Parthian and on his left is a centurion, a traitor to Rome.'

'But neither of those is giving the orders,' Lupus said. 'See to the right hand of the king, in the tunic and the red shoulder cloak, bearing only a shield and a sword? That's the man they're listening to. And he's a Roman or I'm a Gaul.'

'Are you not?' Horgias eyed him in mock horror. 'All those years and I thought you were one of us.'

'So it's Gaulish you are, is it?' Taurus asked cheerfully. 'Is that why you never told us?'

'Horgias is no more Gaulish than I am,' Tears said.

'My bet is that his mother had a late night meeting with a Briton.'

'Or a Dacian.'

'Or a—'

Macer died, with a lead slingshot embedded in the bridge of his nose. He stayed upright a moment, caught in the tight press of men, then I stepped back, cradling him, and eased him to the ground.

When I stood up to the line again, I had the bow in my hand and an arrow nocked, ready to shoot. No one was laughing now. The ease and peace of the morning was gone with the mist, in its place an unyielding hardness and an urge to kill and keep on killing.

'If I live,' I said grimly, 'I will kill the king and the men around him. Just let them come within range so I don't waste the arrows.'

'We shall keep you alive, then,' Lupus said. 'You can be the last one to hold the Eagle.'

Around me, Tears, Horgias and Taurus spoke their assent in their different ways. It was a pact sealed with Macer's blood, heard by the gods who knew our standard and all who had died beneath it already.

Taking the Eagle with us, we began to march towards the oncoming army.

They offered us peace.

A small man with a huge nose stepped forward from their ranks, bearing a shield decorated with the eagle's wings and thunderbolts of the XIVth Martia Victrix, which was renowned for its role in suppressing the revolt in Britain.

He raised a gladius high above his head. I thought both it and the shield stolen, until he spoke in the nasal tones of northern Italy and labelled himself undeniably Roman; three of them, then, at least: three traitors to Rome. I spat on the ground.

'Men of the Twelfth!' That voice carried over us all, hoarse as a crow's. 'You have served your masters valiantly, holding this place while they scurried for safety. Your fight is no longer theirs. There is no reason for you to die here in a forgotten valley. Join with us who fight for Menachem, the rightful king of Jerusalem. He honours us, as the Emperor Nero honours us, and as he will honour you!'

He was met by silence. I was not in the front rank, but I felt no move from them to answer him. Lupus was our leader. I glanced at him and down at my Parthian bow.

'In range?' Lupus asked, barely moving his lips.

'Easily.'

The men around me stepped away a little. Seeing the movement, the Roman smiled and spread his hands in welcome, presenting all his mailed chest as a target.

I could have shot him in the chest, but I remembered Macer and aimed instead for his face. He fell, soundless, just as Macer had done.

For one heartbeat longer, there was stillness. Then the killing – and the dying – began.

I didn't use the bow to begin with; with Macer gone, I was Tears' shield-man. He had no horn; I had no particular command. We were free to fight as brothers, shoulder to shoulder as we had done at Tigranocerta, but not truly since. It suited us.

We held our shields aloft when they showered us with arrows and slingshot, and when these stopped, having killed fewer than twenty of us, we brought our shields down and met the charge of their armoured men, Romans and Hebrews mixed, with a giant Parthian axeman somewhere in their midst and a Roman who commanded Hebrews as if they were legionaries.

I saw none of those. Nor, for a long time, did I see the king on the milk-white Berber mare. By default, we had made a block with each man facing outwards and I was facing west, away from Jerusalem, the rising sun and the king.

His men surrounded us and the fighting was much as it had been at Gabao – except that now we too had nothing to lose, and threw ourselves into the battle with the same careless frenzy as did the Hebrews.

I had not thought we had been restrained by fear of death before, but felt it gone now, and in its place a dizzying joy that gave speed to my sword arm, and weight to my shield, that bathed me in the light of the Eagle, so that I floated above the earth and moved from kill to kill to kill, at times cutting in and down, at times kneeling to come up under a carelessly high shield, and always with Tears at my right hand and Lupus at my left and Horgias with the standard just over my left shoulder and Taurus keeping him safe as a bull with its calf.

A spear stabbed for my face. I batted it down and stamped on it and felt it break and let my foot slide up the haft and my weight with it and put my whole body behind my shield and tasted blood as it crushed the nose of the man who had just tried to kill me.

I spat and stabbed and he was gone and there was another in his place, who lifted his sword too high and was killed by Lupus even as I slashed at the eyes of the man who was trying to kill Tears, and it was this we had trained for over and over, this was the machine we had become, where each man saved his fellows not for love or honour or mercy, but because it was what our bodies knew how to do. Freed at last from the burden of hope, they needed no other calling.

The sun rose over us as our square grew smaller. However well trained, men made mistakes, and when each one died, we stepped back and closed the gap, leaving a corpse on the damp turf. There were no wounded.

Lupus fell first of us who grouped closest to the Eagle. They sent a wedge of six against him, hoping to break us by his loss. He took the leader squarely on his shield, bracing against him, slashing down and up from shins to face and throat. I took the next and Tears the one after and we each killed our man swiftly enough, but someone faltered on Lupus' left and three of them came at him, carving into the space left by one careless man so that there was room for a blade to seek the back of his head.

He saw them coming and turned away, not out of fear, but that I might see his face, and he mine, and that I might hear him when he said, 'Into the centre. Your bow. Now!'

He was gone, hard as a felled tree, and the enemy were amongst us, pushing through the breach in our lines, heading for Horgias and the Eagle, which he had carried into the centre of the formation, although in truth we were so few and so close now that we were more of a bunch than a square.

'Rally! To the Eagle. Stand hard!' I screamed, hoping someone might hear, and felt Tears at my side, hacking, hacking, no longer in good order, slicing at limbs that might have been those of our side, but mostly were not.

I found myself back to back with Horgias, with the Eagle high above.

'The bow!' Tears shouted in my ear. 'Use it now while there's still time. We'll keep you safe.'

I was already unslinging it, feeling for the arrows in the quiver at my belt. Ten; I had thought seven remained, but there were ten. I nocked and turned and scanned the horizon for the king on the white Berber horse.

And saw it, so close; a milk-white mare that my father would have given his soul to see even in a paddock of an evening. Here, in battle, it was a mount of the gods.

I was close enough to see the width and depth of its eyes, to see the broad, flat brow and the ears pricked small, beloved of Xenophon. I saw the red flare of its inner nostril, the soft moleskin velvet of its milk-white muzzle. I saw the prick of whiskers on its face, black on white.

And I saw the face of the man who rode it, who fought from horseback with long, swinging strokes of a cavalry sword. A man whose black hair flowed like a mane from under his gilded helmet, whose eyes were alert, darting back and forth, holding the edge of the battle that we might not break to our south.

And I saw his chest, and the mail that was on it, and remembered Pantera in a forest, who had killed another king. The bow I held now was better than his had been then; the arrows were longer, and the tips designed only for this one task.

I drew, sighted and loosed.

The brief bliss of honey and the hum of droning bees ended in the whistle-crack of a direct hit.

In the battle's fury, very few on the enemy side noticed at first that their king had been struck. He himself sat a moment, staring in weary surprise at the arrow that grew from his breast, much as the treacherous son of the King of Kings had done all those years ago in Hyrcania. But this king fell slowly, not being strapped into the saddle as the usurper had been.

A ragged cheer spilled from half a hundred throats; all of us that were left.

From the Hebrew side came a single cry of anguish, high-pitched, like a woman's: 'Menachem! My lord king is struck!'

And then the enemy did notice who had fallen and it was as if the force of their fighting slammed headlong into solid stone.

Never have I seen the flow of battle stemmed so completely. In one moment they were assaulting us on all sides and we were close to overwhelmed, and in the next we had room to move, to swing our sword arms, to reach out and kill men whose attention was all turned away from us, towards their stricken lord.

'He lives!' The voice cried in Greek, from a Roman throat, but the men that called it afterwards in Aramaic were Hebrew.

'A line!' I dropped the bow and raised my sword.

Stepping forward, I shouted left and right, hoarse from the screams of combat. 'Make a line on the Eagle! Advance!'

Battles can turn on a single moment and we, who had seen enough of them turn against us in the past, felt the gods lay this one open for us to turn it our way.

I felt Tears to my right, Horgias on my left; I think Taurus was still there as his shield-man. With our shields locked, we stepped forward and forward, building speed and power with each stride. I was dizzy with pride. I saw Hebrew men half turn to me and slew them without care, without pause. I sang, I think, but cannot remember what.

The enemy parted before me like corn before a storm. I looked down the long tunnel of space they made and there was a man lying at the end of it, with the stump of a broken arrow rising up from his chest.

A single man dressed in perfect white knelt and cradled his head, except when I looked again it seemed the white-clad aide was a woman: nothing was impossible now, not even that a woman should be on a battlefield.

She raised her eyes and looked at me and I saw darkness and heard the songs of all the dead and knew that he had gone, this self-styled king, and that grief for such a death made men weak.

I raised my shield and drove forward my sword and thought that if we could get to him we could kill also his successors, because the heirs always gather round the death-place of their fallen lord.

And so our line became a wedge, that fabled machine of Alexander that can cleave a battlefield in two if the lead man has only the courage of his charge. I was the tip of the arrow, the nose of the boar as it hurtles at its victim. I had all the courage in the legions.

'*For the Twelfth!*'

I charged, screaming, drawing the wedge with me. Together, we split the enemy asunder.

Men fell over themselves to get out of our way until somewhere near the king a man stood who had been kneeling and in a voice that had commanded battlefields shouted in Greek, 'Stop them! Mergus! Estaph! *Block that wedge!*'

The voice sank into my lungs, my loins, my heart, unsettling all of them. But it did not stop my charge.

I was five paces from the king . . . four . . . two . . . my whole weight behind my shield, bowling fast as a horse, and then—

Stopped.

Stopped on the rock of the giant Parthian who had picked up a shield and punched it at mine. I ran into it as into the face of a cliff.

The full weight of my charge pounded into him and he did not so much as shudder. I felt men crowd in behind me, Tears at my right shoulder, Horgias at my left, and even the three of us, with others behind, could not push him over.

I abandoned the effort, shouted instead, 'Shield ring on the Eagle!' and in three beats Horgias was enfolded within our shields and we stood again, bare yards from the fallen king, while a Latin voice shouting in Hebrew and Aramaic drew order out of the enemy's chaos.

Looking past the Parthian giant's flank, I watched a

small group of men lift the stricken king and bear him from the fray. I saw the Roman with the red shoulder cloak pause in salute, then turn and, still shouting orders, throw himself into combat.

We held our ground but our advantage was gone and they came at us savage with a grief-rage that we all knew too well, but could not raise in ourselves, for we were spent by then, fit only to stand and die.

We were two dozen, and then a dozen, and then eight and then four, me and Tears, Horgias and Taurus, back to back with the Eagle above us and dead men crowding our feet.

I felt Taurus go down and would have turned to help Horgias, but Tears was under pressure from a small, wiry Roman with legion marks on his arms and a look of such impossible anguish on his face that I thought he might die of it, there, in front of us.

Instead, he assaulted Tears with a savagery that made the whole battle seem like the pattering of fools; he struck his shield against Tears' sword hand, batting it down, cut with his gladius under Tears' own shield, then feinted over the top and even as I was turning, trying to get my blade between them, stabbed in and down and through and suddenly my face was awash with Tears' blood and the sounds of his dying and I would have dropped my blade to catch him but that Horgias screamed, '*Demalion!* Look out!' and I swear it was the sun's flame on the Eagle that made me spin to my right and catch the blow that came for my head, and twist it away and stab through to pierce the eye of the one who had just tried to kill me. He died, screaming, clutching at his face. I pulled my gladius free and stepped back.

And now we were only two. Horgias and I were left alone, the last to die, and we did not have to say aloud that we must die together. I caught his eye or he caught mine and we knew it our last look, and cherished it. A last breath, a last sight of the Eagle, of all that we cared for, and in that breath's end, together we raised our blades and hurled ourselves at—

'*Demalion?*'

The sword that struck for my chest jerked away.

A half-remembered face stared at me, blinking, and that inescapably Roman voice, the one that even now commanded the battlefield, said, in astonishment, 'Demalion of Macedon?' And then, 'Mergus, leave him! Estaph, stop! Take them alive! It's over.'

'No!'

I punched my shield at his face and swung my sword in a killing arc around my head, and threw myself bodily at the traitor who had controlled this battle and those before it.

I reached him. I cut straight for his face. He was gone. I slewed to my left—

'Estaph! Take him!'

He was a giant of a man, that Parthian. I felt his shadow fall over me and arms come round me and too late knew what he planned. There was no shield in his grasp, no sword, only two fists like bear paws that met under my diaphragm and rammed the air out of me even as they raised me up and slammed me down; once, twice, three times, until the sword fell from my numbed fingers and my shield was gone and even my helmet rattled beyond my knees.

Horgias was similarly held, though the men who tried to capture him were smaller and he fought like a wild beast until they had to sling ropes about his shoulders to subdue him.

Other men took the Eagle. I saw the sun-kissed gold passed back from hand to hand to hand as if it were just another spoil of war until it was lost from sight in the greater mass of the Hebrew army. Soon there were shouts and a tussle as men fought over its possession.

Locked in the giant Parthian's embrace, I was still struggling, desperate to die. The Roman commander stood in front of me holding the bow I had dropped. The quiver was still at my hip, with the white fletchings plain to see, naming me openly as the one who had killed his king.

He raised his hand. I thought he was about to strike me and braced myself for it, but he turned it into a gesture so eloquent in its futility that I *knew* him: Sebastos Pantera, former spy for the emperor, had turned traitor and was leading the Hebrews.

In shock, I spat at his face. Pantera barely noticed. He was staring past my shoulder to where his men squabbled over the Eagle. He shouted an order in urgent, fluent Aramaic, and others after it, curt, sharp, hard as any legate on the field.

Twisting round, I saw some measure of order drawn from the chaos, enough for a phalanx of men to gather round the body of the dead king and his milk-white

Berber mare. I saw the woman in white raise her arm from the thick of it, a signal of success.

Pantera spun back to me. His tunic was awash with other men's blood; his king's foremost, I think. His skin was as dark as any Syrian's, but his hair, once oak-brown, had been burnished by the sun to a dark straw, with shades of bronze and almost-copper scattered through. A scar notched his right eyebrow, dragging it upward in a perpetual query.

And those eyes . . . In Hyrcania I had thought them aged and cynical and understood now how young he must have been, for a lifetime's pain and weariness had grown in them since then, and only the sharpness remained as it had been: hard-edged and thoughtful.

He raised the bow and held it between us. 'Three mistakes,' he said softly. 'First: I never should have told Cadus that you could shoot with any skill. Second: I should have gone back to look for the bow when I knew I had dropped it. And third . . .' He looked past me again to where men still fought over our Eagle. 'I should have struck Eleazir's head from his shoulders nine months ago, when we first crowned Menachem.'

He slung my bow over his shoulder, reached for the quiver at my hip. 'You have lost your Eagle,' he said, to me, 'but we have lost a king and a kingdom, and may yet lose our lives. I give you a choice: I will leave you here, to die at Eleazir's hand – he will crucify you, of that you can be sure – or you can come with me and we can fight our way out of this mess and there may be a chance afterwards to recover your Eagle. Choose now. Time is not on our side.'

The taste of death was like iron in my mouth, twisting my tongue. The memory of men gone was all around me, their shades but a step away, beckoning, offering peace beyond measure and the welcome of the gods.

More than anything, I wanted to join Tears. But I felt the shadow of fate settle around me and before my courage could fail I answered as I must, for myself and for Horgias, who had been dragged to my side.

'We choose life,' I said. 'If we have the chance to recover the Eagle, it is our duty.'

Pantera left us then, shouting again in Aramaic. I thought for one moment that we were to be given our weapons, and could follow and kill him, for I wanted to do that very badly.

But he felt the thought and turned on his heel. 'Bind them,' he said swiftly. 'And get the horses. I'll bring Menachem. We have to get to the tomb before Eleazir's men. They may have the Eagle, but we have the king and the crown.'

CHAPTER THIRTY

The Eagle of the Twelfth caught the late afternoon sun, magnified it and spilled it down as if from heaven upon the head of Pantera's enemy, Eleazir, who carried it aloft.

It bathed with fainter light the twelve priests of the Hebrew god who paced behind him in their costly silks, with tablets of onyx and gold upon their breasts and crowns of barely smaller wealth upon their heads.

It reached only faintly the first few layers of the vast crowd that surged and billowed around the procession. By their hundreds of thousands they wailed their grief, but did it softly, for they felt the tension in the air, the threat of violence, as keenly as those of us who had been on the hill's top these past hours.

That tension surged up to us in roiling waves. It rebounded off the pale rock wall behind us and fell back through the rows of almonds and of olives, the many-coloured flowers and the camphire at the path's edge, the thorn bushes under which Horgias and I crouched with our eyes to the gaps, seeing down as far as we could while tied at wrist and ankle.

It settled on the body of the man the crowds had come to mourn, the shrouded, anointed body of Menachem ben Yehuda, late king of Israel, who lay on a bier in front of a cave-tomb carved into the rock with his crown on his chest, a trophy for whomsoever had the courage and the wit to take it.

So focused was I on the parade, on the king, that I did not hear the sound of approaching steps. And so it seemed it was as if from nowhere that a woman's voice said, 'I am Hypatia, Chosen of Isis. You are Demalion of Macedonia, last of the Twelfth. Who is it that holds your heart, for whom you grieve with such passion?'

I spun, as fast as a bound man might, and saw the white-robed oracle woman, a vision of black hair and iron-grey eyes, sharp enough to slice open a man's soul. Her face was the epitome of a woman's perfection: smooth-skinned, high-browed, with a nose that would have roused Cleopatra to envy. Even now, in the heat of the afternoon, with dust on her head and runnels of sweat pooling at her collarbones, she was, without a doubt, the most beautiful woman I had ever seen.

I thought of Syrion, imagined what he would have given to have met her, and didn't know whether to weep or to laugh until some sword ended my noise.

I did neither; duty held me still. After a moment, when the woman had not moved, I answered her question. 'His name was Heraclides. We called him Tears.'

'Tears?' Her eyes remained open, but, with a shudder,

I saw her mind go elsewhere, leaving me in the presence of a living spectre.

Presently, returning, she said, 'He was killed, was he not, in the last moments of battle, after you slew our king, but before you were captured?'

I nodded. She made my skin twitch, this woman, and stole the breath from my throat.

She said, 'He waits for you, but you know that. What perhaps you do not know is that he waits in a place outside time. There is no need to rush to him. He will be there when you are ready and will not know if years have passed or an eye's blink.'

I did not say *I am ready now*, but I may as well have done, for I saw her shake her head and shrug her shoulders and make ready to rise.

'If Pantera has his way,' she said, 'if he can sweep Eleazir aside and put Gideon on the throne, with himself the power behind it, he will send you back to Rome with your Eagle as a gesture of our goodwill to the emperor. If Eleazir holds the day, you will not be able to lay hands on the Eagle while it remains in Jerusalem. I tell you this as a truth, not a threat. Think, as you plan your vengeance: what is it that really matters to you?'

She left before I could answer, taking with her memories of Tears that shrouded her like a living veil. In her absence, he did not return to me, however much I begged in the darkness of my mind.

Heartsick, I watched her walk across the small plateau towards the cave-tomb to join the men who waited there. Pantera stood at their head, and now I knew what to look for I saw the signs of exhaustion: his left leg dragged more than on the battlefield, his right shoulder stooped further. I rejoiced at these, watched each one as a wolf watches a wounded bear, savoured them as if the victories they commemorated were mine.

Gideon was with him, the deep-voiced high priest who was their best choice as the next king, and Mergus, centurion of the XXth who fought against the legions. Estaph, the giant Parthian axeman, stood by, and a handful of Hebrews whose names I had not yet found out, who had been sworn shield-men of the king and remained now all around him, except at the front, where he must remain visible to the ascending crowds.

They all deferred to Hypatia, Chosen of Isis, oracle to kings, who walked amongst them as if she had the same powers as a man; more, even, for although I had not once that day heard her say 'I told you he would die', I had heard three men say of her that she had prophesied Menachem's death on the battlefield, and he, hearing her, had chosen to risk the fray and let his god protect him.

And he had failed.

My god, Helios, had proved the stronger.

Ha!

Satisfaction kept me watching through the gap in the thorns and listening as, together, Hypatia and Pantera made a last effort to persuade the still reluctant Gideon to take his nation's crown.

He did not want it; that much had been clear on the ride back from the battlefield, when it had become plain, too, that Eleazir had taken Hypatia's word as truth and, expecting his cousin's death, had held his own men back from the battle, so that by now his followers outnumbered Pantera's faction by four or five to one.

Everything I heard about Eleazir portrayed him as a giant of a man.

'Eleazir will destroy Judaea. He wants nothing more than war with Rome.'

'Eleazir will open the gates to Vologases within a half-month. He will make Judaea a client kingdom of Parthia, and then Nero will be forced to send in the legions. We will not have the power to stop him.'

'Eleazir kills men by slow degrees for the pleasure of it; he's not fit to rule Jerusalem, still less the whole of Judaea and Galilee.'

'Eleazir could have led the charge today, but he had heard the prophecy and chose not to. Do you want a coward as your king?'

This last stung an answer from Gideon. 'I don't want a coward to take the throne, nor one who revels in the pain of others, but I am no more courageous than Eleazir, nor do I have better strategies. The only point in my favour is that I am committed to building a peace with Rome, and there are few left after today who will see that as a benefit. Perhaps if Queen Berenice were to return we might—'

Pantera cut him off brusquely. 'The queen is safe in Alexandria with Iksahra and Kleopatra. She may return when we're sure there is no risk of attack, but for that we need you to be on the throne.'

'Berenice will return to be queen of her land, but not until Eleazir is dead. Menachem trusted you. In that is your strength. If the people will accept you, will you not give them the leadership they need?'

So spoke Hypatia of Alexandria, Chosen of Isis. To listen to her was like listening to water flow in a desert, if water had the power of prophecy, if it could turn the day cold and cause the sky to shimmer with the numbers of listening dead. I would have found it hard to argue against her: what man wants to argue with a woman who can foresee death?

Certainly not Gideon, for I heard him say, 'Very well. If the people will accept me, I will take the crown.'

Thus did Gideon ally himself to Pantera and in doing so became my enemy, just as Eleazir, enemy of my enemy, was my friend.

Soon after this exchange, I had an idea – a gift from Tears, I am sure – of how we who were left of the XIIth legion might yet destroy Pantera and all he stood for.

I shuffled back from my viewing gap and turned a little, so that I came to rest with my bound legs behind Horgias. It took only moments for him to understand what was needed, although the execution took nearly an hour. We had time, though. We had plenty of time.

Eleazir and his men brought the Eagle up the long hill slowly. They were hampered at first by the shifting, grieving crowd, but there came a point near the place where the nut trees ended and gave way to tended gardens, when the air of incipient violence caused movement to falter; when the men, women and children ceased to throw flowers and lay down palm leaves and simply waited, and looked up to their fallen king with tear-washed faces. Thereafter, the procession was able to move more swiftly, unexpectedly so, and I found myself struggling to kneel, that I might not be caught unawares when the clash came, as it must. At my side, I felt Horgias do the same. Together, we saw Eleazir for the first time as he stepped up on to the plateau at the head of his men.

He was not a giant of a man, for all that he was clearly kin to the dead king; they shared a lean face, dark hair, strong brows, and clear, if sunken, cheeks. But Eleazir was the lesser in all ways; slighter, with a narrower visage, so that thin brows made flapping gull's wings over a nose that was too narrow to be noble.

Even so, he was not a man to face lightly. He walked as a lion walks, watching its prey, and although he bore no visible weapons I would have bet my life that he had knives strapped on to the inner parts of both arms, for that is the only reason I have ever seen a man hold himself the way he did, as if the touch of his arms might taint his body.

And he was angry; if ever a man seemed bent on battle, my friend Eleazir was that man.

He stood almost alone on the summit: Pantera and his small group had moved back to stand in the dark mouth of the cave-tomb, shaded from the sun and invisible to the mourning masses. They had the look of men waiting in ambush who do not know how long they might have to wait; relaxed, but sharply vigilant.

Gideon, high priest of Israel, remained alone to stand clearly beside the body of his fallen lord, his white robes dyed a dozen shades of saffron and citrus by the sinking sun.

Alone, he stepped up to meet Eleazir and the lesser priests.

Alone, he spoke the words in Hebrew that sent the dead king to his god, although I knew, because I had seen it on the battlefield, that Menachem had already crossed to the lands of the dead and met whatever judgement awaited him.

Gideon it was who roused the people to bid one last farewell to their king. Menachem lay flat, with gold coins on his eyes, and his arms at his sides, for the Hebrews think it sacrilege to cross a man's arms over his chest as we do, sometimes, in death.

His sword lay at one side and his knife at the other and in the centre, on his chest, lay the filet of gold that had encircled his helmet as his crown.

On possession of that thin gold wire now rested the fate of a nation.

I saw Pantera move, I think, before anyone else; I had kept him in my line of sight so that when he stepped out of the shadows and lifted the thin gold crown I was ready, pushing myself up from my knees, slowly, hidden by the thorns.

The binding cords dropped away from my wrists and ankles. That was the gift Tears had sent me: the understanding that, although neither Horgias nor I could free ourselves, each could free the other while everyone's attention was elsewhere.

We had no plan, no weapons, nowhere to go but down the hill, and there awaited a hundred thousand enemies, but I was ready even as Pantera raised the filet of understated gold and held it high over Gideon's head so that it must seem to the crowds as if the crown had appeared from nowhere and was choosing its rightful owner.

'*People of Israel!*'

His voice boomed out, louder than any normal man's, and I saw that he had turned his head and was using the echo of the cave, and thought that Hypatia had set him to do that.

'See now your rightful—'

Eleazir's knife flew after I moved. To the end of my days, I will swear that: no man can move faster than a thrown knife and I reached Gideon before the blade took his throat, so I must have been moving first.

In a tangle of limbs and oaths, we tumbled together on to the raw earth, leaving Pantera, who stood behind Gideon, as the hurtling knife's new target.

He dodged. The knife missed, and clattered in the back of the cave-tomb. As I freed myself from Gideon's flailing limbs, I saw Horgias dive towards it.

I had no time to look for him; I was caught in the midst of a fight, unarmed and unarmoured, with Pantera on my left and Eleazir on my right.

The crown lay on the dirt between us. All three of us launched ourselves at it, clawing and grasping, fighting like curs over a bone, while all around us was pandemonium.

Gideon fell beside me, caught by another thrown knife. He died gasping, with blood foaming from his mouth and throat.

I ignored him. Two things mattered: the crown and the

Eagle. Scrabbling, clawing, reaching, my fingers found the first of these, wrapped triumphant round the thin, cold wire—

'Demalion!' Horgias grabbed my shoulders. 'The Eagle!'

I rolled to my feet. Somebody dragged the crown from my hand, but my attention was all on the Eagle, twenty paces away and retreating, protected by eight of Eleazir's men.

Around us, Pantera's few were using their advantage of height to good effect, but from below another fifty of Eleazir's men were running up to overwhelm them while the Eagle was heading downhill to the safety of the crowd.

I spun, and came up against Pantera's sword, jabbed at my face.

'Leave it. There are too many of them.'

'For you maybe, but—'

'For anybody.' His sword fell. 'There's a route out at the back of the cave. If you stay here, you're dead men.' And he was gone, shouting in Aramaic to men who lifted the body of the king.

I looked at Horgias. I looked at the Eagle, which was thirty paces away and might as well have been a thousand. I looked at Eleazir's men, at the hate on their faces: they didn't know that we were the enemies of their enemy and therefore their friends; nor did they care.

We had two choices that were only one real choice. I jerked my thumb over my shoulder at the Eagle. 'We can't get it back if we're dead,' I said.

We ran.

*

I rode a Berber colt in the fighting retreat from Jerusalem and hated every silken stride.

He was younger than the mare, and more skittish, an iron grey rather than the full white of age; her son, perhaps, or a distant cousin. Sharp and wary of combat, he jilted and napped and kicked and bolted so that only the horsemanship of the woman Hypatia behind me kept him facing in the right direction and kept us both upright, and unscathed.

I could have held him. I could have ridden him better, but I sat before her, as children are seated, or captive women, and the shame broke my heart.

Pantera rode behind us, last of the line, holding Menachem in front of him on his milk-white mare, for if they had lost the Eagle and the kingdom they still had the dead man, and would not leave him behind, however much he hampered our escape.

Pantera bore the bow I had dropped and my quiver with nine arrows remaining and he used all nine in our flight and others that were brought him, firing back over his saddle in the way of the Parthian bowmen.

In spite of myself, I skewed round to watch and saw him hit at least two out of three that he aimed for and in the end this must have caused our pursuers to drop back because we reached our destination at a walk, unchallenged, with only the old moon rising to show us what we faced.

It was as well, I think, for by then we were exhausted and parched and light-headed for hunger. To have seen in full daylight the jagged mountains that reared high above the desert, to have understood what we must climb – that would have finished us.

As it was, we followed Mergus, the wiry centurion, as he dismounted and led his horse along a winding path in the semi-dark and it was enough to see the horse in front, to keep in line as he climbed an ever steepening gully with a fall on either side. They cut our bonds part-way up that we could hold our balance, and there was no risk to it; by then we were beyond all thoughts of escape.

The way was harsh and hard and we trudged it as men in a nightmare, not knowing where we were going or why.

At the top, the path opened out into a kind of cleft, a valley of sorts, surrounded on three sides by rock and on the fourth by a makeshift wall of rock rubble piled up to keep men from blundering over the edge in the dark.

There were signs of others here before us: fist-sized stones set in rings for fires; a stinking area to the east that had been used as a latrine not long ago; steps cut in the mountain rock leading up to sentry points. Half of Pantera's men went to these now, unasked, to keep watch back down the way we had come.

Horgias and I were given water and food and lay down behind a rock and slept fitfully, to busy, blood-filled dreams.

Chapter Thirty-One

'I will shroud him in nothing less than light itself.'

I woke in the dark from dreams of Tears and this voice, the arrogance of it, dragged me upright.

'Build here, where the sun strikes at dawn and dusk. He will have first light in the morning and last light at night. In this place, it is possible. We didn't carry him all this way for nothing.'

Dreamstruck as I was, I rose and flung myself from the shade of the rock in which I had been lying out into blistering sunshine.

But no Pantera. Instead, I faced a small gaggle of men, just over a dozen in all, the last remnants of his group. Hypatia, the woman, was moving stones and scribing lines on the valley floor where they must create the tomb they needed.

The centurion Mergus was nearby, and Estaph the Parthian axe-giant, and a handful of Hebrews, all of them bearing wounds of varying severity from yesterday's battles. But no Pantera.

I looked around for him, and they, in their turn, looked at me, save for a nearby slave who wrestled with a block of stone the size of a bull calf. The size of the stone and the effort he put into moving it were not exceptional, but what caught my eye, what made me stand and stare when I myself was the object of other men's attention, was the scarring on his back.

Rarely have I seen flesh so scarred on a living man, certainly not on a man of healthy proportions as this one was. His muscles corded like iron as he put his shoulder to the block, but the skin that lay over was white with lines, not of a whip, but of burns, as if men had drawn them with heated irons, over and over, so close together that the scars outweighed the whole flesh.

He turned, stung by my silence, and I saw, with shock, that his chest bore the mark of the IInd legion and this was certainly poker work, for the words *LEG II AUG* were drawn with such clarity that he must have been tied firmly, or unconscious, when it was done.

More than the burns, his right shoulder was a cluster of ruined tissue, caught in sworls that I have only seen when a spear has been passed straight through from one side to the other. His left ankle bore much the same signs of destruction.

I looked last at his face, and only then because he had finally ceased his labours and was standing with his hands on his hips, giving every sign of weary patience, which was not usual for a slave.

'*Pantera?*'

'Demalion.' Pantera swept the sweat from his face with his forearm. 'If you want to help us build Menachem's tomb, you're free to do so. Otherwise, I recommend you drink water and eat and rest. Today is for Menachem; it's already past the time when he should have been laid to rest. Tomorrow, we can begin to work on how to get your Eagle—'

The sun, the skin-stripping wind, the height; all of them were with me. I was as naked as he was; unclothed by strange hands in my sleep, deprived of my weapons.

But in a valley this high, I needed no knife, or blade, or bow. I ran at him, head down like a bull, aiming for the place on his chest where the legion mark had been wrought with fire and pain, crashing into it, powering on, aiming for the lip of piled rocks at the high edge that was all that kept us safe from carelessness, but not safe from anyone bent on dying.

I carried Tears with me, and Lupus, Syrion and Macer, Taurus and Proclion: every man of the XIIth who had died for his treachery. We powered together towards the frail rock wall and the long, long drop below it, and Pantera was swept with us, his fingers fighting for a hold on my back, where was only skin, and nothing for him to grasp.

I heard him cough an oath, felt the moment when he saw the danger, when he felt his own death rushing at him. Then, cursing, he dropped down, slid from my grasp, writhed his sweat-oiled body beneath me and, with the elastic skill of an acrobat, raised a knee, I think, or an elbow, and slammed it into the soft parts of my belly, raising me up, throwing me over his head, spinning towards the high, lethal edge—

I hit the rubble wall and fell, and lay at its foot, crumpled, bleeding from a scalp wound, too winded to move, or even to breathe.

A fist grabbed my hair and dragged my head up. Pantera's face loomed close to mine. 'You can die when you've got your Eagle back,' he said tightly. 'Until then, you have a duty to stay alive.'

He dropped my head and stood. 'Tie him,' he said to someone beyond my shoulder. 'But bring him when the tomb's ready. He needs to understand the enormity of what he's done.'

The dying sun was a rage of red silks flung across the western horizon; a bruised and bloody memory of battle.

As Pantera had wanted, the king's rough-made tomb was bathed in its light, unshadowed by everything else, flooded in ochre and umber, drawn as if by the power of prayer into the bloodied vengeance of the sky.

A pile of high rocks fashioned into the likeness of a cave with the top surface flattened to accept this scarf of sunlight, the king's tomb had not the grandeur of a Latin mausoleum, nor the beauty of a Greek one, but in its very rudeness carried a kind of majesty.

Menachem lay within its heart, as one newly asleep. I have heard it said that Alexander lay in state for months after his death and his flesh was not corrupted. It may be that way for all kings. Certainly this one had not suffered in the day's heat as I had expected. His face had sunk a little, deepening the hollows under his cheeks, but he was still recognizably the man I had killed.

A priest mumbled in Hebrew when they slid him into the cool dark, wrapped in white linen and anointed with oils, but it was Pantera's barely accented Greek that rang over us now, that reached the far corners of this valley and the hills beyond so that the few who were left could hear, and the rocks around could store the memory.

'Men and women of Jerusalem; friends . . . Menachem was our king, but before that he was our brother in arms, the quiet voice in our midst with the strong arm and the swift eye. He it was who had the vision to see how he might rid this land of Rome and yet remain apart from Parthia. He it was, great-hearted, who battled on the field for freedom, and in the temple for justice. He it was whose wisdom held us firm while the legions besieged us. He it was who led the charge out of here, to destroy those legions as they fled from his wrath. He it was who, hearing the oracle's words, still ventured on to the field of battle, not fearing what he knew must come. We grieve him as a brother, as a comrade, as a friend and as a king. Each of these is lost to us.'

He paused there. The sun was losing its fire. Broad, cold shadows chilled us, except across the tomb, where a single sheaf of light remained. Pantera stood with his back to it, making of his own shadow the gnomon that pointed over the dead king and away.

Horgias and I were standing, bound hand and foot, at a place where we could see everyone and everything. We saw how the grieving men drank in Pantera's words as if they might heal the unhealable; how, in that moment, each man was his, to mould as he wished. If he had told them all to turn and leap from the dangerous edge behind us, they would have done it without question.

What he asked for, showman that he was, cost them more than that.

'We who are left now have not the strength of numbers nor the power to assault Jerusalem and remove Eleazir from his throne. What we must find instead is patience. Patience through the long winter, while we gather numbers and find what Eleazir has planned. For it may be that, caught between Parthia and Rome, we must side with one power or the other, to see Eleazir defeated. I will not hold any man of you to this.

'If you wish to leave, to join your families, you can go freely with no shame. Those of us who remain will winter in Caesarea, where we few amongst many will draw no attention. We leave in the morning. You have until then to make your choices.'

Two of the Hebrews chose to stay with Pantera, joining Mergus and Estaph as his bodyguard. The rest went back to their families, leaving singly or together, to ride out into the villages and take the risk of being known later by Eleazir's men.

It was near dark when Pantera came to Horgias and me, bringing a knife.

'You still have the same choice you did yesterday,' he said. 'I will cut you free now, and set you out in the desert with a horse, and you can go where you will. Or you can come with us to Caesarea. There's a chance you might catch up with your general, but I doubt it.

He belongs in Syria and will have gone back to Antioch or Damascus. You may certainly go on to join him, but you will do so as men who have failed. If you stay with us, you have a chance to come back here in the spring and regain what is lost.'

'Why not now?' Horgias said. 'We could go back in now and take it.'

'You can certainly try.'

Pantera rolled his tongue around his teeth and then said something in the native tongue that neither of us understood. When we made no response, he repeated it, more slowly, louder.

We looked at each other, and at him. He smiled tightly. 'I said, "You are Roman and we of Eleazir's party take great pleasure in slaughtering your countrymen. We took five days to skin alive a man who tried to join you. Imagine what we can do now, when we have all winter."'

'Very funny.' I wasn't smiling.

Nor was Pantera. 'If you want to go, I won't stop you. But without fluency in both Aramaic and Hebrew, you will die.'

'We'll find someone to help us who speaks it,' Horgias said.

For a long moment, Pantera said nothing, only regarded us both flatly. But I saw him uncurl his hands at his sides with a steadiness that spoke of infinite control, brought to its limits, and remembered an inn on the borders of Hyrcania, and a horse pushed too fast by this man, who was so afraid of his own rage.

'You just killed the one man who could have made Israel a whole nation,' he said, softly. 'The only reason you're still alive is because I have asked it and the only person who might conceivably help you is me.'

I was not afraid of his rage: in that moment, I was not afraid of anything. I spat on the ground between his feet. 'I'd rather spend the entire winter dying.'

Caesarea, Judaea, Winter, AD 66–67

In the Reign of the Emperor Nero

Chapter Thirty-Two

Winter in Caesarea: four months of excoriating idleness in which nothing happened and everything changed.

Governor Cestius Gallus died the month after we arrived; that was the first change. As Pantera had predicted, he had left Caesarea before we reached it, and marched the remnants of his sorry campaign in through the gates of Antioch. Soon after, he took to his bed and was dead by midwinter.

So said the messages written on onion-skin parchment wrapped to the legs of the messenger birds that fluttered into the dovecote in the yard outside the house in which Horgias and I had our secret billet.

Ishmael, a youth with wide, sad eyes, tended to the doves and to us with equal care. He had the shocked look of one who has brushed too close to death, too young. At other times, in other days, I would have wheedled his story out of him, but that winter in Caesarea I fed on the messages from other cities and took no notice of the messenger.

As Pantera had known we must, Horgias and I had travelled with him to the city on the coast, and done what we could to make ourselves ready to return to Jerusalem. We slept a great deal, ate well, and worked with our weapons as if we were still under Lupus' command. We were harsher on ourselves than any centurion could have been, for in action, in sweat and bruises and curses, we were able to forget. Only when we relaxed did we remember who and what we had lost. Relaxation was rare.

The news of Gallus' death came in the first month. It gave us hope that a new commander might put heart into the remaining legions and march swiftly on Jerusalem. We spent our evenings planning, thinking, creating ideas and dismantling them, piece by piece, until we knew all the ways – the very few ways – by which we might regain our Eagle.

Three months later, after the Saturnalia, the doves brought the name of Gallus' replacement, the new governor of Syria and general of all the eastern legions. Corbulo had been the last man to command all the legions, but Corbulo had been recalled to Greece; his replacement could not be as good, but he could be better than some we had had. We knew hope for the first time.

Seeking more information, I walked through the market listening to the gossip and discovered that our new general, the man sent to quell the unrest in the east, was the second son of a provincial tax collector whose only claims to recognition were that he had commanded some legions in Britain in the heady, early days of the invasion, that his brother had once stood for consul, and that he had been a governor in some African province, where the locals had thrown turnips at him.

Despairing, I returned to the house, and that despair deepened later when Horgias came home with the news that our new paragon of martial virtue had until recently been hiding in Greece, in disgrace for having fallen asleep during one of Nero's recitals in the theatre.

Until then, we had spent each day in training and each night in planning, but that night we abandoned all good living and drank ourselves into a stupor in a tavern.

'He'll be as bad as Paetus,' I said, slumped across the table, drawing hapless sketches of Jerusalem in the spilt wine. 'Worse, if that's possible.'

'We can give up any hope of Rome retaking Jerusalem,' Horgias said miserably and all I could do was use Pantera's money to buy another jug of wine and help Horgias drink it.

And then, before our heads had fully cleared, there came news that wiped away thoughts of everything that had gone before it.

It was a morning like any other. As was their habit, Hypatia and Pantera joined us shortly after dawn, leaving Mergus, Estaph and the two Hebrews, Moshe and Simeon, on watch at either end of the street.

Since we had left Jerusalem, these precautions had proved perpetually necessary. Three times so far, Eleazir had sent his agents to kill us, and three times we had killed the half-dozen men who had slid out of alleyways with sharp knives seeking our throats. Their bodies had gone into the sea, weighted with rocks and sand. We felt no safer afterwards.

On this particular morning, I caught sight of Pantera's face as he pushed through the goatskin curtain and knew that he brought catastrophe with him.

'What?' I asked, and then, guessing, 'Hypatia is leaving?' I didn't consider that a catastrophe, but thought Pantera, who often sought her opinion, might see it so.

'No.' Hypatia had followed him in; in Caesarea they were rarely seen apart. I don't think they were lovers, but they shared a common grief, and a need to find restitution.

This morning, she sat down and helped herself to our flatbread, and she, too, looked more stunned than I had seen before. 'I will leave when you do,' she said. 'Not before.'

It had the ring of prophecy to it, but didn't answer my question. 'Nero, then? Is the emperor dead?'

'Not Nero.' Pantera stood by the wall, just inside the door. His face was grey as parchment. 'The man who should have taken his place.'

Of the two of us, Horgias was the faster to understand; Horgias, who could barely bring himself to look at Pantera, looked straight at him now, his features warped as if the messenger and the message were one ill-made mess.

'Corbulo,' he said. 'He's the only man truly fit to be emperor. It must be Corbulo who's dead.'

'Corbulo!' I exploded from the fireside. 'What have you done to him, you lying, underhanded, alley-bred—'

Horgias caught me. 'Pantera didn't kill him.' He looked back at Pantera. 'Did you?'

'No.'

'But you said he should take Nero's place, which is as good as a death sentence. Men have died in the beast pits for saying less. If Nero were to find out . . .'

I ran out of anger. I had been like that since we came to Caesarea: easily moved to rage, to fear, to loose, unbounded laughter, and then down again, to empty despair.

Pantera had been patient with me all through the winter. He was no less patient now, only that it was clear today what it cost him to keep his voice calm, to stay flat against the wall, with his hands behind his back.

'There's nothing to find,' he said. 'Unless Nero can read the mind of a man halfway across the empire, I am guiltless.'

'If Nero could read minds, he'd have slaughtered every man in the senate and half the empire by now.' Horgias was unreasonably calm, I thought. 'Corbulo was too successful and too popular, that's all. Nero has killed every other man who's shown himself a likely rival. We should have seen this coming.'

Horgias let me go. I felt sick. I had not thought about Corbulo since before we marched out of Antioch, but his loss left me bereft almost as Tears' death had done, as if by his mere existence he had held the last thread of hope; as if he alone could have led the assault on Jerusalem we needed to avenge the disasters of the summer.

I had not dared to think beyond that, even in the privacy of my own mind. Now, I looked up at Pantera. 'Why did you say that he should have been emperor?'

He didn't answer at once, but scrubbed his hands across his face once in a sharp movement that sang to me of guilt, then sank down to sit cross-legged by the smouldering fire, where Hypatia gave him a torn piece of flatbread, and some of the goat's cheese that Horgias bought each morning from the market.

Presently, when I had shown no sign of joining him, he looked up at me again. 'A friend of mine died recently, a philosopher and a great friend to Rome. He asked me a question in a letter sent after his death and now I ask it of you. "Who would you name emperor if you had all the power in the world?"'

'Cadus,' I said, without hesitation.

Pantera laughed, not unkindly. 'Well, yes, but I think not even we four could get a Greek son of a centurion on to the throne. A man must have at least a scintilla of breeding for the senate to accept him.'

'A man who had the legions of the east marching at his back could be bred by a donkey on a mule and the senate would have no choice but to accept him,' Horgias pointed out. 'But Cadus wouldn't want to be emperor; he's happy leading his cavalry. You were asking the wrong question: not who would we name, but who would accept it, did we have the power to make such an offer?'

'Who then?' Hypatia asked. 'Who would you offer it to, and think that they might accept?'

'Nobody,' I said. 'Other than Cadus, I don't know

anybody left alive who's good enough, and if I was I would walk away. Nero kills those who oppose him, and I have better reasons to die.'

Pantera stared at me oddly for a moment or two. 'Let's hope there is somebody ready to try now that Corbulo is gone,' he said.

He left then, and we didn't see him again for over a month and when we did, everything changed one final time, and this time, something did happen.

Chapter Thirty-Three

It was a morning in late winter or early spring; that time between the seasons when frequent storms boiled the waters of Caesarea's harbour and only the maddest of the fishermen dared set sail. Gulls nested in the high towers of the lighthouse and the ewes were close to lambing in the pastures outside the town.

Horgias and I had spent freely of Pantera's gold and bought a dozen unbroken two-year-old colts and fillies brought in from the Syrian lands to the east. They were well matched, well grown, strong in wind and limb, but prone to the fits of hot blood and nerves, by which all their kind are afflicted, that make them such a challenge in the early days of riding.

That we might not be overlooked, we were working them on the rising land outside the city, below the aqueduct that brings water down from the mountains. I sat a particularly sharp blue roan filly and was trying to steady her so that I could shoot my bow – in truth it was

Pantera's bow, but I will for ever think of it as mine – from her back. Actually, I was trying to repeat his feat of hitting two targets out of three while firing backwards at the gallop. Using four different youngsters, I had hit sixty-eight out of one hundred and thirteen tries, and was quietly pleased.

I came to the end of the rising ground, where we had set a cord across the route to mark a turning point. I spun the filly, careful of her mouth, turned to look at the last three targets – and saw Pantera leaning against the last, chewing on a stalk of grass that he must have picked up further down the hill.

'That was well done,' he said.

I felt myself flush. Of all the men I had not wanted to see me try and fail, Pantera was the first.

He raised one shoulder in a kind of apology. 'It took me two years of practice,' he said. 'I didn't hit one in thirty the first few times, and that was on a steady gelding.'

I glowered: I didn't want his praise any more than I wanted his advice. 'Why are you here?' I asked.

'Vespasian is in Antioch,' he said; just that. I frowned, not knowing the name.

'The new governor of Syria.' Pantera pushed himself upright. 'The man who will be your new general, when you finally reinstate your legion. He has arrived here from Greece.'

'He sailed? In this weather?' I had thought he sounded stupid. This confirmed it.

Horgias was on a fine dark colt, the colour of burnt almonds. He brought him over, riding with his legs, his hands barely a feather's weight touch on the reins.

'He can't have sailed in,' he said. 'The sea lanes won't open for another month. He must have marched overland.'

Pantera inclined his head. 'He did.'

'He came overland from Greece?' Not a complete idiot, then. Whatever route he took, that journey could not have been a good one, nor easily accomplished. 'Why are you telling us this? He's the second son of a tax collector who lets marketeers throw turnips at him. He's finished before he starts.'

Pantera regarded me for a while, running his tongue round his teeth. 'You may choose to believe that,' he said at length. 'But you are required to present yourselves to him in Antioch by the month's end. I suggest you go in legionary uniform.'

In uniform, therefore, we presented ourselves to the centurion of the Xth who stood guard outside the door of the general's quarters in Antioch five days later.

As she had predicted, Hypatia had left the night before us, heading overland for Alexandria. I had been surprisingly sorry to see her go. Pantera had accompanied us on the road to Antioch, with – of course – Mergus and Estaph, Moshe and Simeon as our outriders. I was coming to think of them as I might think of another man's hounds; safe and dependable, if sometimes irritating.

Arriving, we were clean and sober and tired and wary of everyone and everything. We were angry, too, because the thing Pantera had omitted to mention was that he was also required to present himself to the new general, and he had gone in first.

And he had been in for an hour and had not yet come out.

A gong sounded from inside. The centurion unhitched his gaze from the horizon on which it had been resting and stared at Horgias and me as if we had recently crawled out of the sewers.

'You were with the Twelfth at Beth Horon?'

I nodded. I didn't trust myself to speak.

'And yet you lived?'

I sucked in a breath. Horgias leaned in to my shoulder and said, 'By the gods' gift we lived, that we might recover our Eagle and the honour of our legion.' He left no room for question or comment.

The door opened. Pantera walked out, and did not favour us with his gaze. The centurion held us both a moment longer, then cracked a salute and let us in.

We stepped from the cool damp of a Syrian spring into the warmth of a hypocaust-heated room. The dry air was scented with smokes of sandalwood, rosemary and something else peppery that caught the back of my nose and made me sneeze, but not unpleasantly.

A slave took our riding cloaks and our swords and led us down a long corridor paved in marble, with friezes on the walls of other generals in other times; Gallus wasn't there, nor Corbulo, and it occurred to me that perhaps all the men depicted in such detail on horseback or on foot, defeating Parthians, Syrians and Hebrews, had never truly existed, but were safely imaginary.

Closed double doors ten feet wide kept the new general safe. Another centurion guarded it, from the Vth. He didn't ask if we had survived Beth Horon. He didn't speak at all, but only nodded and rapped and let us through to the steward inside who hurried us on to stand before a plain wooden desk such as senators and procurators carry with them on long journeys, and behind it a plain wooden camp stool with a canvas seat and no back, and seated on that . . . a man who looked and smelled as if he had just walked in from a hard-fought campaign, or a difficult mountain crossing, which can often amount to the same thing.

There was no incense to be found in here, only the stained air of leather and sweat-sweetened iron and the subtle tones of wood smoke that cling to a man from morning to night when he lives with the legion.

Thus we came at last before Titus Flavius Vespasianus, propraetorian legate of the army of Judaea and governor of Syria, second son of a provincial tax collector and the man who had fallen asleep during Nero's recital and lived to tell of it; the man who had left a trail of mud across the exquisite red and white mosaic of the floor.

Caesennius Paetus would never have done such a thing.

'Welcome!' A big, bluff man he was, with soldier's hands, rough from years spent digging ramparts, or if not that, then something close. He wore mail over his tunic, rubbed gossamer-fine at the armpits and neck, with flecks of rust from a winter's journey.

His face was a round ruin of wind and sun, red about

the cheeks, even now, in the pleasant warmth of his study. His eyes were sharp, more like a wolf's than a hound's, so that they saw round the edges of a man, and knew the mettle of his soul. I found my own colour rising, remembering what I had thought of him.

He grinned. 'Shall we get it over with? I am the younger son of a tax farmer, the mule-driver who got a governorship in Africa and came out of it broke, with vegetables hurtling about his ears. I served in Britain but got the south coast, where were only women hiding in stone forts, not the wild bear-warriors of the Eceni who cut the balls off their living prisoners and stuffed their throats with them before they died. It's all true. Every word you have heard. Except' – and he was not grinning now – 'that they say I shall do to the legions of the east what Paetus did. That is not true at all.'

As he spoke, he came round the desk and leaned his hips against it with his palms flat on the oak behind him. His eyes were level with mine; grey eyes, red at the edges from the wind. They were not the eyes of a man who runs from his enemies.

'I give you my word here and now, on the honour of my name, which matters to me if not to you, that I will never concede defeat to any man or any army. Not even to the King of Kings of Parthia. Especially not to him. You have seen Vologases, I understand?'

He was looking at Horgias, who said nothing, only slid his gaze sideways to me. And so I had to find my tongue from whatever place halfway down my throat it had lodged itself. 'I have, lord,' I said.

'What did you think of him? No, I am forgetting myself. Sit, sit! And take some wine. Anodyces, if you would be so kind? Here. And here. And now, in comfort, what do you think of Vologases and his hold over his Parthian hordes?'

I'd had a few moments' respite while the steward poured the wine and used them to sift through the truths and compare them to the slanderous rumours: that Vespasian was not bred of senate stock; that he was not corrupt, and so had failed to make a fortune in his time as a governor in Africa; that he had fought hard and well in Britain; that he was, in short, a man who actually stood a chance of leading the legions to victory against the Hebrews.

Of all that I had expected through the winter in Caesarea and in the three days' hard ride to get here, this was not part of it.

The steward, Anodyces, had pressed a pewter cup into my hand with a slow deliberation that balanced his master's staccato rapidity. I lifted it now. The wine was dry and sucked at my tongue. I held it in my mouth a moment before I answered the sane, straightforward question he had asked.

'Vologases is honest,' I said. 'And he wants the best for his people. He will do what it takes to get it and if that means crushing every legion in the eastern provinces, he'll do it. He's a good warrior, and he knows how to command armies. I am afraid of him.'

'Good! They said you were quick. Now we find that you are also honest.'

The smile faded slowly from Vespasian's face, replaced by something turned inward and thoughtful. He moved back to his camp stool and grabbed for his beaker of wine, waving away the steward who had rushed to refill it.

Papers lay strewn across the table, maps and drawings of a city and its surrounds: Jerusalem. He glanced down and pushed them aside.

'So tell me how you came to lose your legion's Eagle. I have heard it from the men who fled. I would hear it now from your own mouths.'

He asked both Horgias and me equally, and he did not ask us how we came to be alive when we should have died. Corbulo, I think, would have had the same tact.

We kept our tale short, taking turns in the telling, each filling in the gaps the other left, making sure that we mentioned the names of the men who had died with honour. Vespasian heard us out in silence.

At the end, leaning forward on his stool, 'The Eagle,' he said, 'it remains in Jerusalem?'

It was my turn to speak. 'In Caesarea, the traders said that the new king, Eleazir, has it paraded daily before the temple as a talisman of their victory. The Hebrews take it as a sign of their god's love for the one who sits on the throne.'

'Which is insufferable. I have four legions at my disposal. Will that be enough, do you think, to subdue these madmen before they insult us further?'

Four legions. All the might of Rome bent on Jerusalem's

destruction. How often had we dreamed of this? And how often had we woken, knowing it impossible?

Vespasian was still looking at me, and so I had to say what we had known through the winter, what had absorbed our days and our nights, our planning and our unplanning.

'My lord, I beg of you to consider an alternative. Eleazir will destroy the Eagle as soon as he hears that the legions are marching on Jerusalem. Either that, or he will hide it somewhere in the mountains outside the city and we shall never find it.'

Vespasian studied us through heavy-lidded eyes. 'Could a small group of men get it back before the legions march, do you think? If they were provided with a suitable disguise?'

I felt my throat close up; we had thought to go as deserters, and face whatever we must when we returned. To go with official blessing . . . 'If the men of that group wanted it badly enough, they could succeed,' I said, and heard the catch in my own voice.

'Excellent!' Vespasian's smile was fierce, and his eyes fired with challenge. 'And who wants it more than you two? Which of you speaks Hebrew? Neither? Aramaic? No? That's settled, then: you must take Pantera as your guide. He has expressed his wish to prove his loyalty beyond doubt; let this be his chance. He has gone into the city to make ready his disguise.

'My steward will give you the details of where he may be found. He has asked that you give him three days before you go to him, and that you use the time to work on your own guises. The legions need another month to be ready for the full assault on Jerusalem. Bring your Eagle to me before then or not at all. When we besiege Jerusalem this time, no man will escape it, I promise you.'

Chapter Thirty-Four

'What do you want?'

We were outside a tiny stinking hut at the darkest end of a snake-alley on the edge of old Antioch, right up against the western walls. In front of us, a small windowless room stank of unwashed camel-hair rugs and burning ox dung.

The question came from inside, rattled in rough northern Greek, thick with phlegm, as if he were half-way to death with the coughing sickness, this grubby grandfather who limped to the doorway, with his grizzled hair and a whitening beard and skin dark enough to be an Egyptian.

He smelled of ox dung and spat at our feet and leaned on the door jamb and asked again, with rising hostility, 'What do you want?'

Anodyces' note had very clearly led us to this place: out of the governor's palace, south into the city centre and then through a series of ever narrower alleys to this last one where the sun never reached.

The pass code had been at the foot of the note. In a voice not at all my own, I said, 'The moon is fine and full tonight.'

He stared at me a moment longer, then gave a short, dry laugh. 'If we go fishing, we may have luck. Indeed.'

He smiled, showing a mouth with three teeth missing on the lower jaw. His accent was suddenly less rough, his throat less filled with catarrh. 'You had better come in.'

Stepping back, he stooped in under the lintel and thrust back the woven camel-hair mat that formed a door. Inside was an ox-dung fire and a sleeping mat; nothing else that I could see and little room for more. When we joined him, Horgias and I took up most of the space.

In the firelit dark, Pantera said, in Pantera's voice, tinged a little with wonder, 'Demalion of Macedon. I truly would not have known you. Nor Horgias. It *is* Horgias?'

'It is.' Horgias took off the shapeless hat he had been wearing. Underneath, his filthy hair kept the shape of its crown. It made little difference. Even to me, he was barely recognizable as the Horgias we knew; he looked like some savage ready to cut your throat if you looked at him wrongly.

In the three days of waiting, we had let our beards grow, had not washed, had worked with our small band of horses until we stank of horse muck and straw and had the filth of the streets on every part of us. We were, I was quite sure, as unlike two Roman legionaries as it was possible for any legionary to be.

Pantera was easily as well disguised, but I would have known those eyes anywhere, and as they met mine the anger that had been building since we left Vespasian's study reached boiling point in my head.

'Why?' I asked harshly.

'Why am I going to Jerusalem to regain your Eagle? Or why am I taking you with me?'

His face was bland, as far as it was possible to read anything in the strange concatenation of age and cunning that seemed to cloak him. His gaze was not bland at all and I was learning to read him.

'You're not taking us with you,' I said. 'We're taking you. Or not. We've been planning this for months. So stop playing games.' I was tired, suddenly. I sat down opposite him, and found that my head was below the smoke and it was easier to breathe.

I held his eye. 'Vespasian said you have to prove your loyalty to Rome and I'd say he was understating the case. You fought for at least a year for the Hebrews. You helped lead the attack on Jerusalem that wiped out the garrison guard. You organized and led the defences against the siege organized by Rome's governor in the east. You let Eleazir take the throne when you knew he favoured Parthia.' This last was unfair, but he said nothing to stop me and I wasn't in the mood to back down. 'What is amazing,' I said, 'is not that you feel beholden to help us regain the Eagle, but that Vespasian has let you live at all. What did you tell him?'

'That everything I did while I was in Judaea was for the good of Rome. That I had contained an insurrection and held it to one city when it could have inflamed an entire province. That I had done all one man could do to prevent Judaea from making an alliance with Parthia—'

'You didn't stop them making an alliance with Adiabene,' said Horgias. 'One of Monobasus' sons led a cavalry charge against us when we first came through Beth Horon.'

Pantera shrugged. 'I was not the king, only his adviser: some things I could not change. But yes, I should have killed Eleazir in the battle for Jerusalem. The *first* battle for Jerusalem. I had the chance and I took the time to kill someone else whose death seemed more important. Everything that flows from that is my responsibility: the cataphracts who fought against you, the tilting of Judaea towards Parthia . . . the loss of your Eagle. I could have held it safe on the battlefield but I was so lost in grief for Menachem that I didn't realize Eleazir had sent his men to bring it out. So yes, I have a lot to prove – to myself as much as to you or Vespasian.'

Horgias had come to sit beside me. 'I didn't feel blamed by Vespasian,' he said. 'I blame myself daily and nightly, but he showed no signs of it to me.'

'He knows, I think, how much we blame ourselves.' Pantera leaned in and tossed another chip of ox dung on the fire and watched as it puffed smoke, and then burned with a greasy flame. 'Who does he remind you of?' he said to me.

'Corbulo.' I surprised myself, but it was true. 'He'll

have to go more carefully if he doesn't want to find himself forced to fall on his sword.'

'He's survived so far when many others would have died. Not many men have slept through one of Nero's recitals and lived to see the next dawn.'

Pantera leaned back, looping his hands behind his head. I studied his face in the falling firelight, to see if I could find the line where he had dyed his skin. I failed.

When he spoke, he was more cautious than I had ever heard him. His eyes flicked between Horgias and me, testing the impact of each phrase.

'Vespasian warned me that I would have to earn your trust before we left Antioch, or the mission was destined to fail. I told him I had spent the winter doing exactly that. He told me it would take more than simply being in your company.' His smile was as dry as it had ever been. 'He hadn't met you; I thought I knew better and that he was wrong.'

I said, 'He was right.'

'Obviously.'

He looked down at his hands, at the fire, back at us. Dirty orange flames etched out the lines on his face that were not, now, the disguise, but the first and best signs of a new tension.

In Hyrcania, he had killed a king's son and it had cost him less than this. I leaned forward, devouring his words.

'Moshe and Simeon are prepared to accompany you back into Jerusalem,' he said. 'Each is fluent in Hebrew and Aramaic. Neither has any experience of horse-trading and so you might need a different cover story – I am assuming that's what the youngstock were for? To sell in Jerusalem? Yes? Well, it won't work with them and you'll have to think of something else. You can't afford to have a weak cover. But they have said they will go with you if you ask it.'

'And leave you behind?' I had to be sure.

'Obviously. This endeavour will work best with fewest at risk. The more men involved, the greater are the chances of disaster. You know by now that Eleazir will have no mercy if he suspects there are spies in his city.'

Of all possibilities, I had not expected this; that we might leave Pantera and go in other company, risking other men's lives for a quest in which they had no stake.

I glanced at Horgias, but his half-shrug left the decision to me and I . . . I found myself like a man who has set himself to shove against a shield, and has found that shield suddenly removed. With nothing to push against, where was there to go?

'Why?' I asked. 'Why are you stepping back now?'

'When I've worked all winter to get you to take me?' Pantera was not smiling now. His eyes fed on my face. 'Because you need to go and I don't. Because it's your right, and only my wish. Because if one of us has a chance to survive, to win, to make this happen, it is you. I have pride, and as you have noticed, I have a lot to prove, but not so much that I will endanger your legion for my own sake.'

He waited then, not speaking. The fire smouldered in the space of his silence.

I said, 'Moshe and Simeon are your men. They won't follow me.'

He laughed at that, quietly. 'The man who walked out of the sick tent to lead the archers that nearly wiped out our slingers on the walls of Jerusalem? Who led the battering ram that came so close to breaking open the north wall gate? Who killed their king with a single shot on the battlefield and then was last left alive beneath the Eagle? They are warriors, and they have seen you fight. Trust me, they've seen in life what I saw only in promise in Hyrcania. They'll follow you as readily as they follow me; more so, for you shine the brighter on the field.'

It may be that he was humouring me, but if so it succeeded, for my anger broke apart like a ripe grape crushed underfoot.

I studied Pantera afresh, not seeking the evidence of his disguise this time, but of the man beneath. In Hyrcania, I had mistrusted him, and he had not only kept me alive, in circumstances more dangerous than I had ever understood, he had sent me home with the best mare I had ever ridden and enough gold to arm half a legion. I know: I spent it later doing just that.

In Jerusalem, he could have killed Horgias and me and we would have thanked him for it. Afterwards, he could have abandoned us in Caesarea. Until now, I had hated him for each of these. Now . . .

I thought of Moshe and Simeon, both good men, and what I knew of them, and whether I trusted them with my life, in the centre of a city run by a man who would spend five days skinning us alive if we were caught.

The long wait lengthened. The heat became stifling and the smoke from the fire barely bearable.

At long last, I pushed myself to my feet. 'The blue

roan filly's in season,' I said slowly. 'If we were to cover her with your grey Berber colt, the foal would be worth a fortune.'

Pantera raised his head. 'But why would you want to sell such a paragon?' he asked. 'If you kept it, it would be the start of a dynasty.'

'She will not be for sale. But to found her line, we need to bring her out alive, with ourselves and the Eagle.'

Pantera rose, unevenly, hawking a cough. Even here, now, with Horgias and me as his only audience, he did not forget that he was an old and crippled horse-trader, not a man with the suppleness of an acrobat and the reflexes of a trained assassin.

That was when I knew I had made the right choice. I said, 'What will we need to do before we go?'

Pantera rubbed the side of his nose but failed entirely to hide a flush of pleasure. To Horgias, he said, 'What languages can you speak besides Greek and Latin?'

I winced. Not one of us who were his friends had ever dared ask that.

But Horgias only nodded, as if it was the right question for the time. 'I speak this,' he said, and let fly in a tongue that I did not recognize and had never heard.

I was alone in that, evidently, for when Horgias paused for breath, Pantera said, 'Thracian? Am I right?'

Thracian! All these years we knew him a barbarian, but not of that calibre. I felt my throat grow tight at the thought of Proclion, of Taurus, of all the men who would have given a month's pay to know this. Pantera looked me a question, but I shook my head, unable to speak.

'So we are Greek-speaking Syrians and you are our Thracian brother,' he said, to Horgias. 'With a skill, I think, perhaps, in bone-setting? Can you do that?'

'A little. Enough to set a horse sound for a day or two.'

'It'll do; we'll try not to put it to the test. For now, take this' – Pantera hefted me a pouch of silver – 'and buy some brood mares: they want fertility in Jerusalem, as well as youth. Put your filly to the colt tomorrow and then again two days later if she'll still stand to him.' He flashed a smile and was young again, vital; the man who had laughed as he fletched arrows in Hyrcania. 'We'll leave to get your Eagle the day after that.'

Chapter Thirty-Five

'You came to sell that? It's broken in wind and leg. I wouldn't pay to eat it, much less ride it. How much do you want?'

They were eight, the youths who stopped us outside the small northern gate at Jerusalem: eight dark-haired, olive-skinned Hebrew zealots, swaggering as they halted us and laying their hands ostentatiously on the knives at their belts, in case we were blind and hadn't seen them.

Our own knives were in our packs, on the backs of our horses, and however easy they were to reach, however often we had practised – and we had practised until we could reach them in our sleep – it was never going to be fast enough. I looked at Pantera, who was looking at his toes as if the sight of armed men terrified him.

Sighing, I stepped ahead of Horgias. 'My lords, I offer deepest apologies, but my brother is Thracian. His

Greek is not good and his Aramaic is pitiful. He can ask for a whore and pay her, but when it comes to setting the price for youngstock of the quality of these—'

'Why did you hire him, then?' They spoke Greek as if they hated the feel of it on their tongues, these young Hebrew men.

'He's our brother!' I was fulsomely affronted. 'And he is the best bone-setter we have ever met. If, may the gods forbid, one of these mares were to break a leg, well . . .' My spread hands offered the assumption that these were intelligent men of the world, who understood the ways of trade, and could see why we might forgive some basic lacks, language, perhaps, and manners, for someone so patently valuable.

The youths stared in flat-eyed silence. I began to calculate how fast we could mount and run, and whether we could take with us at least a bright copper mare, pregnant to a good stallion, in whom I had some hope.

Before I could move, Pantera spoke in a rattle of phlegm from just behind my left shoulder. 'My brother here . . .' he laid a lazy hand on my arm that stopped me from going anywhere, 'knows horses better than any man east of Gaul, where they breed the best chariot horses the world has ever seen. He wouldn't sully his reputation by bringing rubbish to sell in the newly free Jerusalem.'

Along with the youngstock, we had brought an additional ten mares to sell, good ones, though not the best.

Pantera kept talking fast and thickly so that they had to concentrate to understand him. I had to admire that; a man who is straining to listen is not planning an attack. It was the density of his words that grabbed the young Hebrews, and the obvious passion therein.

'Ten denarii for each of the barren mares and fifteen for the copper-chestnut and the colt foal she carries within her or we have made a loss on the journey from Antioch.'

'Antioch?' The leader had a slight bronze cast to his hair that set him apart from the others. He was neither the eldest nor the tallest, but he had the cold, flat eyes of a man who has killed and found that the experience did not touch his soul. He spat at our feet. 'You are spies, then? Our cousin will be happy to see you.'

'Spies?' Pantera's laugh rattled into a cough. His own gobbet of spit was directed respectfully away. 'If we were spies, would we tell you where we came from? You can pay us for our horses, our good, Alexandrian colts, as different from the broken-winded donkeys and mules you have here as the sun is from a candle, or you can tell us now that you will not pay and we will leave you to your fastness and misery. What is Rome to us? What is Israel? We are traders; we care nothing for your wars. Will you show us the colour of your silver? Or shall we leave now?'

His hand was still on my arm. He turned me away from them and I, in turn, pulled on the halter of the copper mare with the kind eye who was pregnant to a lively bay colt that Pantera had left behind in Antioch.

'Wait!' One of the younger men ran round ahead of me. 'How do you know she's carrying a colt?'

'There's a witch in Antioch who tastes their piss,' I

said. 'She sniffed at half a cup and swore it was a colt. I've never known her wrong.' I had never known her at all, but Pantera had found her and swore she was genuine and found a dozen men to testify and I was happy to believe him. 'She's due in two months' time. When we come this way again, I'll give you two denarii back if it's a filly, but you won't be disappointed even if it is. She'll be the best brood mare you've ever had.'

They stared at us, and seven of them waited while the leader made his mind up.

'Antioch,' he said, at last, when we had begun to fear he might not have swallowed the hook. 'What did you see there?'

I was wet-kneed with relief and hid it behind a creased brow. 'We saw the legions massing under their new commander. Vesu . . . Vesari . . . Vespa—'

'Vespasian,' Pantera said helpfully. 'The son of a tax collector. The Romans know how to pick good men.' He favoured them with his lopsided, gap-toothed leer and picked his nose. They looked away, rolling their eyes.

'I saw the standards of the Fifth and Tenth,' I said, as if only now remembering. 'They were performing manoeuvres for the new general. And men were saying that his son, Titus, has sailed from Alexandria with the Fifteenth. They've got King Agrippa's forces and the garrison from Caesarea which has been sent to join them. All of them need horses, but we chose to come here, because you Hebrews have been good to us, and promise lower taxes if Rome is defeated, and we thought you might need good fighting horses more. If you don't, the quartermasters of the legions will pay good silver, far more than we have asked from you.'

The flat-eyed leader nodded at that last, as if I had finally spoken some pass code that only he had known.

'Come.' He jerked his head back towards the city. 'There are men who will want to know all that you know, in as much detail as you can tell it. For that, we may consider buying your broken beasts. As a favour.'

They formed a guard on either side of us, like a tent-party of legionaries. I mounted again and fussed the blue roan filly when she did not need it as a way to keep walking, not to panic and run. Horgias caught my eye as we passed in through the gate and gave a bleak smile that showed all of his tension and no humour at all.

At my other side, Pantera was whistling tunelessly, as a man will who has lost three of his lower front teeth, which was little short of terrifying given that I knew he had blacked them again just that morning, and that all it would take to expose the subterfuge would be for a man to hold him still and run his hand across his mouth.

I remembered him holding a bow at full draw, facing the combined ire of the petty kings of Parthia after he had killed Vardanes II, King of Kings. I had forgotten that he had nerves cast in iron, and did not know the taste of fear. It was a poor time to remember.

Now, we were inside the walls of Jerusalem, oldest of cities, built on a high table of rock with ravines of vicious steepness curving round its southern side and edges. We were kept safe by our mares, or must believe so; with fifteen horses in our train, we could not be diverted down some winding alley and killed in the dark. Thus we kept to wide, open streets and moved at the pace of the slowest horses' walk, which gave us time to look about.

Where Rome is built on seven hills, Jerusalem, it seemed to me, is built on seven valleys. Or at least, it has been forced to bend itself around the schisms that knife into the plateau. And in that winding is great, great age: some of the houses here must have dated back fifty generations, each one showing in the gently sloping walls and the layer upon layer of additions that had expanded each one outward until it met its similarly growing neighbours.

They were strewn along the sides of hills and valleys and none showed any sign of damage from our catapults; we were, I think, too far away from the battle front. When we had advanced with the XIIth, we had come from the north and west and reached Herod's palace, which was set against the wall there. Now the temple and the tower of the Antonia stood proud on the plateau a long way to our right, for we had entered at a small northeastern gate, well away from the destruction we had wrought at the other side of the city.

I didn't know if they had rebuilt the wall yet, and brought the market back to life in the place we had camped. I was trying to find a way to ask without giving us away when Pantera said, 'We heard you had suffered the legions' assault, and sent them packing. Is it true?'

They preened, these young men; they grew half a hand taller, just walking at our sides. I wanted to break their heads on the paving stones and instead had to grin at them admiringly and wait for their leader to tell us what we already knew.

'We smashed them into pieces. We held out against the worst they could throw at us and when they had run out of arrows, out of rocks, out of men with heart, we turned them back and took their Eagle for ourselves. The battle of Beth Horon will live for ever in the mouths of men as the first of Rome's many defeats.'

It would have been easy to ask, then, 'What of this Eagle?', to have wheedled out of them all they knew: where it was kept, when and where paraded through the streets.

I was halfway to asking when Pantera, swaying a little, trod on my foot and I bit the words back and glanced at Horgias, who had seen and gave the barest nod and continued to grin in the mindless manner of a man who only understands one word in every dozen that he hears. The Hebrews didn't notice; they were too busy reminding each other of their victories, of the men killed, the stones dodged, the slingstones hurled.

They brought us in time to a tavern marked by the sign of a cedar tree. It took up the entire length of its own short, broad street, with the horse stalls below and a barn full of last season's hay that must have been brought in since the siege. Above were rooms for hire and a wide galleried room from which came the scents of garlic, spices and meat, so that we were slavering before we came near it.

'You have silver to pay your rent?' asked the flat-eyed leader.

'Of course.' I could afford to be imperious now. 'We shall settle the stock and give them time to recover from the journey before we consider whether Jerusalem is a fit place to receive them.'

'A fit place . . .' He coughed a crow's dry laugh. 'I, Nicodemus, will take you to the man who will buy them. You will sell. Tomorrow, after the Roman Eagle has been shown to the sun.'

Chapter Thirty-Six

Dawn crept up on us quietly; a footpad stealing our sleep.

We rose from our disparate dreams. Mine had been of battle, with Tears alive, and then dead, with Lupus thrusting his shield high over my head, and slingstones raining down, so that Pantera had to wake me carefully, as he had done every recent morning, by grasping the big toe of my left foot and pressing ever harder until I woke and kicked him off.

Horgias was already awake, sober and watchful, too alert to be a horse-trader. Before my eyes, he dimmed himself to a more suitable boredom.

Pantera was filthy; he stank of garlic and old sweat and hot, mouth-burning spices I could not name and this morning, as every morning, the clash between this and the fastidious, careful man I had known threw me so that I had to stare out of the window for a while to bring myself back to being Demalion the horse-trader, who despised the legions and had no particular hatred for the Hebrews.

Our window faced west, towards the Hebrew temple. The sky had blushed a faint peach at the sun's touch and was fading now to citron, deeper in the far west where night still held the edges of the world. Against that, the Hebrew temple stood out like a clay brick on a white marble floor. It was not a beautiful thing, but it had command of the whole western part of the city; it and the tower of the Antonia that reared above like a raised phallus.

I saw a flurry of movement at its height, where the wall met the steps, and a scurry of men, made small by the distance, and a spark of gold, warmer than the sun, and moving at the pace of a walking man.

'The Eagle!' I spun from the window and only as I spoke remembered to keep my voice low. 'They're parading it at the temple now!'

Horgias was already moving. Pantera stood in the doorway and blocked our leaving.

'Slowly,' he said. 'We go there slowly and with a lot of staring at the markets, at other people's horses, at anything and everything but the Eagle. There is no quick way out of here if they find we are not what we seem.'

He was serious then, and it was as if the stench of unwashed tramp dropped away only to return moments later with his black-toothed leer as he let Horgias pass and ran searching eyes over me. He nodded and handed me my own knife, taken from my pack and concealed somewhere on his person; up a sleeve, I think, although I hadn't seen him take it.

'Let's go and explore the city,' he said, in his nasal northern accent. 'We can see if the Hebrews have silver enough to buy our horses. Don't show your weapons unless you must.'

The Hebrew priests were the same as every priest of every god I had ever seen; small men, full of their own self-importance, wearing their god's gold and jewels as if they were their own personal wealth. Today, they were at the forefront of the procession, and they bore themselves with more pride than they had done on the day of the funeral half a year before.

Gideon's replacement as high priest was a nervous man, prone to much glancing at the crowd, which was not surprising given that he was the third to hold his post in the last twelve months and his predecessors had met summary, and not necessarily painless, ends.

He wore his gold as if it were armour, guaranteeing his life; a headdress so weighted with bullion that he must have had a neck brace to keep it upright, and on either breast, tablets inscribed with the names of the twelve tribes of Israel that clashed with each stride.

Jewels the size of duck eggs stitched down the front of his tunic glowed in the rising sun: emeralds, rubies, turquoise, amber; a walking melody of light and all of it irrelevant beneath the blistering wash of gold that was the Eagle.

The Eagle. Our Eagle; close enough to touch. We could have done that, I think – touched it – before Eleazir's men killed us.

Instead, we watched it borne along behind the high

priest, carried by a younger man with the now familiar bearing of a zealot, who wore no gold but held aloft the greatest prize any Hebrew army had ever won.

He blazed with the pride of the victor, but in our eyes, if no one else's, the Eagle's blaze was the greater, flooding the street below the temple, and the crowds that stood in silence, here in Jerusalem where there was never silence, even in the middle of the night. On them, that blaze lay like a blanket beneath the shimmering gold of the sun-touched bird and held even the children to wide-eyed awe.

We stood with the rest, feigning a paltry interest, and believed ourselves inconspicuous.

A hand grabbing at my shoulder spoke otherwise. I turned, schooling my face to avarice. 'You have silver? You wish to buy a good copper-chestnut mare with a colt foal in her belly?'

I faced a drawn knife with its blade honed so fine the iron had turned blue. Behind it I recognized the flat eyes of Nicodemus, the leader of the Hebrew youths who had brought us to the city. He did not smile. He did not so much as lift his lip.

'You will come with me.'

'Only if you're going to buy a mare,' I said.

Pantera leaned across me, favouring the youth with a wash of garlic, setting himself between me and the knife.

'Better go with him,' he said thickly. 'There are more behind. We'll never sell anything if they make a fuss here.'

They were eight again, and I was beginning to be able

to tell them apart: Nicodemus of the subtly bronzed hair and flat eyes; Levius and Gorias, the twins with identical dark hair, dark brows, dark eyes and a particular curl to their lips that made them seem to laugh more often than their cousins. Manasseh was the tallest, and the most silent; in many ways he was like Horgias and I counted him amongst the most dangerous. Matthias was his cousin, thicker set and duller of wit, while Yohan, Sapphias and Onias made another small sub-clan of brothers or close cousins, all with the same gingery lift to their hair, the same stubble on their not-yet-adult chins.

They led, we followed, only today we were not protected by our horses, not held to wide, open streets where murder might conceivably be harder, but drawn into the dark winding alleys that stooped down into the deep heart of this city where the priests never went, and the small markets became smaller and smaller and finally stopped.

On the edge of a slope, with the wall not far away, we turned left and then left again and came to a halt at a door. Nicodemus rapped a particular rhythm and then stood back as the door opened, sending us alone into a house whose interior was quite at odds with its modest location and appearance.

Inside was not modest by anyone's standards, but not ostentatious either. In the best Greek tradition the wealth of its owner was evident in the subtlety of its restraint: the marble on the floor, the nine-branched candlesticks in silver, the wall hanging of velvet in deep midnight blue, the oak and cedar table, inlaid here and there with subtle cuts of ivory and ebony, the carp pool, and the pad of well-trained Hebrew slaves.

The master stepped smartly forward. 'Gentlemen, welcome.' His voice was smooth, soft, unthreatening. 'I apologize for the way you were brought here, but these days I'm afraid we must proceed with the utmost care. Even now, when we are winning all our wars, there are men who would betray us to Rome. You are the leader, I am told?'

He passed the velvet hanging and came to stand at a certain place where the water light of the pool met candlelight from the many-branching candlesticks, and both met fine sunlight filtering in from the ceiling.

Harlequin shades played across his face and I could not see him clearly, only enough to say that he was of middling height, with a beard that grew far more fulsomely than did the hair of his head, that his nose was the most prominent part of his face, and that his eyes hugged his soul tight beneath brows black as drawn charcoal. He looked tense and trying to hide it.

Pantera, by contrast, looked more slack-lipped and disreputable than ever.

The master smiled pleasantly enough. 'I am Yusaf ben Matthias, elder of the sanhedrin of Jerusalem. You are . . . ?'

He was looking at me. Startled, I said, 'Demalion of Macedon. My father was a horse-trader of great repute in our land. I, who am unworthy of his name, nevertheless do my best to honour it. We have brought a dozen mares of good breeding and one in foal to—'

'Yes, yes. I have heard.' Ben Matthias held up his

hands. 'They are fast as the wind and will go all day without rest. But you come also straight from Antioch. You will forgive me if I have little use for your mares, but my master Eleazir, who is king here now . . .' his restless gaze settled on Pantera a moment, so that their eyes met in passing, 'is interested in what you know. We will recompense you for your time here if you will but talk to me about all you saw of Rome's preparations for war.'

At the mention of money, gold flashed between his fingers: a sun-spark in the dark folds of his velvet gown. Pantera leaned in towards it and Yusaf ben Matthias swept his arm back, towards his table.

'Sit! Please, do sit!' He smiled again, and it was no more real than the first time, with no less tension about his mouth. 'I shall call for food and drink and you can tell me all you know.'

I spoke for most of the time, with irregular interjections from Pantera that wandered far off the point but appeared to be telling ben Matthias things he found interesting, plus the occasional grunt from Horgias when a name came up that he evidently recognized with his paltry Greek.

In between these, I told the story we had arranged, which was not all we knew, but close enough to ensure that other spies who brought their own tales would concur with all we said. All of it had been cleared with Vespasian before we left. He had been enthusiastically helpful. *The more they know, the more they will fear us. Tell them all you can. Within reason, of course.*

So we told again of the gathering legions, of the auxiliaries, of the rumours of the new commander, the second son of a tax farmer who had fought with astonishing success against the terrifying warriors of Britain; the governor who was so incorruptible that he made no money out of his governorship in Africa; the man who had offended Nero so greatly that he was lucky to be alive.

'If he was any good, he would be dead by now,' Horgias said in his barely comprehensible Thracian Greek, and we, astonished, spun to look at him. Encouraged, he went on, 'Nero kills all the men who are good enough to oppose him.'

His accent was so thick that ben Matthias stared at him for a good dozen heartbeats before he broke into a hesitant smile.

'Indeed. Nero does our work for us. We should send him gold in gratitude. Perhaps one day we shall do so. When we are our own nation again, under the protection of the King of Kings.'

We were merchants. We cared nothing for Vologases or Parthia. You could have fallen asleep, lulled by our boredom. 'Does he buy horses?' Pantera asked.

'I'm sure he will do.' Yusaf stood, clasping his hands to himself, as if warding off cold in the midst of a warm spring day. 'I will ask his envoy when next I am called to meet him; soon, I think. In the meantime, you should return to your lodgings and see to your mares. I fear no one will come buying now; the time for trade is the first hour after dawn, and it is already beyond noon. In the morning, men will come to you. You might like to watch the parade of the Eagle again at dawn. There is always something new to be learned and Jerusalem is a place of constant change, particularly now, when we have your news of the forces ranged against us and the man who leads them. In the meantime, the day is yours and you have earned your gold.'

The coin spun, flashing. Pantera caught it, leering, and tested it openly with his teeth. Ben Matthias' smile grew fixed and his eyes offended. 'My best wishes in your endeavour,' he said. 'If we are fortunate, we may never meet again.'

We left the house alone; Nicodemus' gang had gone and nobody came with us. As Pantera led the way, it became clear that he had not memorized the route as we came but knew it already in all its twisting, winding complexity.

'How do you—' I had sidestepped to avoid a dead chicken on the road and bumped into Pantera, so that my voice carried nowhere but his ears and his barely carried to mine.

'We can't talk now. We're being followed. Yusaf is a man of great courage. That's all you need to know.' He cursed at me fiercely and pushed me away and I pushed back and tried to get the gold coin off him and he fought back again until Horgias came between us to keep us apart, and like that, wrangling, we returned to the inn of the Cedar Tree, there to spend the day tending to our horses, eating our meals, and arguing hotly over how to spend our unexpected windfall in full view of anyone who cared to watch.

We never saw who they were, but we all three felt their presence.

Chapter Thirty-Seven

Another day, another dawn, another blurred wakening to a pinch on my toe; another scurry under a peach sky to the temple, there to wait and watch while men wearing a country's ransom in gold and too-big jewels paraded themselves before the crowds.

There is always something new to be learned. So had said Yusaf ben Matthias, and Pantera said that he was a trusted agent, and so I watched, wondering what that new thing might be, awaiting the fall of a hand on my shoulder.

There was a moment when Horgias flinched and I thought he had fallen to a zealot knife, but he was whole, still gazing up at the Eagle, and before I had time to speak to him a large man with blacksmith's shoulders and old, linear scorch marks on both arms wormed his way to my side.

'You sell mares?' he asked.

Turning slowly, I looked the prospective buyer up and

down with a hauteur I remembered vaguely from my youth. 'For the right price,' I said, 'we may do. Your name?'

He bared thick teeth. 'I am Zacchariah. My price will be right. You show me now?'

In that moment, ten generations of horse-traders counted for more than half a lifetime in the legions. I was my father made young again, itching to make a sale. Abandoning the Eagle – I was a horse-trader, what did I care for a gold bird on a stick, however venerated by the Hebrews? – I gathered Pantera and Horgias about me, and trekked back to the inn of the Cedar Tree.

Along the way, we collected Zacchariah's well-muscled younger relatives, three other, unrelated, horse merchants who gazed at him with undisguised venom, a woman who claimed she could more accurately assess the sex of the foal our pregnant mare carried, a bone-setter who set to arguing with Horgias but gave up when his poor Greek met Horgias' worse Greek – and Nicodemus and his seven zealots who stood about as we conducted our business, obviously waiting for a chance to inflict violence upon us.

Over the course of the next few hours, I sold the pregnant mares, the barren mares and eight of the twelve youngstock. The bargaining this entailed took up the better part of the day and I found I was enjoying myself more and more as time wore on and the haggling became faster, harder and more brutal.

It was only near the end, therefore, as we were sealing our promises with clasped hands and silver, that

I chanced to see the tension on Horgias' face and the urgency in his eyes.

I came back to myself and closed the deals, sending the men off with their mares, making excuses for why I was no longer able to grace their homes with my presence, declared myself bereft not to share their evening meal.

'What?' I asked, after the last one had gone. We were leaning against the all but empty stalls, seeming to count our money.

'It wasn't the Eagle,' Horgias said.

I stared at him, my mind still full of sound hocks and good wind, and the relative worth of silver and horse-flesh. Pantera, who had done little to help but had, as far as I could tell, picked everyone's pockets, examined the contents and returned them to their rightful owners untouched, said, 'But yesterday it was?'

'Yes. Yesterday it was the Eagle. Today, it was a replica cast in bronze and dipped in gold.'

'How do you know?' I asked.

'There was a crack under the left wing. I had filled it with lead and burnished it, but you could still see it. I saw it yesterday as it passed over us. Today, no crack.'

'They could have mended it,' Pantera said.

'No.' Horgias was adamant. 'This is a new Eagle. A counterfeit.'

'Why?' We asked it of each other and ourselves.

Pantera sat on the floor, juggling silver coins thoughtfully. 'They've moved it,' he said. 'There was always a chance they would do so when they knew the legions were on their way.'

'But where have they taken it?' Horgias' face was a

landscape of despair. 'It could be anywhere. We could search the whole of Jerusalem and—'

'It won't be in Jerusalem,' Pantera said. 'They'll have taken it somewhere safe in the desert. Yusaf will know where; that's what he was trying to tell us yesterday.' Throwing down the silver, he lurched to his feet. 'We need a fight,' he said, and swayed back, roaring. When he came forward, he hit me.

We fought as men do who have earned too much silver and let it go to their heads. Horgias thrust himself between us, cursing, flailing his fists and feet and once cracking his head against my cheek, missing my nose by a finger's width.

I screamed abuse at him, at Pantera, at the innkeeper who came to see what was happening and left again swiftly. I was my father in his cups, but without the need for drink. I flailed with intent to injure, and did not care who I hit.

Pantera defamed my father, my mother, all three of my brothers and the memory of my dead sister in language that was barely Greek. Ducking under my punches, he grabbed the greater part of the silver that had been scattered on the floor and ran for the street.

Horgias held me about the chest, pinning my arms to my sides, until he was sure we were alone.

He released me slowly, warily. 'Are you sane?'

I shook my head. The world became more solid, less threatening. 'I think so.'

'Let me buy you a drink. He left us some of the money.' Horgias bent to the dirt and picked up the remaining silver, neat-fingered, finding the smaller coins where they had rolled into the empty horse stalls. Rising, he held his palm out in a flash of shining metal. 'Most of it, actually.'

'And Pantera? Do we wait for him?' I was still sore where he had hit me.

Horgias, all solicitude, held up the flat of his blade for me to see the growing edges of a bruise reflected in its surface. He said, 'We're to wait until tomorrow's dawn, and if he's not back we're to get out as fast as we can.'

He said it with assurance, as if he had orders in detail.

'How do you know that?'

'That last curse . . . every third word was Thracian.'

'Very clever.' I felt oddly deflated. My head ached. My fists ached. My belly screamed for food. I nodded towards the stairs that led to the upper dining rooms. 'I didn't know he spoke Thracian, too.'

Horgias shrugged. 'There's a lot about him we don't know,' he said. 'But if he can find out where they've taken the Eagle, I won't care how many languages he speaks. Or what he does with men's purses.'

It was dark. Horses ate sweet hay from racks below us, and their breath smothered us; sweet exhalations, thick with memories of summer pastures, and foaling fields and sleep.

A hand fell on my foot. I jerked it away and sat up. Two hands caught my shoulders, pressing me back on my pallet. Lips near my ear, a voice behind them, so silent it had no character. 'Get up. Dress. Come downstairs, silently. Wear your cloak. Bring your knife.'

I am a legionary. I follow orders, particularly when they are given by Pantera in that tone.

In the horse barns, my blue roan filly was already saddled, her colour dulled to slate under the light of a starved moon. Horgias was mounted on his burnt-almond gelding. Pantera was a dozen paces behind me. He still had the black on his teeth, but he no longer slouched; rather he padded past on silent feet, lithe as a lion.

'Where to?' I was awake suddenly, my head clean, clear, sharp of mind and ear.

'Out of the city first. Then east to the sea of floating, which is death to drink. There are caves set high in the rock at the sea's edge, looking down towards the water. The Eagle is held there by Eleazir's men; it's their last refuge in case Vespasian takes the city.'

'Yusaf ben Matthias told you so?'

'He did. Could you appear to be drunk, do you think? Particularly if we are stopped. Don't show your knife unless you must.'

With which Pantera smiled his crooked smile and mounted in one smooth movement and that was the last I saw of his face, for he led us out of the city into the black and quiet night.

We travelled in single file behind him, stoop-shouldered and swaying and watching every unlit side street for a gang of eight young Hebrew zealots and their stone-throwing friends.

When we passed under the gate and out into the open pasture beyond, the air felt cleaner, the sky less oppressive. It was easier to see, although still not perfect. Pantera sat up straight in the saddle.

I pushed my filly up beside his. Horgias came up on his other side. We rode abreast, and the freedom lit my heart, so that I pushed my horse faster, and faster, and they theirs, until we were running under the starlight, over the rising and dipping ground, letting the horses have their heads, and the wind clear the last of Jerusalem from our hair.

In time, we slowed, and came back to a walk. 'Where are we going?' I asked.'

'East,' Pantera said. 'And east and east, until we see the water of the killing sea. Then we rely on Horgias to find out which caves hold men.'

'What is the chance that we're riding into a trap?'

'There's always that chance.' Pantera turned in his saddle. He was a vague shape under the poor starlight, but as he looked at me his teeth were white. The shock of seeing him with a whole mouth set me silent. 'Yusaf owes me his life,' he said. 'He's cleaving close to Eleazir because I asked it of him and so I trust what he tells me, but if you wish to leave now and go back into Jerusalem you're free to do so.'

'Do I look that tired of life?' I laughed, loosely, and found that it was real, which made me stop.

Pantera looked at me a long moment, but said only, 'Good. If we ride hard, we'll be at the shore before dawn.'

Chapter Thirty-Eight

We tasted the sour, cold brine before we saw it; in the near-dawn chill, I licked my lips and found them salty, and knew we were close.

Shortly after, the smooth, undulating land became harder and more dangerous, cut across its sweep by lethal steep-sided clefts that struck deep into the rock beneath us. Here we rode on the backs of cliffs whose top surface was clean of detritus and dust, as if floods swept this place often. Ahead, the last stubborn star-light stitched sparks across the wide, slack sea.

Pantera raised his hand and we slid from our horses on his either side. 'Tether them,' he said, and they were honest beasts and stood for us as we tied the off fore to the near hind, loose enough for them to walk, not so loose that they could run. We gave them clean water from our cupped hands, then scattered grain for them to eat.

The rock was sculpted in shades of grey so that when

Pantera lay face down he became part of it, lost in the grey night, and we only knew where he was by the rasp of his linen tunic on the stone as he edged forward to the lip of the plateau.

Horgias and I went down on our bellies and followed him and looked down, all the long way down, until we saw the treacherous Judaean sea fully for the first time; vast and slow and greasy to look at, as if the water had been mixed with egg white and then beaten to a froth at the edges.

It held us only a moment before we tore our eyes away and looked south down the uneven line of the cliff that stood higher than the tower of the Antonia all along the sea's edge.

And there, along its face, as Pantera had said, cave after cave studded the ghosted grey stone like so many holes in a cheese. Some were big enough for a horse to walk in, some so small, a child crawling would have become lodged.

I tried to count and gave up; even those nearby were too many, and by a hundred paces distant the rock and the night had merged, making counting impossible.

'How many?' Horgias asked.

'According to Yusaf, no man has counted them all, but there are at least a hundred, all linked by tunnels and other caverns as a honeycomb deep in the rock. The only way to reach any of the caves passes down there.' Pantera wriggled back from the edge and pointed out a gully that ran steeply down in front of us from right to left. 'Everyone who comes here must follow that path. Can you track men on bare rock?'

'I can,' Horgias said.

'Before dawn?'

We turned to look east, where a silver line creased the horizon far beyond the sea. It promised enough light in under an hour to render us visible to anyone who chanced to look down from the cliff-caves to the paths below.

'If we start now.' Horgias had risen to his knees and was wrapping his tunic tight about his legs. Tying the last knot, he turned to us. Even in the un-light, the fire in his eyes burned bright. He laid a hand on my arm. 'Ready?'

'Ready.'

We clasped arms, like brothers, and turned, and would have run then, but Pantera held us back.

'A moment.' He slid a long, narrow knife from his sleeve, thin as a reed and fluted down its length. I had seen its like only twice, on men who had bought them from barbarians who were supposed to be able to throw them with such accuracy that they could split a held hair at a hundred paces.

This one, he used as a pen to draw on the hard rock. 'According to ben Matthias, this is not only home to the Eagle. Everything the Hebrews want to preserve from Rome is to be hidden here, including the scrolls of the most sacred of their writings, and they won't leave such things alone.'

'They'll be guarded,' I said. The thought of combat made my blood sing. I rolled my shoulders and checked the slide of my own knife from its sheath.

Pantera, watching, said, 'If we have to fight, it may

be that only one of us can get away, so you both need to know the way back to Vespasian from here.'

I barely glanced down at the route he had drawn on the rock. If ever a man knew his death-place, this was mine, and I was certain that if one of us had to stay and fight so the others could run, I was that man.

Then I looked at Horgias, and found the same truth written on his face. We made a silent vow, there and then, that we would stand together at the end, and let Pantera go back to Vespasian alone.

The salt-stiff air parted reluctantly before us as we eased down the path towards the foot of the cliff. Every dozen paces or so, we paused while Horgias bent and searched the bare rock for signs of men's passing. If he found them, I never saw what they were, but he led us on with a steady confidence. He was less Roman now than he had ever been, and completely given to the legions.

Near the sea's edge, the path turned hard right so that we were heading towards the cliff face. We followed, and there, where rock and mud and sand were one, I saw the first footprints, and heard Horgias' grunt of triumph before he led us, loping onwards and upwards, along the path that led to the honeycombed cliff.

The cliff became more alive the closer we approached; what had seemed a flat, vertical face was hewn by wind and water to a wavering surface that put me in mind of a fine curtain's billowing.

Shadows played along it, sent by the ever-rising sun, so that Pantera and I glanced up often, expecting a shout and the first hail of stones or spears. Horgias alone kept his eyes on the ground and would not be hurried lest we take the wrong track.

Presently, the path began to rise, so that we walked uphill ever more steeply, then scrambled up on broad rocky steps, like a giant staircase leading to the skies, and then, finally, took to the rock face where we must set hand and foot on the cliff, searching for handholds, footholds, for places to press tight to the rock with face turned sideways simply to breathe.

The climb was no more than thirty or forty feet, but it was long enough to bring me to the last hold with my hands slick with sweat.

'Here.' Horgias had been first up. He took my wrist and pulled me the last few feet on to a ledge a hand's length wide and long enough to take all three of us. I turned carefully and crammed my shoulders to the living rock behind. Like that, I could see land and sky and a little of the sea and not know how high up we were. Beside me, Pantera was shivering, finely, like a leaf in a tight breeze.

He caught my eye, gave a wry smile. 'We've done it. The sun can rise now and they won't see us. All we need is for Horgias to find the way to the right cave.'

That was easy to say, less easy to do. We were in the midst of an embarrassment of caves; too many to count, but none within easy reach. Horgias was searching the rock like a blind man, running his fingers over it, pausing here and there to snatch back and examine what he had found.

I eyed the ledge left along its length, and saw where it tapered away to nothing, and where, fifty feet beyond it along the cliff face, was a cave that we might enter.

Above us was another, a mere twenty feet away, and another a little to our right and above, that might be reached in two strides by any man who had legs twelve feet long and arms to match.

And then, because I wasn't thinking, I looked down.

I snatched at Pantera's arm; he was closest. '*Below.* We're not alone.'

Eight men walked where we had been. Eight young Hebrew zealots, each bearing a large pack on his shoulders, and one of them with showy bronze locks that glimmered in the pale morning light and labelled him Nicodemus as surely as a placard bearing his name.

He didn't look up, none of them did, for they were deep in the shadowed part of the path where they had to watch their footing – but only for now.

'We have to find the cave.' Pantera breathed it, no more a sound than the rising of the moon. 'Horgias? Which one?'

Horgias shook his head. 'I don't know. There are fragments of wool and linen on the route to each of the three closest. The Eagle could be in any one of them.' He chewed his lip, looking up. 'We could draw lots?' he offered doubtfully.

I had a better answer. Even as he spoke, three white birds came from the south and rode the strong air that lifted over the deathly sea. I pointed, and we watched them turn west, back towards Jerusalem, and, ultimately, towards Rome.

'Three,' I said. 'Sacred to the gods and pointing our way. We need to go in through the third cave, counting along from south to north.' I pointed to the smallest of the three caves nearby; the one up and twelve feet to our right that a long-limbed man might reach.

Horgias squinted sideways at me. 'You saw the birds first. Do you want to lead?'

I looked up at the rock and found that in the better light of dawn the shadows had grown smaller and deeper and the route across was suddenly obvious even to such as me who did not have the stature of a giant.

I eased past Horgias, and if I was not fearless as I stepped to the end of the ledge and reached for the first small pinch of rock to anchor me, I was at least lifted by the gods and their promise.

My foot slid out to a shelf no wider than my thumb and I felt the cold stone grow warm beneath me as it took my weight and held it so that I might bring my left hand to a slight crack and my left foot to a knuckle of rock and then I was crabbing sideways across the rock face with a fall of a hundred feet straight down if I let go.

Don't look down. My own voice in my head, the old memories hazy now. I did look down and saw the sun-washed sea and the men still making their way up the path, and prayed to the same god that had sent the white birds that Nicodemus and his zealots might not look up.

My hand reached the edge of the cave and found it not a flat ledge but a lip, like the edge of a beaker, that I could wrap my whole hand around and so haul myself up as on to the branch of a tree, then inside to the floor about a foot down.

The air moved past me fast enough to lift my hair, but it was too dark to see more than a yard or two of the interior. I found an iron ring embedded deep in the rock, but nothing else to show that the cave had ever been inhabited. No men came to assault me; no guards set about their sacred writings. I was relieved and disappointed all in one messy round.

Safe, I guided Pantera with silent signals until he, too, scrambled over the lip and went on past me to explore the dark interior, and then Horgias swarmed up smooth as a lizard and came to sit beside me inside the lip of the cave, far enough back to be lost in the dark should the zealots look up, and yet close enough to the front to watch them as they took the path below us, each one humped like a she-camel with a linen-bound pack.

'Their packs look as if they weigh heavy,' I said. 'It won't be easy climbing with those on.' I tried to imagine making the last crab-crawl across the rock with a pack on my back the weight of a sheep and shuddered at the thought.

'There are weapons on top,' Pantera answered, from behind my right shoulder. 'You can see the ridges of sword blades in their sheaths.' He took a step back into the gloom. 'This cave has two openings about twenty paces back that lead deeper into the mountain. There may be men through either of them, but the mouths of both are silent. If Nicodemus and his group come up to here, we can hide in one and hope they take the other.'

'And if they don't?' Horgias asked.

Pantera's grin was the only part of him we could see.

‘If they don’t, then we fight.’ He drew a broad-bladed knife from one forearm and held it up, mirror to our eyes. ‘If they bring a rope, try to tie it to the ring. It’ll make getting down a great deal easier afterwards.’

Chapter Thirty-Nine

We lay on our bellies on the cold cave floor and listened to the Hebrews' progress.

They climbed more slowly than we had done, pausing often for rest and water. When they reached the rock face, they dropped their packs, drew rope from each one and tied them together in pairs, attaching the long line to the waist of each second man.

On the rock itself, they followed the route we had done, so that the first one was at the lip of our cave as the sun touched it.

We had backed away before they began, and found the two openings Pantera had described. 'No white birds here,' he said softly. 'Do we have any reason to choose one or the other?'

'There's more of a draught from the left hand one,' I said. 'If I were going somewhere, I'd choose that way. I say we hide in the one to the right.' The others did as I bid; today, I was the god-marked wayfinder.

We lay together, shoulder to shoulder, that each might know where the others were. Dark held us like a blanket, still and dense and tight, warmer than the air outside, and it brought us the Hebrews' voices long before they reached us.

Nicodemus of the bronzed hair was first into the cave. He stepped over the lip and sank down, speaking aloud prayers to his god. The rope tied to his waist sprang tight as he finished and he leaned back so that Manasseh, who was second, might climb up more easily after him. Between them, they hauled up all eight packs, and then the remaining six men swarmed up the ropes like rats on to a ship.

We could see them easily against the light of the cave mouth, and so we had warning when Nicodemus produced a flint and tinder from his pack and began to spark a light, buzzing all the while in his native Aramaic, which sounded to my ears ever more like a flight of bees trapped in a box.

I felt Pantera flinch beside me before the first strike took light. 'They found our horses.' His voice in my ear, soft as death. 'Tell Horgias we have to move back.'

As snakes, we writhed backwards, soundless, or as near to it as living men can be. The tunnel curved along its length and there came a point when we could see the light of the spark and the shadows it cast, but only against one wall, and knew we were safe from the men in front. I was about to stand up when Horgias caught my arm and dragged me round. 'Light!' he hissed in my ear. 'Men behind!'

I turned, and followed where he led, to another

bend, and there was the shine of strong light from many torches, with shadows that barely flickered. And in those shadows were men seated and standing, men leaning on spears, or against the wall.

And something that was not a man, something that made my head spin and my heart burst wide in my chest.

'*The Eagle!*' I nearly said it aloud. Pantera reached past me to catch Horgias in the moment before he launched forward.

'*Not yet!*' The words were holes breathed into the silence. 'They are too many. We have to hide.'

'Where?'

'Back.' I tugged at them both. 'There's a draught behind us.'

And so we hid again, writhing backwards into a fissure barely wide enough to take a man, which grew progressively lower as we squeezed inside.

Without thought or comment, I went first because I had found it, Horgias next because Pantera was herding him away from the Eagle as a leopard herds a stag, and Pantera last, as the cork in our bottle, holding us in and the Hebrews out.

I crouched in the sweating dark, and peered past both of them as the growing lights from outside merged with those from ahead that had moved to meet them, and then grew dimmer as men set lamps and torches down on the cavern floor to greet each other.

In near dark, I listened to the shouted names, to the sounds of men embracing, to the murmurs of thanks given to their god, all the same as when the legions met.

They spoke briefly and with vehemence, and through

the crook of Pantera's elbow I saw Nicodemus spit to emphasize the end of one short, sharp comment. The men he had met looked around them, as if danger might come from the dark. I felt Pantera press himself ever backwards and dip his head, that the shine of his eyes might not betray us. I held my breath and felt my bladder clench and renewed my grip on my knife and tried to move my arm from where it was trapped against the rock, and failed.

From some distance, someone called Nicodemus' name. The word ricocheted around the caves and came to rest in a dozen places. There was a shout of laughter, and some animated chatter and the whole small mob moved back away from us into the cave where the Eagle was kept, leaving us in almost-darkness and almost-silence.

A long time later, Pantera eased his way forward. Horgias and I followed, easing the cramp out of our knees, our elbows, our necks. At length, we stood in the cave and watched the shadows and barely dared to move.

'How many?' Horgias asked.

'Sixteen.' Pantera shook his head. 'Too many for us to take.'

'But we don't need to take them,' I said. 'We only need to take the Eagle.'

In the near-dark, I saw Horgias smile.

We drew lots. We argued over the result – silently, in mime, with grimaces for words. We drew lots a second time with different results and did not accept them this time either. We stood in the dark and not one of us wanted to leave the other two and be the hare that drew the Hebrew hounds from their lair.

In the end, in the compressed whisper that was all we dared manage, Horgias said, 'Demalion and I are of the Twelfth. The Eagle was ours to lose and ours to take back. You can make convincing noise for three of us and have a chance to get away. If we don't come out, you can tell Vespasian that the Twelfth is dead, and it will be true.'

Pantera closed his eyes. When he opened them, he was a changed man, shorn of the irony he held about him like a shield. He nodded to us both and it was as heavy as a salute. 'If you don't come out,' he said, 'make sure you're dead. Eleazir can keep a man alive longer and in greater pain than either of you wants to think about.'

There was no more talking then. We drank from our flasks together, as men sharing the last wine, then Pantera took a few moments to check his knives while Horgias and I rolled our shoulders and eased our joints, the better to run when we had to.

Pantera said, 'They've left the rope tied over the lip to get down with. Remember it's there if you need to leave in a hurry.' I felt the weight of his hand one final time on my shoulder and then he was gone, a black shape lost in the black cave.

Left alone, Horgias and I backed into the fissure again to sit tight in the dark with our heads down. The waiting was worse than it had been before. We knew how many we faced now and Pantera's last words, well meant as they were, repeated in an endless echo in the ears of my mind.

Make sure you're dead . . . dead . . . dead . . .

I felt sick. I felt the rock shudder to the hammer of my heart. I heard the slow hiss of our breath and thought it a wonder that the men in the neighbouring cavern didn't smell the waves of sour battle-sweat that flushed my armpits and rolled in wet lines down my limbs.

Horgias was no better. However often we had waited before battle, it had been in the open, with sword and shield to hand. I bruised my palm, so tightly did I hold the knife, and rehearsed the track it would have to take to my own heart if I needed urgently to die, but there was no comfort in that, and nothing of the battle-rage that buoyed us up before a fight.

I felt the shudder of Horgias' breath and put my hand on the small of his back, and felt his foot creep back to press against my elbow, and in that small touch was more intimacy, more closeness, more sharing of souls than I had known since the battle at Lizard Pass.

I loved him then, and would have said so, perhaps, and cost us both our lives, had not there been a movement in the outer cave whither Pantera had gone: a whisper; a foot scuffed against stone; a man's voice that cursed softly in Greek, and another that rebuked him, less softly, in heavy Thracian.

In the Hebrews' cavern, the crackle of talk, which had been animated and sharp, fell to shocked silence. The air grew tight with a dozen breaths held and one stifled cry of joyful vindication, fiercely hushed.

In the outer cave, where Pantera wrought his subterfuge, Nicodemus' rope scraped across the rocky lip over which we had all climbed and a third voice cried out in Latin, rising with fear at the end. To my ears, it sounded foreign, but I have no doubt that the Hebrews believed they had heard me.

It was more than enough: sixteen men hurtled out of their cavern, heedless of the noise they made, the lamps they kicked over in their haste, the Eagle they left behind.

Their passing caused a sudden lift in the sullen air, flavoured it with garlic and citrus and sweat. The slap of their bare feet sounded like a full cavalry ride and their voices, raised in rage and rejoicing, were those of any hunt on the closing trail of their quarry. They passed us in a mass, and were gone.

'Now!' I pushed on Horgias' back and we writhed free of our hiding place, turned away from the havoc Pantera had brought on himself, and sprinted ahead into the Hebrews' wide, airy, lamplit cavern – where we stopped, stunned by the vision that lay before us.

The cavern was vast; easily as big as the biggest audience room in the governor's palace in Antioch. An opening halfway along the far wall led deeper into the heart of the cliff and another to our left opened out to stark morning sunlight, and the dense blue sky.

By my reckoning, this was the middle one of the three cavern entrances we had seen from our ledge. I gave thanks to the watching gods that the three birds had turned us away from it to the smaller entrance we had used.

The cavern's interior was as well furnished as any

Hebrew home. Many men had climbed up many times carrying many packs to create the comfort and ease they had here: thick rugs covered the walls and bedding rolls lay in a careful row for half the length of the far wall, stopping just before the place where daylight reached.

Near the mouth, where the morning sun painted gold across the cave's floor, was a line of low desks with cushions behind them and scrolls laid open on top, pinned down by the small lead stones, the size of songbird eggs, that the Hebrews used to such effect in their slings. Other scrolls lay in tiered groups set with care to the side beyond a clearly demarcated line that was the limit of the sun's reach.

And there, exactly where the hard light of morning met the soft light of a dozen oil lamps left in niches in the walls, stood our Eagle.

They had left its wings outstretched to catch the sun. I felt its touch then: the reflected light washed me clean from crown to foot, scouring me free of guilt, care, fear, shame; all the things that slowed me.

I reached for it, but Horgias was there first, moving as a man in a dream who finds that his lover, believed dead, has returned to him living with gifts of ambrosia and wine.

He swept it up and, although he bore no mail, and the wolf did not snarl from his head, he was what he had been born for: the aquilifer of the XIIth; glorious, full of honour, full of might. In a single moment I saw the changes in the planes of his face, the winter's pain swept away for ever, the bitterness sweetening to the man I had known.

He grinned at me and there was such joy on his face that I could not help but weep a little. We embraced as victors, as men who have shared the same sweat, eaten the same sour terror, and come through victorious. My heart soared, and I felt the leap and press of his heart as he lifted the Eagle high into the sun.

'The Twelfth will live,' he said. 'We'll march at its head when Vespasian rides to take Jerusalem back for Rome.'

'First we have to get to safety,' I said. 'And we may have to climb.'

'Always so sober, Demalion. You need to learn to love the small victories we are given.' He pulled a face at me, laughing, but the shaft was sliding through his hands as he did so, bringing the Eagle down to stare us fiercely in the eyes, prideful as any living bird.

The god looked through it then at both of us and we ceased to laugh and were silent while Horgias began to dismantle that which held the soul of our legion.

Whatever else they might have done, the Hebrews had looked after it well, for it came off the shaft as easily as the day it had first gone on, with a twist and a pull and a slight suck of grease as wood parted from metal.

The wings each lifted off, each rounded end popping cleanly free of its mooring, and I saw for the first time the crack under the left one that Horgias had mended, and knew that only a man who had lived with it every day for years on end would have noticed it, and then seen it gone.

'Your cloak,' he said, and I tore a strip from the hem, and Horgias wrapped the gilded body with the skill of repeated practice until he had a small anonymous bundle.

Which he held out to me.

I took a step away. 'It's yours.'

'No.' He pressed it urgently against my chest. 'It's ours. You take the body and I'll take the wings. That way, if only one of us makes it back, we'll still have enough to start the legion again.'

He turned away and tore a strip from his own cloak for the wings and I was left holding the body of our Eagle.

For something with such power, it was so small; not much larger than the head of a yearling ewe, made to fit in the front of a man's tunic that it might be taken secretly from the battlefield in case of near-defeat. The big standards of cohort and century were designed to be left behind; they didn't matter.

I slipped the body down the front of my tunic to nestle against my belt and felt it warm, like a living thing, a lamb to be nurtured, an eagle chick, awaiting its first taste of hot, bloody flesh.

Horgias wrapped the wings and tied them to his belt, then flexed his fingers, grinning. He was like a boy who steals apples for the fun, not the taste. 'Shall we go back to where we hid before?' he asked. 'Or on into the dark?'

I had already looked around for the answer to that, but there were no birds to see, no spiders, ants, or beetles; nothing from the living world by which the gods might speak to us.

'What does the Eagle say?'

He closed his eyes a moment in question, and then

frowned, listening to the answer. 'It says that we should go back,' he said slowly. 'If we go deeper, there's no clear way out.' His eyes sprang open. He caught my arm. 'Quickly then, before they realize Pantera is alone and come back for us.'

We ran. Near the entrance, he said, quietly, urgently, 'If they come back once we're hidden then as soon as the last one is past us, count a slow fifty and get out. Keep running, don't look back.'

'If you'll do the same.'

'Agreed,' he said, and I knew he didn't mean it, and he knew the same of me.

Chapter Forty

Voices from the small outer cave ahead reached us faintly as men argued, and called from where the rope was anchored on the iron ring to others who must have followed Pantera down it to the foot of the cliff.

We reached the crevasse where we had already hidden twice before, but the thought of crawling in there a third time left me sick.

Horgias, too, was hesitant. 'They took no light with them,' I whispered. 'We could go on?'

I felt his nod, and we drew our knives and went on step by wary step through the tunnel that led to the cave at the front.

The dark held us close. Ahead, eight of the Hebrews were caught in the brilliant morning light that bathed the cave's mouth. We could count the hairs on their heads and their faces, the beads of sweat rolling down the backs of their necks as they leaned over the lip of rock and shouted imprecations, advice, curses down to their brethren below. Their god did not tell them we were there, nor did any instinct let them feel our gaze on their backs.

We edged as far as we could away from the mouth of the tunnel, that they might not discover us by accident when they returned to their cavern.

And then we waited again.

The making of a legionary is in learning to wait, everyone knows that, but this waiting was as new as had been the others of this day. Here we sat, armed, within touching distance of our enemy – and we did nothing.

This once, our lives mattered more than honour and so we kept still and breathed slowly and ignored the straining ache in our bladders as the sun crawled across the sky and the light at the cave's mouth became ever more finely angled, until there was no sun spilling over the lip at all, but only the perfect blue sky outside, and the ever more somnolent men whose outlines marred it.

'Nicodemus!'

We all jerked awake. One of the men leaned over and shouted the name a second time, loud in the liquid silence. Nicodemus' voice from below shouted up a stutter of angry Aramaic and the men at the cave mouth moved from near-sleep to frenetic animation. The rope hanging over the ledge sprang tight and five of the absent eight men were hauled up into the cave.

We didn't need to know the language to understand that three of the group were missing and probably dead: one of the twins – Gorias, I think – Manasseh who had been like a brother to Nicodemus, and his cousin Matthias; all had disappeared.

Both Nicodemus and Levius, the remaining twin, had smears of drying blood on their tunics. Levius wept a torrent of grief and would not be consoled. He raged around the cavern so that I shut my eyes and set all my thoughts inwards, lest he be drawn to Horgias and me purely by the power of his passion.

He moved away. I breathed again, but did not look up. Presently, amidst much swearing of oaths and promises of retribution by heaven – the sounds of a man in anguish are the same in any language, and the vengeance he craves rarely varies – the entire group swung back towards the dark, to the tunnel, on their way to the rug-bedecked cavern.

Nicodemus led them.

Two more came after him. Three . . . five . . . ten out of thirteen passed us safely into the dark and I let my eyes open and began to measure the distance from where I sat to the cave's mouth. I flexed my fingers and slowly rolled my neck that I might rise smoothly when the time came to move, and not alert the enemy to my presence by the crack of joints grown solid with sitting.

The remaining three ran at last into the tunnel. I counted to fifty as Horgias had said, and felt him move as I did. We scented the first heady wine of freedom, and raced towards it.

At the cave's mouth the rope was still in place, tied to the deep-sunk iron ring and hanging loose over the edge. Freedom was truly ours. All we had to do was slide down it and run. I passed the rope to Horgias.

He shook his head. 'You got here first.' He clapped my shoulder. 'Go!'

Eight men and then five had safely come up it. I told myself that as I grabbed hold and looped my leg over the lip of the cave.

Thirteen men up. Others down. Including Pantera.

Safe. Safe. *You will be safe.* Both legs over the edge and a moment's blinding terror as I swung free in space with only my sweating hands on the rope holding me up. I found a knot that gave me some purchase, and breathed out, and my questing feet found another. My chest was level with the lip. I looked up at Horgias.

'There's a knot for your feet; you—'

A noise behind. He spun away from me. His knife arm jerked. In the dark heart of the cave, a man screamed and fell.

'Horgias!' I tried to pull up on the rope, to come to his side where he needed me. The rope slid on my sweat and I fell back to the knot. Luck and panic held me, nothing more.

'Go!' Horgias could have come over the lip to join me. He could have drawn his other knife and thrown it. He could have done any one of a dozen things.

What he did was to wrest the wrapped wings of the Eagle from his belt and thrust them down the neck of my tunic to join the body nestling at my belt.

'Go!' He shoved my chest. 'I'll keep them from cutting the rope.' And, when I didn't move, he said, desperately, 'Demalion, please. For the Twelfth. And for me. Please *go!*'

'Horgias—' But he had turned and this time he did have his blade in his hand, and was slicing with it, fast and sharp and hard, so that the iron was a blur in the part-light above me. 'Remember me!'

I heard a blade meet flesh and did not know whose it was.

Would you have stayed and lost the Eagle? I wanted to. Perhaps I should have done, but it shifted like a living thing against my breast and the fervour in Horgias' voice ran onward through my ears. *Please go! For me . . .*

His voice and his will pushed me down so that I loosed my hold on the rope until it slipped through my hands and I slid down fast and faster, skidding over the knots set every ten feet, losing skin with every foot until I hit the bottom, with the raw flesh of my palms bleeding.

But nobody had cut the rope while I was on it and nobody leaned over to hurl spears at me, or rocks or knives or the small lead pellets they used in their slings. Looking up all the while, I backed down the great rock stairway that had led to the foot of the cliff.

'*Demalion!*' I heard my name. You must believe that; I heard Horgias call my name, and I looked up at the cave in time to see the rope snake down towards me, cut clean through at its top end, so that none of the Hebrews could speedily follow me. Nor Horgias, who must still be alive.

Make sure you're dead. Eleazir has ways of keeping a man alive . . . Pantera's words burned again in my head so that I prayed for a swift battle-death for Horgias.

And if I had heard him call me earlier, then he heard me now, for the prayer had only just gone to the gods when I heard his voice again, like the voice of a living god speaking aloud the names of the dead men who were waiting for him: Proclion first, and then Taurus, and then the oath to the Eagle. I saw him hook his knee over the cave's lip and, slashing at the hands clawing him backwards, thrust himself off the edge.

Like the Eagle he had so loved, Horgias flew down from the heights of the cliff. A fierce, burning joy lit his face as he sailed towards me, and at the end a kind of peace I had not seen in any man.

'*Demalion, don't stay with me. Get the Eagle to Vespasian.*' He said it in my head, not my ears; there was not time enough to speak aloud before he ended his flight on the hard rock of the Hebrew cliff-foot.

The crack of his landing spun me backwards. I turned to see him lying not five paces away on a flat shelf of rock with his eyes open to the blue, blue sky and peace still etched deep on his face.

I didn't need to feel at his neck or his wrist for the hammer of his heartbeat to know he was dead, but my heart ruled my head and I had hope, even then. My seeking fingers rested on the great vein at his neck, waiting for a beat that did not come.

His skin was warm. His flesh was whole and solid. His smile had not yet faded, but the back of his head had cracked open like a hen's egg and yellow fluid was leaking out and his life had leaked out with it.

I wanted Hypatia there, suddenly; she knew how to send a man cleanly to the lands of death. But she was long gone, and I was his friend.

Standing, I took a step back, and sent him to the gods, mine and his, in the only way I knew how.

'Given of the god,
Given to the god,
Taken by the god in valour, honour and glory.
May you journey safely to your destination.'

I spoke it aloud, why should I not, here, where the gods were all around? Shouts came from the cave mouth above. I ignored them and fumbled in my belt pouch for two of the silver coins that were left from the sale of the mares. Speaking the last words, I placed one on each of Horgias' eyelids, weighing them shut.

Truly, I don't know if the ferryman requires payment for his services, but in that moment all that mattered was that Horgias travel whole across the Styx to greet the men who waited for him on the other side.

I wept as I placed them, slow tears that might have unmanned me then, but that a stone lumbered down past my shoulder and, looking up, I saw Nicodemus lowering another rope down from the heights.

Even at this distance, the hatred on his face was as pure and undiluted as I have seen on any battlefield. It shocked me to sense, and as I stood Horgias' shade touched me, whispering in my ears. *Go! The Eagle is all. Don't let them take it a second time.*

I bent and kissed the cooling skin of his brow, tasting his sweat, and then turned and ran for the path that had brought us here, and on, and round and up to where the horses had been tethered.

Three dead men waited there, feasting-tables for a legion of fat flies. The blue roan filly was safe; with Horgias' burnt-almond gelding and Pantera's bay, she had moved into the shade of a rock and stood dozing, slack-hipped in the heat.

I looked around for Pantera and saw nothing but uneven rock, set about with potholes and scoured clean by sun and wind. I was set to cut the tethers when I caught sight of a particular mound of grey that was not exactly as it should have been. I reached it just as Pantera thrust himself to his feet.

He began to dust himself down and then stopped, his eyes searching my face. I wasn't weeping by then, but the signs of it must have been clear. 'Horgias?' he asked.

'Dead.'

'Are you sure?'

'Would you go back for him if Nicodemus had him alive?'

'If necessary.' He meant it. I could read the truth on his face. Strange that he was so easy to read now, when I had least need of it.

The Eagle burned against my chest. I busied myself loosing the tethers from the horses. 'There's no need. He heard what you said as well as I did. He cut the rope after I climbed down it and then threw himself from the cave mouth. He landed at my feet. I left him silver for the ferryman.'

'And Nicodemus?'

'He's coming for us. We need to ride.' I mounted, and took Horgias' horse by the reins. 'I have an Eagle to deliver to Vespasian.'

Epilogue

Antioch, Syria, April, AD 67

In the high blue sky, an eagle, soaring.

Beneath it, closer to the ground, a gilded Eagle, radiant in the careful sunlight, spills its own light across the two hundred men gathered beneath.

They are not a legion yet, but the beginnings of one: on each shield, the crossed thunderbolts of the XIIth Fulminata, the Thunderbolt legion; on the helm of the standard-bearer, a wolfskin; on the arms of the men, bands in gold that tell of valour in battle, and on their faces a pride that catches the spilled light of the Eagle and spins it back up to the podium.

From their throats, two hundred voices, offering anew their oath to the emperor, to their general, to their legion, the XIIth, brought back from the dead.

And on the podium, Vespasian, governor of Syria, legate of the eastern legions; a ruddy-faced, wind-blown general who knows the value of his men.

He hears their oath in silence and lets the wind lift the banners and the eagle cry its response from the heavens before he steps forward and raises his battle-honed voice.

'Men of the Twelfth! In blood and battle were you lost, but never bested. In courage and care was your heart recovered, here to stand. Now do we salute those who died in your defence, and honour those who brought your Eagle to safety. For ever shall their names be known, and always with honour shall they be spoken.'

A brisk step sideways, a sharp cutting motion with his palm, and a sheet of purple silk billows down from the wall behind him.

Two hundred men gasp at what they see; they did not expect this. But they see and they read and soon two hundred swords batter two hundred shields, for how could they not?

HORGIAS.

LUPUS.

SYRION.

MACER.

PROCLION.

TAURUS.

HERACLIDES, KNOWN AS TEARS . . .

The names are chiselled indelibly into the wall of Antioch, Syria's greatest city, the third greatest in all the empire after Rome and Alexandria. And above them all, an Eagle flies for ever, and the number of their legion: *XII: WITH HONOUR DID WE DIE FOR YOU.*

*

I meet Pantera later, in the house that they have given us. He stands in the doorway, looking in at me.

'Did you see it?'

'I heard. It was a good speech.'

'But you didn't watch?'

'No.' I have a flask of wine in front of me. I have not drunk. I have not drunk at all since my return. I hold it out to him as he enters.

He shakes his head. 'You could still join,' he says. 'He'd make you camp prefect even now, if you asked for it. Or primus pilus. Legate of the horse. Anything you wanted.'

'I don't want anything.'

He comes into the room and sits down opposite me. We are on the third floor. The view from the window looks out over green and brown hills, but if I close my eyes I could be in a tavern in Hyrcania, watching him fletch an arrow with which to kill an upstart king. I have his Parthian bow. He has not asked for it back.

I say, 'I've given to the Twelfth all that I can. Vespasian will let me go if I ask it. He will sign my manumission himself.'

'Do you want that? Truly?'

'I don't know.' I have water in my beaker. I dip my finger in it and draw a picture of a running horse; a thing I have not done since childhood. It is a child's drawing, not at all lively. I smear it away with the heel of my hand.

I say, 'Hypatia could tell me what I want. She sees into men's souls better than they do themselves.'

'You can see as well as anyone. You just need to accept what you see. You were born a horse-trader, but it's not who you are now.'

'No?' I do look up then. Pantera is regarding me quizzically, his head on his arm and his arm propped against the wall just inside the door. He kicks the door shut with his heel, and it shudders on the door jamb.

'What will you do?' I ask.

'What I am ordered to do. As ever.' And then, because I am still looking at him, 'I am ordered to Rome.'

'By the emperor?' I cannot keep the disdain from my voice.

Pantera shakes his head. 'By the spymaster who serves the empire,' he says, and I am reminded of the sick colour of his face, relaying the news of Corbulo's death. *Not Nero. The man who should have taken his place.* And then, at another time, *Who does he remind you of?*

Corbulo.

Thoughtfully, I draw another picture. We both look at it. I say, 'Vespasian has asked me to be part of his personal bodyguard. That way, if I don't want to be part of the new Twelfth, I can still be with the force that takes back Jerusalem.'

'He knows the value of a good man when he sees one. Like good horses, they are few enough, and to be cherished.' Pantera stands. Neither of us is good at saying goodbye. He says, 'I'm leaving in the morning. I've left the Berber colt in your care. You'll need a good mount while your roan filly becomes a brood mare.'

I blink at him. 'When will you come back to claim him?'

He is looking down at the Eagle I have drawn in water on the oak table. 'If I come back,' he says, 'it won't be to claim him. Or the bow.'

He leaves me, then. I sit a while longer, before I smooth out the drawing and stand.

I drink the water, and a little of the wine, and then I go to tell my general that I will be honoured to serve in his bodyguard for as long as he has need of me.

Author's Note

I am indebted to Rose Mary Sheldon for her excellent work, *Rome's Wars in Parthia, Blood in the Sand* which was published bare months before I began the research for this book.

Barbara Levick's *Vespasian* is a decade older, but still one of the best biographies of one of Rome's best emperors, and I have drawn on it extensively for details of his early life, with Suetonius as back-up at all times.

Josephus and Tacitus, as ever, provided the primary detail for the movements of the XIIth and its near destruction, while my bible for military accuracy has been Bishop and Coulston's *Roman Military Equipment*, which has done much to shape my beliefs of what was (and wasn't) standard in the first century.

I was particularly struck by the assertion that representational evidence for *lorica segmentata* is 'virtually non-existent with a few possible (and debatable) exceptions before the second century AD' (second edition paperback, page 255). My mid-first-century legionaries, therefore, only rarely wear the armour we have come to associate with later centuries.

Brigadier Allan Mallinson was kind enough to direct me towards memoirs of modern wars that, to him, best encapsulated the bonding of battle. Of the three that he recommended, *Quartered Safe Out Here* by George MacDonald Fraser was easily the most moving and the most informative. The scene in which my characters share out the property of their dead comrade, Proclion, is adapted directly from this book in the belief that such actions must have been common to all armies in all eras.

I have taken minor liberties with Vespasian's known movements in the spring of 67, which was necessary for a rounded narrative.

I am ever in debt to my friends and colleagues of the Historical Writers' Association for their thoughts, conversations, debates and arguments over accuracy and detail. It's a joy and a wonder to have a community to call on; thank you.

My agent, Jane Judd, made everything possible, while my editors, Selina Walker and Bill Scott-Kerr, continue to be founts of sanity, support and strength, while my partner, Faith Tilleray, is the light that brightens every day. Nancy Webber is my constant, much-lauded copy editor and Vivien Garrett has cleared the way to a smooth production.

To all of these, my grateful thanks, knowing that, as ever, any mistakes are entirely my own.

ROME

THE EMPEROR'S SPY

M.C. Scott

'Stop this fire, whatever it takes. I, your Emperor, order it'

THE EMPEROR
Nero, Emperor of Rome and all her provinces, feared by his subjects for his temper and cruelty, is in possession of an ancient document predicting that Rome will burn.

THE SPY
Sebastos Pantera, assassin and spy for the Roman Legions, is ordered to stop the impending cataclysm. He knows that if he does not, his life – and those of thousands of others – is in terrible danger.

THE CHARIOT BOY
Math, a young charioteer, is a pawn drawn into the deadly game between the Emperor and the Spy, where death stalks the drivers – on the track and off it.

From the author of the bestselling *Boudica* series, ***The Emperor's Spy*** begins a compelling new series of novels featuring **Sebastos Pantera**. Rich characterisation and spine tingling adventure combine in a vividly realized novel set amid the bloodshed and the chaos, the heroism and murderous betrayal of ancient Rome.

'As exciting as Ben Hur, *and far more accurate'*
Independent

'A gripping tale, with more to come'
Daily Mail

ROME

THE
COMING OF THE KING

M.C. Scott

AD 65, SEBASTOS PANTERA, known to his many enemies as the Leopard, is the spy the Emperor Nero uses only for the most challenging and important of missions. Hunting alone, not knowing who he can trust, he must find the most dangerous man in Rome's empire and bring him to bloody justice.

But his prey is cunning, subtle and ruthless. Saulos has pledged to bring about the destruction of an entire Roman province and has even now set the means to do so in motion.

It will take the strategies of a master hunter to combat the brilliance of Saulos' plan, and so Pantera must set forth into the wild lands of Judaea to set an equally deadly trap for his arch-enemy and nemesis . . .

'Religious and political tensions, passion and intrigue, superb action sequences and real and imagined characters are seamlessly woven together to create a fascinating and exciting story on a truly epic scale'
Guardian

'A dramatic new version of the past . . . grippingly sustained'
Independent